MAMA'S SECRET

An Enid Gilchrist Mystery

SYLVIA A. NASH

Published by Fractured Time Press.

First Edition: October 2017
(Revised August 2021)

Printed in the United States of America.

ISBN-13: 978-0-9977267-2-5 (Paperback)

Scripture quotations are from The Holy Bible, King James Version.

Cover Image (Family Tree)
© Yaroslav Borysobych / Dreamstime.com
Cover Image (Background)
© Vyacheslav Plyasenko / Dreamstime.com

"Stories," © 2017, Sylvia A. Nash

IN LOVING MEMORY
OF MY FATHER
DOUGLAS NASH
1928-2016

STORIES

Share with me your mothers
and your grandmothers.
Touch me with their stories
and their history.
How else can I know you?

ACKNOWLEDGMENTS

I could not have written *Mama's Secret* without the help and advice from many individuals: Law enforcement officers in Tennessee and Michigan, professors and librarians at several universities, archivists at several institutions, attorneys and other public officials, an auto body technician, a medical and forensic expert, and members of the professional writers' organizations to which I belong.

I owe a special debt of gratitude to these three individuals:

Rebekah Nash Alhashimi, Teacher of English as a Second Language, for editing and proofreading.

D. P. Lyle, MD, story consultant and award-winning author, for advising me on medical and forensic details.

Toni Shiloh, author and member of American Christian Fiction Writers (ACFW), for reading an early version of this story.

As important as all of the help and advice, all of my personal research, and all of the work that went into this story was the support of family and friends without whom I might never have finished *Mama's Secret*.

Any errors or misinterpretations are my responsibility alone.

CAST OF CHARACTERS

Mama's Secret spans nine generations of women descended from two women whose lives were intimately intertwined. Not all of the women appear in this story, but for those who do, keeping Granny Olivia separate from Granny Maude could prove distracting. Genealogists are accustomed to such distractions, especially in families who name descendants after ancestors from generation to generation. Family trees help them identify family members. The lists below are designed to help you identify the mothers and daughters of *Mama's Secret*.

The Firstborn Daughters of Charlotte and Her Descendants
> Charlotte Abbott Goodwin
> Olivia Goodwin Woodson (Granny Olivia)
> Savannah Woodson Smith
> Beatrice Smith Baker
> Maude Baker Everly (Granny Maude)
> Isabel Everly Parker
> Natalie Parker Croft
> Abigail Louisa Croft (Abby)

The Firstborn Daughters of Hannah and Her Descendants
> Hannah Abbott Jacobson
> Miriam Jacobson Michaels
> Lydia Michaels Jones
> Ida Jones Ethridge
> Hallie Ethridge Beale
> Zora Beale Maston
> Marian Maston Ross
> Alexa Irene Ross

CHAPTER ONE

Monday, August 1, 2011

Enid Gilchrist leaned against Patrick Mulhaney's strong shoulder and watched as her best friend Rachel and her goddaughter Miranda pulled in behind the huge moving truck. When Patrick slipped his arm around her waist and pulled her closer, she blinked back tears and glanced at him with a wistful smile.

"The movers didn't act the least bit upset at having to make a second stop to pick up Miranda's antique dresser."

"Why would they? They do get paid for whatever they do."

"True. Silly of me, I guess, but she loved that dresser, and I wanted her to have it."

"To remember you by?"

"Don't tease."

"I'm not. I understand you and her. She's taking a part of you with her."

"Exactly. Benjamin's death ripped a piece out of all our hearts, and now Miranda and Rachel are leaving. Bakersville will never be the same without them. I will never be the same. If and when I see them again, Rachel won't recognize me, and Miranda won't need me anymore."

"Alzheimer's is a cruel disease, but both Rachel and Miranda will always need you, Enid. You'll be all right. They will, too. The sun's shining. It's already pushing eighty-eight degrees. A good omen for a good beginning."

"If you call this heat good." Enid wiped at the beads of sweat on her brow. "But for them, yes, they'll be fine, and I'm happy for them. Imagine Miranda all grown up, practicing medicine on real people instead of her dolls and pets. As for me, I'll survive, but I won't be all right. They were all the family I had left. So much for the joys of my retirement years."

"You're not retired."

"I am from teaching, and I am sixty-five."

"You haven't stopped working—or living."

"I didn't expect so many changes."

"Life changes."

"I know. So does weather." Enid squinted at the sky, but she didn't see sunshine or clouds. Instead, she saw faded images of Luticia, gone three years now, and Bryce, gone ten years. She saw Patrick and Luticia's boys, Raymond and Shawn, as children squirting each other with their water guns. She glimpsed shadows of the children she and Bryce never had.

Patrick squeezed her shoulder and brought her out of her reverie. "You still have me."

"And don't you ever leave!" She slapped at his arm playfully without disturbing the sleeve of his uniform.

"You have my boys, too. They always claimed you and Bryce as honorary aunt and uncle."

"They did."

"Besides, as many irons as you poke into that fire of yours, you'll find something new to focus on before Miranda and Rachel reach their new home."

Enid slipped her arm around Patrick. Neither said a word for several minutes until she drew an audible breath and extracted herself from their embrace.

"Well, then." She smoothed imaginary wrinkles from her royal blue pantsuit and straightened the sapphire teardrop hanging from the sterling silver chain around her neck. "Half the day will be gone by the time I get to the library, and I'm sure you need to get to the station. Crime stops for no one."

"Will you be all right?"

"You said I would." She raised an eyebrow.

"I did, didn't I?" He grinned.

"So off with us. I need to find that something new to focus on." She brushed a piece of lint from the pocket of his shirt. "You could call me tonight, though."

"I can and will."

"Good. Come to think of it, by then I should have my new focus. Maude Everly plans to come to the genealogy room this afternoon. She called me at home this morning all excited about something she discovered concerning her great-grandmother. She hopes it will help me help her find something else for which she has been searching for a very long time. She may be our oldest patron, but she's also been our best patron and supporter since shortly after Benjamin named me Director of the Douglas Genealogy Room. She's always a delight to work with. I hope I can help her." Enid frowned. "I'm not sure why, but she's afraid she'll run out of time before she finds what she's searching for."

Patrick leaned over and gave her a peck on the cheek, then picked up his hat from the front porch swing. He settled it over his thick, dark brown hair and tipped the visor forward over eyes of the same shade of brown as his hair.

Enid reached up to push a few escaping strands back under his hat. "I could run my fingers through those locks every time I see you."

Patrick glanced up and down the street, a hint of pink touching his cheeks.

"No one's watching or listening. I'm not that daft."

"There you go. The thought of a research partner has roused the tease in you and added to the sparkle in those cornflower blues." He touched her face and brushed back a short wisp of her hair. "Speaking of hair, have I ever told you those honey-colored tresses are the perfect frame for your eyes?"

"Now who's teasing and tempting the neighbors?" For a moment, Enid lost herself in Patrick's gaze.

"Are you ready then?"

She returned his kiss.

"I am. Let me get my bags and lock the door."

As she stepped off the porch a few moments later, she paused to enjoy the sunshine. She squinted into the rays bouncing off the two vehicles in her driveway—Patrick's police cruiser, a new white Ford Crown Victoria Police

Interceptor, and her own not quite two-year-old navy Subaru Impreza Sedan.

Looks like we both sprang for detail jobs this weekend.

Lost in her thoughts, she deadheaded a spent daffodil and its seedpod before following Patrick across the walk.

* * *

Once inside the library, Enid stopped at the door to Benjamin's office on her left, not yet able to think of it as Mary's office. She spoke briefly to her friend and now boss before heading back to her right, past the circulation desk, and down the hallway to the genealogy room. She found the door locked. Ellen Randall, her volunteer for the day, had not returned from lunch.

Enid scratched through her purse for her keys and let herself in. She glanced at the wall clock hanging to her left over the copier. "Twelve thirty. I have time to do some work before Maude arrives."

She glanced between the rows of shelves in front of her before turning toward the copier and crossing the room to the door of her tiny office. After she unlocked it and stashed her bags inside, she returned to the main room and rolled a loaded book cart to the stacks. While her hands worked instinctively returning source books to the shelves, her mind wandered, imagining the new life Miranda and Rachel would soon have. She was so preoccupied with her imaginations she didn't hear Ellen enter the room.

"Anyone here?"

Startled, Enid dropped the last book. It hit the floor with a thud. "I'm here. I'll be right out." She bent over to pick up the book and placed it on the shelf before exiting the stacks. "I didn't hear you come in. I was lost in my own little world. How did things go this morning? Anything new? Any problems?"

"No problems. An out-of-town couple visited first thing. They were quite surprised at our holdings. They found several relevant records and plan to return during their next vacation. After they left, something odd happened though. Miss Maude called. She wanted to be sure that you would be here when she came in this afternoon. I told her you planned to be back right after lunch. She said she'd call you at home."

"She did. That is unusual for her. She's quite content for you or any of our volunteers to help her and quite capable of searching on her own when she wants to. She has something she wants to show me, though."

"I know. She told me that, too. There's something else. She didn't sound right."

"How so?"

"I'm not sure. She sounded…old."

"She is old. Her voice quavers. Although I will admit, she sounded worse than she did."

"Much worse. She reminded me of my great-aunt during the days before she died."

"Maude hasn't mentioned any ailments that I can remember. She always jokes and says, 'I'm as fit as a long-forgotten fiddle.' Her voice has quavered for some time, but not as much as it has recently. I've noticed a decline in her over the last several weeks in other ways, too. Then again, she is ninety years old."

Enid tugged at her collar. Maude might be ninety, but her decline had come on abruptly. When she searched the stacks a week earlier, her eyes had lost their twinkle. She didn't joke or smile as usual, and she leaned heavily on a walking cane. Enid shook her head as if to rid it of cobwebs, but it wasn't cobwebs she feared.

"Age creeps up on the best of us, and then one day it isn't creeping. It's racing against time itself. In Maude's case, I hope we're overreacting."

Before Ellen could respond, the phone in Enid's office rang.

"I'll get it," said Enid. She hurried to her office and pressed speaker. "Hello?" She heard what sound like words, but she couldn't make them out. "Who's speaking, please? Hello? What did you say?" She thought the caller was Maude Everly, but the woman spoke in such a brittle whisper.

"This is Maude. Can you understand me? Are you there?"

"Yes, Maude. I'm here. This is Enid. I'm having difficulty understanding you."

"I'm sorry, Enid. My voice weakens as the day progresses. I'll try to speak up."

"No problem. What can I do for you?"

"As I mentioned earlier, I'm afraid I don't have much time. You said you could help me this afternoon, but Abigail is running late, and she has to leave for school. I wanted to be certain you were at the library before we left the house."

"You come on in, Maude. I'll meet you at the front door. Abby won't even have to get out of the car." When Enid first met Maude's great-granddaughter, she cringed inside every time she called her by her nickname, but Abby insisted no one but her granny call her by her birth name. Maude never corrected anyone, and in time, calling her Abby sounded natural. "If you're ready to leave before she returns from school, I'll take you home."

"Thank you. We'll leave the house now."

Enid stared at the phone on her desk, listening to the beeping, unaware she had not hung up.

"Is something wrong?"

"What?" Enid looked up to see Ellen standing in the doorway. "No. Yes. That was Maude." Enid lifted the handset and placed it back in its cradle. "You're right. She sounds awful. Worse than this morning. Cryptic, too."

"How so? The cryptic part, I mean."

"She said again she's afraid she doesn't have much time."

"Her doctor might have told her something she hasn't told us. Is she coming in?"

"Yes, she is. Maybe she meant she didn't have much time this afternoon. Can you take care of any other patrons who might come in so I can work one-on-one with her?"

"Sure."

"Good. She's on her way. I'm going out to meet her. I might also take her home when we finish. Maybe she'll shed light on both mysteries—her research and her health."

CHAPTER TWO

Enid waited outside the double doors of the library for Abby to pull her red Honda Civic into the handicap parking space next to the short ramp. She winced as the younger woman now supported Maude when she leaned out of the car and struggled to stand with a walker. Only a week ago, Maude managed with a cane and without assistance.

Maude motioned behind her, and Abby grabbed the worn, soft leather briefcase lying on the seat before shutting the car door. They made their way up the ramp one careful step at a time.

As Maude drew closer, Enid could not help but notice the thinning of her friend's white hair, the trembling of her wrinkled hands, or the loose fit of her favorite peach-colored pants and matching top. The slight creak of one of the walker's wheels deepened her somber mood. She pressed her hand against the heaviness in her chest.

How could anyone decline so much in so little time? Enid brushed away her thoughts, forced a smile, and stepped forward.

"Abby, I could have helped Maude. You need to get to class."

"Thanks, Miss Enid, but I'm used to it. Granny and I have learned to work as a team. I'll only be a few minutes late. Granny, if you think you and Miss Enid can manage, I will let her help you inside. It's all flat from here."

"Yes, of course." Maude patted Abby's arm and then shooed her off, holding onto her walker with her free hand. "We'll make it fine. You go on now. Call me when you're ready to leave campus to see if I'm here or at home."

"Will do! Here's Granny's briefcase, Miss Enid. Thanks."

"You're welcome."

Abby ran back to her Honda, and Enid turned her attention to Maude.

"Here we go then." Conscious of Maude's pride and independence, Enid tried not to hover as she shadowed her progress and opened one of the foyer doors for her. As the door closed behind them, a fresh, clean floral scent of gardenia, lilac, and jasmine wafted through the air.

Enid smiled. She had associated that fragrance with Maude for at least twenty years and maybe longer. She always would. She stepped ahead to open the inner door and held it while Maude made her way into the library proper.

They stopped long enough to speak to Mary at the circulation desk before heading for the genealogy room. There, after a cursory hello to Ellen, Maude headed straight for Enid's office. A few feet from the door, she stopped.

"Enid, I do need to speak with you privately before we go to work. I didn't think to ask. Do you have time?"

"I always have time for my fellow researchers." Enid reached around Maude to open the office door, afraid for her to turn loose of the walker. She stood back and waited for Maude to enter the small corner office and sit in the straight-back chair beside the old teacher's desk. The chair scraped against the hardwood floor when Maude dropped into it.

Enid set the briefcase on the floor between the chair and the desk before slipping past Maude to her own soft leather desk chair. Before she sat, she asked, "Would you prefer to sit here? It's a much more comfortable chair."

"No, thank you. Those chairs make it harder to stand, and this chair's straight back will support my back better."

Enid sat and swiveled to face Maude. "Now then. What can I do to help you speed up your research?"

"Dear, dear. I'm afraid it's much more complicated than that. I have to tell you a story first. One that begins with my own great-grandmother." Maude glanced at the open door. "Would you mind closing the door? I must begin with a secret."

Without a word, Enid nodded, stood, and crossed to the door, closing and locking it in a single motion. She returned to her chair.

"Now, tell me your story."

* * *

Enid leaned back and crossed her ankles. Maude's stories were never short. She might as well get comfortable.

"As a small child," began Maude, "I remember my great-grandmother Olivia Goodwin Woodson—we called her Granny—telling us children about her mother, Charlotte Abbott Goodwin. 'My Mama had a secret,' she would say. 'Someday I'll tell her secret to one of you.' She would wink at me when she said it. Granny Olivia lived with her oldest daughter, my grandma. Grandma Savannah always tried to shush Granny when she mentioned her secret."

Maude picked at the hem of her top before continuing.

"'Now Mama,' she would say. 'You know that's an old tale and not true. I do not want you telling any of my grandchildren such nonsense. None of them want to hear it anyway.'

"Granny Olivia would snub her nose and say, 'One of them will, and one of them will find my sister, my baby doll.'

"When I was nine years old, Granny Olivia took to her bed all of a sudden with pneumonia. She was only seventy-four. Mama would go every day to help Grandma Savannah take care of her. She would take me with her to help out, but she would forbid me to go into the sick room, as she called it, which makes me guess Granny's pneumonia was caused by a viral or bacterial infection.

"One day, I heard her and Grandma whispering about how sick Granny was and how she might not live long. I loved my Granny Olivia. I always suspected she favored me over her other grandchildren. Maybe because I looked and acted so much like her that she and everyone else called me her *spit and image*. Maybe because we liked the same games. I didn't know for certain, but I did know I wanted to see Granny again before she went to heaven.

"So I sneaked to the sick room to see her. I eased the door open and peeked into her room. She appeared so small in her big four-poster bed, as if she had shrunk, and so washed out against those white sheets. Mama had brought fresh cut flowers and they were in the room, but their fragrance couldn't cover the smell of sickness. I gagged.

"When Granny saw me, she managed a faint smile and whispered, 'Cover your mouth with your hankie and come sit in the chair beside my bed.' I did. I had to sit close because her voice was so weak.

"'Maude,' she said, 'I'm going to tell you about Mama's secret. I meant to tell you before now, but I wanted to wait until you were older. I'm afraid I've waited too long. When I tell you, will you promise to find the secret? To find my baby sister, my baby doll?'

"I crossed my heart with my finger and said, 'Yes, Granny, of course, I will.' Then I asked her something that had always puzzled me. 'But why haven't you looked for them?'

"She glanced at the door and whispered even lower, 'I've always known Mama's secret. I didn't have to look for that. I knew where it was hidden. I also knew where she had hidden a treasure and the clues, but I couldn't tell anyone until I found my baby doll. I did look for her, every chance I got, but I had to keep my search a secret as well until I found her, and I never found her. I'm trusting you to do what I couldn't do. I've left you all I have to help you find her—and Mama's secret.'

"Her instructions confused me. It sounded to me like more than one secret needed to be found. I opened my mouth to ask her to explain what she meant and to tell me how to search, but before I could say a word, Mama and Grandma Savannah burst into Granny Olivia's sick room.

"'Here she is,' said Mama. She and Grandma ran into Granny's room so fast their skirts and petticoats sailed behind them. Mama flew into me for being so careless. Grandma flew into Granny for allowing me to stay in the room.

"Granny raised her head and said with all the force she could muster, 'It was meant to be. She knows, and she's promised, and there's nothing you can do about it.'

"I had never seen Grandma Savannah so angry or Granny Olivia so defiant. Grandma looked at Mama and jerked her head toward the door. Mama jerked me up and pulled me out of Granny's room.

"I turned back and yelled, 'I love you, Granny!' She whispered, 'I love you, too, Maude. Don't forget the secret. Don't forget I've left you my dower chest and all Mama's needlepoints, her family Bible, her three precious books, and the pillow from her grandmother. Don't let anyone else have them. Don't let anyone take them away from you.' She lifted a frail hand and blew me a kiss. She gave Grandma a hard stare. Grandma pursed her lips together and didn't say another word.

"As Mama pulled me out of her bedroom, Granny Olivia pushed against Grandma Savannah to rise up on one elbow. 'Wait,' said Granny. She reached toward me and motioned for me to return to her. Her words were broken up by fits of coughing. 'I have to…tell Maude…one more thing. I have to…the account….' Mama kept pulling at me, and Grandma eased Granny back onto her pillow. Grandma said, 'It will wait. You can tell her later. You need to rest now, and she doesn't need to be in this room.' Only later never came. I never saw Granny Olivia alive again. She died that afternoon.

"Grandma spent every free minute that night and the next day telling me I needed to forget Granny's ramblings. 'Your Granny's always been a little eccentric,' she said. 'And you don't need to feel obligated to keep that silly promise she insisted you make.'"

* * *

As tears filled Maude's eyes, Enid reached for a tissue and handed it to her. While Maude wiped her eyes, Enid pulled a bottle of water from one of her bags and twisted the cap loose.

"Here. Take a sip or two."

Maude nodded and drank several sips.

"I never considered my promise silly, but I was only nine years old, and Granny was the first person I'd ever known to die. The next few days were so difficult. The next few years were difficult, too. Granny died in January of 1930. The Great Depression had begun. Mama had to take in laundry to help buy food. I was the oldest, so I had to help with the laundry and the younger children. I had little time left for thinking or remembering much less playing.

"Somewhere in the middle of it all, especially with everyone insisting none of it was true, I forgot about the secret and the sister. I only remembered my promise to search for Granny's missing baby doll. I might have forgotten about her dower chest and its contents if I hadn't secreted them away the day after she died.

"That dower chest held everything she promised me plus several other items—except for two of her books. I knew what items it contained. Granny had told each of us what we were to receive when she died, but after Grandma and Mama acted the way they did, even at my young age, I didn't trust them to give me my inheritance. The day after she died, I made Daddy drag that chest down the stairs, bumping from step to step, and take it home before anyone else had time to think about it or claim it or remove anything. Daddy never questioned my motives. He and Grandma Savannah had locked horns enough over the years that I guess he knew how she could be.

"Afterwards, I searched high and low for Granny's baby doll and the missing books. I searched through every box and chest left at Granny's house. I couldn't find them anywhere. Before they sold her old house, I went through it again, through every room, every closet, every corner of the downstairs, upstairs, and even the dusty old attic. There was no baby doll nor any books to be found in the dower chest other than the Bible and the *New England Primer*. I never found the other two books, *The Scarlet Letter* and *The Sketch Book*.

"Whenever I tried to talk to them about the baby doll, both Mama and Grandma shushed me. Grandma said, 'I told you Granny Olivia was eccentric, always had a wild imagination, and at the last her mind wasn't right because of her age, her sickness, and the fever.'

"Mama chimed in, too. 'Forget that baby sister nonsense, too,' she said. 'I've never heard anything about a baby sister. I do recall one of the aunts telling me how Granny had a falling out with her own grandmother over a lost doll.'

"Grandma didn't comment on the falling out or the lost doll, but both of them insisted I put it all out of my mind and forget the ramblings of a sick old woman. I didn't quite forget it, although to my shame, with Granny's death, the Depression, and life, I did more or less shove it to the back of my mind. It stayed there until long after I began researching our family history, which if you remember I did only because of your encouragement. Even after I began to remember, I never came across anything that might shed light on Granny's last words."

Enid frowned and rocked against the back of her chair. "What a sad story." Then her frown softened. "I do remember how much encouragement it took to get you interested."

"It took a lot, didn't it? I did it for you, not for me. I thought my family and its history were well documented, especially Mama's side. We had names, dates, and photographs of every ancestor from every generation on both sides of the family. We had mementoes from many of them. Why would I need to spend hours and hours researching? It was your first time to offer a family history workshop after assuming the directorship. What was it? Twenty years ago?"

"Yes, indeed."

"You told us at our Woman's Missionary Union meeting that Benjamin Alexander, rest his soul, needed to know the workshops would be a sound investment and a self-supporting endeavor, so you needed a good class turnout. Half of us signed up for your first workshop."

"Every one of you continued your research after the workshop ended, too."

"That we did. For different reasons. Some found a new hobby. Some wanted to add branches to their family trees. Some, like me, enjoyed learning about their ancestors and the times in which they lived, things they never knew in spite of having a well-developed family tree.

"I have to confess, I also fleshed out my tree a bit. We knew from Charlotte's family Bible the names and dates for Mama's maternal line back to the mid-1700s in Pennsylvania. We knew Daddy's paternal line back to the early 1800s in Virginia thanks to his grandfather's records, but we certainly didn't know all the siblings and their descendants or all the interesting details. More importantly, we didn't know much on the other lines that married into the family through the years. My goal was to trace each line back to the 1700s beginning with my grandparents.

"Along the way, I learned such fascinating bits of history— about both my family and our nation. One of those bits was the list of items found with many of the earlier will and probate records—from geese and chickens to cows and horses, stores of wheat and corn to flax and straw, plows and anvils to axes and hoes, pewter and tin to beds and bureaus, and wool and tobacco. One ancestor's list was three typed pages long. Not every family had such good fortune, but some farms were self-sufficient little communities. I began with my more recent generations, and I had so much to keep me busy that I hadn't made my way back to such records for Charlotte and Peter.

"Except for Abigail, my family thinks of my research as something to keep me occupied, hobby or not. For me, it was and is a fascinating occupation. I could not imagine how one family could move here and yon and all still live in the same county or that they could all have lived through so much of our nation's history.

"In addition to learning about my ancestors and our history, the research kept my mind sharp. Until lately, that is. I'm still somewhat sharp, but I get things mixed up some days and feel a bit confused. Instead of a sharp tack, I think of my mind more as a blade dulled by years of use. I don't suppose that can be helped, though. Time dulls us all.

"The sad thing is that it took my research for me to finally find evidence of Granny's mama's secret, and what I've found is quite worrisome." Maude stopped to sip her water.

Enid leaned forward, eager to hear the rest of Charlotte and Olivia's story.

CHAPTER THREE

"Maude, before you begin again, would you like some coffee?" Enid bent over to retrieve her thermos from her bag.

"No, I'm not a big coffee drinker. I'm fine with water. You go ahead."

Enid poured a cupful from her thermos and leaned back in her chair. "So you discovered the secret?"

"Not exactly. Evidence of it though. As I said, I had forgotten about the secret. Then about six months ago, I was zipping through microfilm of old issues of *The Bakersville Guardian*. I was skimming the pages for anything to do with any of my ancestors, more to jumpstart the day than anything else because I didn't have anything in particular in mind.

"Quite by accident, I came across a newspaper advertisement about runaway slaves, two who belonged to Granny's daddy, Peter Goodwin, and one who belonged to Granny's granddaddy, Abraham Abbott." Maude pulled a copy of the advertisement from her briefcase and handed it to Enid. "The advertisement includes copies of two photographs, one of a young man named Daniel, the other of a young mother named Hannah and her child, Miriam. The child looks to be about two years old.

"The advertisement is black and white, of course, but Daniel appears to have short, black hair and to be very dark complexioned, tall, and muscular. Hannah appears to be much lighter, although she too has black hair pulled up behind her head. Miriam is even lighter than her mother, but her black curls are just as dark."

"The advertisement describes Hannah as 'a young mulatto woman' and Miriam as a 'quadroon child.'"

"Yes. Something about that photograph triggered a memory or a thought or something that brought my promise to Granny back to my conscious mind. It also reminded me of a photo I had seen of Granny as a child. You will no doubt think I'm crazy. At first, I thought I must be, too, but I got it into my head that the slave child was Granny's baby doll, maybe even her sister.

"That thought drove me to keep my promise to Granny, but I had no idea how to discern the truth much less research the lives of slave descendants during or after the war. I had no way of determining where the runaway slaves might have gone, what surname they might have used when they stopped running, or even if they kept their given names. However, I believed with all my heart that if there was a way, I could find it, determine what happened to Granny's sister, and find her descendants before I left this world.

"Until the last month or so anyway. Now I'm not so sure I can." Maude wrung her hands. "Enid, I'm slipping away a little more each day physically and mentally. I'm afraid I don't have much time left. I'm afraid I'll be forced to leave the search and the promise with my own great-granddaughter. That has forced me to make the difficult decision to allow someone else to be privy to our family secret whether this is it or it's something else. I need your help before it's too late."

"You know I'll help you, Maude, in any way I can, and keep any confidence you request."

"Yes, I do. Knowing I could trust your discretion made my decision easier. Especially in light of the opposition I've gotten from certain family members and perhaps others."

"I'm confused. Why would your family care? What would it matter to anyone else? Wait. Before we delve into that, you said you found evidence of your ancestor's secret. What in the world does it have to do with runaway slaves, and why do you think the child was her sister? Are you basing it solely on the picture? Even if she was, how could it affect anyone now? The secret had to have been from…when…prior to or during the Civil War?"

"Precisely. Prior to, during, and after the Civil War. No, I'm not basing my suspicions solely on the picture. As I said, the first evidence I found was the advertisement. It was placed in *The Bakersville Guardian* on Wednesday, October 1, 1862, about a year and a half after the war began. Granny's father, Peter Goodwin, placed the advertisement to request any information anyone might have on the whereabouts of the three runaway slaves who had disappeared the previous Friday night. He described them, forbade anyone to harbor them, and offered a reward for their capture.

"After I saw the photograph of Hannah and Miriam, I searched Granny's mementoes and photos and found the one I remembered. It was of Granny Olivia and her mother Charlotte when Granny was about six years old." Maude pulled another sheet of paper from her briefcase. "Place this copy of Granny's photo beside the one in the advertisement. Anyone can see the women and children were photographed at the same time in the same room. Not only was the lighting the same, but the two women sat in identical Queen Anne armchairs made of carved walnut sitting on either side in front of a stone fireplace.

"And notice their clothing. Both women wore similar dresses with full skirts, fitted bodices, and bell-shaped sleeves of a solid color without trim of any kind. So did both girls although their dresses were shorter and high waisted. Because of its rough edge, I had always thought someone had trimmed Granny's photo. Seeing the picture in the advertisement convinced me that it was the other half.

"More to the point of my theory, I couldn't help but notice that not only did the women resemble each other, but their daughters resembled each other. That's when I got it into my head that Miriam must have been Granny's baby doll! That thought prompted the recollection of another forgotten memory.

"When I was a small child, Granny Olivia would set me in her lap and show me photos from her childhood. In one of them, she held a baby girl whom she called her baby doll. Granny said she was four years old in that picture. The baby appeared to be one or two months old. Their ages in that photo corresponded to the ages in the later photo.

"Granny would always say, 'She was my baby doll, but she was more than that. Someday I'll tell you how much more.' Then I remembered sneaking into Granny's room after she died to look through her photograph box for that very picture. It was not in the box. I never discovered what happened to it. I remembered thinking, 'Grandma took it,' but I never knew for certain.

"Enid, I'm convinced Miriam was Granny's half sister, and I wouldn't be surprised if the mothers were half sisters, too."

"All by the same father?"

"No, no. By two fathers. From the recording of a deed of gift at her marriage and from the family Bible, I know that when Granny's mother, Charlotte, married, the items given to her by her parents included a young house slave named Hannah."

Maude handed Enid a transcription of the deed of gift. Enid read the first part of it aloud.

> Know all men by these presents that we Abraham and Mary Abbott of the State of Tennessee and County of Henry For and in consideration of the natural love and affection which we have towards our daughter Charlotte Abbott hath given granted and conveyed and by these presents do give grant and convey unto our said daughter Charlotte Abbott her heirs and assigns a certain Negro girl named Hannah about fifteen years of age To have and to hold the Said girl Hannah with her increase and all the profits and benefits arising therefrom.

"Enid, such a transaction in and of itself is enough to make me sick, but to think that Abraham fathered both Charlotte and Hannah and then Peter fathered both Olivia and Miriam makes my blood boil." Maude accepted another tissue from

Enid and dabbed at her tears. "I'm sorry. I don't mean to act foolish."

"You're not acting, and you're not foolish. I've seen such reactions on a number of occasions from descendants of both slave owners and slaves for the atrocities done and those received. Do you think that's Charlotte's secret?"

"I'm convinced it's one of several secrets but perhaps the first. In the advertisement, Peter accused the young man, Daniel, of stealing money out of Peter's house in addition to absconding with Hannah and Miriam. The actual details of the theft could be another secret. Then there is the missing child."

"Another little girl?"

"No. A young boy. Hannah's first child, Isaac. You see, Charlotte's mother Mary—and then Charlotte herself after she married—recorded the names, births, marriages, and deaths for family and slaves in the family Bible. Charlotte recorded the sales dates for those slaves who were sold before the war and the emancipation dates for those freed after the Emancipation Proclamation and after the war.

"However, she never recorded anything about the recapture or emancipation of the runaway slaves or about the status of Isaac. Both Bible records and census records show that Hannah had two children, first the boy named Isaac and then the girl named Miriam. The Bible records the birth and death of another boy, Joshua, who died days after his birth.

"For Isaac, though, I can find no other date except his birth date and no other information of any kind. Would his mother leave him behind? If so, why is there no entry concerning his sale or emancipation or death? I believe I must account for two children, which means I may now have at least three secrets to uncover. The relationships between the mothers and their daughters, the theft of Peter's money, and the disappearance of the child Isaac."

"Maude, tell me what your search has entailed so far, and then we'll map out a new search plan."

"Thank you, Enid. I should have come to you sooner. I thought I had learned enough to find them on my own. I also wanted to avoid sharing any of this with anyone but family until I discovered the details of the secret. Of course, I also thought I had plenty of time." Maude scowled and tapped her fingers together.

"What's wrong, Maude?"

"I wish I hadn't shared what little I did share with family, either, but that and their opposition is a conversation for another time. Right now, we need to leave such thoughts so you can tell me how to find an escaped slave. How and where do I search for Hannah and Miriam's descendants? How do I discover the whole of Charlotte's secret—or secrets? If I find Miriam's descendants, what do I do then? If the two women were sisters, would DNA tests prove it?"

Enid wasn't sure she wanted to leave the topic of Maude's family until later, but she had always made it a point to follow a patron's lead before making suggestions of her own. She hoped she wouldn't regret doing so now.

CHAPTER FOUR

"How do you search for an escaped slave?" repeated Enid as she sank back into her chair. "As a rule, I would tell an African American researcher the same thing I would tell any other researcher. Begin with what you know and work your way back."

"We don't have that option."

"No, we don't, but we can address that and your other questions later. For now, I want to think about the advertisement and see what census records you've checked. You've no doubt searched the 1850 Census and Slave Schedule."

"I have—as well as both of those for 1860 and the census for 1870."

"Not all census enumerators for 1850 and 1860 recorded the names of the slaves. I don't believe they did for either census in Henry County."

"They did not. They recorded only age, gender, and race. Black or Mulatto."

"We need to move to the other room so we can spread things out. Can you manage?"

"I can with a little assistance. I need to stretch a bit anyway."

Once they settled themselves at a table in the research room, Maude opened the soft leather briefcase she held in her lap and began spreading the document copies on the table in front of them.

"I have printouts of the census and slave schedule pages and transcriptions of the census information for the family of Peter and Charlotte Goodwin. Peter and Charlotte married in 1850 prior to the taking of the census, so they are in the household together. Charlotte is sixteen. Peter is thirty-six. Their slaves are enumerated but not named.

"I knew from family stories and the family Bible that Charlotte's parents and Peter owned slaves and from my research that Charlotte brought one slave with her when she married. I searched the Deed Books and found several records relating to purchases, sales, and transfers of slaves to and from our ancestors. Two were relevant to my search. You've seen the copy of the Deed of Gift to Charlotte at her marriage naming Hannah and giving her age as fifteen, making her a year younger than Charlotte.

"The second, which occurred sixteen years earlier, is the Bill of Sale for Daniel, his parents Esther and Jacob, and Celia." Maude handed a copy to Enid. "Charlotte's father, Abraham, purchased the four of them in 1834 together from a man from Alabama. The entry for Daniel says 'Daniel, infant son of Esther and Jacob.' Celia apparently had no children. Hannah, her first child, would have been born the following year. Both transactions are recorded in the family Bible as well. Jacob's death was recorded a few months after his purchase.

"The 1850 slave schedule lists only one fifteen-year-old mulatto female slave in the household of Peter and Charlotte. She has to be Hannah.

"The 1860 slave schedule also lists only one mulatto female slave in Peter's household who is a year younger than Charlotte. Two children are listed for Charlotte and Peter, Mason nine and Olivia, my great-grandmother, four. Two children are listed in the slave schedule immediately below the mulatto woman, a boy seven and a girl a few months old, both mulatto and the only mulatto children listed in the household. Their genders and ages match the information recorded in the family Bible for Hannah's children, Isaac and Miriam.

"Also in both schedules on Abraham and Mary Abbott's farm, I found one black male who was a year older than Hannah. I'm thinking he must have been Daniel. The advertisement for the three runaway slaves confirms everything except for the existence of Isaac after 1860.

"In 1870, I again did not find Isaac in the area. Nor did I find Peter and Charlotte. I did find Mason listed as head of household at the family home. Olivia, who was fourteen, was listed with her aunt and uncle, Isaiah and Nancy Kessler. This would confirm that both Peter and Charlotte had died by 1870. This is supported by the family Bible, which gives their deaths as 1867 and 1869. As we had this information, I had never bothered to look for their obituaries but more about that later.

"I also searched for Hannah, Miriam, and Daniel in the 1870 records in three states—Tennessee and the two states bordering us to the north and northwest, Kentucky and Missouri. I searched by their given names. They would now be free and could establish their own household, but I did not find any household with all three names. I even did a page-by-page search of the counties closest to us on the off chance that their names had been transcribed incorrectly."

"You must have spent hours searching through the 1870 census."

"I did and found nothing on the three runaways. I also searched the Freedmen's Bureau for marriages in case Hannah and Daniel were still in or had returned to the south and married here. Nothing. I attempted to search birth, marriage, and death records from 1860 to 1870 in general but using only Hannah and Daniel with no last names. In the U.S., I found over one hundred and fifty thousand records. When I selected African American records, I came up with over six hundred thousand records, which did not make any sense at all until I realized that set included records from other countries as well.

"Next, as slaves often took the surnames of their former owners, I added Abbott as a last name for Daniel, which reduced both numbers to fewer than fifty, but no records for a Daniel and a Hannah together. That's when I reached my frustration limit, and that's why I'm here today. It doesn't appear that I've uncovered much in six months, but I had other projects as well, and I didn't think about my time running out."

"You've done well, Maude. Abbott would be the logical surname for Daniel to choose if he had remained on the Abbott farm. Under the circumstances, though, with the warrant and all, I would think he might have chosen a different surname. We are, of course, assuming he and Hannah married, and for now, I think that's a safe assumption to work with.

"The next step would be to continue your search for an 1870 household with Daniel, Hannah, and Miriam but in other states. However, as you found for Kentucky and Missouri, there are bound to be thousands of such households, so we need to limit the number of states we search. It would help if we knew the route they took and whether or not they actually crossed into Canada, which considering when they left, they might not have done."

"Why not?"

"As they left in October of 1862 and Lincoln issued the Emancipation Proclamation in January of 1863, they might not have reached Canada before they learned of it. They might have settled in one of the northern U.S. states. If they did go north, they might have taken any one of three primary routes from West Tennessee—through Kentucky into either Illinois, Indiana, or Ohio. Of course, that's assuming they took one of the primary routes."

"A lot of assuming, Enid."

"We have to pick up your search somewhere. Based on the bill of sale, Daniel was born around 1834 in Alabama. Hannah was born the following year in Tennessee. Let's add that information to our search and start with Illinois."

Enid stood and waited for Maude to pull herself up. She followed the elderly woman as she pushed her walker over to the microfilm readers. Maude eased into a chair in front of the first reader and waited for Enid to gather their microfilm.

After an afternoon of searching, resting, adjusting parameters, and searching again, Enid had managed to help Maude identify only one couple named Daniel and Hannah in Illinois, but Hannah was too young, and the couple had no child named Miriam. They turned their search to the other two states. They found no such couple in Indiana or Ohio. By the time they stopped, Ellen had left for the day.

Maude closed her eyes and leaned back in her chair.

"You're tired, aren't you?" asked Enid.

"I'm frustrated, but yes, I'm also tired, a little more so than usual. We should stop for now and continue tomorrow. It's getting late, and I'm surprised Abby hasn't called."

"I agree. It's almost six o'clock. I shouldn't have allowed you to stay so late."

"Enid, you're old enough to know better than try to tell an old person what to do. Besides, I need to finish this—soon."

"I do understand. For now, though, we both need to rest and eat. I'll tell you what. I'll turn off the reader and stack the microfilm in the to-be-filed box for tomorrow. You call Abby and tell her I'm taking you home. We'll stop for fried chicken dinners on the way. After we eat, if you'd like, you can show me what you've found in your Granny Olivia's dower chest. I'm eager to see your chest of treasures."

"I do like that idea. Maybe you can see something that neither Abby nor I have seen among the items. For the life of me, I haven't been able to see a clue in anything although I do have a thought or two about the clues." She pulled her phone from her purse and dialed her great-granddaughter.

Enid returned to her office and gathered her belongings. Back in the genealogy room, she helped Maude up from the chair and over to the door."

"Thank you, dear." Maude's voice was scarcely above a whisper. "Abigail was getting ready to leave, but as you're taking me home, she asked if it would be all right for her to stay a little longer and check out some research materials she needed. Do you mind staying with me until she returns home?"

"Not at all."

"I didn't think you would. I told her if she happened to arrive before we did, I wanted her to wait for us before entering the house. I don't know why, but I worry about her entering the house alone. I like to be there. Silly of me, I guess."

"Not silly at all."

At least, I hope it's not silly, thought Enid. *I've never known Maude to be unduly frightened by anything. Maybe it's part of her decline.*

CHAPTER FIVE

As Enid pulled into Maude's driveway, she whispered, "Thank goodness."

"What did you say?" asked Maude.

"I said thank goodness. I didn't mean for you to hear me. I dreaded the trip up those steep steps with the walker. I didn't realize you had added a ramp."

"I didn't want to. I had no choice. My son Barton knew a man—good, quick, and efficient. We had him build it a couple of weeks ago. It doesn't detract too much, do you think?"

"Not at all. It looks fine. Let me take the food and set it on the table on the porch. I'll come back and walk with you up that new ramp."

"I'll be glad to wait."

As she hurried up the ramp, Enid admired the workmanship. The ramp blended in with the house itself, a beautiful old country farmhouse with two stories, an attic, and a wraparound front porch. When she returned to her Subaru, she found Maude staring at the top of the house. Worry lines creased her forehead.

"What's wrong?"

"Nothing, I'm sure. These old eyes. That's all. I thought I saw a shadow cross the attic window."

Enid glanced up at the window.

"It's not there now. Let's go in. I don't want that chicken to get cold."

Both women laughed as they eased up the ramp.

Once inside, Maude shuffled into the dining room and sat at the table to rest while Enid went to the kitchen for glasses and a pitcher of iced tea. When she returned, she poured tea into two of the glasses, left one empty for Abby, and sat the pitcher on a wooden tray. She went around the table to sit on Maude's left facing the doorway.

Maude lowered her head. "Enid, please say grace."

As they lifted their heads a moment later, Enid noticed that Maude's hands trembled, so she opened all of the containers.

"May I fill your plate, Maude?"

"Yes, please."

Both women focused on the food in front of them. When they finished, which did not take either of them long, Enid refilled their glasses.

"I'll wait until after Abby eats to clean up. We can rest until she arrives."

"Which I hope is soon. It's almost eight o'clock."

"While we wait for her, tell me more about the dower chest and its contents. The Bible must be old."

"It is. It had been in the family at least one or two generations before it came to Mary Abbott. Mary passed it down to her daughter Charlotte, who passed it on to Granny Olivia."

"That would make it over two hundred years old."

"Two hundred and twenty to be exact. It's an Isaac Collins's Bible, King James Version, printed in 1791 in New Jersey."

Enid twitched in her seat.

"Now don't get in a dither," said Maude. "Granny kept it in a wooden Bible box. I kept it in that same box except for when I took it out to gaze upon it or read from it until I began attending your workshops twenty years ago. After your lecture on caring for antiques and old books, I bought an archival-quality paper board box for it. I wash my hands and dry them thoroughly before I take it out. And the attic, which used to be a spare bedroom, is ventilated and stays at a reasonably constant temperature."

"You've done well," said Enid.

"I thought so, too." Maude leaned back, a satisfied smile on her face.

"Does it include the Apocrypha? Collins made the Apocrypha optional to purchasers."

"Yes, it does have the Apocrypha."

"It's also recognized as the first family Bible printed in America."

"It seems I have more than I realized."

"I would say so. Do you have any idea how valuable it is?"

"No, no idea at all. I'm sure it's worth a little, being that old, but I've never given it much thought."

"Give it thought, Maude, much thought and soon."

"Oh, my."

"Yes, oh, my. You need to decide who is to receive it at your passing and get it in writing if you haven't already." Enid paused long enough to lick her lips. "You also need to have it insured. Personally, I would store it somewhere under lock and key when I didn't have it out to read or display." Enid stopped again to rub her hands together. "I can't wait to see it!"

"By the way," said Maude, "I've only read a few passages at a time from the old Bible. It's in good shape but it is fragile, so I've been careful with it. With those passages I have read, I didn't notice any differences from the King James Version I use today. Do you know if there were any differences?

"The reason I ask is that some of the framed needlepoints in the dower chest have Bible verses on them in addition to scenery or floral designs, but they don't all correspond to what I think I remember from the Bible I use today. I've always wondered if the old Bible was a different translation, if Charlotte didn't know the scriptures that well, or if maybe they contained the clues Granny Olivia mentioned. I haven't taken the time to check them. Maybe because I've not felt well lately, but that's no excuse for all the years prior to this."

"That I don't know for certain, but I doubt there would have been significant changes. We should compare the needlepoints to both your Collins Bible and your personal King James Bible."

At that moment, a floorboard creaked above them. Both women flinched at the sound.

"Enid, tell me you heard that, too."

"I did hear it."

Then the front door slammed. Enid jumped up from her chair. Maude grabbed at her chest.

"Granny, I'm home!"

"Thank goodness," whispered Maude.

"We're in the dining room, Abby," called Enid.

Abby rushed in, dropping her books and bags by the door.

"Food! Great! I'm starved!" Abby stopped halfway to the table. "What's wrong? You two look as if you've seen ghosts."

"Heard them."

"What?" Abby's eyes got wide.

"We heard something. It sounded like a board creaking in the attic," said Enid.

"And I thought I saw a shadow at the attic window when we pulled up in the driveway," said Maude. "We need to check it out."

"Not we. Miss Enid and I can do it," called Abby over her shoulder as she raced to the stairs.

Enid followed the agile young woman into the hallway and up the stairs. She was halfway up when Abby pulled open the attic door.

"Abby, wait! We need to call someone."

"No, we can't wait. We need to catch the intruder."

Abby disappeared through the door.

When Enid reached the top of the stairs, she heard a thunk of wood against wood.

"Abby?"

"I'm all right! But he's getting away!"

Enid blinked as she entered the attic lit now only by the soft glow of twilight. Then she saw Abby leaning out an open back window. She rushed across the room and pulled the girl back in.

"I saw him running across the back yard. He's getting away."

"He's gone, Abby, and we need to check on Maude. She'll be terrified. Let's lock this window and get back downstairs."

"You're right." Abby locked the window and stacked empty boxes under it. "Maybe if he tries again, he'll fall through the boxes, and we'll hear him."

"And maybe he won't come back."

Abby raised an eyebrow at her. "Yea, right."

They returned to the stairwell and descended the stairs, Abby again in front and covering ground faster than Enid. Maude met them at the newel post at the bottom, gripping her walker and gasping for air. Abby took her arm and guided her toward the dining room.

"Granny, you should have waited in here. We're fine." She embraced the frail woman and held her close.

Enid could see the trembling of Maude's body against Abby's. She turned a chair out. "Here, Maude. You should sit."

While Abby eased her into the chair, Enid poured her a glass of iced tea and helped her hold it as she drank. Abby still stood at her shoulder.

"Maude, you don't try to climb those stairs, do you?"

"Heavens, no, Enid. Not anymore. I had my bedroom moved to the first floor years ago. Abigail does any climbing that needs to be done."

"If you think you're okay now, I'm going to check out back. Abby, stay here with your granny."

"I will."

Before heading out back, Enid checked the front door.

"Locked and no scratches."

When she checked the back door, she found it locked as well with no scratches. Outside, she found a ladder still propped against the house. There was enough twilight left for her to see where the intruder had landed hard on one foot.

"A man's shoe." She surveyed the back yard. "The back is hidden by trees on three sides. Someone could have cut through the trees at the back onto Maude's property and then crossed her yard. The trees on either side would have prevented the neighbors from seeing him." She tapped her chin with her fingers. "But how did he get into the house? That window was unlocked from the inside. I'll have to ask Maude and Abby about that."

She spun around, locked the back door behind her, and returned to the dining room.

* * *

When Enid returned, Abby had filled her plate.

"Granny said I should eat. I didn't argue. I'm glad you got the herb battered chicken. I like the crispy, but this pleases my taste buds more."

"It's also easier to chew," said Maude.

Enid braced herself to say what had to be said.

"Maude, you need to call the chief. Patrick needs to be made aware of what's happened, and he needs to gather any evidence he can."

Maude stiffened. "No. Absolutely not. My family already thinks I'm crazy. They'll have me in a home before the sun rises. I won't have it."

"Maude—"

"No."

"Abby?"

"Granny's the boss."

"Okay then. On another note, Abby, you kept saying *he*. Are you sure you saw a man?"

"No, I'm not positive, but he did look like a man and run like a man, and he moved like someone in shape, athletic even."

"The footprint I saw suggested a man's shoe. We can't rule out anyone, though, at this point. Man or woman, have either of you considered how the intruder got into the house?"

"Up the ladder through the window, right?" Abby sipped her tea as she waited for one of them to answer.

"Toting a ladder onto the property is unlikely," said Enid.

"It's probably mine," said Maude. "It stays on the back porch. Anyone could have moved it."

Enid tapped the table. "That would mean one of you left the attic window unlocked."

"No way, Miss Enid. I checked all of the windows and doors after I moved in. Nothing was unlocked then. I haven't unlocked anything except the front and back doors since then, and I make sure they are both locked when we leave the house and when we go to bed at night. No. Unh-unh. We did not leave that window unlocked." She frowned at her tea glass. "But it doesn't unlock from the outside."

"Exactly."

"Thank goodness Abigail had moved the dower chest downstairs."

"Who knew you originally stored it in the attic?"

"To my knowledge, only family knew anything about it, much less where it was stored. But back to that window. Even if I could have climbed the stairs, I never would have left that or any window unlocked."

"Which means someone would have to be in the house in order to get to the attic window."

"Yes."

"Someone who had been in the house could have gone to the attic and left the window unlocked for a return visit. Have you had any unusual or infrequent visitors lately?"

"No, not that I recall."

"Granny, are you sure?"

"No one has been in the house the last couple of days except the two of us."

"Both doors were locked, and I didn't see any scratches on the locks. What about keys, Maude? Who has keys?"

"Besides Abby and myself?" Maude squinted as she thought. "More people than should and maybe more than I can remember. All of my children have keys. Some of my grandchildren, including Abby's mother. My lawyer, Lowell Franklin, which means any of his staff probably have access. Jedidiah Goodwin, a distant cousin who is also my handyman. Janet Baker, another distant cousin who is a nurse. She checks in on me from time to time. My neighbor to the right. I can't think of anyone else."

"One more at least," said Abby.

"Who?"

"Not who. Where."

"Yes, the key taped to the bottom of the flowerpot at the end of the back porch."

"Everybody in the family knows about the key under the pot."

Maude's sheepish grin made them all laugh.

"As I got older and heard stories about other old people, I began to fear something would happen to me and no one could get in."

"Maude, someone could always break a door down or break a window."

"I was afraid of that, too! But I've lived here since I married, and I've never had a break-in or even been frightened."

"Until now."

"Until now. Not much help, is it?" She laughed. "Is that not the cat's meow? Give no one keys and die alone, or give everyone keys and get knocked over the head."

They all laughed together but quickly got serious again.

"Maude, you need to have all of your locks changed."

"I think you're right. I'll call my cousin tomorrow."

"Maybe you should have someone other than a family member install the new locks. Maybe you don't need to give everyone a key. In the meantime, Abby and I will make sure all the windows are locked."

"I agree, Granny. More than Miss Enid knows. I don't suppose you've told her the other stuff."

"No, not yet."

"What other stuff?"

Maude pressed her lips together. "Don't you go getting all daughterly on me, Enid Gilchrist. I get enough of that from my own daughters."

"I won't, but if I'm to help you, don't you think I need to have some idea of what I'm up against?"

"That might be helpful."

"Okay, then. What stuff?"

Maude stared at the empty plate in front of her. "Maybe you two could clear the table and let me go to the living room before we get into that."

"I'll clear, Miss Enid, if you'll help Granny."

CHAPTER SIX

Enid helped Maude into the living room. Abby soon joined them.

"Let's get this over with," said Maude. "Remember how I told you how I thought I had learned enough to find the runaway slaves on my own and how I wanted to avoid sharing any of this with anyone but family until I discovered the details of the secret?"

"Yes."

"And then how I said I wished I hadn't shared it with family, either?"

"I do. You also said that was a conversation for another time."

"This is all a part of the same conversation, and this might as well be that other time." Maude twisted the hem of her blouse. "I did share a little with the family. Not long after that, I…I received a note, a threatening note."

"From one of your family? What did you tell them, and what did the note say?"

"I didn't really tell anyone anything specific. It was at our last family reunion of the Goodwin and Abbott descendants, about six weeks ago. What I did was ask questions. I asked every person there who was of mine or my daughter's generation if he or she remembered any stories or had any photographs from our Goodwin and Abbott lines from the years before, during, or after the Civil War.

"I tried to be discreet. I reminded them I was researching our family history and told them the information from those years wasn't as plentiful as from other years. Different ones told me I needed to leave those years alone. I got all kinds of indignant comments. Why dredge up that part of our history? Why embarrass the family by acknowledging publicly that our ancestors owned slaves? A few voiced sentiments I'd heard growing up but never thought I'd hear in this day and age."

"Like what?"

"Mostly about how our family struggled after the war and how those struggles were a direct result of losing property without any recompense for it and how it took generations to overcome the loss. They were talking about the freed slaves, of course, but it didn't take generations to recoup any supposed losses. It took those first generations a little longer than later ones because they weren't as successful at running their farms with hired labor as they were using slaves. They had to learn new ways of conducting business. A few of my extended family still find ways to attribute current situations in our country to the War Between the States. I've never understood how individuals in the same family could have such opposing views."

"Did you share your suspicions about the women being half sisters?"

"I didn't dare! I've told Abigail, of course, but no one else. Some members of my family deny any *mixing of the races* ever occurred at all and certainly not in our family. Some go so far as to say doing so is sacrilege. By the end of the day, I had almost decided to keep any future research efforts—and findings—to myself. Receiving the note settled the issue. I didn't dare mention anything to anybody after that. I even tried to distance Abigail from my research, but she wouldn't have that."

"Maude, what did the note say? Did the writer threaten you personally?"

"Not exactly, but maybe. The note…. It said the secret must die with me, which could be nothing more than someone telling me to keep the secret and take it with me to the grave whenever I die."

Enid couldn't stop the furrows from crossing her brow. "It could also mean the person is threatening your life if you try to make the secret public."

"I know. It could. I'm not so worried about me, though. I feel like I'm on my last leg anyway. It does worry me about Abigail. She is a champion of the oppressed of the world. She saw the note, too, and she will not let this go." Maude sighed and patted Abby's hand. "I never should have told her about the secret or the baby doll." She grew still and quiet, her only movement the wringing of her hands. "I wish I hadn't. Especially after the note, my sudden decline, and…another piece I found in the newspaper."

"I worried about your health. The changes came on rather sudden, it seemed. But what bearing does this news piece have on that?"

"The reunion took place a little over six weeks ago. On Saturday, the eighteenth of June, to be exact. I received the note on the following Friday, the twenty-fourth of June. By Wednesday of the next week, I noticed a drop in my energy level, not enough to see my doctor but enough that I didn't feel like driving to church that night. I called a friend to pick me up instead. I've declined a little more each week since then."

Maude paused long enough to stop her lip from quivering.

"Anyway, about a week later, I found my great-great-grandmother Charlotte's obituary. Of course, she had passed long before I was born, but I knew about her. I had seen pictures of her. Her birth, marriage, and death dates were recorded in the family Bible, but I knew none of the details about her death. My own sudden decline and the response I received at the reunion stirred me to search for her obituary."

"Did it give her cause of death?"

"Not exactly. It did say she died unexpectedly after a short illness in August of 1869. She was thirty-five years old. I had never really paid that much attention to the dates in the Bible before I took the family history workshop, and I guess I had it in my head that she lived much longer than that because of this one photograph I remembered of her and Granny Olivia. Granny was thirteen. Charlotte looked old in the picture, much older than thirty-five, but her name was on the back. I did question whether or not the photo had been mislabeled and the older woman was Charlotte's mother Mary.

"I hadn't given it another thought until after I read the obituary. I found that photo. The date and names were inscribed on the back. Charlotte and Olivia. The picture had been taken the week before Charlotte died. She looked like such an old woman. She was thin. Her hair, which in earlier pictures had been full and beautiful, had also thinned. She appeared fragile and feeble. I've learned to pay more attention to photos, that's for sure. More to the point, her picture made me think of myself even if I am as old as I look. Then I found something else." Maude studied her hands.

"Go on."

Maude sighed. "Charlotte's obituary said Peter had preceded her in death, which I confirmed with the dates in the Bible. So I went back to the microfilm another day to find his obituary. I wound forward to hers with the intention of rewinding to find his, but I was winding the film so fast, I went past hers. I slowed down and rewound from where I was. If I had been going any faster, I would have missed it."

"His obit?"

"No. The piece concerning the inquest for Charlotte."

"Inquest?"

"Yes. There was some concern on the part of Charlotte's sister Nancy that she might have died of arsenic poisoning, and the sheriff had called for an inquest. It was held here in Bakersville. The doctor stated that he suspected some form of cancer, either stomach or female. The sheriff stated that he did not find any evidence at the house, in the outbuildings, or in the slave quarters of any poisons that she might have taken intentionally or by accident. Neither mentioned any tests for poisoning. Of course, back then in a small rural town, they might not have had the means or even known how to test for poisons. The jurors agreed that no evidence existed to support poisoning and that the doctor's statement concerning cause of death would stand. I printed it out but tried to dismiss it. I continued winding backward until I found Peter's obituary. He died following a *fit of apoplexy*, which I assume was a stroke."

"I would like to see copies of the original obituaries and the inquest piece."

"Of course. After I found the newspaper piece, I found the corresponding entry in the Henry County Circuit Court Minutes and printed that out. It said basically the same thing. I think you'll see what I finally saw, but the relevance of what I found quite by accident didn't hit me until several days later."

"How so?"

"My family already thought I was both senile and paranoid. They, especially my oldest daughter Isabel and her oldest daughter Natalie, Abigail's mother, had suggested several times I needed to consider moving out of my house. I would be in a nursing home by now if Abigail hadn't stepped in.

"She had been admitted for the fall semester to UT Martin as a history major. She planned to live at home the first year to save money. Then she decided to take one class this summer. After the hoopla over the nursing home idea, Abigail insisted she should stay with me. Somehow, she convinced her mother that not only would it save her time and gas money, it would give me more time in my own home. Though neither Isabel nor Natalie liked the idea, they couldn't argue with her reasoning. Natalie lives about thirty minutes farther east than I do. Living here would cut an hour off Abigail's travel time every day, and she could keep an eye on me. They finally agreed, albeit reluctantly.

"As it happened, Abigail came to stay the next night after I found the obituary even though it meant she had to go back and forth every day to her mother's house to move her things a few boxes at the time. Once she got settled in, she began helping me clean out my attic and search through all of Granny Olivia's things. With her dad's help, she brought the dower chest downstairs, and we examined and admired the contents, especially the family Bible and the needlepoints, but we also tried to determine what clues they held. However, we may have spent too much time admiring and not enough discovering.

"Then the following Wednesday night after coming in from a Women's Missionary Union meeting and before Abby returned from the school library, I heard someone or something in the house, in the attic. Of course, I couldn't go up the stairs to see who or what it was. I sat terrified on the edge of my bed with my bedroom door closed until Abigail returned from school. She insisted on checking the attic to see if a squirrel or something had climbed in. She found nothing. That was about two weeks after my health began declining and a week after I saw my doctor and found the obits.

"My daughter and granddaughter convinced themselves I had imagined the intruder and repeated the story to anyone who would listen. I didn't know what or who made the noise, but I knew I didn't imagine it. Afterwards, everyone began to attribute my *imaginings* to my age and failing health the same way Granny Olivia's family did with her."

"Maude, how does that connect to the relevance of the inquest?"

"With the threatening note and my own decline, I…I got it into my head that maybe someone had poisoned Charlotte because of the secret and that maybe someone was now poisoning me for the same reason. Then I feared maybe everyone else was right, and I was growing senile. Charlotte died over a hundred and fifty years ago. No one from then is still alive."

"Did you discuss your thoughts with anyone? Did you discuss the dower chest with anyone?"

"Yes and yes. With Abigail, of course. To my regret, I also discussed my thoughts with my daughter Isabel, my lawyer, and my doctor. Isabel, of course, discussed it with my other children and my siblings. As for the dower chest, anyone who came to visit during that time would have seen it. We kept it in the living room for a week or two before moving it to my bedroom."

"Maude—sorry for interrupting—but have you looked for any poisons that might be in your house that you've forgotten you have?"

"That was the first thing Abigail and I did after I got the notion about it after the intruder and everyone dismissing it as my imagination. We searched everywhere, and we didn't find anything poisonous. Of course, I have bleach and laundry detergent and such, but I would think I would know if I had routinely ingested any of those. I don't even have ant spray in my house. I have the house treated every other month by a local company."

Enid sat silent, staring at the floor, for several minutes.

"What are you thinking, please?"

"If tonight was the second time your intruder has been in the house, this is more of a problem than any of us imagine. And we made it worse tonight."

"How did we do that?"

"The two things we discussed. The first would be the family Bible, its historical value, and its possible monetary value. The second would be the possibility of the needlepoints holding clues to Charlotte's secrets, which apparently, someone does not want you to make known."

"Now I'm not only weary from this day, I'm also frightened even more than before."

"Me, too, Granny. Me, too. Maybe we should do what Miss Enid suggested and call Chief Mulhaney."

"No, Abigail. I will not budge on that. At least not yet. Enid, I'm afraid your visit may be for naught. I don't think I'm up to looking through the contents of the dower chest tonight. On the other hand, I'm afraid to go to bed for fear someone will sneak back in, knock me over the head, and steal the chest."

"Where is the chest?"

"In my bedroom closet, sitting on an old blanket for pulling it, and covered with another blanket for protection."

"Good. I have an idea. You are willing to have the locks changed, right?"

"More than willing."

"Would you consider allowing me to sleep over tonight?"

A tiny bit of the sparkle returned to Maude's eyes. "Of course! You can sleep in one of my granny gowns in the bedroom next to mine."

"I can go home in the morning early enough to shower and change," said Enid.

"And I'll cut my class tomorrow afternoon if necessary and stay here until the locksmith comes." Maude opened her mouth to protest. "No arguments, Granny. I'm staying here until I know you'll be safe. If he comes early enough, I'll go on to class."

"Maude," said Enid, "will you also promise me you will talk to Patrick if this happens again?"

"All right." Maude frowned. "That's what happens when you get old. Everyone tells you what to do." Maude smiled. "Sometimes you don't mind." She patted Abby's hand. "Enid, can you come back tomorrow after work to look at the obituaries and inquest report?"

"I can. If I can also see and touch your Bible!"

"That you can."

"Now this old lady needs to go to bed." Maude's shoulders drooped. "I hope we all sleep without anything else happening, at least not tonight."

Later, as Enid prepared for bed, Patrick called. She shared the events of the day up until the point where she and Abby chased the intruder out of the house. She also declined to mention where she was sleeping that night. Her stomach churned at the omissions, but the alternative was to break her promise to Maude.

Moral dilemmas complicate matters, she thought. She decided the best alternative was to hang up before she divulged everything.

After she hung up, Enid sat on the edge of the bed and reviewed the details of the two intruder events. Something didn't fit.

If the intruder had anything to do with Maude's decline, especially if he introduced some kind of poison, his first intrusion must have been within days of the family reunion.

The significance of that hit her as she drifted off to sleep.

That means he has been in the house three times instead of two, the first time to plant the poison and to unlock the attic window. It also means he is most likely a family member or a very close friend.

CHAPTER SEVEN

Tuesday, August 2, 2011

Enid had been tempted to rummage through the dower chest the night before, but she had felt almost as exhausted as Maude had looked. Besides, she wanted Maude to have the privilege of sharing her family mementoes.

Unfortunately, exhaustion did not prevent her from sleeping fitfully and dreaming of intruders carrying bags of poison up and down the stairs.

She overslept and then had to drag herself out of bed.

"The bags under my eyes this morning pay tribute to my restlessness more than to my oversleeping and rushing home without breakfast or coffee." Her reflection in her mirror did not respond. "Maybe a little concealer will improve my appearance. My denim pantsuit will be more comfortable than my usual attire."

A short time later, she pulled herself out of her Subaru and into the library. Mary stood at the circulation desk.

"Enid, what happened? You look awful."

"Thank you very much. Nothing happened. I didn't sleep well."

"There's fresh coffee in my office. Pour yourself a cup."

"Thank you for sure. I'll do that."

Enid walked around like the zombies she refused to watch on TV until midmorning when multiple cups of caffeine finally kicked in. By then, she and Ellen had assisted all of the early researchers, and the room was empty and quite again.

"I have some paperwork, Ellen. I'll be in my office if you need me."

"I'll work on the stacks until someone else comes in."

"Sounds like a plan."

Enid went to her office and closed the door. She plopped into her chair, continuing her ongoing argument with herself.

"I should call Patrick, but I promised Maude I wouldn't, but my promise was against my better judgment. It still is. But I promised. Fine. One more incident, though, and I call him. There was one more incident. The first one. But Maude meant one more new incident. All right, all right. I'll wait. For now, I'll check on her."

She tapped speaker and dialed Maude's number.

"Good morning. How are you?"

"Better. The locksmith has come and gone. All new locks are in place. Abigail not only had time to make it to her class, but she also left early enough to go by the school library for some additional research material."

"That's great, but it also means you're alone, right?"

"I am, but every lock is locked. I'm fine. I'm about to have another cup of tea, although I'm drinking more and more and getting less and less benefit from it. I wanted to come to the library today, but I don't think I'm up to it."

"Tonight, we'll make search plans. Then I can work on them whether you come in or not."

"Excellent idea."

"I'll check on you this afternoon."

"Thank you, Enid."

"You're welcome. Goodbye until then."

Enid lifted the handset and dropped it back into the cradle. She leaned back in her chair. "What should I do? Hmm. I could do paperwork later. I could go ahead and expand our census search now. I need to set search parameters so I won't lose my train of thought if I need to stop and help another patron. I really do suspect they traveled through Kentucky, but we've searched Illinois, Indiana, and Ohio." She rocked her pencil back and forth, tapping the table with each end. "The next logical step would be to search Canadian records."

She nodded once, gathered paper and pen, and left her office to begin her search. By noon, she had examined the records for every household in the Canadian census records between 1861 and 1901 with a Daniel, Hannah, or Miriam in them. She had found no households with all three names and only a few with two of the names. None of them matched both the ages and race of her search targets. Ellen approached her.

"Are you going to take a lunch break?"

Enid rubbed her eyes. "Yes, I believe I will. Has no one been in since ten?"

"Not a soul. Eat a hearty lunch, though, because I've heard from several people who plan to be here this afternoon."

"Thanks for the warning. You go on. I'll leave after I rewind the film and turn the machine off."

When she finished, she glanced at the map on the wall showing the primary Underground Railroad routes. "Two of the primary routes through Kentucky pass through Indiana to Michigan, one through the southwest tip of the state where it borders Lake Michigan and the other through the southeast edge where it borders Lake St. Claire. The third primary route through Kentucky passes through Ohio to Lake Erie near where the lake borders Michigan. I wonder. If so, that search will have to wait until another day."

Enid collected her belongings from her office and locked the doors on her way out to lunch.

* * *

After what did indeed prove to be a very busy afternoon, Enid finally sank into her office chair. Ellen stuck her head through the doorway again.

"I'm leaving. You want me to lock the door behind me?"

"No. I'm leaving, too, after I make a phone call. Thanks for your hard work today."

"My pleasure. See you tomorrow."

I need to ask Mary to consider hiring Ellen, thought Enid. *She works as hard as I do and always comes in when no one else can. Like this month with everyone else on last minute vacations. Maybe when this other situation is resolved. Right now, I need to call Maude.*

She again tapped speaker on her reliable old desk phone and dialed Maude's number.

After several rings, a feeble "Hello?" greeted her.

"Maude, is that you?"

"Who else would it be?"

"Right. This is Enid."

"I know."

"Okay. Your voice…."

"It comes and goes. I'm not worse."

"Good. I plan to come to your house straight from the library—almost. I'll pick up dinner again if that's okay with you. What would you like?"

"Hmm. I'm sure Abigail would enjoy pizza for a change. It's been a while. I might enjoy pizza, too. You could get original crust, though. It's easier for me to chew."

"Me, too. What kind?"

"We both prefer sausage and pepperoni. If you want something different, get that also. I'll pay for them."

"I like your choice, and this is my treat. What do you want to drink?"

"Dr. Pepper for Abigail. I'll drink tea. It's already made."

"Enough for me?"

"A whole pitcher full."

"Good. Is Abby home yet?"

"Yes. She's been here a while."

"I'm on my way, then."

Enid clicked off and sat back in her chair.

"Maude sounds worse than when I left this morning. This bothers me to no end."

After a few moments of staring at her desk, she shook her head, gathered her belongings, and left.

* * *

"I cannot eat another bite," said Enid. She pushed her plate back.

"That was so good," exclaimed Abby. "You'd think I'd never had pizza before. Come to think of it, we haven't had it since the family reunion!"

"I'm glad you enjoyed it. Maude, you didn't eat as much as we did. Did it taste all right?"

"Yes, it did. Neither my appetite nor my taste buds have been quite normal since I started feeling poorly. What little I do eat seems to leave a taste of metal in my mouth. Tonight, however, my taste buds didn't fail me. My pizza tasted spicy instead of metallic. Thank you for bringing it."

"My pleasure. I'll clean this up. Let Abby get you settled in the living room, and you might pull out the copies of the obituaries and inquest piece. When I finish in here, Abby and I can pull the dower chest into the living room."

Soon they were all seated around the old chest. Abby yanked off the blanket covering it.

Enid's eyes widened. "This looks like—"

"A hand-painted Pennsylvania German dower chest made of pine and in excellent condition except for a small chip out of one of the feet," said Maude with pride. "I could hardly wait for you to see it. I knew you would appreciate its value and history."

Abby grinned from ear to ear. "Isn't it great? I've heard Granny call it a *dower chest* all my life. When I was younger, I never thought to ask her what dower meant. I'd always heard the phrase *dour old lady*, and I assumed that's the word she was using, but I couldn't figure out what *stern* or *sour* had to do with a chest, especially not this chest. At some point along the way I made the connection between dower and dowry and dower chest."

"You never told me that, Abigail."

"I didn't know any better until I figured it out, and then I was too embarrassed."

"It is called a dower chest. It's also sometimes called a blanket chest or a plain old storage chest. Same difference. But of course, as you did figure out, the purpose for the dower chest was for a young girl to store the things she would make through the years for when she got married."

"I'd hate to see something I made when I was a young girl."

"Maybe knowing it was for when they married gave them reason to do the best they could. This chest first belonged to Great-Granny Charlotte. She gave it to Granny Olivia. I've often wondered if she passed it down as a keepsake or if Peter was too stingy to make a new one for Olivia. Of course, his family's heritage was different from that of Charlotte's family."

Enid found her voice. "I've seen pictures of dower chests with tulips painted on them before, but I don't remember ever seeing one with daffodils."

"Yellow daffodils were Granny Olivia's favorite flowers. She once told me they were also her mother's favorite flowers. I don't know the story behind their love for them, but I rather like them myself, too."

"They are beautifully painted. Do you know by whom?"

"I don't. I suspect Charlotte's father or mother painted them. So many things we don't know about our ancestors. Lifetimes of memories lost."

Maude touched a spot on the flower-filled side. "Both Charlotte's and Olivia's names are painted here in the corner along with the years of their marriages. 'Charlotte Abbott married 1850' and 'Olivia Goodwin married 1872.'"

Maude lifted the lid, its hinges creaking as she did. They gazed at the items inside.

"This small compartment is so cool," said Abby. She pointed to the lid of a small built-in box on the left.

"It's called a *till*," said Maude. "It's where Charlotte kept her one piece of jewelry—a necklace—given to her as the firstborn daughter by her mother on her thirteenth birthday. Charlotte gave it to Olivia on her thirteenth birthday. Granny Olivia said she kept it here, too, until she gave it to her oldest daughter on her thirteenth birthday. That would have been Grandma Savannah. Grandma should have given it to my mother, Beatrice, who was her oldest daughter. She didn't. What she did with it, I have no idea."

"The lock looks broken," said Enid.

"It is. I'd forgotten about that. It was broken before I took it home from Granny's. I don't think either that or the chip in the foot would affect its value, do you, Enid?"

"I wouldn't think so, not much maybe, but I don't know. I have seen pictures of dower chests that were not nearly so well preserved, and they were...quite valuable."

"Before we get too involved in the contents, I forgot to ask you if you got a chance to search any today."

"I did. For two uninterrupted hours, I searched Canadian census records using the same parameters we used for Illinois, Indiana, and Ohio. Unfortunately, I turned up nothing."

"How frustrating," said Abby.

"Yes and no," said Enid. "That's part of it. Family history research is as much about excluding as including. You keep narrowing the field until you find the person you're looking for."

"So frustrating and time consuming."

"You'll have more patience for it when you get old like us," said Maude. "Of course, Enid is younger than I am, but she is a senior citizen." Her eyes held a hint of a twinkle.

"That I am! Nevertheless, a little success here and there helps every researcher. Genealogical research is a little like a gambling addiction. A single win can carry a gambler through a hundred losses. A single name or date can carry a family historian through weeks of combing the stacks and staring at microfilm." Enid grimaced. "Not a very appropriate analogy, is it?"

"No, but I get the point," said Abby.

Maude pulled several sheets of paper from a side table.

"And it is a great lead-in to the copies of the obituaries and inquest article I transcribed. They helped feed my addiction." She handed the sheets to Enid, who scanned each of them.

"There's nothing unusual about either of the obituaries except their ages and causes of death. Charlotte died young in 1869 of a mysterious illness. She was only thirty-five. Peter died two years earlier, but he was twenty years older than his wife. She would have been thirty-three when he died from apoplexy at fifty-three in 1867. Even so, he was young to die of a stroke."

"It does happen," said Maude.

"True. The obituary doesn't say whether or not he had been in ill health, but apparently, there was no cause to question it. You didn't find an inquest for him, did you?"

"No. I didn't even think to look for one for him."

"As to Charlotte's inquest results, I can see how you got it in your head after reading how someone suspected she had been poisoned with arsenic that it might have been because of her secrets and that now maybe someone was trying to poison you for the same reason. However, as you pointed out, that was over a hundred and fifty years ago, and no one from then would be walking around today. If you didn't know about Charlotte's suspicious death or her secrets, I can't imagine anyone else living today would know."

"Nevertheless—"

"But why would anyone want to kill Granny because of her family history research? It makes no sense."

"Charlotte's decline was similar to mine, Abigail. Except for the stomach issues, of course. I've been fortunate not to have those."

"Perhaps it's nothing more than a coincidence," said Enid.

"It has to be, Granny."

Enid grimaced. *I dare not remind them of the story behind Benjamin's death. I hope I am not seeing evil where none exists.*

"What are you thinking?" asked Maude.

"I am a little disappointed that nothing from the three documents helps move us forward with our search or your illness. Not that they aren't important. We have dates and names and such, and hints of what to search for, but we don't have any clues as to the whereabouts of the runaway slaves or to Charlotte's secrets. Also...."

"What?"

"Something other than research and documents. I suspect your intruder entered the house one other time. He had to have been here before the first known visit to get upstairs and unlock the window, and it had to have been early during the week after the reunion before your energy levels dropped if your decline is due to something he or she has done."

"I hadn't thought about that."

"Do you remember anyone who visited you that week? Family members? Friends? Anyone?"

"Not right off hand. I'll give it some thought, though."

"Good. Maybe for now we should turn our attention to the dower chest contents. Even if we don't learn anything new, it can't help but be a fascinating look into the past."

"I need something to lift me out of this—"

"Funk," said Abby as she leaned toward the chest.

The two older women chuckled.

"Not the word I was looking for," said Maude, "but yes, funk certainly describes what I'm feeling. Let's look at the Bible first. Abigail?"

"Sure." Abby moved two of the framed needlepoints and lifted the box that held the old family Bible. She carefully removed the Bible and placed it on the coffee table in front of them.

Enid reached out to touch the cloth covering the Bible. "Maude, did you make this?"

"No, I didn't. It has covered the Bible from the time I first saw it. I have no idea who made the cover or put it on the Bible. Although I suspect either Charlotte or Granny Olivia did. The cover is a work of art. Two layers of square pieces of light blue and light brown worsted wool patched together with tiny delicate stitches, several sheets of stiff paper placed between them, and the whole sewn together with larger, ornate stitches to form a cover."

"We may be admiring one of the first homemade book covers." Enid turned the front book cover back to gaze at the inside of the cloth covering. "Look at the stitches connecting the squares. They are so tiny and so perfect." She turned to the title page and lightly ran her fingers over the words. "Imagine. These words were printed two hundred and twenty years ago. Amazing." Taking great care, she turned the yellowed pages.

"Cover to cover," said Maude.

"What?"

"Cover to cover. One of the needlepoints says something about 'cover to cover.' It should be close to the top of the pile."

Enid picked up the two needlepoints Abby had removed earlier and turned them over. Neither said anything about covers. Abby grabbed the next one in the chest.

"Here it is, Granny." Abby held up the needlepoint for Maude and Enid to see. Beside the scripture, Charlotte had stitched an open Bible resting on a small table, all in brown and black. Around them, she had stitched a pale blue background and a border of flowers in subdued shades of red, yellow, orange, and green. "It reads, 'Search the scriptures from cover to cover; for in them ye think ye have eternal life: and they are they which testify of me. John 5:39.'"

"Wait," said Enid. "That's not right. Or is it?" She stared at the Bible in front of them. "I don't remember the words, *cover to cover* being in this verse."

"This is one of the needlepoints that puzzled me. I thought it sounded different from what I knew, too, but I thought it might be a different version or translation or something. Could that be it?" asked Maude.

"No, I don't think so," said Enid. "Maybe. No, I think it's misquoted, but that could have been unintentional. One way to be sure. Let's compare the needlepoint to the text in the Collins's Bible." Enid turned the pages to the passage in John. "Here it is. 'Search the scriptures; for in them ye think ye have eternal life: and they are they which testify of me.' That's what I thought."

"So what does that mean?" asked Abby. "That Charlotte didn't have the verse memorized correctly?"

"Maybe. Maybe not." Enid turned the Bible back to the front cover. She stroked the pages. "Feel this, Maude."

Maude traced her gnarled fingers down and around the cloth cover. "Even with these old hands, I can detect two sets of papers."

"I don't understand," said Abby, wrinkling her brow.

"Here," said Enid. "See this rise?"

"I do. I still don't see the point."

"One set of papers is stitched to the cloth, perhaps to make it stiff. The other set is loose within the cloth cover. Look at the top. See the two rows of stitches?"

"Yes."

"The sides and bottom have only one set of stitches."

Abby's eyes widened. "You think she hid something under the front panel?"

Enid nodded and flipped the Bible so they could examine the back panel. "She did the same to both the front and back—cover to cover. Maude, we'll have to snip the stitches at the top."

"We'll be snipping stitches on the cover, not on the Bible. But maybe we should remove the cover before we snip anything."

"Good idea. Abby, would you get a pair of scissors?"

"Yes." The excited young woman jumped up and ran out of the living room.

While they waited, Enid and Maude held the Bible between them and carefully bent the back panel of the Bible enough to remove the cloth cover. As they slipped the cover off the front panel, a scream pierced their ears and jarred them so, they almost dropped the Bible.

* * *

As Enid grabbed the Bible and placed it back on the coffee table, Maude pushed herself up and yelled, "Abigail?"

"Sit back down. I'll go." Enid eased Maude back onto the sofa and raced to the doorway and into the hall. She met Abby running toward her, the scissors in one of her outstretched hands. "The scissors! Be careful!"

Abby stopped, terror in her eyes. She lowered her head to see the scissors she gripped so hard her knuckles were white.

Enid took her by the shoulders. "Abby, what's wrong?"

"When I came out of Granny's sewing room, I saw someone at the back door trying to unlock it!"

"Go to the living room. See to Maude. I'll check the door. And watch the scissors!"

As Abby ran past her, Enid blew out a long breath, threw her shoulders back, and strode toward the door at the end of the hallway. She peered out the window and then unlocked and eased the door open. She leaned through and turned from side to side but saw no one. She glanced at the lock on the outside of the door and shook her head. After one more glance into the back yard, she locked the door behind her and returned to the living room.

"Good thing you had the locks changed, Maude."

"I know what you're thinking. This makes four times. Call the chief."

Several hours later, Enid jumped when the hall clock struck midnight and Patrick stood to leave. Maude had recounted the intruder events from the beginning but had been evasive about her personal concerns.

"Mrs. Everly, can you think of anything else you haven't told me?"

"No, chief. I told you more then than I wanted to." Maude leaned back, a grim expression on her face.

"I appreciate that, ma'am, but this is serious. Four possible intrusions and nothing to identify the intruder. He wiped the new lock clean and no doubt wore gloves. My men found no fingerprints at all even on the flowerpot. They did find scratches around the keyhole, and the key is missing from under the flowerpot. I'm assuming that you had not replaced the old key with a new one." Maude and Abby shook their heads. "Thank goodness. We did find some partial footprints in some loose dirt at the back of the porch. They appear to be similar to the print Enid described from last night when you heard someone in the attic. None of that points to a particular individual."

"Chief Mulhaney," said Abby, "don't you think it odd someone would try again so soon after we saw him and while we were still up?"

"I do. However, when I arrived, none of the lights were on at the back or in the hallway, and the living room curtains are so heavy or opaque that I wasn't sure but what the glimmer of light I did see was a night light."

"Granny is somewhat conservative with her utilities, and it isn't uncommon for her to go to bed this early. Huh. I answered my own question, didn't I?"

"Maybe. Enid, do you plan to stay again tonight?"

"I hadn't planned on it, but I do now."

Maude shook her head. "I cannot have her life interrupted, too, Chief. She has a job. Besides, my children will take notice and expect the worst. I'll never hear the end of it."

"How about one more night, Mrs. Everly? In the meantime, I'll have an officer drive by several times a night for the next couple of nights."

"I don't want that."

"I know, but I need to do my job, too."

"Very well. But don't you dare call my daughter."

"I will refrain from doing that—for now." Before Maude could respond, Patrick turned his attention to Enid. "Walk me to the door?"

"Of course."

Once they were out of hearing distance, Patrick twisted his hat in his hands and studied Enid's face. "Are you sure you all are telling me everything?"

"Well…there is one other thing, but it may not be relevant."

"Tell me."

"Maude's ancestor that we're researching…. A family member suspected poisoning, but there was no evidence."

"That was what, over a hundred years ago?"

"Way over. Here's the thing. Maude is also declining with no apparent cause."

"She's ninety years old. It happens."

"I know, but—"

"I'll talk to her doctor about it."

"Will he tell you anything?"

"Probably not much without proof of legal or medical necessity unless Maude gives her permission. However, her health is at issue. He and I can dance around medical necessity enough for me to determine whether or not I need to know more. In the meantime, as you're in and out, you might check for anything suspicious."

"She and Abby have already searched for poisons, but I'll check, too."

"Thank you. If her doctor gives me anything, I can have her house searched officially."

"I hope were not too late."

Enid locked the door behind Patrick and returned to the living room.

"Maude, maybe we should postpone snipping the threads on the cover. It's late. We're all tired and shaky. We don't want to damage anything."

"I agree. Although I'm not sure I'll sleep much wondering what might be sewn into the covers." Maude stood with Abby's help and headed toward the doorway. "Can you two put everything back and take the dower chest into Enid's bedroom?"

"We can."

"Good. Maybe I can sleep a little knowing it's safe."

While she waited for Abby to return, Enid paced the living room floor, popping her knuckles and trying to make sense of the events of the last few days. Another concern kept pushing through her tangle of thoughts.

"The chest isn't the only thing I hope will be safe."

CHAPTER EIGHT

Wednesday, August 3, 2011

The next morning, Enid made plans to go home first for a shower and a change of clothes and then to go to the library and stay until Ellen, who had an early appointment, arrived. Then she would return to Maude's so they could continue with their plans, especially to remove the pages from the family Bible's cloth cover.

"Enid, you can wait until this evening. I've already taken up too much of your time."

"Not a problem. I'm happy to help—and a little excited about it."

As she dashed out to her Subaru, Enid chewed at her lip.

I didn't lie. I am happy to help, and I am excited about such finds, but maybe I didn't tell the whole truth, either.

She slid under the steering wheel and started the engine.

Maybe I'm concerned about time running out, too. But only because of Maude's age. All right, maybe because I'm afraid someone else might also think time is running out but for an entirely different reason. Besides, whatever time Maude has left, I want her to discover as much as she can about what happened with Charlotte and Olivia.

She backed into the street.

And maybe I'm also afraid to leave Maude alone.

* * *

By ten o'clock, Ellen had returned from her appointment. Enid closed the accounting ledgers she was trying to balance and grabbed her bag.

"Ellen, one of these days, your willingness to work will be rewarded."

Ellen's eyes lit up. "You think? Seriously, I need something to do. I enjoy helping others with their research, and when no one else is here, I get to work on my own research. Thanks, though. I do appreciate being appreciated."

"You're welcome again—until you're better paid."

They both chuckled, and Enid left for Maude's house. Abby met her at the door.

"No school today?"

"Not until this afternoon."

"I keep forgetting you're taking only one class this summer."

"Besides, I couldn't miss this." Abby bounced on her toes. "Exciting, isn't it?"

"It is! Who would have expected us to find such a firsthand account by anyone in our family? Granny is waiting in the living room with the Bible, the cover, and the scissors on the coffee table."

Enid followed Abby into the living room and sat beside Maude on the sofa.

"Which one of you is going to snip the stitches? My hands are too shaky. I'm afraid I'll cut more than stitches."

"I suspect Abby's hands are steadier than mine," said Enid. "Will you do the honors?"

"Yes!"

Abby pulled a chair up to the coffee table and with painstaking care snipped the second row of stitches along the inside top of the front cover. "Whew! One down. Let's check its contents first and let my fingers rest before I snip the stitches on the back cover."

"I agree," said Maude. "I can scarcely stand it."

Abby moved to the empty spot at the end of the sofa and turned the cover toward Enid. "You do it."

"I'd be honored," said Enid. She slipped a finger underneath the pages inside the cover and eased them out. She placed them on top of the cover. The three of them stared at the handwriting on the worn pages.

"The paper is yellowed, and the writing is different," said Abby. "It's so pretty and neat. Painstaking is the word that comes to my mind. Some of the letters are different, too. See how some of the *s* letters are longer than others?"

"The writing is old," said Maude. "It was a time when those who could write took as much care and pride when writing journals and letters as they did when writing legal documents. As for the long letter *s*, there were rules that determined when you used a long or a short *s*. Read the pages, Enid, word for word."

Enid lifted the first of the three pages. It was blank except for three lines. She read those lines.

My Journal
A True Record of Daniel's Innocence and Other Events
Charlotte Abbott Goodwin

"Impossible," said Abby. "How could she have had the forethought to write everything down?"

Maude chuckled. "Whom else do I know who does that very thing?"

Abby giggled. "Hmm. Maybe my granny? Maybe me? Maybe we came by our habits honestly."

"It appears we did. Read on Enid. May these pages shed light on Charlotte's secret."

CHAPTER NINE

The Journal of Charlotte Abbott Goodwin
A True Record of Daniel's Innocence and Other Events
Entry #1, Friday Evening, October 3rd, 1862
The Purpose of My Journal

It is with a heavy heart that I begin this journal—not for the writing of it but for the reason I feel compelled to do so. Only by recording the true story can I hope to offer any protection to the ones I love. May good arise from the evil that precipitated our decisions and the events that followed.

My Dearest Hannah, one week has passed since your departure on Friday night, September 26th. I hope you will soon be safely housed in the North. We were wise to plan your escape and send you on your way. I was wise to insist you keep your destination from me. Peter has beaten me twice in his effort to force me to admit I knew you were leaving and to tell him your destination. He then threatened my precious Olivia. She clung to me. Her body trembled against mine. I begged him to believe me and not hurt our child. He finally relented, but I am not at all sure he believes me.

I hope the three of you are well. I miss you and Miriam more than words can convey. If possible, Olivia misses you more. She cried every morning upon waking and every night at bedtime for five days until Peter threatened her if she shed another tear. She is terrified of her own father. We are adjusting, but at times, I wish Olivia and I had left with you.

I did err in one part of our plan, and that is why I am beginning this new journal, one that will tell the true story in the event you or Daniel is captured or has opportunity to return safely at some future date.

If that day does not come and I outlive both Peter and Mason, I will make your story known so that Daniel will not face charges or conviction as a thief. If I do not outlive them, I will leave this journal with Olivia.

Of course, I will continue writing my usual journal entries about our daily lives, which Peter often reads, so that he will not suspect me of keeping a secret journal. I must, however, devise a way of hiding the entries of these secret pages separately.

If you have managed to make contact with your mother, you know about the charge of theft against Daniel and the reward Peter has posted for Miriam's and your return. I did not expect Peter to suspect anyone, much less Daniel, assisted you in your escape, nor did I expect him to check on his money box, at least not so soon. He only adds to the box when he sells crops or livestock. To my dismay, he did both immediately. How could I have been so naïve?

As to hiding places for these journal pages, perhaps I will place some of them behind one of my embroidered Bible verses, overlap the edges, stitch them inside the pocket formed, and either hang them in Olivia's room or place them in her dower chest.

I stitched my latest one for her after Peter forbade her to cry. "Jesus wept. John 11:35." She remembered the story of Lazarus, and in her childlike wisdom, she said to me, "Mama, Jesus cried for his friend who was gone. Why can't I cry for my Miriam?" I held her close and told her we could still cry in our hearts, and Jesus would comfort us.

On further reflection, I cannot hide every entry behind a needlepoint. If Peter were to discover one, he would tear them all apart searching for others. No. I must devise more than one hiding place.

I could, however, embroider errors in several of my needlepoints to give clues to the hiding places for the journal pages and for the money I mean for you to have, so that if I die before I hear from you, someone might note the error, take a closer look, find the pages, and know to search for others. Especially Olivia.

Peter returns. I must stop writing for now. I may have to wait until next Friday to continue, but I will take up my pen the moment he leaves rather than waiting until I finish my chores. When I write next, I will record the events leading up to your escape. I love you and miss you. I know you will remember to kiss Miriam for Olivia and for me and tell her we love her. I tell Olivia the same each night for you. I hope to hear from you soon.

Maude raised an unsteady hand to her cheek. "I cannot wait to find out what is under the back cover. After we read the next pages, we can stop and discuss both sets."

Enid picked up the scissors and handed them to Abby, who, without a word, reached for the book's cloth cover and began snipping the second row of stitches on the back. Enid turned to Maude.

"While we wait, I have a question. Have you ever run across her other, non-secretive journal entries?"

"No, not at all. They weren't in the dower chest, and I've never heard anyone mention them. Thank goodness Charlotte hid these pages."

Abby finished snipping and handed the back cover to Enid, who extracted the second set of pages with care. She counted seven pages this time. She glanced at Maude, who gestured for her to begin reading again.

CHAPTER TEN

The Journal of Charlotte Abbott Goodwin, cont.
A True Record of Daniel's Innocence and Other Events
Entry #2, Friday Evening, October 10th, 1862
Events Leading to My Decision

Here begins my account of the events leading up to the escape of Daniel, a man slave belonging to my father and mother, and of Hannah and Miriam, mother and child, the mother gifted to me by my parents on the occasion of my marriage.

I need to record these events for myself now but more for anyone who might read them in the future. Perhaps I want someone to forgive me, perhaps only to understand me. I can do neither for myself.

I must confess. I am terribly conflicted over this war that some call the great rebellion, this war that is tearing families and communities apart. What are we fighting about? A state's rights? An individual's rights? Slavery itself?

Whatever the reason, it has served to make matters worse for myself and for those I love. I was born into a world, into a home, where slavery was and is the expected way of life.

Not everyone owns slaves. Many of our neighbors and others across the state are opposed to slavery. Father says that is why Tennessee's laws governing slaves and masters are numerous and strict.

Of those who are not opposed, not all have the means to purchase even a single slave. Both Daniel and

Hannah are valued at more than a thousand dollars each, though Peter has never paid that much. Instead, he purchases older men and women, able to work but not in their prime.

The truth is that my father's slaves fare better than the poor white families who live in this and surrounding counties. Even Peter's slaves have better food and clothing than many of the poor whites. His slaves sometimes ridicule those whom they call white trash but never if they are aware of my presence.

My father says slavery has existed since the beginning of time and was practiced in Biblical times. Slaves are purchased and cared for by their masters. Slave owners accumulate their wealth and provide for their families and the slaves by their labor.

If that were the end of it, I might still question the institution of slavery, but perhaps I would not be so conflicted about it. Are not all hired hands slaves of a sort? That is not the end of it, though.

I personally know men and women who have been beaten without mercy for the smallest of infractions. I personally know children who have been put out to work before they were old enough to understand the meaning of the word work. Those are not the worst atrocities. Some masters do not even consider their slaves to be human beings.

Not all masters are guilty of such thoughts and actions, but they still own their slaves, dictate to them what their lives must be, and purchase and sell them at will, sometimes separating husband and wife, mother and child.

My father is a good man, and he is good to his slaves in material ways. He has always provided them food, clothing, and medical care when they were sick equal to that he provided for his own wife and children.

Nevertheless, he does punish what he considers wrongdoing or slackness, and I am certain now that even he has other faults. Neither as a child nor as a young

woman did I ever dare to question Father or Mother—
nor Celia for that matter—but I often wondered
whether or not Hannah and I were half sisters.

Celia has a husband now, and all of her other children
are as dark as she and George, but not Hannah. Then
there is the resemblance between Hannah and myself.
We have our differences. Our coloring is different.
Though lighter than Celia's, Hannah's skin is darker than
mine. Though we both have curly hair that is thick and
silky, hers is black as night while mine is the lightest of
browns. Our amber brown eyes and the similarity of our
facial features, however, cannot be denied.

I might have expected this of Peter, but I did not
want to believe it of my father. I did not expect it of
Peter before we married.

How could I? I was a child, barely turned sixteen,
when he and father decided we would be married. That
was in 1850. Such a short time ago and yet a lifetime.

I had but one say in the matter: Which slave I would
carry with me to my new home as a wedding gift from
my parents.

Had I known the turns our lives—her life—would
take, I would never have asked for Hannah. I would not
have asked for any of my parents' slaves. Peter had
slaves, male and female. I had no need of more.

Indeed, I have often thought since then I would not
have come to this house by my own choice, though I
have no idea how I could have persuaded father
otherwise.

At the time, although Peter's very appearance
frightened me—his straight hair black and coarse, his
brown eyes so dark they appeared to be black, his skin
baked brown from the sun, his demeanor gruff, and
himself twenty years my senior—I looked upon it as an
adventure. My father was sometimes gruff, and he
treated my mother and his children well. I convinced
myself that father would not have me marry a man less
good-natured than himself.

My marriage to Peter also meant I would have a new house, newly built by Peter and, of course, his slaves. Though smaller than Papa and Mama's home, it was equally fine in every respect with a porch and several rooms. I would not begin married life in a cabin or worse. Such were my thoughts at sixteen.

As for Hannah, she wanted to come with me as much as I wanted her to. She and Celia had been our house slaves all our short lives. I was one year old when Hannah was born. We grew up together. Played together. Studied together. I thought of her as my best friend and felt closer to her than to any of my sisters. My other sisters.

Mama often crossed wills with Celia, embarrassing both Hannah and myself, but I had never commanded Hannah to do anything. I always asked, and yet even I did not question that her duty belonged to my parents and then to Peter and myself after I married. Not until later that is. Not until after our children were born.

I am no longer a child. I am also no longer blind to the similarities between our daughters, Olivia and Miriam. While Olivia has milky white skin and thick light golden-brown hair and Miriam has tawny skin and thick black hair, both have silky curls, similar facial features, and eyes of the darkest of browns.

Had Hannah stayed with Mama, she would have been married to Daniel by now, another of our slaves with whom we grew up. Daniel and Hannah had always been sweethearts. Daddy had promised they could be married when they were older. He told Peter the same and offered to send Daniel with us when we married, a very generous offer on the part of my father, but Peter declined. I expected Peter to give his consent to their marriage in time, but he forbade it. I did insist upon one thing, that he allow Hannah and later her children to visit Celia two full days each month. I expected her to spend some of that time to be with Daniel.

When I found the courage to broach the subject of the similarities between my Olivia and Hannah's Miriam with my mother, Mama dismissed me with a wave of her hand.

"This is the way with men," she said, "and if you question it, you will make life harder for both Hannah and yourself."

I never imagined how hard life would be for both of us but especially for Hannah. Or how hard it could be for sweet little Miriam. Even with my blind acceptance of slavery, I could not fathom why it should be so for Hannah and Miriam. If I am correct in my assumptions, Hannah is half white, and Miriam is three-fourths white. They are identified as mulatto. Some would call Miriam a quadroon. Whatever term one might use, even though Celia is a slave, should not Hannah and Miriam be free? And why would such terms be used at all?

What does all of this have to do with keeping this secret journal? Perhaps nothing but to show how difficult—and how easy—it was for me to make the decision I made and for Hannah to accept it.

What happened to Isaac pushed me to act. If only I had acted sooner. That awful day came years after we left our childhood home together.

In 1851, one year after my marriage to Peter, I had my firstborn, a son whom Peter named Mason. Two years later, Hannah had her firstborn, also a son. Hannah named him Isaac.

When Mason was five years old, I gave birth to my second child, a daughter whom Peter allowed me to name Olivia.

Two years later in 1858, Hannah gave birth to her second child, Joshua, but he lived only a few hours.

The following year, 1859, a week before Olivia's third birthday, Peter called Hannah outside. His countenance frightened me. I listened at the door.

"You should've been with child by now," he said. "It's time for you to give me another living slave child.

If you cannot—or will not—I'll sell you down south and keep Isaac here."

I caught the gasp that rose in me. His words chilled my bones and gave proof to what I had suspected all along. But what could I do? Bile caught in my throat.

I wanted to slap Hannah for not telling me. She and I had always confided in each other, but she had never told me that Peter went to her.

I wanted to slap myself for pretending that Isaac's father was one of our field slaves, for not asking Hannah for the truth.

Even though I had suspected—feared—Peter had fathered Isaac, I was naïve enough to think that if he had, he had gone to Hannah because he was drawn to her because of her beauty. I never thought he might have used her for the purpose of procreating additional slaves.

As soon as Peter left and Hannah came inside, I embraced her in tears and sorrow to ask her forgiveness for what Peter had done and said but more for my turning a blind eye to it.

She grabbed both my hands. "Charlotte," she begged, "please, do not say anything to Peter. We both know my Joshua died because of the beating Peter gave me before he was born. I fear for Isaac every day, and I fear for any children I might bear him in the future. You know neither of us can do anything about this."

I responded with a new heaviness in my heart. "I promise, Hannah, I will hold my tongue as long as I can. Promise me you will come to me if he...hurts you or Isaac."

Hannah smiled sadly and, as I think on it now, with an understanding that I did not possess. "I promise I will come to you."

I did not broach the subject of our own possible relationship nor did Hannah.

I felt worse for my promise after than I did for my ignorance before. Neither of our promises did anything to prevent what happened to Isaac.

A year later—on September twelfth in 1860 to be exact—Hannah gave birth to Miriam. Olivia was four, Isaac seven, and Mason nine. Two boys and two girls between us. I loved Isaac and Miriam as much as I loved Olivia and Mason. Isaac had the sweetest disposition of the four.

I thought Peter would be satisfied. I could not have been more wrong.

When he saw Miriam, he yelled at Hannah. "A girl? I don't need another house slave! I need a field hand! Mark my word, she will work in the fields. And so will you if the next one isn't a boy."

That was two years ago last month.

Peter's temper grew in the weeks and months that followed. In the year and a half after this rebellion, this civil war, began, his temper grew even worse and his behavior even more cruel. He struck both Hannah and me when things did not go to suit him. He beat his slaves over nothing and threatened them daily with the promise that if they ran away, when he caught them, the men would be hung, and the women stripped and beaten.

Not even Mason and Isaac, both old enough by then to assume chores, could escape Peter's wrath. He often whipped them both for trivial offenses, but he whipped Isaac harder and more often. He never broke skin on Mason, but Isaac's small back bore many scars.

In time, Mason began emulating his father and ordering Isaac about and beating him when Isaac failed to do as he said or failed do it quickly enough. If Hannah intervened, Mason would threaten to inform his father. If I intervened, he ignored me.

By this past summer, Isaac had grown taller and stronger than Mason. He had also grown more and more resentful of Mason's treatment. His disposition now bordered on surliness with everyone except Hannah, Miriam, Olivia, and myself, but he refrained from acting out.

The day came, however, when Isaac could take no more. The day after Miriam's second birthday, he fought back when Mason struck him, and to Mason's humiliation, Isaac overpowered him. Hannah and I were hanging out wash when we heard them arguing. We turned and saw their punches. We dropped the clothes into the basket and ran to separate them.

Mason pushed me away and scowled at Isaac, blood flowing from his nose. "You will pay for this." When he turned away, he glared at both Hannah and me as if to dare us to say a word.

Peter was in the field at the time. Mason went directly to him to report the incident, but he told Peter that Isaac had started the fight. He followed his father back to the barn where Isaac had returned to work cleaning out the stalls. Peter knocked Isaac down and then jerked him up off the ground by the straps of his overalls. I cannot write the words he used as he yelled and cursed the frightened but defiant child.

When he did lower his voice, I watched in terror, fearing what would follow.

"Who do you think you are, striking the son of your master?"

"Sir." Isaac's voice did not waver, nor did he. "I did not strike him first, and he struck me for no reason. I defended myself."

"You what?" Peter's voice rose again. "You defended yourself? You have no right to defend yourself. You are my property and that means you are his property, too. You will never strike my son again for any reason. You will never backtalk me again."

Peter reached toward Mason, who held his father's whip in his hand. I had never seen such evil on the face of my son. I knew at that moment Mason was lost to me. To my sorrow, Isaac was lost as well.

Hannah and I both pleaded with Peter to no avail. He whipped Isaac for starting the fight and then whipped him for lying about it. He whipped him so severely that the child died two days later from his injuries.

Something worse than I had dared to imagine had come about in spite of Hannah's and my promises to each other.

Peter's rage at Isaac went further. He refused to allow us to acknowledge Isaac's death. He refused to allow me to enter his death in my own family Bible. He buried the child in the spot of ground he had reserved for slave burials, but he did so that night, I suspect so no one would realize what he and Mason had done. I knew from stories told by my father that by the laws of our state, a man could be punished for killing a slave, even his own. However, I also knew that interpretation and implementation of the law rested on the local citizens and their leaders. I did not expect our neighbors to turn on Peter, but apparently, Peter chose not to take that chance.

He said he would tell anyone who asked about the boy that he had sold him down south. He threatened Hannah's and my very lives if we disputed him.

He stood over us and said "If either of you tells anyone what happened to Isaac, you may find yourselves joining him on that patch of ground. And just because I've allowed you to mark the other graves with a wooden cross, don't even think about marking Isaac's grave with one."

At least Isaac did not rest alone. Four graves lay to his left—his baby brother Joshua, another infant who had died at birth, and two elderly slaves—each grave marked by a simple wooden cross. Only the sycamore tree to his right marked Isaac's resting place. Again, I was afraid to act.

I tossed about all night. I worried about a marker for Isaac. I worried about Hannah and Miriam's safety. Two plans came to my mind. I acted on the first one the next morning.

After Peter and Mason left for town on an errand, I asked Hannah to go with me to one of my yellow daffodil patches.

"What are we going to do?" Her voice gave away her wariness of my intentions.

"We're going to fill the ground above all of the graves with daffodil bulbs." I walked out the door, determined to do so.

Hannah followed me. "Charlotte, we cannot defy Peter."

"We're not. He said we could not mark his grave with a wooden cross. He said nothing about flowers."

Hannah shook her head at me the whole time we worked. Even the birds marked the solemnness of our efforts with their silence. The only sounds we heard were the spades hitting the ground. Long before Peter returned, we had transplanted enough bulbs to make a bed of them across the five graves. We had left the withered leaves attached to the bulbs in hopes they would continue to nourish them and produce an abundance of the large yellow daffodils the next spring.

When we finished, we leaned back on our heels to view our handiwork.

"Why daffodils?" asked Hannah. "If you want to mark their graves, why not plant flowers that bloom longer?"

"For two reasons. First, they are my favorite flower. Second, they are the most appropriate flower to mark Isaac's resting place. They have a beautiful but short life as did Isaac."

Hannah smiled through her tears and whispered, "Thank you."

When Peter returned and saw what we had done, his face turned an ugly crimson, and the vessels on the side of his head swelled. He yelled at us.

"You have neglected your work to plant weeds over a grave I forbade you to mark."

"They are not weeds." I spoke in as calm a voice as I could, though my body trembled. "You told us no wooden cross. You said nothing about flowers. Anyone who doesn't know of the other graves will think they are simply another patch of daffodils. Anyone who does know of the other graves will think I finally got around to planting flowers over them. No one will suspect the flowers are there for Isaac. How can you object to a patch of flowers that will bloom for such a short period of time?"

I am not certain which convinced him, my argument or my audacity. Whichever it was, he relented but stomped out of the house without another word.

Hannah and I both exhaled as if we had been holding our breaths forever.

In the days to come, the patch of withered leaves brought some comfort to Hannah, but they did not lessen the tears she wept for her son.

On the third day after Isaac's death, Peter responded to Hannah's tears. He struck her so hard that he knocked her to the floor. Then he jerked her up and told her, "You have grieved long enough. You should have taught the boy his place. Because you didn't, his death should be on your conscience. If you can't control your own emotions, you'll receive a thrashing equal to the one I gave Isaac."

That was the day I affirmed my second plan. I would send Hanna and Miriam away.

Enid turned the pages face up. Maude reached out to stroke them. Abby brushed away tears.

"I am too overcome to talk about this right now," said Maude.

"Perhaps we all need to take a few moments," said Enid. "I'll take out the sandwiches I brought and arrange everything on the dining room table. Rest until I call you."

"Thank you." Maude leaned back and closed her eyes.

As Enid stood, Abby slipped behind her to sit beside Maude and place her head gently on her granny's shoulder.

CHAPTER ELEVEN

Later, as the three women ate lunch in silence, Enid watched Maude pick at her food more than she ate it. She didn't want to intrude on Maude's thoughts, but she did want to make certain she was okay. She cleared her throat.

"Maude?"

"I'm fine. I am afraid I have no appetite. What we learned this morning makes me sick to my stomach."

"Me, too, Granny." Abby pushed her plate back. "What Charlotte said about slavery existing since the beginning of time and being practiced in Biblical times—I know that's true, and I believe in my heart all slavery is horrible and wrong. What I don't understand is why slavery in the U.S. seems to be considered so much worse than slavery in all the other places down through history."

"I've often questioned that myself. Enid, any thoughts?"

"A few. Some from others. Some my own. Historians speak of American slavery as being parochial and race-based versus economic and military, of slaves being viewed as nonhuman versus human. I can't answer as an historian," said Enid, "but I can speak for myself. What I'm going to say may be oversimplified, but it does have merit. A long time ago, I asked an African American colleague a similar question. She said she believed the thing that most distinguished historical and Biblical slavery from slavery in the U.S. was the destruction of the family. The husband-wife bond could be forced and severed at will. Children could be sold out of the mothers' arms the same way the young of livestock were sold off. I've no doubt those things happened in other eras and in other countries. However, in the U.S., they were the norm."

"That makes sense to me," said Abby, "and it breaks my heart. You'll both probably think what I'm about to say is because I'm young, but before today my thoughts and feelings about racism and the many other forms of prejudice—not just in America but also in other countries—were somewhat superficial. History has always been fascinating to me but...impersonal. I am aware that time passes and history happens, people are born and they die, but it's always been kind of like a movie running in my head, not like something that ever really happened to anyone important to me.

"Even researching and learning about my ancestors didn't make them all that real to me...but Charlotte's journal entries...reading them is like reading letters from someone still living. I mean, of course, she's not, but she was living when she wrote them. She experienced things I've only read about in books. I'm a part of her. A part of her went into making me who I am. What scares me is that a part of Peter also went into making me who I am."

"My dear Abigail, you are nothing like Peter. You have a heart that takes in the whole world. You always have."

"Three things, Granny. One, I got that from you, but if I did, why didn't Mama and Grandma? Two, if I had lived back then, would I have been like Peter or like Charlotte? Three, even if I would have been like Charlotte, would I have stood by while such things happened?"

"How can any of us know with certainty what we would have done?" Maude grimaced and pushed her plate back.

Enid tapped the table with a fingernail. "Abby, none of us can know with certainty what we would or would not have done. Charlotte, like all of us, was influenced by the times in which she lived and by the family into which she was born. She was a victim of Peter's cruelty as well. She finally did the only thing she could think of to do."

"Does that mean we have no choice in the person we become?"

"No!"

Enid grabbed her chest. "Maude, you startled me. You haven't spoken with such force in weeks."

"Conviction sometimes boosts whatever we have left in us. I do not believe that any of us have no choice. That whole nature versus nurture thing. Of course, we are influenced by both, but at the end of the day, we have to make our own choices, and those choices determine the person we become. Even Mason. Of course, Peter influenced him, but Mason chose to accept his father's influence rather than his mother's."

"Well put, Maude. I think you're right. I also think what you say occurs on two levels—that of the individual and that of society."

"Individuals make up societies," said Abby, "so maybe as our hearts and thoughts change us as individuals, we change society. For good or for evil. Either one takes time, though. Too much time as often as not." Abby pushed remnants of her lunch around on her plate. "My, aren't we waxing philosophical?"

"We are." Maude's smile did not diminish the sadness in her eyes as she reached over to touch Abby's cheek.

Abby grasped her hand. "Maybe we can't change the world, but we can try to change a small part of it by discovering what happened to Olivia's baby sister and by making things right with her descendants."

Maude frowned as she tore strips off her napkin "Which brings us back to the other side of this coin. Beginning in the twentieth chapter of Exodus, God says He visits 'the iniquity of the fathers upon the children unto the third and fourth generation' for hating God and for sinning against Him. I understand that we all suffer the consequences of what our fathers and forefathers did, but that scripture doesn't say I'm to be judged for what my ancestors did or considered racist simply because I'm white or possibly descended from slave owners. I'm responsible for my actions—good or bad—but not for theirs.

"Nevertheless, what's right is right. What's wrong is wrong. What's hers is hers. I'm not responsible for Peter's mistakes or his sins. I'm responsible for no one's thoughts or actions but my own. However, Charlotte intended for an amount of money to be given to Hannah. If we find it, I can see to it that it goes to her descendants." Maude shook her head. "That doesn't prevent me from being afraid to tell any of my family what we've learned. I was afraid I would die before I could find Granny's baby doll because of my age. Now I am more afraid someone is trying to kill me to prevent me from finding her, and if anyone in the family—especially anyone who still holds to the old ideas—is aware of this part of our history, I understand why they want me dead. Olivia was old. They said she was senile and imagining things. I'm old. Everyone seems to think I'm senile—or crazy. I suspect my intruder is using that to his advantage."

Enid agreed with Maude but did not want to add to her fear, so she tried to keep her expression and her words neutral. "Then we need to do two things. Watch out for each other and continue our search."

"Amen," said Abby.

"Agreed," said Maude. "So Charlotte's first two journal entries confirm what we have discovered so far. Daniel, Hannah, and Miriam did run away together. Money was stolen. Isaac did disappear from the scene. The entries add three facts not in the newspaper advertisement. Peter was a cruel man. Charlotte took the money, though I wouldn't call it stealing. And Isaac disappeared because he was murdered."

Abby shook her head. "Poor Isaac. Murdered by his own father and brother."

"Yes," whispered Maude.

"The entries confirm other things, too, that Great-Granny Olivia told you."

"Yes." Maude raised her head. "She did have a baby sister, and her mama did have that and other secrets she planned to pass on to her daughter. How many secrets have we identified so far? The murder of the child Isaac. His burial place. The escape of Hannah, Miriam, and Daniel. The theft of money. Where the money is hidden. The kinship between the women. The kinship between their daughters. Where the runaways settled. How Charlotte died. Nine secrets of which we are aware. All of which lead to more questions and mysteries."

"Wow. How in the world are we going to discover all the answers, solve all the mysteries?" Abby threw her hands wide.

"We must continue searching census and other records for the three runaways," said Enid.

"Yes," said Maude, "and we must determine what other clues are stitched into the remaining needlepoints and then follow those clues."

"Granny, you don't suppose the money is in the dower chest, do you?"

"Somehow I doubt it. I've been through its contents so many times over the years. Nothing is large enough to hold much money. Of course, we have no idea how much was hidden."

"Shoot!" Abby jumped up.

"What's wrong, Abigail?"

"I've got to go to class!"

"Go! I need to take a nap. We can pick this up tonight or tomorrow. However, I do have something I want you to do when you return home."

"What's that?"

"I want you to record Isaac's death in the family Bible."

"I'll do that first thing. For now, what about the dishes?"

"Go," said Enid. "I'll take care of the dishes."

Abby ran upstairs to collect her books and back downstairs to the front door. "I'm gone!"

"Be careful, dear!"

"I will, Granny."

The door slammed behind her.

"Enid, you'd better check to make sure she locked the door."

"I will. Where do you want to nap, in the recliner or in bed?"

"In bed. I plan on taking a long nap."

"I'll walk with you."

Enid brought the walker to the table and helped her frail friend to ease her chair back and stand. Once in the hallway, she checked the front door before walking with Maude to her bedroom and settling her in.

"Will you stay until I wake up, Enid?"

"I will. I'll be in the kitchen or the living room. Call when you awaken."

Maude didn't reply. She just closed her eyes and inhaled deeply as she drifted off to sleep.

Enid inhaled as well. The floral scent she associated with Maude was stronger in the bedroom but still pleasant, not overpowering. It eased some of her tension.

Enid left the bedroom door ajar as she tiptoed out to clear the table. She soon had everything clean and back in place.

"Now. What shall I do? No, I won't open the dower chest without Maude and Abby. Hmm. I could take this time to go through drawers and cabinets to see if I can find what might be poisoning Maude without poisoning Abby."

Enid spent the next two hours going through every drawer, cabinet, and closet in every room except Maude's bedroom and bathroom. "Humph. Nothing. Surely that's a good thing." She glanced at her watch. "I'd better check on Maude."

The elderly woman lay in the same position as when she closed her eyes. Enid stepped to the side of the bed. Her heart skipped a beat. She could not see Maude's chest rise and fall. She leaned over and then released her own breath of relief.

"Maude? Would you like to wake up and have some tea and cookies?" She gently shook her by the shoulder. "Maude?"

"Wha...what? Enid! you frightened me."

"I'm sorry. You've slept for two hours, and I was a little concerned."

"My, my. I never nap that long. Here. Help me up." Maude reached up for Enid's hand. With a bit of difficulty, she managed to sit up. Enid pulled the walker to the side of the bed.

"Maybe you should wait a few moments before you stand."

"That might be a good idea. Right before you woke me, I was having the worst dream."

"About yourself?"

"No. About Abigail. Something was happening, but I couldn't see what. She was calling out to me, but I couldn't reach her. I hope she's all right."

"When do you expect her home?"

"She should be leaving school about now."

"Would it ease your mind to call her?"

"Yes, it would." Maude reached into her pants pocket. "It's not here. Where did I put it?" She glanced around the room. "I don't believe I ever put it in my pocket this morning." She slapped her hand over her mouth. "I didn't take it off vibrate when I got out of bed. I put it on vibrate at night because I don't want to be awakened by wrong numbers, but I leave it on in case I need to call someone. It's in the top drawer of my bedside table. There."

Enid pulled the drawer open and handed the phone to Maude.

"I have a voicemail message. I hope it wasn't Abby calling me. Here. Will you check it for me? I'm not awake enough to do it."

Enid opened the message and pressed speaker. She almost dropped the phone when she heard the whispered voice.

If you don't think enough of your own life to stop this nonsense, you would do well to think of your great-granddaughter's life.

"That's the only one."

"Call Abigail now. Her speed dial number is two."

Enid punched the two and hit send.

"Hey, this is Abby. Not available at the moment. Leave a message, send a text, or call back later."

The recording did nothing to relieve the fear of the two women who stared at the phone.

"I have to call Patrick."

"I won't argue. Call him."

His phone went to voicemail, too. Enid left him a message. Maude wrung her hands. "What are we going to do?"

"We're going to the living room so we'll appear calm and nonchalant when Abby arrives. Until she arrives, we're going to keep calling—both her and Patrick."

Though she did wobble, Maude managed with Enid's help to get to the sofa in the living room.

For the next fifteen minutes, Maude continued dialing Abby's number. Enid continued dialing Patrick's number while pacing the floor.

"I would pace, too, if I could, but your pacing is making me more nervous."

"I'm sorry, Maude. I'll sit down." Enid sat halfway down and shot right back up when her phone rang, startling both of them.

She accepted the call and hit speaker with a single sweep. "Yes? Hello? Patrick?"

"Yes. I see you've dialed my number several times in the last few minutes. What's up?"

"It's Abby. We can't reach her."

"How did you…? I'm on my way to her now. I'll call you when I know something."

"What do you mean, you're on your way to her? Patrick? What's happened?"

"Uh. She said she had a little problem of some kind with her car. Sgt. Cantrell, Bonnie, answered the phone. Abby asked her to have me call her. I did. She was a little hysterical, so I'm not sure what's happened. I will call you."

Patrick hung up before Enid could ask any more questions.

Maude collapsed back against the sofa, her face ashen and her eyes wide with fear.

CHAPTER TWELVE

Enid stood close, fearful Maude would fall when she pushed herself off the sofa to grab Abby.

After touching and hugging her great-granddaughter over and over and with both Enid and Abby's help, Maude finally sat down, tears flowing from her eyes, her voice cracking.

"I cannot allow anything to happen to you, Abigail."

Enid glanced at Patrick and didn't like the expression she saw on his face, but she didn't comment.

"Granny," said Abby, "it was kind of my own fault. Not the phone call, of course. I didn't recognize the number, so I let the call go to voicemail. When I listened to it after class, I panicked. I was driving too fast, and the car in front of me slowed down. My brakes took forever to grab. I had to pump them. I'm fine. My Honda, on the other hand, may need a little work. Chief Mulhaney suggested I have it checked out."

"Do what he says. You can drive my car until yours is repaired if there's anything wrong with it."

"I love your Lincoln Town Car, Granny, but it's only three years old. I hate to drive it even around town. I'm scared to death I'm going to scratch it. Any little old scratch would show up on that black paint."

"Nonsense. It's a car. You are more important to me than any old car. Enid, Patrick, sit down." They complied. "Now Abigail, what about this message you received?"

"I hate for you to listen to it. What happened might not have anything to do with it. I mean, my Honda is in good shape, but it is ten years old. Things do happen."

"Abigail."

"Yes, Granny."

Abby played back the message she had received.

*You need to talk some sense into your great-grandmother.
She needs to stop digging into the past and let the dead stay
buried. If she doesn't stop, sooner or later she's going to rest
with them.*

Maude clenched her teeth. "Sooner or later I'm going to rest
with them anyway."

"Granny, we can't stop searching for the answers, but I
have to keep you safe."

"And I have to keep *you* safe. He called me, too, and
threatened your life."

"I can't hole up in the house."

"Then we need to reconsider your transportation problem.
Maybe you should accept the offer of your nice young man
who keeps asking you to ride to school with him. At least until
the end of this semester."

"Granny...."

"Tell him your Honda is in the shop, and you'd like to
carpool for a few days. I doubt he'll mistake need for interest."

"His name is Robbie Garrett." Abby shrugged her
shoulders at Enid and Patrick.

"Your granny has a point. Riding to school with someone
is a good idea." Patrick raised one eyebrow. "Don't you agree?"

"Yes...in theory. But if I do, Granny, I'll have to go and
come on his schedule. I'll be away from the house longer
periods of time."

"I'll be fine."

"I'll check on her so much she'll beg me to stop," said Enid.

"If only Mama...."

"Don't even think about bringing Natalie into this. If Isabel
dismisses my concerns, you know Natalie isn't going to take
them seriously."

Abby bit her lip. "On one condition."

"What?"

"You hire someone to stay with you when I'm gone and
Miss Enid has to work." Maude raised a hand. "Granny, don't

interrupt and don't say it would be too expensive. You have the money. You know that I know that you do. So. End of discussion if you want me to ride to and from school with my nice young man." Abby raised both eyebrows.

"Fine. I'll hire someone to stay with me when neither of you can." Maude shook her head. "If your grandmother and mother get wind of this, though, they'll cause a commotion."

"So, we don't tell them." Abby winked at her granny.

"I suspect we'll all rest better with that settled," said Patrick. "Now, would you mind if Enid walked me to the door? And would both of you please put me on speed dial and call me if anything untoward happens?"

"We will, Chief," said Abby. Maude nodded.

Enid followed Patrick to the door.

"So what's up?"

"I'm not sure Abby's mishap was an accident. Her brakes were leaking fluid. Not enough to stop working altogether but enough that she had to pump them to stop. That's why I'm having her Honda checked by a police mechanic. Enid, do you think they need to continue this research business? If someone tampered with Abby's brakes, it won't take him long to figure out with whom she is riding to school."

"Do you think either of them is going to give it up?"

"No, probably not. You're in the middle of this, too."

"I know. I've already thought of that."

Patrick leaned over to give her a peck on the cheek. She smiled and squeezed his arm.

"Thank you for caring, Patrick."

"You're welcome. Care enough about me to be careful."

"Will do. Call tonight if it's not too late when you leave the station."

Patrick left and Enid returned to the living room.

"Enid," began Maude, "you need to sleep in your own bed tonight. I insist. Abby's going to sleep in her sleeping bag on the floor in my room tonight, and she's going to move the dower chest back into my closet. We've programmed speed dial numbers for you and Chief Mulhaney on both of our phones. We'll be fine."

Enid shrugged. "Whatever you say, Maude. It is your home."

"Thank you. However, before you leave, and I can't do much more today, but I would like to read at least one more needlepoint. Then we'll have something new to work on between now and the next time you come to the house or I come to the library."

"Sounds like a plan to me," said Abby. "I'll get one. Any particular one?"

"No. You choose."

Abby crossed the room to the chest and opened it. She flipped through the needlepoints and pulled one out.

"I confess I didn't choose this one at random. I chose it because Charlotte used most of the same colors of thread in this needlepoint as in the one that led us to the first two journal entries. I'm hoping this one will lead us to journal entry number three. What can I say? I like things in chronological order."

"So do I, Abigail."

"If it is another scripture," said Enid, "we also need the Bible again."

"It is." Abby lifted the Bible box from the chest and brought it and the needlepoint to the coffee table. She sat beside her granny, opened the box, and lifted the Bible from it.

Maude picked up the needlepoint and stroked the soft wool threads that formed the words and the design. This time the scripture was stitched in red and set against a white background. The border was formed by the letters of the alphabet in red intertwined with tiny flowers and leaves in the same subdued shades of yellow, orange, and green.

"Such amazing workmanship." After a moment, she read the words. "'Come now, and let us reason together, saith the Lord: though your sins be marked as letters in scarlet, they shall be as white as snow; though they be red like crimson, they shall be as wool. Isaiah 1:18.'"

Abby turned the pages of the Bible to the verse in Isaiah. "Now to compare the needlepoint to the Collins's text. 'Come now, and let us reason together, saith the Lord: though your sins be as scarlet, they shall be as white as snow; though they be red like crimson, they shall be as wool.'" She pointed at the words. "Instead of 'though your sins be as scarlet,' she sewed the words 'though your sins be marked as letters in scarlet.'"

"We have our puzzle for the night, then, don't we?"

As Enid left for home, she called Patrick to tell him where she would be and to ask him to drop by instead of calling.

* * *

Later that night, Enid and Patrick sat in the swing on her front porch facing each other.

"I've never known anyone as contrary or stubborn for any reason as Maude has been about telling her family she and Abby might be in danger."

"Ha! Really?" Patrick drew back to gaze at her in disbelief.

Enid slapped his thigh. "This is not funny, and I'm not that stubborn." Her face crinkled. "Close maybe."

"Very close."

"Nevertheless, I would consider your advice if my life was in danger."

"Yes, you would consider it, and then you'd do whatever you wanted to."

"Probably. That wouldn't stop you from advising me."

"No."

"By the way, have you talked to Maude's doctor yet?"

"No. I've called his office several times, but we've played phone tag all day. Either he's with a patient, or I'm on a call."

"I'm going to advise Maude to schedule another appointment."

"You still think someone is trying to poison her?"

"I find it difficult to believe anyone would, but yes, I do. Enough so that while Maude napped this afternoon, I searched every nook and cranny in every room except for her bedroom and bathroom for anything that might be poisonous. I didn't find anything. I even opened containers of things like flour and sugar and tea, and nothing appeared suspicious."

"Depending on the poison, if there is a poison, you might not be able to tell if it was mixed with something else. If Maude does agree to see her doctor, tell me what he says."

"If she agrees to it."

"Between you and Abby? She'll go."

"Humph."

"Changing subjects—which might be wise—you mentioned a new needlepoint clue. What was it and have you figured it out yet?"

"The needlepoint read, 'though your sins be marked as letters in scarlet.' The Collins's Bible read, 'though your sins be as scarlet.' I read the verse in my own Bible to be sure I wasn't confusing myself, and it also reads 'though your sins be as scarlet.'"

"Sins marked as scarlet letters."

"Remind you of anything?" asked Enid.

"No. Should it?"

"Yes. It should. Think a little harder."

"Sins. Marked. Scarlet letters. Ah! *The Scarlet Letter!* Could that be it?"

"I suspect so."

"But why?"

"Maude said that, in addition to the Collins's Bible, the dower chest contained three of Charlotte's favorite books. One of those was *The Scarlet Letter.* I suspect she hid the next journal pages inside the covers of *The Scarlet Letter* the same way she hid the first ones inside the covers of the Bible."

"Have you told her yet?"

"No. She needs to rest. I'll talk to her tomorrow. I hope she's well enough to come to the library so we can continue researching—and be safe. Then I'll take her home so we can examine the book."

"I hope she's well enough to do so, too."

Later, when they stood for Patrick to leave, Enid took an odd comfort in the stubble that brushed her face as he kissed her goodnight.

CHAPTER THIRTEEN

Thursday, August 4, 2011

The next morning, Enid waited at the top of the library's ramp for Abby and her friend Robbie to drop Maude off. Her heart ached as she watched Maude extricate herself from the car and shuffle toward the ramp, her knuckles white against the walker, her face tight with the strain. She met her and Abby at the end of the ramp.

"We'll manage from here, Abby."

"Thanks, Miss Enid." Abby kissed her granny on the cheek and turned to leave, worry creasing her brow when she glanced back over her shoulder.

Inside, Enid insisted Maude sit at one of the tables for a moment while she pretended to check in with Mary. Once in the genealogy room, she guided Maude straight to the microfilm reader.

"You sit. I'll get whatever we need."

"What records will we search?"

"How about probate and land records? They are bound to exist, and they might give us something, anything, useful until we discover more clues from the needlepoints and other contents of the dower chest. We need those records anyway."

"Good idea. It will also give us a sense of accomplishment—and feed our addiction as you call it. Speaking of needlepoints, did you and Patrick come up with any ideas?"

"We did. What about you and Abby?"

"We did, too. Abigail solved it before she went to bed, but I had fallen asleep already, and she wouldn't wake me. I must have mulled it over in my sleep, though. I may not be a retired English teacher or have studied English literature as recently as Abigail, but I woke up this morning mumbling 'a scarlet letter' and from that to shouting, *The Scarlet Letter*. I frightened Abigail half out of her wits. We had a welcome chuckle over it. I suspect you came to the same conclusion we did."

"We did. Four heads with the same idea must be right."

Maude shrugged and sighed. "Unfortunately, I have no idea where the book is. It's not in the dower chest."

"We'll worry on that one later. For now, let's search microfilm."

"Yes, let's."

The morning passed quickly with both their own search and the constant interruptions from other researchers, more researchers and interruptions than usual in a single morning. Ellen assisted as many as she could. When she needed Enid's help, Maude didn't mind. She took advantage of the interruptions to nod off. Enid kept an eye on her, afraid she would fall from her chair. By lunchtime, Maude had gone her limit.

Enid patted her on the shoulder. "We need to stop for the day. We've found everything we hoped to find and more. Probate records for both Peter and Charlotte. Deed transfers for Peter's land showing his original purchase, the transfer to Charlotte at his death, the transfer to Mason and Olivia at Charlotte's death, and the transfers of Mason's half to his firstborn son and to every subsequent firstborn son. As well as the sale and transfer of the tract of land Charlotte received as part of her dowry. Besides, I'm hungry."

"I believe I am, too," said Maude. "Do you mind carrying me home?"

"Of course not. We'll pick up something on the way. Would you like a hamburger for a change?"

"That actually sounds good to me, but make it a cheeseburger. With fries and a coke maybe."

"Definitely. After we eat and you rest, we can act on a theory I have about the missing books."

* * *

After Maude finished her nap, Enid pulled the dower chest out of its hiding place and into the living room. It took more effort without Abby's help, but she managed. She sat on the sofa beside Maude.

"Whew! Got that little job done. Now let's think this thing through."

"You know," said Maude, "I am surprised that Charlotte would hide the copies of either *The Scarlet Letter* or *The Sketch Book* when she brought them with her to her new home. It makes me think she knew Peter would disapprove."

"Which brings me to my theory. What if you're right? What if he did disapprove and she had to hide them from the beginning. Where do you think she could have hidden them?"

"Hmm. If she did put them in the dower chest—and her admonitions to Olivia would suggest that she did—then there must be a secret compartment."

"My thoughts exactly."

"We need to remove all of the items and knock around on the inside."

"I'll push the coffee table out and place the items there. Then we'll have room to pull the dower chest up close."

Several minutes later, the two women commenced knocking about the top, sides, and bottom of the chest.

Maude scrunched her face. "The chest does not appear to have any pockets sewn into it. Everything appears uniform. However, the bottom does sound different from the sides and top."

"Yes, it does, and look here." Enid leaned backward and forward again scrutinizing the chest. "The bottom is thicker than the sides and top."

Maude ran her hand across the bottom inside and outside. "The outside of the bottom of the chest is smooth. The inside of the bottom, however, is unfinished, almost rough. Something a farm girl—or one of her father's slaves—"

"Like Daniel?"

"Yes. Something one of them might do—"

"To form a second or false bottom in a hurry."

"Yes. Maybe," said Maude.

"That's what I suspect, too."

"How do we remove it?"

"Look here. See the slight indention in the bottom? Right in the middle at the front?"

"Yes. As many times as I've gone through the contents, I've never noticed that.

"A flat tool could be inserted there." Enid looked around the room.

Maude leaned over to open the small drawer in the side table nearest her. "You mean something like this letter opener?"

"Something exactly like that."

Enid took the letter opener and inserted it into the indention. It fit. She held it at an angle and lifted carefully. The rough-hewn board came up with little effort on her part. A musty old book smell rose along with it.

Maude clapped her hands together. "The two missing books. They've been hidden here all these years." She reached for *The Scarlet Letter* and opened it. "See here. The paper on the inside of the cover does not match the paper used for the book, and it appears to have been glued down at the edges." She ran her fingers over it. She blew out a tiny breath of air. "Enid, there's something in here."

"Check the back panel as well."

Maude turned to the back and again ran her fingers over the panel.

"Here, too. We'll have to remove the paper glued on. It may damage the book." She paused. "But we have no choice."

"It's already loose in places. Perhaps we can steam it off."

Enid went to the kitchen and brought a pot of water to a boil. She returned to the living room with the pot and two potholders on which to set it.

The two women held onto the sides of the book to prevent it or any journal pages it might contain from dropping into the water. The old glue soon warmed enough for them to loosen and lift the two paper coverings. Underneath each were pages similar to the first journal pages.

"We must wait for Abigail." Maude peered at the clock on the mantel. "It's almost four o'clock. She'll be here soon."

"She'll need to eat."

"I've waited this long. A few more minutes won't hurt."

The two women jumped as something hit the floor. They turned to see Abby standing in the doorway and her books lying on the floor.

"Does this mean you've found the next entries?"

"We have," said Maude. "We didn't hear you come in."

"I didn't sneak in. You two were so intent on what you were doing you wouldn't have heard anyone. As for eating, I can wait."

"You need to eat, Abigail."

"Granny, I had lunch before class and a candy bar after class. I'm good. I'll take this pot of water back to the kitchen so we don't spill it on anything. I'll be right back."

By the time Abby returned, Enid had the folded pages spread open. She shifted to one side so Abby could sit between them.

"Granny, I want to read these entries."

"Please do."

Abby took a deep breath and picked up the yellowed sheets of paper. She leafed through them with care.

"This group includes three separate entries. Shall I read all three before I stop?"

"Yes, please."

Enid and Maude gave their full attention to Abby as she read the next of Charlotte's journal entries.

CHAPTER FOURTEEN

The Journal of Charlotte Abbott Goodwin, cont.
A True Record of Daniel's Innocence and Other Events
Entry #3, Friday Evening, October 17th, 1862
Plans and Preparation for the Escape

I left off abruptly last week when Olivia woke up crying, although I did manage to record more than I expected to. Friday nights are the only time I can find to write in my secret journal. Last Friday night, Peter and Mason left early. I will begin tonight where I left off.

I soon set my plan in motion for Hannah and Miriam to leave for the north with money, clothes, and Daniel.

"Others have done so," I told Hannah. "There are those who will help. I've heard tell of a railroad. I don't think it's an actual railroad but rather a way marked by stations where you can rest and hide during the day."

Hannah stared at me with fear in her eyes, a different kind of fear than usual. "Charlotte," she said. "How can I travel alone with a two-year-old? It wouldn't be safe. She would be safer here than out there with me alone. At least until she's a few years older."

"I don't plan for you to travel alone," I said. "I want Daniel to go with you. I know he's one of my father's slaves, and I'll be going against both my husband and my father, but you and Daniel have loved each other since you were children.

"I'm also hoping Daniel has more knowledge than I do about this railroad. Perhaps he's acquainted with someone who can help you. I wish I knew of someone myself, but as the daughter and the wife of slave owners, I doubt anyone would confide in me or trust my intentions.

"I've no doubt you both can find your way and don't need my advice, but I am compelled to give it. Always travel at night if possible. Follow the North Star. If you must travel by day, watch for moss on the north side of the trees."

The hint of a smile crossed Hannah's face. "We will," she said. "We'll also need to carry some clothes and supplies with us."

"Yes, you will. Daniel should have suitable clothing such that he might pass for a free Negro. Father has seen to that though not for this purpose. You and Miriam have suitable clothing for passing as well. We'll pack as much as we think you can carry."

Hannah nodded, her fear somewhat allayed. She still wrung her hands and kept turning towards the door, no doubt fearing Peter's return as I did.

"I'll provide enough food to sustain the three of you for at least three days, more if you can manage, but on foot and with Miriam to carry, you must travel as unencumbered as possible. I worry about you traveling on foot, but we cannot take a chance on someone accusing you or Daniel of stealing a horse. We'll pass the time between now and when you leave by devising a means for you to carry Miriam and for Daniel to carry supplies."

"Mama can advise me on that."

"Yes, but you must not say anything to anyone other than Celia."

"I won't."

The next morning, September 19th, also a Friday, I sent Hannah to my parents' home on an errand so that she might speak to Daniel, get her mother's advice, and say goodbye to her.

That night, Daniel slipped away from the slave quarters on my parents' farm to meet with Hannah and myself after Peter and Mason left the house.

For the first time, I was thankful for Peter's Friday night absences, which he continues to this day. He spends most of every Friday night at a friend's house drinking with a group of likeminded men. Even more helpful, after the fight between Mason and Isaac, he insisted on taking Mason with him.

"Mason is old enough to learn men's ways," he said.

I did not like the ways Mason was learning, but I had no say in the matter.

This served my purpose, however. When the time came, Peter would not realize Hannah and Miriam were missing until the following morning.

Ten minutes after Peter and Mason left, Daniel tapped on the back door. Hannah ushered him in. When we were younger, the three of us stood eye to eye. Now Daniel stood a head taller than both Hannah and myself.

We discussed every contingency we could imagine before finalizing our plans.

"I allow I might know of a man and a place concerning this Underground Railroad," said Daniel. He said no more, and I asked him nothing.

Our plan was for the three of them to leave the following Friday night. By the time Peter awakened on Saturday morning and found Hannah and Miriam gone, the three runaways would be some distance away and hidden for the day.

That and the clothes and supplies they were to carry were the extent of my input. Hannah and Daniel were to make their remaining plans themselves and not share the details with me.

As Daniel was about to leave, I informed them of one other item they were to carry.

"As part of my plan to supply you for the trip," I told them, "I intend to take Peter's money box as soon as he leaves the house and hide it. He sometimes forgets where he last hid it, especially if he has been drinking. I know how much is in the box—an amount at least equivalent to the dowry of land my father gave us at our marriage, which, of course, Peter saw fit to sell. I'll give Hannah some of the money when you leave. Once you're safe, I'll send the rest to her to use in establishing your new home."

I could tell by Daniel's expression he did not approve of that part of my plan, but he did not question me.

Fear again showed on Hannah's face. "Charlotte, that will put you and Olivia in danger."

"No. We'll be fine. It will be some time before Peter checks the box again. He'll never connect its disappearance to me."

I, too, had the smallest of doubts, but I did not dare to share this with Hannah.

I wanted to take no more than the amount of my dowry from the box, but I could not return the box to its hiding place with only part of the money. Peter would surely suspect me of taking it if I did.

I reasoned, however, that if the box with all of the money was gone, he might think he had forgotten where he had put it—which he often did for a spell—or that someone else had stolen it. In either case, he was not likely to open it again until the following week when he planned to sell livestock in town.

When the evening of Hannah's departure arrived and Peter and Mason left the house, I put Olivia to bed early with much protest and tears from the child. I hesitated but for a moment. While I wished she could spend those last hours with Miriam, I could not risk her having a memory Peter could wrest from her little mind.

Thirty minutes later, I had sewn the money into Hannah's petticoat and packed a flour sack with the supplies set aside earlier that day.

As we waited for Daniel, I gave Hannah something else. I gave her the paper I had written for her and

Miriam, their freedom paper signed by me. Tears flowed down both our faces as she read the paper aloud.

I kept a copy, and I will transcribe it here.

> To all to whom it may concern, this deed witnesses that I, Charlotte Abbott Goodwin of Henry County Tennessee, do hereby manumit and set free Hannah, my negro slave woman aged about twenty-seven years, being light-skinned, standing about five feet four inches high, bearing some scars across her back, also Miriam, child of said Hannah, aged about two years, being light-skinned and bearing no scars, releasing said Hannah and Miriam from all manner of servitude to myself or my heirs as fully and completely as if each had been born free. Witness my hand and seal this 26th day of September 1862. Charlotte Abbott Goodwin.

When she finished reading, I gave her my warning and my regrets.

"Hannah, if you are caught and returned, Peter will disavow this paper as it has only my signature and not his although you were given to me as a wedding gift, not to him. Regardless, if you get far enough away that no one knows Peter, it should serve you well enough. I regret that I cannot forge my father's signature on a paper for Daniel. I also regret that we cannot register your papers with the court as required by state law, as someone would surely alert Peter. However, as soon as you settle somewhere, you should be able to have them registered."

"Thank you, Charlotte, for me but especially for Miriam."

My heart broke. "Hannah, you've no need to thank me for giving you something that was never mine to have."

We embraced. Then I lifted Miriam out of the carrier Hannah and Celia had made for her and held her close. Hannah paced the floor while I rocked little Miriam until Daniel arrived.

He arrived sooner than I wished, but I knew the travelers had to leave as soon as possible. Amid our last whispers and tears, Hannah and I hugged each other repeatedly and said our goodbyes. I gave her my last instructions and admonitions.

"Hannah, do not come back here as long as Peter lives. Do not contact me directly. Find a way to contact your mother if you can—a way that cannot be traced back to you—so that I may send you the rest of the money. If I outlive Peter and you hear of his death, please let me know where you are and how you are. Take care of our precious Miriam. I've placed one of the photographs of the four of us with your clothes so that you might remember Olivia and me. I'll keep my copy forever so that Olivia and I might remember you and Miriam. Hannah, though neither of us has ever broached the subject, I have no doubt that you are my half sister. That my father is your father. Which would make Miriam and Olivia cousins as well as half sisters."

The look in Hannah's eyes before she turned her face to the floor told me she had always known what I had only suspected. I choked back a sob and continued.

"You and Miriam will always be a part of us and we a part of you. You will forever be in our hearts and prayers. Be safe. Hold Miriam close."

We embraced once more as Daniel waited, the only sign of his impatience the tapping of his foot. I kissed Miriam on the forehead one last time, shook Daniel's hand, and watched them disappear into the night.

In spite of our planning, I did not foresee all of the possible flaws in those plans.

I must stop. Peter has returned. I must hurry to hide this before he and Mason enter the house.

CHAPTER FIFTEEN

The Journal of Charlotte Abbott Goodwin, cont.
A True Record of Daniel's Innocence and Other Events
Entry #4, Friday Evening, October 24th, 1862
Events Following the Escape

Another week has passed since I last wrote in my secret journal. I write with a heavy heart as I relate the events of the days following Hannah's escape.

As I noted in my last entry, I did not foresee all of the flaws in our plan. Perhaps the most important of these was not considering that Peter might check his money box sooner than expected and accuse Daniel of its theft, for this led to additional warrants being issued against Daniel. I had no doubt this would prevent Hannah from ever contacting me directly and perhaps indirectly even after Peter died.

When Peter realized Hannah and Miriam were not in the house that Saturday morning, he searched the barn and other outbuildings looking for them. He searched the slave quarters and questioned the men and women.

When he returned to the house, his face blood red and the vessels on either side bulging as on the day we transplanted the yellow daffodils, he struck me and yelled, "Did you have anything to do with this?"

"With what?" I cried.

"With their escape!" He drew back to strike me again.

I threw up my hand to defend myself. "No, of course not. Why would I?" I held my own tears as I grabbed up Olivia, who clung to me screaming. I held her close until her tears subsided, but I kept an eye on Peter, who stared at me, his mind churning and his anger boiling over.

"If not you, then who? She would not have left on her own. Not with a small child." He looked round the room as if he could find the answer hidden in the walls. When he returned his gaze to me, his eyes narrowed in realization or anger or both. "Daniel," he said. "Your father asked me if I wanted Daniel when we married. He said they wanted to be married, but he told them they must wait until they were older. I told him no, I had no need of a possessive buck. He helped her, didn't he?"

My fear mounted, but I had to continue my lie. "Peter, how could I know that?"

He closed his eyes and whispered, "Daniel." Then he stomped across the floor and cursed, calling Daniel words not even my father would say. At the door, he stopped and spoke in a calm, icy voice more frightening than his yelling and his curses. "I'm going to your father's. If Daniel's gone, too, I'll find them. I'll have him hung for stealing my property. I'll sell Miriam down south. I'll make Hannah wish she'd never been born."

I jumped up, frightening Olivia and sending her into another screaming fit. "Peter! You can't do that!" I yelled back at him over Olivia's cries.

"I can and I will." His stony glare froze my very heart. Then he turned and stomped out of the house.

Again, Olivia's screams subsided, but her tears continued to wash over her cheeks. I tried to comfort her, fighting my own tears as I did.

I prayed, "Dear God, what have I done? Give them safe travel. Hide them from Peter. Please."

Peter did not return until midafternoon. His horse's sides, white with lather, rose and fell. Peter, covered in dust streaked with sweat, looked through me with a stone-cold glare as he told me the details of his search.

"Daniel disappeared last night as well. Even with the help of several of our neighbors, we did not find a trace of them. Someone helped them. I will find them if it is the last thing I do. In the meantime, I plan to place advertisements in Wednesday's *Guardian* asking for any information on them. Bring me the picture of the four of you. I'll get a picture of Daniel from your father."

"But why?"

Peter turned to face me and yelled. "Bring it to me!"

I retrieved the photograph from our bedroom.

Peter clenched his fists but lowered his voice. "Cut it in half. Give me the half with Hannah and Miriam."

I clutched at the photograph with one hand and at my stomach with the other. My heart throbbed like an open wound as I picked up my scissors and tried to cut straight down the center of the photograph. I wiped away a single tear as I handed him the half he demanded. It would be the last time I would see the faces of Hannah and Miriam as they were in the days before they left.

Peter turned but stopped abruptly and stomped across the room to the latest hiding place for his money box, the back side of the bottom shelf of my pie safe, which he claimed for storing his ledgers and other items. My breath caught, but I dared not show any sign of emotion that might rouse his suspicion. He opened the doors and squatted to reach over the items in front for the money box he expected to find at the back. He cursed and began throwing the ledgers, quill pens, and other items, even the ink bottle onto the floor as he dug deeper. I grabbed the ink bottle before it could spill but quickly stepped back. Peter stood and began pulling canned and baked goods from the upper shelves. At least he did not throw them, but he did slam them down on the nearby table. When the shelves were bare, he pushed the doors shut and slammed his fist into one of the punched tin panels. He froze but for a moment. He swung around to face me with a more fierce hatred and vile contempt than I had ever seen before.

"You would not have dared," he said. "You…you…." He glared at me and took several sharp breaths as he stepped toward me. "You could not be that stupid, could you?"

He turned on his heel and headed for Olivia's bedroom. I grabbed my chest and held my breath. I watched from where I stood as he lifted the outer lid of my dower chest and tried to lift the lid to the till inside. It was locked. He pulled his knife from his pocket and pried the lid open, breaking the lock in the process. He lifted the necklace I kept in the till and then dropped it. He stood staring into the chest then slammed both lids shut. He stomped back into the front room.

"You would not have taken the box. You would not have taken all of my money." He gritted his teeth as he again studied the room. He closed his eyes and shook his head. "But Daniel would have. Hannah would have told him about it. He not only stole two of my slaves, but he also stole my money! I'll have him beaten before he's hung! I'm going to town. I'll be gone some time. In addition to placing the advertisements, I'll have warrants issued for Daniel for the theft and for aiding and abetting two runaways in addition to the single warrants for each of them for being runaways. Do not leave this house."

Peter stormed out the front door. I sank to the floor with Olivia clinging to me and gulping tiny sobs.

"Mama, why is Daddy so mad? Where is my Miriam? Where is my Hannah? Why are you crying?"

I prayed again for the safety of Hannah and Miriam and Daniel. I prayed I could keep my own little one safe.

The advertisement did appear in *The Bakersville Guardian* the next Wednesday. I hoped those few days gave my friends time to be well away from anyone who might recognize them.

I continue to pray daily for theirs and our safety. Both my fear and my prayers have escalated to a fever pitch. I cannot imagine what lies ahead for Olivia and myself any more than I can for Hannah, Miriam, or Daniel.

CHAPTER SIXTEEN

The Journal of Charlotte Abbott Goodwin, cont.
A True Record of Daniel's Innocence and Other Events
Entry #5, Friday Evening, December 26th, 1862
Events Following the Escape, cont.

A dismal Christmas has passed and an unpromising New Year approaches.

When I last wrote in my journal, I did not think it possible for Peter to become more bitter or brutal, but he has. The past two months have proved to be the most difficult of my life.

I thanked God each night that Peter had not turned his anger on Olivia and that Hannah, Miriam, and Daniel had not been found in spite of the advertisements and the warrants.

I prayed that the three travelers had found sanctuary. Nevertheless, I worried about them constantly. I had heard the stories of slaves who had been found. Of those who had been hung on the spot. Of others, both men and women, who were beaten savagely. Of women who had suffered worse.

If they avoided capture, what of their travel hardships? Making their way with a child in bad weather and good, through woods and brambles, through swamps, and up rivers. Would they be able to procure the food they needed? Had I sent Hannah to freedom or death or worse? How could little Miriam make such a trip?

I had no doubt Hannah and Daniel were of sturdier stock than I, but would that be enough to keep them alive? Of the thousands of Negro slaves, how many actually tried to escape? Of those who tried, how many succeeded or lived to reach their destination? Of the slaves in our town and the nearby countryside, I knew of only four others who had tried. I did not know if they had lived to reach safety.

For more than a month, I wished for news from Hannah but prayed she would not send it for fear Peter would hear of it. Three weeks ago, we did hear from Hannah, but we managed to keep it from Peter.

A traveling free black man slipped into the slave quarters on my parents' farm and delivered a brief message by word of mouth from Hannah to Celia. It was old news, but it was news. It brought us joy and heartbreak.

The man had seen the three travelers, they looked well, and they had made it to the border between Kentucky and Ohio. However, they had also learned of the warrants against Daniel for the theft of the money, for being a runaway slave, and for aiding in the escape of two other runaways. Because of that, they did not dare risk sending another message or ever returning to Tennessee.

Celia moaned and rocked as she shared the message with me. We had always known the likelihood of this end, but hearing it in a message from Hannah made it a reality. When Celia finished, she sobbed as she poured out her grief. "I will never see my firstborn child again."

I wrapped my arms around the woman who had been as much of a mother to me as my own mother had. "I'm so sorry, Celia. I should never have sent her away."

Celia drew back and fixed me with fire in her eyes, "Don't you ever say that again, Miss Charlotte. If she had stayed, who knows what might have become of her and that child. We lost Isaac. We lost Joshua. I could not bear to lose our little Miriam, too. No. Better I never see them again than lose them at Peter Goodwin's hand."

I held her close again as I tried to reassure her with words I did not believe myself. "I won't give up hope of seeing them again. I cannot. If Lincoln wins this war, he may bring about a blessed change. Freedom."

"Miss Charlotte, don't you dare let anyone hear you say such words! You know better than that." She grabbed her chest. "Forgive me. I forget my place."

"Celia, you watched over me from a babe in my Mama's arms. Your place is in my heart."

"I know that, child, but you still know you can't say things like that. Besides, what if Mr. Lincoln loses this war?"

"I cannot think on that, Celia. I will hold my tongue, but I will also pray for Mr. Lincoln's victory and for Hannah, Miriam, and Daniel's safety."

"Amen to that." Neither of us spoke for a time, each of us lost in our thoughts. Celia broke our silence.

"Miss Charlotte, it don't matter if Mr. Lincoln wins this war or not for me seeing my child or my grandchild. With those warrants on Daniel, they can't come back. No matter you have it all written down in that journal of yours. Ain't nobody around here going to believe what's in your journal."

Celia may be right, but I can hope for change. My journal is part of my hope.

The news that Hannah would never return gave me another concern—what I could and should do with the money I had secreted away and how I could prevent Peter from finding it.

However, by the following Friday, I had decided on a new hiding place for the rest of the money. After Peter and Mason left the house to be with their men friends, I put Olivia to bed early. When I was certain she was asleep, I moved the money box, returning to the house frequently to check on Olivia, fearing Peter's early return every step I took.

Once the money was safely hidden where no one would ever think to look, I spent the rest of the night finishing the needlepoint that pointed to its location. If I have passed and Olivia or one of my descendants has found these journal pages and read them, I trust that you have also discovered my method and found the needlepoints I will leave in Olivia's care.

I have created and framed such needlepoints for family members on special occasions since I was a child. Many of them are decorated with scenes, others with flowers. Most have scriptures on them.

They have become one of my few options for gift giving over the years, as Peter does not approve of wasting money on giving presents. He doesn't, however, object to my giving away needlework done with scraps of canvas and thread, especially as I call them patterns that I may follow and share with others to follow and as I stitch them at the end of the day after all work is finished. Peter adheres to the admonition that idle hands are the devil's workshop and even mistakenly attributes it to the Bible though he himself doesn't care to indulge in reading the Bible, another pastime he allows me with reluctance. The result is that neither Peter nor anyone else will give any thought to seeing a new needlepoint project in my lap or on the wall.

The latest ones are different, however. Each scripture will contain an error that will provide a clue to the location of something I have hidden. This is the only way I know to prevent Peter from uncovering my secrets. He is not a spiritual man, nor does he attend church or read the Bible. He has even forbidden me to take Mason to church or to teach or read the scriptures to him.

While I must grieve for both their souls, it has given me this way to hide my words in plain sight. Neither Peter nor Mason will suspect the needlepoints contain errors much less clues.

It is, of course, another Friday night, and I hear voices at the barn. Peter and Mason have returned. I must stop for now.

Enid touched Abby's hand as she continued to stare at the journal pages on the coffee table in front of her.

"Are you all right?"

"Yes. No. Charlotte had to make several difficult decisions. So far, we've seen nothing but heartache as a result."

Maude placed her arm across Abby's shoulders and pulled her close. "But she made the right decisions, Abigail. She never expresses any regret for her decisions except once and that was for Celia's sorrow. What she regretted was the results."

"Maude's right, Abby. We have to try to do the right things in life without the expectation that all will turn out the way we want or expect. Charlotte did a good thing by sending Hannah, Miriam, and Daniel away. She also did a good thing by leaving her story for someone to carry out the rest of her plans if she couldn't. We've learned more of Charlotte's story, more about her, and more about the time in which she lived. We know she left clues for where she hid the money and her journal entries. I suspect some of the clues will lead to *The Sketch Book* and the *New England Primer* as the hiding places for more journal pages."

"I think so, too," said Maude, "but I don't think I can sit here any longer. I need to rest. Abigail needs to eat. Perhaps this is enough for one day."

"Perhaps you're right, Maude."

"I do hope I have enough days left to read the rest of Charlotte's journal. At least we now know they traveled through Kentucky to Ohio. Maybe that will help us when we search again. Abigail?"

"Yes, Granny?"

"If I don't live long enough to find them, will you carry on for me—for Charlotte and Olivia?"

"Of course, I will. You know how tenacious I can be. I will find Hannah's descendants, but I want you to be there with me when I do."

"I want to be there, too, dear, but I'm not so sure that's going to happen at least not in body. If not, rest assured I will be there with you in spirit."

Enid cleared her throat.

"I don't like that look, Enid. What is it now?"

"Maude, before we go any further with this line of thinking, I…. I'm not family, and it's not for me to say, but…I'm going to say it anyway. I want you to see your doctor. Abby, I want you to go with her and tell him we are concerned about…outside influences."

"He won't listen to me, Miss Enid. He hardly listens to me when I go for my own appointments."

"Abigail is right. He doesn't take it well when patients have their own ideas or question his. When I first began feeling more tired than usual, he and Isabel both insisted it was age. All I needed to do was slow down and take care of myself." Enid frowned. Maude continued. "I'll tell you what. I have wanted to go back, but I didn't see the need of it given his attitude. However, if you will go with us, I'll go. Surely the three of us can get his attention."

"That's a great idea," said Abby. "However, you both need to be ready to deal with Grandma. She will not like it at all."

"I don't mind going with you," said Enid. "I don't even mind speaking my piece if you're sure that's what you want."

"I am. I'll tell you both what else I want. I want to see my lawyer and our funeral director. Don't make a face, Abigail."

"I know, Granny. I'm happy and willing to do whatever you decide, but again, we need to be ready for the opposition, which will no doubt include Mama as well as Grandma."

"Maybe it's time for them to grow up. We can do this." Maude nodded once to show her determination. "Enid, I want you to go home again tonight. I love having you as a houseguest, but I don't want to take advantage of you or keep you from your own concerns. I'll call first thing in the morning to schedule appointments. I'll let you know when I know."

"I'll prepare myself for a full day," said Enid.

CHAPTER SEVENTEEN

Friday, August 5, 2011

As Enid backed out of Maude's driveway the next morning, her worry lines testified to her concerns about the day's plans. The usual calming effect of the lilac and jasmine in Maude's fragrance did nothing to relieve her tension. Abby, who sat in the back seat, seemed tense as well, her knuckles white as she gripped her seat belt with both hands.

Maude, however, acted anything but tense in spite of what she said. "Enid, I'm sorry to pull you away from the genealogy room again today and on such short notice. However, the next appointment time Dr. Finley had available was a week from Monday. But what if I don't have a week?"

"It's not a problem, Maude. How did you manage to get in today?"

"They had a cancellation, and I took it. Abby and I would have gone on if you couldn't have gotten away."

"I'm glad you called me."

"After we finish at the doctor's office, I want us to go to my lawyer's office. If you can stay and attest to my state of mind, I would appreciate it."

"I've taken off the whole day. I have several days of vacation built up. I'll be happy to attest to anything you want."

"I'm taking the day off, too," said Abby. "I haven't missed a class yet. I called my professor to explain. She said she understood, and I could make up the work."

"When we leave the lawyer's office, Abigail and I need to go to the funeral home and get my final wishes settled. You could take us home to get my car, but I wouldn't mind if you accompanied us there, too. I have this awful suspicion that Isabel will get wind of all this and show up at some point."

"I'm happy to go with you for moral support. However, I'm not sure I'll be much help if Isabel does find out."

* * *

Aware of the questioning stare in the nurse's eyes, Enid helped Maude to the chair nearest the doctor's desk and slipped into the chair nearest the door without comment. Abby sat beside her Granny.

"Dr. Finley will be with you in a minute."

Enid watched the hands of the wall clock creep forward. Fifteen minutes later, the doctor entered the room. He stopped short when he saw Enid and Abby and then crossed to his desk before greeting his patient.

"Miss Maude, how are you today?"

"I've been better, Dr. Finley, and I'm worse than I was at my last appointment, which was one month ago today. Before we begin, you know Abby. And you know my friend Enid Gilchrist, don't you? She drove us here today."

"Yes, I know Mrs. Gilchrist from the library." He nodded in Enid's direction. "Was Isabel busy today and not able to accompany you?"

"Something like that. Dr. Finley, the last time I came in you insisted nothing was wrong with me other than old age. The fact is even old people have problems that can be treated. Furthermore, I didn't live to be ninety years old without learning a little about my own body along the way. Something is not right. I want some bloodwork done and maybe some other tests as well."

"Perhaps we should review your symptoms first. Except for moving a little slower, you've always been very healthy for your age."

"If you can't remember my symptoms from last time, I certainly can. I have some to add, too. It's all come on gradually. This. That. Something else. Through it all, I've kept feeling weaker and older and more tired. Some nights I don't sleep well. What bothers me the most is my decline in mobility. Two months ago, I was walking fine on my own, maybe moving more slowly as you point out, but fine. Then walking became more difficult. In time, I had to begin using a cane. Now I'm using a walker. I'm afraid not to. Sometimes I experience a little pins and needles sensation in my hands and feet, sometimes a little numbness. My legs have gradually gotten weaker, and I'm unsteady on my feet. Little tasks are more difficult. Abigail has to help me get dressed sometimes."

"Do you have any problems with your bowels or bladder?"

"No, no more than I have for the past few years."

"Anything else?"

"My hair is thinning. There's not only less of it, but the strands themselves have thinned. I have more skin irritations than usual. I've kept an itchy skin rash on my body for a couple of weeks now. I apply hydrocortisone cream before dusting with powder. That helps the itch, but the rash doesn't go away. Then I have these dark spots. I thought I was going to get through life without them. I'd think they were liver spots if it weren't for the other problems."

"I'd think so, too, but not all dark spots are liver spots. What about your memory and other cognitive functions?"

"I don't notice any difference until I get tired. Then thinking takes more effort, but for the record, my mind is intact. Both Abby and Enid can attest to that, can't you?" Maude glanced from one to the other.

"I can for sure," said Abby.

"I can, too," said Enid. She bit her lower lip to avoid grinning.

"Now. As to the bloodwork I want—"

"Miss Maude, if it will give you peace of mind, I'll have blood drawn. We'll run all of the usual blood tests. If anything shows up, we'll consider other tests."

"I want to add another one or two tests to the usual ones."

Dr. Finley peered at Maude over his glasses. "What tests?"

"For common poisons. In particular, arsenic."

The doctor glanced from Maude to Enid to Abby and back to Maude. "Are you serious? Whatever for? You've lived in your house most of your adult life. If there were anything in it with arsenic or even lead, you would have had symptoms long ago."

"Humor me."

"Why would you suspect arsenic poisoning? You didn't say anything about having gastrointestinal problems."

"That's the one thing I don't have, thank goodness, at least not any more than usual. My appetite isn't what it was, and things don't always taste like they should but nothing else."

"Let me see your fingernails."

"What are you looking for?"

"Mees lines, white lines across the nails. You don't have them. I'm sorry, Miss Maude. I can't justify those tests as medically necessary. At least not until we get the other tests back for review. Insurance may not cover them if I can't justify them and may not if I can."

"I'll pay for them. You don't have to submit them to insurance if I pay for them."

"Miss Maude—"

"I have rights, you know. This is my body and my money. Either you do the tests, or I'll find another doctor who will."

Dr. Finley sat back in his chair, placed his palms together, and closed his eyes. None of that prevented the hint of color creeping up his face.

Enid glanced at Maude, who gripped the arms of her chair.

"Dr. Finley," said Enid, "you'll be drawing blood anyway. One or two more tests won't add much to the collection time, and Maude said she would pay for it. Of course, if your conscience won't allow you to run the tests to rule out something, I believe we can find sites online where an individual can schedule tests on their own at reputable labs. Maude could also get a second opinion."

"I'll order the tests," he growled, "but for your information, testing urine levels is the most reliable means for assessing arsenic exposure. It can also be useful for checking for anemia and for calcium levels."

"So add the urine test," said Maude. "I need to go anyway."

Dr. Finley looked at the ceiling and shook his head. "Fine. I'll run them all—CBC, thyroid, and arsenic blood tests—as well as the urinalysis. I'll have to send them to the hospital, and it may take a few days for the results to come back. Maude, I suspect all of these changes are simply signs of aging. You may have even had a couple of TIAs, as Mr. Everly did. Frankly, you've had a good run with your health. Nevertheless, you should inform Isabel of your concerns."

"Thank you, Dr. Finley, for respecting my wishes in spite of our disagreement," said Maude. "Now, let's get this done. I have an appointment with my lawyer. I don't want to miss it and have to put off making the changes to my will until next week especially as I'm aging faster and faster by the minute."

"No need for sarcasm," snapped the doctor.

Maude rose, winked at Enid, and turned toward the door. "I know where the lab is. Let me know as soon as you get the results back."

Abby hurried to the door and opened it. Maude pushed her walker through and headed for the lab.

Enid hesitated a moment, expecting the doctor to say something before they left. Instead, he frowned, opened his mouth as if to speak, then returned to his notes without another word. She suspected that did not bode well for any of them.

CHAPTER EIGHTEEN

Enid drove Maude and Abby straight from the lab to the lawyer's office. Abby eased Maude out of the Subaru.

"Here we go again," said Maude. "I hope my lawyer isn't as contrary as my doctor was."

Inside, they were ushered directly to Lowell Franklin's office. He stood to greet them, distinguished looking as always in an impeccable dark gray suit that set off his salt and pepper hair, but he did not come around his desk.

Enid admired the desk, an antique Victorian mahogany pedestal desk, and the mahogany and leather desk chair, both old but well cared for and in pristine condition.

No grandchildren played in this room, she thought.

By comparison, the guest chairs and small sofa, also mahogany and leather, were modern but chosen to complement the older furnishings.

"Maude, come in, come in." Lowell continued to stand, wringing his hands while he waited for Abby to help Maude settle into one of the guest chairs, his lean but muscular physique evident even under his suit, at odds with his demeanor.

Abby sat in the guest chair beside Maude. Enid crossed behind them to the sofa against the wall. As she turned to sit, she caught Lowell staring at her. He snapped his attention back to Maude and Abby.

"Maude, it's good to see you out and about. Abby, it's nice to see you, too." He glanced back at Enid "What brings you along this morning, Enid?"

"I'm along for the ride," she answered.

"And to help Abigail attest to my mental stability," said Maude. "She went with me to my doctor's appointment this morning. He agreed with them that my mind is good."

"I've no doubt of that, Maude."

"So we're all in agreement, I'm in my right mind?"

"Yes, Maude, we're in agreement. You are in your right mind."

"Good. I don't want there to be any questions about the changes I wish to make to my will and other final wishes."

Lowell's jaw dropped and his eyes widened. He dropped into his chair. After a moment, he found his voice.

"I've never known a family with such a penchant for changing their minds over their last wishes. My daddy and my granddaddy said the same thing. Whatever would you want to change? I thought you had finessed every detail."

"I did. Now I want to change a few of those details. They shouldn't be a big deal."

"I'm sure they won't be. Tell me your changes."

"Abigail is taking care of me now, and she's more attuned to my wishes so...."

"Wait. Is Isabel aware of this meeting and the changes you want to make?"

"She will be. Besides, it's my business, not hers. She's no spring chicken herself. She could go before I do."

"Right. So then. What were those changes?"

"First and foremost, I want Abigail to have durable power of attorney for both my financial affairs and my health care. She is to see that all of my wishes are fulfilled and is to make any decisions not specified in those documents or in my will if I am incapacitated or dead."

"Are you certain—"

"I am positive. Now moving on. She is also to be named executrix of my will and for my estate."

"In place of your sons and daughters?"

"That's right. Too many noses in the business and some are bound to get knocked out of joint."

Lowell studied his desktop, tracing imaginary circles in the wood. When he looked up, he focused on Abby. "How old are you?"

"She's eighteen years old," answered Maude. "Old enough and wiser than other family members, all of whom are older."

"Right. Abby, are you agreeable to all of this? It's a great deal of responsibility and could be a heavy burden."

Enid caught the note of condescension in Lowell's voice and heard Abby's intake of breath before she spoke.

"First, yes, I am agreeable. Second, I am a responsible person even if I'm not as old as the hills. More importantly, it is not and never will be a burden. I am aware of Granny's wishes, and I'm happy to carry them out for her."

"Yes, of course, you are. Maude, will you be increasing her inheritance?"

"Don't be daft—or insulting—Lowell Franklin."

"I wanted to be certain."

"I'm sure you did. Can you have the papers ready for me to sign by Monday noon?"

"I'll see to it."

"Good. I'll come in Monday afternoon to sign everything and get my copies."

"Someone should contact Isabel."

"I'll take care of Isabel."

Maude pushed herself up from her chair. "Now, ladies, to the funeral home and then to lunch."

As they left, Enid could not help but hear the sound of a pen tapping back and forth on the wooden desk behind them. She held her comments until they settled themselves into the Subaru.

"Whew! I've known Lowell Franklin most of my life though from a distance. I never knew he could be so persnickety."

"His disposition has changed over the years. It began after he entered law school. He didn't choose to be a lawyer."

"He told you that?"

"No. He would never share such intimate thoughts and feelings with me. Lucille, on the other hand, loves to tell all. Lucille is Lowell's wife and one of my distant cousins.

According to her, Lowell loved his father, but he never wanted to follow in his footsteps, especially into law. He wanted to be a scientist of some kind. To his father and his grandfather, however, the firm meant everything. They were disappointed with his decision and refused to provide any more than his tuition for college. Scholarships provided his basic living expenses, but he worked weekends pumping gas for spending money.

"Then his grandfather died at the end of Lowell's senior year of college. His father needed him to help in the practice. Without a second thought, Lowell finished his B.S. degree, went on to get his J.D. degree, passed the bar, and came to work at the family firm. Fortunately, for his father and the firm, Lowell had a strong academic, service, and extracurricular record that prepared him in many ways for law school. Lucille says Lowell's favorite saying is, 'You do what you have to do for family and firm.'"

"That explains the contrast between the two undergraduate degrees on the wall in his office."

"That explains his disposition, too, but it doesn't excuse it. He is an astute lawyer, but I feel battle weary every time I have business dealings with him. Isabel encouraged him. He'd best leave informing her of this meeting to me. I hope we can leave the funeral home less on edge."

CHAPTER NINETEEN

Enid pulled into the New Eaves Funeral Home parking lot. She held the walker steady while Abby tugged on Maude to get her out of the Subaru.

"I hope I have enough energy for this one last stop," said Maude, "although I don't expect this meeting to be as difficult as the first two. Afterwards, I would like some lunch." She stopped for a moment at the glass door of the funeral home. "If lunch restores me at all, I'd also like to read the next journal entries if we can find them."

At that moment, Timothy Foster, the funeral home's director, opened the door.

"Good afternoon, Miss Maude. I have everything out and ready for our visit."

The three women followed Timothy to his office. Again, Enid waited for Maude and Abby to settle into the guest chairs before settling herself onto a nearby sofa. She glanced around the room, taking comfort in the soft, restful earth tones that drew her gaze from the sofa to the landscapes on the wall to the plush carpet on the floor. All elegant but contemporary, including the streamlined executive desk. Timothy's voice drew her attention back to the business at hand.

"Now, Miss Maude, you said you needed to make changes to your arrangements."

"No. I need to make sure they're carried out. I want Abigail to have sole responsibility for my final arrangements."

"I see. It is usually handled by the next of kin."

"She's my executrix. She'll be paying the bill."

"Ah. Of course, we'll follow her instructions then."

"I thought you would."

"Mr. Foster, I believe Granny gave you instructions and made all the arrangements on a previous visit."

"Yes."

"All I'll need to do is see that they're carried out."

"Of course." He smiled.

"We're having power of attorney and executrix paperwork prepared by my lawyer, Lowell Franklin," said Maude. "Do you have any such paperwork that needs to be completed?"

"No, not at this point. When the time comes, if there are...uh...problems with anyone, it might be wise for Abby to bring a copy of those documents with her to my office."

"I understand."

"Let me take a moment to update our records with Abby's information, and then I'll print out a new copy for you."

Timothy made the changes and sent the document to the printer. As the last page printed, a door slammed, startling them. Heels clicked hard and fast down the hallway toward Timothy's office. When the clicking stopped, someone shoved the office door open. Timothy puckered his lips for a silent whistle and glanced at Maude. She turned sideways to see who had burst in on them. Her oldest daughter, Isabel Parker, stood there, stock-still, staring at them, jerking her head and her attention from one to the other of them.

"Mother! What do you think you're doing? As for you Abigail Croft, don't you think you've overstepped yourself? And you, Enid Gilchrist, what are you doing here?"

"She's here at my request." Maude straightened her back, wincing as she did so. She cut short a groan. "This is my business."

Isabel took a few steps toward Enid. She stomped and waved her hands in Enid's face.

"Enid Gilchrist, how dare you interfere in our family matters? How dare you encourage my granddaughter in this and put her life in jeopardy! That's right! I heard about the incident with the brakes."

"Grandma," said Abby, "Miss Enid has done nothing of the sort. She has even stayed with us to help me keep Granny safe. We're not doing any of this at her encouragement. Granny is calling the shots. I would think, with all that's happened, you would appreciate someone helping us. Do you not even care someone might be out to harm Granny?"

"Of course, I care. I also care about whether or not you get hurt, too, but you both need to let the police take care of this. It's their job. Not yours. Mama, I'm not the only one who feels this way. The whole family is up in arms at you over your current antics. It's bad enough that you've hounded Dr. Finley into doing unnecessary lab work. It's bad enough that you've made your great-granddaughter your executrix and put her in charge of everything over your own children. What's worse is that you're doing all of this over dredging up age-old family secrets. For what? For the life of me, I cannot understand your fascination with the past. They're all dead!"

"Grandma! Stop it! Leave Granny alone. I'm going to do this, and there's nothing you or anyone else can do to stop me."

"Before we end this little test of wills," said Maude, "who told you about the lab work and the change of executrix?"

"Who do you think? Your doctor and your lawyer called me and told me. That's what they've been instructed to do."

"You can rest assured that will change. Until I'm declared incompetent, they will no longer be informing you or anyone else except Abigail of anything."

"Mother!"

"Don't *Mother* me, Isabel Everly Parker. This discussion has ended. I'm worn out, and I'm hungry."

Isabel glared at Enid. "I hold you responsible. You and this genealogy nonsense. The past is the past. It should be left in the past. If you're not careful, you could find yourself joining those whose bones you delight in digging up."

Enid could not resist challenging this often-repeated nonsense. "Why would you not want to know about your ancestors? They make us who we are. We exist because of them. Besides, it's only by understanding the past that we can make the future better."

"And be judged for what those ancestors did in the process? That's not right. It's not any more right than what they did." She glared at her granddaughter. "I wash my hands of this whole matter, Abby. Whatever happens next is on you." She turned to stomp out of the funeral home, the sharp rat-a-tat-tat of her heels clicking up the hallway and out the front door.

Abby wrinkled her nose. "You know, Miss Enid, I hate to admit it, but I do understand Grandma a little. I thought about it more after Granny brought it up. I can't imagine that anyone would actually judge us for what our ancestors did. But like Granny, I don't want someone to think I'm a racist because I'm white or because I'm descended from slave owners."

"I do understand, Abby. We still have much ground to cover in that respect. Unfortunately, those who continue the prejudice and hatred of the past get more recognition than those who do not."

"Enough of this topic, both of you," said Maude.

"I know, Granny. Food."

"Soon. Timothy, I do apologize for my daughter's outburst. At the very least, she could have done it in the privacy of my home. However, perhaps this does show you why I'm so insistent about Abigail handling everything."

Timothy smiled. "Don't worry about a thing, Miss Maude. I've seen worse. I will respect your wishes."

"Thank you."

"You're welcome. Miss Maude, we have a wheelchair on hand. Would you like for me to get it?"

"I don't want you to, but I'm going to go against my own wishes on this one. Please do. Then we're going home to eat, rest, and read another journal entry."

"I'll be right back."

As they waited for him to return, Enid couldn't push her concern over Isabel's threat out of her mind. How could Isabel—or anyone else—be so angry over Maude's family history research to want to harm them, especially Maude? By the time Timothy returned with the wheelchair, her concern had settled into the pit of her stomach.

CHAPTER TWENTY

Enid waited for Abby and Maude to ascend the ramp one slow step at a time and go into the house before she left again to pick up lunch. She had brought them home first as much for Maude to rest as for herself to have a few moments of peace and quiet.

"Whew! What a morning. Worse than working. I am thankful Maude accomplished all she did, but I do hope this afternoon will be less stressful."

When she returned, Abby met her at the door. Enid caught her breath.

"Is Maude all right?"

"Yes, but she is exhausted. I have her propped up in her bed with a bed tray. I also have a couple of TV trays set up if you don't mind eating in the bedroom with her."

"I don't mind at all."

The two soon had roast beef sandwiches, curly fries, and drinks spread out and ready to eat.

Halfway through her sandwich, Maude leaned back against her pillow. "That's all I can manage. I'll just close my eyes a few minutes while you two finish eating."

"We can move to the kitchen."

"No you don't. I want to find more of those journal pages."

"Granny, you need to rest."

"I'll rest long enough when I'm dead."

"Granny!"

Maude winked at her great-granddaughter. "Well, I will. Right now, though, I have things to do. Now let me close my eyes for a bit so I can get to those things. Eat."

"Yes, ma'am."

"When you finish and before you rouse me, find another needlepoint and its journal pages. Then we'll read."

"Will do, Granny."

By the time Enid and Abby finished eating, Maude was fast asleep.

* * *

Enid watched as Abby placed the remaining needlepoints side by side in two rows on the coffee table in the living room. Some, she was certain, had no errors in them. She picked up two that didn't sound right.

"Let's check one of these two against the Collins's Bible. Which one do you want to do next?"

"Let me see." Abby glanced at them. "No contest. This one."

She held one out to Enid. It depicted a teacher standing beside a student working diligently on some task at her desk. Colorful geometric designs formed the border.

"Why this one?"

"Look at the threads."

"It has the same colors as the previous two. It's as decorative as they were as well."

"Right. Look at the other one."

"It's sparser of decoration and stitched mostly in darker threads, colors that were used sparingly in the earlier ones."

"Like maybe she was running out of thread and energy."

"Good eye and good deduction, Abby. We begin here then." Enid picked up Abby's choice and read the scripture. "But after that faith is come, we are no longer under a schoolmaster reading from a primer. Galatians 3:25." She raised an eyebrow at Abby.

"Has to be a reference to the *New England Primer.*"

"I agree, but let's compare it to the Bible first."

Abby opened the Bible to the middle and turned the pages a few at the time to the third chapter of Galatians. "Here it is," she said. "But after that faith is come, we are no longer under a schoolmaster."

"But nothing about 'reading from a primer.' The clue must be for the *Primer*. It's there in the top part of the dower chest."

Abby lifted the well-worn book and placed it on the coffee table. She turned back the front panel and felt along the edges.

"Same as *The Scarlet Letter*. A different color paper but glued over the original panel with papers under it."

"Check the back panel," said Enid.

Abby turned to the back.

"Same here. Boil some water?"

"Yes. I'll place the needlepoints back in the chest and the Bible in its box while you do."

After they had removed the journal pages from their hiding places and returned the pot of water to the kitchen, they carried the pages to Maude's bedroom.

Abby touched the sleeping woman's arm. "Granny? Can you wake up?"

"I'm only half asleep. Do you have new journal pages?"

"We do."

"I'm fully awake then. Help me sit up."

Linking arms with Abby to brace herself, Maude scooted upright in her bed. Abby and Enid sat in their chairs.

"Who's going to read?" asked Maude.

"Do you want to, Granny?"

"I do, but I'm afraid my voice won't hold out."

"Then I'll let Miss Enid read this group. I'll read the next group."

"You think there is another group?"

"I know there is."

"Let's begin then."

"There are three entries, but they're short. I'll read all three of them straight through if that's okay with you."

"Yes." Maude circled her hand for Enid to begin. "I hope these three tell us what happened to the runaways and to Charlotte and Olivia, of course."

Enid picked up the first sheet of paper and began to read.

CHAPTER TWENTY-ONE

The Journal of Charlotte Abbott Goodwin
A True Record of Daniel's Innocence and Other Events
Entry #6, Friday Evening, July 3rd, 1863
Events Related to the Emancipation Proclamation

We are now halfway through 1863. We have received no other word from Hannah. Earlier this year, as Olivia approached her seventh birthday, Celia and I again grieved our loss. I tried to comfort us both by turning our conversation to Lincoln's recent Emancipation Proclamation. Celia would not be comforted.

"Miss Charlotte, what's this Emancipation Proclamation got to do with me or with my Hannah? Nobody we know in this county is ready to follow that proclamation. They plan to wait it out to see what comes of this war. If your mama and papa did follow it, where would I go? I'm nigh on sixty years old. I'm a house slave. What would I do? As for Hannah, like I told you once before, even freedom don't take away that warrant on Daniel for stealing Peter Goodwin's money box."

"Celia," I said as I grabbed her hands. "If freedom comes and Mama and Daddy send you away, you can come work for me. As for Hannah, I wish I had never taken Peter's money. I don't know if what I sent with them did them any good or not, but I know what I kept to send later has done them no good!"

"You did what you thought was best at the time," Celia told me. "We'll do the same now. One thing I know, though, as much as I love you and Olivia, I cannot come to live in that house as long as Peter Goodwin lives in it." Celia brushed away a tear. "How is Olivia?"

"Celia, she still cries for her baby doll. She hasn't called Miriam her baby sister since Peter whipped her for it all those months ago. She still cradles the straw doll you made for her. She whispers to it from sunup to sundown. Sometimes I worry for her—for her mind. Peter tells her Miriam is all in her mind. Mama and Papa do, too. Even Mason tells her she's off in the head. I try to tell her the truth and help her remember when none of them are around, but she's too young to be tossed about so."

I remain concerned about Olivia although she has begun to resume a somewhat normal life. I also worry about what will become of Celia and her family.

I wish Hannah could have seen the daffodils this past spring. They grew more beautiful than ever and lasted days past their usual season.

The Journal of Charlotte Abbott Goodwin
A True Record of Daniel's Innocence and Other Events
Entry #7, Friday Evening, August 4th, 1865
Events Related to the Ending of the War and the Leaving of Celia

It has been almost two years since I have written in my secret journal. It has been a difficult time for all of us.

The war ended May 9th of this year. The peace we prayed for has caused Olivia's heartbreak to redouble on itself. Celia has left us.

In time, some of our neighbors did follow the mandate of the Emancipation Proclamation to free their slaves. Others did not. They used various tactics to keep their men and women enslaved. Father and Peter forbade anyone to leave with even the clothes on their backs without paying for what they took with them.

They were required to work until they had earned enough to pay for what they would take.

Others forbade mothers to remove any children fathered by their former masters, a wickedness not limited to Father and Peter as I have learned. Rather than leave a child behind, those mothers chose to remain, oftentimes joined by a husband.

However, at war's end, Father and Peter had no choice but to free their slaves unconditionally.

Mama asked Celia to stay on with them for wages, but Celia chose not to do so. She and George left with their youngest daughter and her husband for Illinois where she hopes to live out her days in peace, albeit a peace overshadowed by her longing for Hannah and Miriam.

A few older ones did stay on to work for wages for both Father and Peter, but Peter promised those who stayed with him nothing more than a place to sleep, food to eat, two changes of clothes per year, and a percentage of what the crops bring in—a small percentage. How will they discern whether or not he cheats them? Unlike my parents, Peter refused to allow his slaves to learn to read and write much less to cipher.

Even so, Peter cannot raise what he once did without the help of younger, more able-bodied men and women. Times are difficult.

The Journal of Charlotte Abbott Goodwin
A True Record of Daniel's Innocence and Other Events
Entry #8, Friday Evening, September 7th, 1866
Peter's Contrariness

Thirteen months have passed since my last entry, and still we have had no word from Hannah. I have had no word from Celia, either. When I visit Mama, I slip away to Celia's rooms in the slave quarters. I must stop. The empty, soundless rooms bring me no joy, and Mama complains incessantly about the time I spend there.

Peter grows more contrary every day. We are not as well off as we once were, but we are comfortable—much more so than some others. He has to work much harder now. Of course, Mason helps. He also complains about it every day.

Peter blames everything—our lack of money, his declining health, everything and anything that goes wrong in our small town and in these United States—on the war and on emancipation.

He has become miserly and hoards any profit he makes. He is more protective of his precious money box as well, hiding it in a different place on a daily basis, reduced to a state of panic when he forgets where he put it just a day earlier. He has become even more suspicious of others—including me—than I thought possible. He stomps about, jumps at the least sound, and glares at me whenever I speak to him.

His doctor expresses concern about some kind of condition that often leads to such changes. Peter refuses to see him again and forbids me from speaking to his doctor about him. I have obeyed in spite of his condition worsening.

I hate to think what Hannah's and Miriam's lives would be like if they had remained. I have no doubt Peter would have forbidden Hannah to leave with Miriam. She would not have left without her. I thank the Lord every day they are safe from him. I hope they have found a good life with Daniel wherever they are.

When I am out and about, if Peter is not with me, I ask every colored person I meet if they remember Hannah or Miriam, if they have seen them or heard from them. Even Olivia has taken up the task by asking the same of the children. Not one person admits to having any knowledge of their whereabouts, although upon occasion one or another will appear to be ready to tell me something but then stop and say instead that they have heard nothing from them. I cannot find fault with them for this. Those from here know Peter well. Those

who are new to our town soon find out about him. I fear
no one will ever tell me anything even if anyone does
hear from them. I fear I will never see Hannah and
Miriam again this side of death. Olivia promises me she
will continue to search for them even after I am gone.

Nevertheless, I put away a few coins every month to
send them should we ever find them. If Hannah does
not want the money for herself, I hope she will accept it
for Miriam's sake. In addition to my remaining dowry
money, Miriam deserves an inheritance from her father
as much as do Olivia and Mason.

I pray the time that passes between this and my next
entry will be a happier and less stressful time.

* * *

Enid shifted in her chair beside Maude's bed.

"You're uncomfortable, aren't you?"

"I'm fine. Maude. I needed to stretch my muscles and joints.
That's all."

Enid handed the journal pages to Abby. Abby took them
and placed them on the dresser beside her. She traced the grain
pattern of the dresser's dark red-brown cherry wood surface.

"What are you thinking, Abigail?"

"How people manage to survive such hard times."

"The time between these entries says as much as the entries
themselves," said Maude. "The years after the war must have
been difficult for everyone. Unfortunately, the entries don't
add much to our search or tell us much about the secrets."

"I'm not so sure about that, Granny. One of Charlotte's
comments reminded me of some things I heard at the reunion.
It didn't fit what we read earlier, and we had so much to discuss
and do, I just put it on the back burner and kept meaning to
bring it up but didn't."

"Abby's right. We've been so caught up with the past that
none of us has been paying close enough attention to the
present—especially your present, Maude."

"You mean the intruder and my health."

"I do."

"So how do we work in the present?"

"Have Abby tell us what she overheard at the reunion and then see what else either of you can remember about who said or did what that day, especially anything suspicious. Abby?"

"When we first began reading the journal entries, I did remember one thing I heard, but I thought the men at the reunion might have been talking about Peter's first money box and simply had the details wrong. Now, if Peter did indeed continue keeping his money in another box and hiding it, then I suspect the men at the reunion were talking about the new money box."

"You're losing me, Abigail."

"Sorry, Granny. Here's the thing. I'm young enough that I'm still learning things about the family and hearing some things for the first time. I'm also young enough that to most of the older ones, especially the men, I'm sort of invisible. At the reunions, I've always enjoyed walking around unobtrusively listening to the stories they tell. I happened to hear a few stories this time that I'd never heard before.

"After your request for help, I heard Uncle Lawson talking to two of Mason's descendants, Charles and Arthur Goodwin. They've always been good friends. They were all leaned back against a picnic table like kings of the mountain, telling jokes and family stories. The jokes I could have done without. Some of them were crude. As for the stories, it seems a few have come down Mason's line that none of Olivia's descendants knew or told."

"What were they, dear?"

"You've got to realize I didn't think anything about them at the time. I had nothing to connect them to. Now they make some kind of sense. One was about Peter's *lost money*. It went missing at the time of his death. He apparently got and kept another money box, which we now know he did, but when he died, Mason couldn't find it. According to the family story, Charlotte said she didn't know where it was, but if it were to be found, it was hers by the stipulations in Peter's will."

"No one ever found it?" asked Enid.

"Nope. Not according to those three. And if I understood them correctly, that farm has been handed down from generation to generation and is still owned by one of Mason's descendants, Charles Goodwin."

"Which we confirmed with the land transfer records," said Maude.

"But, according to Charles, the property has been searched over and over down through the years."

"Hmm. We'll need to pay him a visit," said Maude. "While we're there, I'd like to see if we can locate that patch of daffodils. I won't tell him that. I'll only say that we're trying to find a slave burial site. Now what about the second story?"

"Mason bragged about Peter's efforts to father his own slaves so he wouldn't have to purchase any new ones when the other ones got too old to work. After the war, Mason complained that if Lincoln hadn't interfered, Peter's plan would have worked, and the family's story would have been very different. This one was shared at a whisper with a caution not to mention it to any of the women of the family."

"The very idea. That fits with what Charlotte wrote in her journal. How did your Uncle Lawson respond to that?"

"He didn't act all that upset about Peter's plan. He did say he thought Lincoln messed things up for everyone."

"I'd like to teach Lawson a thing or two, but I'm too old to do it, and he's probably too old to learn it. Mama tried, but he's always had a prejudice streak in him. I never could figure out where he got it. Maybe now I know—from Charles and Arthur. What was the third story?"

"The third story was about two interest-bearing trust accounts that Charlotte set up at the bank for Olivia, neither of which Mason could access. Mason had known about one of the accounts, which was set up to match what he received from the farm transactions, but he had no knowledge of the second account until after Charlotte's death. When he learned of the second account, he thought he should get half of it, but both were in Olivia's name, and neither the bank manager, who was the successor trustee, nor Mason's lawyer could do anything about it."

"If I were a betting woman, I'd lay odds the second account was meant for Miriam. We can follow up on that, too. Anything else?"

"Not that I heard. I moved on to another group."

"So now to Enid's suggestion. Who at the reunion did what? What exactly should I concentrate on?"

"Well," said Enid, "I would concentrate on four groups of attendees. Those who acted offended, threatened, or worried when you brought up your family research. Those who visited your house during the week or so following the reunion. Those who attributed anything you said to your health. Those who did or said anything suspicious or out of character."

"You don't ask for much from an old woman, do you? Do you realize how many people attend our reunions? Never mind. I can do this. I'll begin with those who acted the worst.

"Lucille, my cousin twice removed, considers herself high society and always manages to project that. She's married to Lowell Franklin, my lawyer, so I try not to act too senile around her. She stared down her nose at me and said, 'Who cares what any of our ancestors did? Let them and their sins rest in peace. You need to live in the present. Join the living, Maude.' I had no idea to what sins she referred, and I didn't ask. Lowell was with her, of course. He didn't say anything. I did notice him shaking his head when I asked for information, but why would he care? I know for a fact he gossips with his employees about people in town. I've heard him. So I'm sure he told them all about the incident when he got back to his office.

"Then there was one of my sons and one of my daughters, Barton and Julian. Barton has always idolized Lawson and mimicked his attitudes toward others. I've tried to convince myself he didn't truly hold those attitudes. However, I did notice him sneaking a grin at Lawson when someone mentioned the slave issue.

"I've never known Julian to be prejudiced toward anyone. Nevertheless, she did say, 'I agree with Miss Lucille. Almost. If there's any money to be had, dig all you want, but you ought to keep the other stuff to yourself, Mama.' Her comments were tacky but not unusual for her. Her husband is a slacker, and they are always in need of money.

"We can't forget Isabel and Natalie, who get in a dither anytime they get it in their heads that something will threaten their community status or inconvenience them in any way. They definitely expressed those sentiments at the reunion. Charles and Arthur, the two Mason descendants Abigail overheard, were also quite vocal about not wanting me to dig into Mason and Peter's slaveholding. Those were the most vocal though several folks murmured out of my hearing range and accompanied their murmurings with fingers pointing directly at me. Mercy. My voice is about to give out. Abigail, please get me a glass of water."

Maude rested until Abby returned with the water. She took several sips before continuing.

"Now to my visitors the following week or so. I'm sure every one of my children visited sometime during the week. They always do. As do two of my distant but somewhat younger cousins. Jedidiah Goodwin, my handyman, checks with me weekly to see if I need lightbulbs changed or odd jobs done. Janet Baker, a nurse, periodically checks my vitals and my mobility. She's been more concerned about me than Dr. Finley or Isabel. Lucille also dropped by with Lowell. She came to visit. Lowell brought a form for updating some of my information. A few days later, his assistant Vance brought me the original of the paper for my files. I can't remember if anyone else came by.

"Every one of them either asked about my health, commented on it, or suggested I should slow down because of it—and my age. I tuned them out after a while. I never thought of anything said or done as being suspicious. In my opinion, we're all a little eccentric, and age has nothing to do with it. I expect people to apply that to me, and I certainly apply it to everyone else."

Abby laughed out loud. "Sorry, Granny, but I've always thought that very same thing."

"Nothing to be sorry about, Abigail. Enid, we've considered all this present-day stuff, but I'm afraid I'm not ready to say any of the people we've identified is...suspicious."

"You mean *a suspect*?" asked Enid.

Maude raised her eyebrow and tilted her head. "I'm hard pressed to see any of them as suspects, although each of them does appear to have something that could be considered a motive, but surely none of our family expects an inheritance after all these years."

"Wait!" said Abby. "One of the remaining needlepoints says something about a *letter of inheritance*. I know you don't want to read it today, but what might Charlotte have meant by that?"

"The only thing I can imagine is a will, which I'm sure she and Peter both had. I've always been told our family has used the Franklin Law Firm since the days of Peter and Charlotte. The firm might even have copies of the old files."

"Hmm. Maybe Monday you could ask about it," said Enid.

"I certainly can, but I'm done in for the day."

"Your day would have been exhausting for a young person. I don't how you managed it, Granny."

"Force of will, that's all. I'm going to rest over the weekend. As Enid pointed out, I have the appointment with Lowell midafternoon on Monday. Perhaps we could pay Charles Goodwin a visit at noon."

"I have class, Granny, and I'll have to leave early if I ride with Robbie."

"I certainly don't want Isabel taking me."

"I'll take you, Maude," said Enid. "It's the least I can do after making you suspect your relatives."

"I would appreciate it, but I do feel I'm imposing."

"Not at all."

"Thank you. Let's all rest over the weekend and begin again on Monday."

"It will be all right if I study a little, won't it, Granny?"

"Yes, it will. You do need to do that." Maude gave Abby a hint of a smile before lying back against her pillow.

"I'll call you Monday morning," said Enid.

Maude nodded and closed her eyes.

Enid slipped out of the bedroom and left for home.

As she drove, she prayed for rest for all three of them and for clarity of mind as they searched for answers.

"We need to identify the opposition before…." She shook her head and chose not to finish her sentence.

As she pulled into her own drive, her cell phone rang. As she didn't recognize the number, she didn't answer.

"I'll check for a message once I'm inside. I can always call back if it's important."

She trudged up the walk and into the house. After checking the doors, dressing for bed, and pouring herself a glass of milk, she settled into her recliner.

"I am determined to read a few chapters before I go to bed. I hope losing myself in an imaginary mystery will relax me enough to fall asleep." Then she remembered the phone call. She pulled her phone out. The caller had left a voicemail message. Her hand trembled as she listened.

Enid Gilchrist, you need to stop encouraging Maude Everly's search for skeletons in her family's closets. If you don't, the two of you may find yourselves communing with them in person.

Enid slapped her phone shut and jumped up from the recliner. She rechecked every room, window, and door in her house before returning to her living room. She drank the whole glass of milk in a few swallows and carried the glass back to the kitchen.

"Reading is not going to help me sleep tonight." She reached for the kitchen light switch. "No. I believe I'll leave a couple of lights on tonight."

Before crawling into bed, she dug in her closet for an old baseball bat of Bryce's and set it against her bedside table.

"I won't go down without a fight, you old coot." She pulled the sheet up to her neck. "I'd rather not go down at all."

CHAPTER TWENTY-TWO

Monday, August 8, 2011

Enid awoke with the same sense of apprehension that had plagued her since Friday night. This morning, it took her a few moments to remember the cause of her apprehension. She had debated with herself all weekend about whether or not to tell anyone, especially Patrick, about the call. In the end, she had chosen not to tell anyone.

She had used caution, however, at every stop she made and with every person she met throughout the weekend. Her concern extended to Maude and Abby, whom she called every few hours all day Saturday and Sunday, disrupting their schedules and their naps. She herself took no naps nor did she sleep well either night.

Now she had to face another week. She stumbled her way into the kitchen. As her mind sorted through Friday's activities, her plans for the day, and her fears, she managed to make coffee and pour a cupful with her eyes half open.

"Here it is Monday morning, and nothing has happened. So why do I feel like a vise is tightening its grip on my chest?"

She lifted her cup to her lips. "Ouch. Pay attention, Enid. Hot coffee burns." She set her cup on the table, scrambled eggs, fried sausage, retrieved her toast from the toaster, and sat down to eat. She stared at her plate.

"Enough. I'm fine. I have a busy day ahead of me. Research. Meetings. I need to concentrate and kick it into high gear." She bowed her head for a word of thanksgiving for her food and her friends and a request for safety and health.

"I suspect I'll need to stay in high gear. It may not be Monday attire, but this day calls for blue jeans, a T-shirt, and walking shoes.

Soon she was ready to walk out the door and begin her day. With every step across the walkway, she pushed the nagging in her stomach farther and farther down.

* * *

As soon as she stepped inside her office, Enid dropped her bags and called Maude.

"How are you this morning?"

"I feel both rested and exhausted physically and mentally. It's quite frustrating."

"I can imagine."

"I hope your weekend passed more peacefully than ours did. Almost everyone I know knocked on my door. Isabel took pleasure in sharing the details of my doctor's visit with anyone who would listen. Some feared my imagination had run away with me. Others convinced themselves I was knocking at death's door. Isabel never did understand what zip your lip meant even as a child. Enough of my complaining. Can you still take me to both places this afternoon?"

"Yes, I've told Mary and arranged for Ellen to stay."

"I keep telling you how sorry I am for inconveniencing you, but I'm so thankful you're involved with all of this. Especially as I can't shake my fear for our safety—in particular Abigail's—and I'm sinking faster and faster."

"I understand on all counts." She did not explain how real her understanding was. "I consider it a privilege to help you both. In fact, before I leave here, I plan to follow a hunch I had a day or so ago and research one other state for census and other records for Hannah and her family."

"Which state?"

"Michigan."

"Why Michigan?"

"Because the three primary routes from West Tennessee through Kentucky end up passing into Michigan or close to the Michigan border."

"You think they might have gone there instead of going into Canada or stopping in one of the other states?"

"It's possible."

"Good luck!"

"Thank you."

Enid did indeed have good luck. At eleven thirty, with a bounce in her step that defied her earlier apprehension, she turned off the microfilm reader and exited the computer program she had been running. She returned the microfilm to the cabinet and prepared to leave. She wanted to jump up and down, but she didn't want to frighten their newest out-of-town patrons. She thrilled at the prospect of telling Maude of her discovery but decided to wait until after their visits with Charles and Lowell when Abby could be with them.

* * *

Before Enid could pull in behind the white Dodge Ram pickup parked in the driveway, Charles Goodwin strode out of his house and stood waiting for them on his front porch, thumbs hooked in the straps of his overalls. When Enid pulled the walker from the back seat of her Subaru and opened the door for Maude, he grabbed plastic chairs from the porch and set them on the ground beside the steps. He waited until the women sat in them before sitting himself. Enid rubbed her nose to prevent the sneeze that threatened to react to the strong tobacco odor. Charles spoke first.

"I must apologize for not having a ramp, Maude. I figured I'd need one by now, but I've been fortunate."

"No apology needed. We can enjoy the fresh air."

"That we can. Little warm, of course, but I'd rather be out here than in the house any day. What brings you and Enid out my way? Not still digging up old dead bones, are you?" He snorted and turned his head to spit tobacco juice. "I mean, you're both dressed in jeans. Unusual for you two."

"As a matter of fact, I am, but I'm also interested in living bones, especially if they have something to say about those old dead bones. You're Mason Goodwin's oldest living descendant, aren't you?"

"That I am. I'm eighty-eight years old. I'm closing in on you, Maude." He winked and spat again. "So what do you need to know?"

"Abigail heard you, Arthur, and Lawson discussing Peter's missing money. Tell me about that."

Charles squinted sideways at her and then at Enid.

"Can't imagine why you'd be interested in his money. Simple story, it is. You are aware this farm I own belonged to him, handed down from eldest son to eldest son?"

"I am."

"Whatever else Peter Goodwin may have done, he built a good house. Or rather, his slaves built a good house with his oversight. It's stood the test of time. Both the house and the story about the money were handed down from generation to generation, only the money was called Peter's *lost money*. Mason spent a lifetime searching for it. One reason he never sold the farm. Reason he didn't marry until later in life. Each of his firstborn descendants has done the same, including me. Not the marrying late part but the searching part. None of us ever found it, either. Why, your own daughter Julian, has been out here searching for it. She talked me into allowing her to scour house and grounds for half the proceeds if she found the money. I figured why not. At my age, half would be more than enough and better than nothin'. She didn't find it neither. So, now you want to search, too? Might as well. We've searched for over a century, and no one's ever found it. Or maybe you want to buy the whole place instead so Abby can search after you're gone."

"You never know, Charles, I might do that."

"Make me an offer I can't resist, but don't tell my young'uns or your'n. If you do, all bets are off. You've got to know every one of them would fight it."

"I do."

"None of my boys is interested in the farm. They'd let it go to seed and say they were letting it lie fallow right up until the day they sold it and divided the proceeds. If you bought it, at least it would be in the family, and you might put it to use. One thing, though."

"What would that be?"

"That you'd make a provision. If you ever sold it, you or your'n, you'd give my descendants first option to buy it back if they could meet your price."

"If I decide to buy it, which I might, your provision would be perfectly acceptable. My price if I sold it would be fair."

"So you gonna think on it?"

"I'd like to, but I need to hear your price first."

"I'll think on that and let you know."

"Good. Charles, I can't stay long. I have an appointment with my lawyer. I wanted to ask you something else, too."

"Ask away."

"Do you know the location of the burial sites for Peter's slaves?"

"Maude Everly. Now you got Miss Enid doing research for slaves' descendants?"

"No, Charles. At least not yet. I am curious as to where they might be buried."

"Don't have a clue. You've got Charlotte's family Bible. Don't it tell?"

"No, it doesn't. It gives names and dates but not the burial spots."

"Sorry. I can't be no help to you there. My pappy might a' knowed, but I don't remember him ever saying. I do recall talk of wooden crosses marking them, but they're long gone."

"Thank you anyway. We should leave now."

"No problem. Nice to see you, though. Miss Enid, too. Don't get many visitors, not like I did when I was younger."

"It was nice to see you, too, Charles. You call me if you come to a decision about a price for the farm."

"I'll do that. Maude, one more thing about this researchin' of yours. It don't bother me none. I'm mostly all talk, don't really have nothing against nobody, but you might want to have a visit with Arthur. He's mightily against it. Maybe you could reassure him that whatever you find is for family only and not for the public, like puttin' a file in that drawer in the genealogy room."

"I'll think on that, too, Charles."

Maude and Charles shook hands. Enid nodded to the old man and assisted Maude back to the Subaru.

As they walked, Maude stopped and pointed to several patches of withered daffodil leaves growing wild nearby. The two women gave each other a look but didn't say a word until they reached the car.

"Enid, one of those patches must be where Isaac and the others are buried. If I buy the farm, I want to get someone out here to confirm which one it is. Then using the Bible records, we can set headstones for each of them."

"That's a wonderful idea, Maude. Are you thinking seriously of buying the farm?"

"I might be."

"If you do and we find the burial site, we can provide the information to the genealogical society and the descendants as well as record the information in the file Charles mentioned."

"I'd like that." Maude took a deep breath and blew it out. "I'm tired already, but I have to pretend to myself I'm not so I can deal with Lowell."

* * *

Enid pulled in beside a brand-new silver Mercury Grand Marquis Sedan parked in front of Lowell's office, leaving plenty of room for her to open her door without touching the Mercury.

"Whose car is that?" she asked.

"Why Lowell's, of course," said Maude. "He gets a new one every year."

"Business must be good." She chuckled at her own sarcastic remark and eased out of her Subaru. Before she could open the door to Lowell Franklin's outer office, a striking young African American man with short black hair and dressed in a black tailored suit opened the door for them. His brown eyes sparkled as he smiled and said, "Please come in."

They stepped into the luxurious front office.

"Miss Maude, how are you today?"

"I'm fine, Vance. How are you and your family?"

"We're all well, thank you. I see you've brought someone new with you today. How are you, Miss Enid?"

"I'm doing well, too, Vance."

"My wife has so appreciated your help researching her family. African American research can present some serious obstacles. She's promised to work on my line when she finishes hers. I'm not sure that will happen in my lifetime, though. I'm beginning to think she will never finish with her family." His good-natured laugh lit up his face.

"She has been a pleasure to work with and together we have uncovered more African American records than even I knew existed. I'm indebted to her for that."

"She will be pleased to hear that. Mr. Franklin is with another client in the conference room, but he won't be long. He said if you arrived before he finished for me to show you to his office."

"Thank you."

"You're welcome."

Enid followed behind as Vance held Maude's elbow, led her to Lowell's office, and helped her situate herself in one of the guest chairs. He then held out a hand for Enid to sit in the chair beside her before he turned to leave.

As soon as Enid sat down, Maude grabbed her arm. "I forgot to ask you earlier, did you have any luck with your Michigan hunch? Did you find Hannah and Miriam? Were they with Daniel?"

"I believe so. I'd planned to wait until Abby could be with us to give you the details and show you the records, but I'll tell you this much. I do believe I've found all three of them, and I'm hopeful the findings will lead to her descendants."

"This is wonderful news."

Enid heard a noise and turned her head. Vance was handing a file to Lowell at the door.

I wish Maude had waited about bringing up my Michigan search. If either of them heard us, though, they don't appear to be interested in it.

Lowell entered the room and walked to his desk without a word. He sat behind the desk and made himself busy shuffling papers.

"Do you have everything ready for me to sign?" asked Maude.

"Yes, I do. Will you be making any additional changes?"

"I may and I may not." Maude's agitation was obvious in her voice and the tilt of her head. "Whatever I decide, you will remember in the future that my business is my business and that you have an obligation to me to keep it confidential from everyone except Abigail. Do you understand me?"

"I understand perfectly."

"Good. Let's get this over with. You keep a copy and I get the original, right?"

"That is correct."

Lowell stood and came around to Maude's side of his desk. He handed her a pen and indicated each place where she was to sign and Enid was to witness. When they finished, he called out, "Vance, will you come back in here please?"

The young man returned and stood beside Lowell's desk.

"Ahem. Vance, would you please make copies of these papers for our files and return the originals to Miss Maude as soon as possible?"

"Of course, Mr. Franklin."

Vance picked up the papers and winked at the women as he turned to leave. When he was gone, Maude said, "Vance Abbott has been one of the better additions to your firm, Lowell. I understand members of his family have been here since before the Civil War."

"Yes, well, that's the case with many of us now, isn't it?" Lowell strummed his desk with the fingers of his right hand. "Can I do anything else for you?"

"Possibly. Something came up in conversation with Abby about our ancestors, Peter and Charlotte Goodwin."

"Yes?" Lowell's strumming became incessant.

"The Franklin Law Firm has been here since the early 1800s, has it not?"

"Yes, it has."

"And one of the Franklin family has always been the senior member, right?"

"Yes. Your point?"

Vance returned but stood to one side as Maude continued.

"It's always been my understanding that the Franklin Law Firm has represented our family since the beginning."

"Yes, I believe that's right," said Lowell.

"Would the firm still have copies of the records of the previous generations?"

"I.... Yes, I believe we have boxes filed away in the basement from the early years."

"Do you have those records on microfilm?"

"Maybe, some of them anyway. Why do you ask?"

Enid caught a glimpse of a one-sided smile on Vance's face as he watched Lowell squirm in his chair.

"I want to see the documents in any files you have for Peter and Charlotte, especially their wills."

Lowell glanced at Vance and reached out to take Maude's papers from him.

"Thank you, Vance. Maude, here are your originals. Perhaps between now and your next visit, I might find the time to see if we still hold the Goodwin files. I doubt any from so far back have been microfilmed though."

"If you do find them, paper or microfilm, please call me."

"Of course." Lowell stood. He nodded at Vance, dismissing him. "Vance on your way out, perhaps you could escort Miss Maude and Miss Enid."

"Yes, sir," said Vance.

As Vance helped Maude to her feet, Enid pondered his earlier peculiar smile.

A few minutes later, Enid backed out into the street. She hesitated a moment before speaking.

"Maude, wasn't Charlotte's maiden name Abbott?"

"Yes, it was. Why?"

"I wonder...."

"What?"

"Vance's surname is Abbott. You said his family had been here since before the Civil War. You don't suppose...."

After a pause and a sharp intake of breath, Maude said, "That Vance's ancestor was a slave on Charlotte's parents' farm? Why, it's possible, isn't it?"

"Yes, it is. Of course, other Abbotts could have lived in the area."

"I don't believe they did. Charlotte's parents traveled here from Pennsylvania when she was a child. To my knowledge, no other family members came with them."

"Hmm."

"Another person to consider?"

"Possibly. Whether as a suspect or a relative of Hannah, I don't know, but let's not say anything until we learn more. Perhaps we could speak with Vance at some point."

"Yes, that would be an excellent idea. Enid, will you stay for dinner? I may not be able to do anything more tonight, but Abby is going to get carryout from one of the local restaurants on her way home. I told her to call me to see if you would stay."

"I'll stay with you until Abby arrives, but you do need to rest, and I need to get on home tonight. Truth is, Patrick was busy all weekend, and I didn't spend ten minutes with him. I'm hoping he'll come over tonight."

"That sounds nice." Maude turned toward Enid. "The two of you were high school sweethearts, weren't you?"

Enid smiled. "We were. Then we went our separate ways. Now our ways have come together again."

"How nice for both of you. You will stay long enough to tell us the Michigan news, won't you?"

"Yes, I will do that."

"I do hope Lowell is cooperative and looks for the old files. This search crosses so many paths."

"Something only family researchers can fully grasp."

* * *

When Abby arrived, Enid set the table. The three women gathered around it once again, and Abby said grace.

"Thank goodness," said Maude. "I've been holding in my anticipation all afternoon. Please tell us what you found for Michigan."

"I am almost certain I have found all three of our runaways in two census records. I searched every household for Michigan for 1870 and 1880 with any person of color named Daniel or Hannah or Miriam. I found a couple of households with two of the three names, but the ages weren't right. I found one household in Lansing, Michigan, in both censuses with all three names and their ages and birthplaces match. I also found them in the 1873 Lansing, Michigan, directory at the same house. I did a deed search and found where Daniel and Hannah purchased the house in 1870.

"Last but not least, I found a marriage record for Daniel Jacobson and Hannah Abbott in Detroit, Michigan, in March of 1863. I can't say for sure they are the same couple that's in Lansing in 1870 because the marriage record does not indicate race, but I can find no other marriage record in their names. If it is them and if they remained in the area and Miriam married in the county, I have no doubt we can trace them through the 1930 census."

"Why not after 1930?" asked Abby.

"To protect people's privacy, census records are not released to the public until seventy-two years after the census is taken. The 1940 census records won't be released until April of 2012."

"I am so excited," said Maude. "I cannot believe we may have finally found them! But how can you be sure? We have no way of knowing what surname they took."

"That is the one problem left. This Daniel chose the surname Jacobson. In every place, all three of them go by Jacobson except for the marriage license where Hannah goes by Abbott. Her surname strengthens the case for her being Celia's daughter, but I can see no logic in Daniel choosing Jacobson."

Maude rubbed her chin for a minute then startled them with her shout. "I can! Remember the bill of sale recorded for Abraham's purchase of Celia, Daniel, and Daniel's parents Esther and Jacob? Jacob. Son of Jacob. Jacobson. Is that not a logical explanation?"

"It's possible. It makes sense. If you hadn't found that bill of sale...."

"I am more fortunate than many researchers tracing African American heritage with what records I have found and with Charlotte and her mother keeping such a detailed record in the family Bible. One of the ladies with whom I took that first course had spent years trying to trace her family's history and migration with little success all because she had been told emancipated slaves always took the names of their last owners. You told her some slaves refused to take the name of any of their masters. Some selected another name with meaning for them, perhaps even a previous owner. Some already had surnames spoken only in private and not known to any of the whites in the community. With your help, she found them by searching through every bill of sale for the county. They did not take the surname of their last owner but of the first person to purchase them when they were brought from Africa to Alabama."

The three women were silent for a moment.

"I believe this must be our Hannah's family," said Maude. "I feel it in my bones and in my heart, a sense of peace. I think I shall rest better tonight than I have in weeks."

"I hope so, Maude."

"Me, too. Go, then, and Abby and I will head to bed, too."

"Let me give you the copies of today's findings, and then I'm on my way."

Enid pulled the research copies from her briefcase and gave them to Maude. Then she left for home, overcome by exhaustion. The return of her apprehension as soon as she turned her key in the ignition did not help.

"All the more reason I need to see Patrick tonight whether or not I tell him about my Friday night voicemail."

* * *

Halfway home, Enid called Patrick. He had not left the station. When he answered, he sounded exhausted, too.

"Patrick, I almost hate to ask, but can you come by the house tonight?"

"I can, but it may be late. It's been a grueling day, and I may not be able to leave for an hour or so. Will that be too late?"

"No. That's fine. What about dinner?"

"I've eaten a sandwich, but coffee would be good."

"I'll put a tray of freezer cookies in the oven and put on a pot of coffee while I wait."

"I'm good with cookies, too."

"See you later then."

By the time she hung up, Enid was in her driveway.

She pulled her belongings closer to her.

She put one foot on the ground and leaned out the car door.

Before she could reach back for her purse and briefcase, a loud whack against the side of her head brought stars to her eyes and drove her back into her Subaru.

As she lingered on the edge of consciousness, struggling to push her way back, she became vaguely aware of the engine starting up, her briefcase floating in front of her, and a figure disappearing into a squat at the back of her car. Then she was aware of nothing.

CHAPTER TWENTY-THREE

From somewhere far away, Enid heard someone calling her name.

"Enid! Enid! Wake up! Can you hear me? Can you see me?"

"Wha…what's happening?" She tried to focus on the faces hovering above her. She grabbed at the metal beneath her, afraid she was falling off.

"Enid. Can you hear me?"

One of the faces hovering to her left came into focus.

"Patrick. Why am I down here? Where am I?"

"We'll answer your questions in a minute. Right now, you need to answer the EMT's questions. Okay?"

"Okay. If you think I need to."

She turned to the face hovering at her right. She blinked. A young woman shined a light in her eyes.

"Please take the light away. I'm just now able to see you."

"I need to check your reflexes, Mrs. Gilchrist. You've had a nasty knock on the head. We're going to transport you to the emergency room."

"That's not necessary. Is it Patrick?" She attempted to raise her head.

"It's necessary, Enid. It won't hurt a thing."

"Except my pride."

Enid snarled and lay back on the stretcher, catching sight of a couple of officers hovering around the back of her Subaru before she blacked out again.

When she woke up the second time, she found herself in the emergency room. She looked around for Patrick. He stood in a corner. She reached for his hand, and he moved to her side.

"They need to do their jobs. We'll talk when they finish."

* * *

When the ER doctor finished, Enid had unwittingly consented to an overnight stay for observation due to a slight concussion and inhalation of carbon monoxide as much because of Patrick's insistence as the doctor's concern.

"Enid, if I hadn't changed my mind and left the station shortly after you called, I might not have found you in time." Patrick's voice broke and he swallowed. "I…uh…think you need to ask Mary for hazard pay."

"Patrick, that's not funny."

"I didn't mean it to be funny."

"Humph. Who would have ever thought being a genealogist could be hazardous to your health? Tell me. What happened?"

"Obviously, someone knocked you out. That resulted in the concussion, however slight it might be. Then he pushed you back into your car and turned on the ignition. At some point, he placed a long piece of hose over the end of the exhaust pipe, rolled the front window down enough to poke the hose through, and taped cardboard over the remaining opening. You got enough carbon monoxide in your lungs for concern but not enough to…."

"To kill me?"

"You don't have to be quite so direct. You are talking about the woman I…care about."

"Thank you, Patrick, for caring and for getting to me in time."

The ER doctor cleared his throat. "If you two lovebirds are finished, I'll have one of the attendants carry you up to a room."

"Just for tonight, though, right?"

"Depends on how you're doing tomorrow. When I do send you home, I want you to take it easy for a few days. I don't want you to drive or go to work. You may have a lingering headache and feel like you've had the flu, and you may not. I'd also like for you to see your regular doctor by the end of the week. Tell him if you have any memory problems or other effects. Think you can follow those instructions?"

"You both act as if you think I can be difficult."

"Stubborn was the word that came to my mind," said Patrick.

"Your humor is beginning to annoy me. Stubborn would be refusing to wear this excuse for a gown. I do not need this much ventilation. Take me to my room so I can sleep this off."

Soon Enid was settled upright in a stiff hospital bed with Patrick sitting in an equally uncomfortable straight chair beside her.

"You plan to stay all night?"

"Only a little while."

"Good. I can't sleep with you staring at me. What's next?"

"Enid, I have no doubt Maude's intruder is responsible for this. I also have no doubt he is escalating his activities. Someone did tamper with Abby's Honda. The line was cut just enough for fluid to leak and cause problems with the brakes but not enough to prevent her from pulling over and finally stopping. However, if she hadn't pulled over when she did, she might not have been able to, and she could have been injured or killed. It should be obvious, this person's intent for you was much more determined, much more than a threat. Enid, are you listening?"

"Yes, I am, but I thought of something else and was distracted. My briefcase and my handbag. Did you find them?"

"Your handbag was on the seat beside you. Your briefcase was on the ground beside the car."

"I thought I saw it floating in front of me."

"What was in it?"

"Nothing, thank goodness. I never carry library materials home with me. I sometimes carry copies of research material to review them. I did have copies of my latest research in my briefcase earlier, but I left them with Maude. I left another set at the library. Patrick, I'm more worried for Maude than for myself. My recent primary research efforts have been for her. If someone is this determined to stop her, stop us, then she's in more danger than I am, and I'm more convinced than ever that someone is trying to poison her. What's strange is that they may be mimicking her great-great-grandmother's murder."

"How so?"

Enid gave Patrick an account of Charlotte's inquest report. "Patrick, did you ever talk to Dr. Finley about Maude?"

"Finally. He returned my call late this afternoon after his office closed. He had been out all day and happened to see he had several voicemail and handwritten messages from me. He's convinced that her physical decline is a result of old age and that she's imagining everything else. He implied that she could be suffering from dementia. He said her daughter agrees with him. After Abby's and your narrow escapes, I'm inclined to disagree. I thought you said she was going to see him again."

"She did. This past Friday."

"He didn't mention her visit to me."

"She insisted he do lab work including testing for poisons and metals, especially arsenic."

"He didn't mention that, either. Why arsenic?"

"Because of the inquest for her great-great-grandmother and because her decline began after her request for information at their last family reunion."

"How does that suggest arsenic?"

"It doesn't unless you use our unique sense of logic. The inquest suggested a family member might have poisoned Charlotte with arsenic. Family members attended the recent Goodwin and Abbott reunion, and many were unsupportive to say the least of Maude's interest in their family history. After the reunion, her health began to decline."

"I see. But the inquest for Charlotte Goodwin found no cause to suspect poisoning."

"I said our sense of logic was unique."

"When did Dr. Finley say he'd get the reports back?"

"He had to send them to the hospital lab. He said it could take a few days. Could you speed things up?"

"I'll give the lab a call."

"Maybe Maude needs to call Dr. Finley again."

CHAPTER TWENTY-FOUR

Tuesday, August 9, 2011

At one o'clock the next day, Enid sat dressed and waiting when Patrick arrived to take her home.

"You did understand that your doctor is releasing you with an admonition to take it easy and to not stay by yourself for a couple of days. Right?"

Enid compressed her lips and stared at the ceiling.

"Don't be difficult. I don't want you staying alone, either. Whom can you call to stay with you?"

"I've taken care of that. I've talked to Maude, and we've agreed to stay with each other at her house."

"You two will be a pair. Neither of you can do anything if something happens to the other one."

"We can call someone if we need to, and it will allow us time to continue to search through her great-grandmother's dower chest for more clues."

"Like that's going to give me any comfort."

"Patrick."

"Fine. Fine. As you said, at least one of you can call someone if the other one needs help. You will, of course, keep all the doors locked, right?"

"Patrick!"

"I'm done. We're leaving now. Although I do have one other concern."

"What?"

"Both Maude and Abby received a warning threat. You didn't, which makes me think he's stepping up whatever schedule he has. Enid? Why are you looking at me like that?"

"It's a good thing you brought this up before we leave the hospital."

"Enid?"

"I did receive a threat. Friday night. But nothing happened that night or the rest of the weekend or all day yesterday. I thought it was a bluff."

Patrick adjusted his hat on his head. He stared at the floor, one hand on his hip, the other against his forehead. After a moment, he looked up. The softness of his voice did not match the hardness of his eyes.

"Enid, you of all people. You could have died. What good would your death serve?"

"I didn't want to worry anyone. I am aware of how foolish I acted. I don't want to discuss it further. I want to go home to pack a bag and go to Maude's. Now."

* * *

Much to Enid's frustration, after not saying a word on the drive from the hospital to her house, Patrick insisted on helping her pack a bag and following her to Maude's house. By the time he had her settled in, it was four o'clock, and Abby had returned home from school.

"Remember, Enid. All doors locked at all times."

"I don't think any of us will forget to lock the doors."

"I hope not. I'll check in with you later."

"Thank you, Patrick. I'm sorry for being so prickly. I'm worried, and I'm angry for these interruptions in our lives."

"I know. Talk to you later."

"Yes."

Enid returned Patrick's peck on the cheek before he left. She closed and locked the door behind him and joined Maude and Abby in the living room.

"Enid," said Maude, wringing her hands, "I cannot endanger either Abigail's life or your life anymore. Maybe we should end this."

"Granny, I'm going to do this with or without you and Miss Enid."

"Besides," said Enid, "I'm here and on rest detail for a couple of days. Furthermore, if I'm here and we're working, you won't have to hire anyone to stay with you while Abby is at school."

"Did you two get together and make this all up to persuade me?"

"We didn't, Granny, but is it working anyway?"

"Yes. Yes! I give in. We will continue. Together."

"Good," said Enid. "What do you want to do next?"

"I want to finish with this needlepoint business. I'm fascinated, and I hate to rush through it, but I'm afraid I don't have time to drag it out any longer."

"I'm eager to finish the needlepoints, too, Granny, because I want to hear the rest of Charlotte and Olivia's story. Not because I plan on you leaving anytime soon."

Maude smiled. "You must be realistic, Abigail. Whether I've been poisoned or not, my allotted time is limited." She patted Abby's hand. Abby smiled back at her but with sadness in her eyes. "So what after the needlepoints? We need to have a plan."

"After that," said Enid, "we must discuss possible suspects."

"Can't the police do that? I hate to consider anyone in my family, but I don't think I have a choice."

"The police will handle it, but they need something to go on. We're the only ones who can give them that at this point."

"You mean I'm the only one. Let's do this. We can begin by comparing the scriptures stitched onto the remaining needlepoints with their counterparts in the Collins's Bible to rule out those with no misquotes and write down the correct version of those with misquotes."

"Good idea. First, however, you should call Dr. Finley to see if he has your bloodwork reports back."

"You're right. He should have called by now."

Abby dialed the doctor's number and handed the phone to Maude.

Maude's frown deepened as she listened. "Then please have him call me first thing in the morning." She snapped her phone shut with a slap. "He's out of the office today. You'd think someone else could tell me something. Time's wasting. Let's get to it."

They spent the next thirty minutes comparing the remaining needlepoints to the corresponding verses in the Bible.

* * *

"Good work, ladies," said Enid. "We've reduced our probable needlepoints with clues to four. Now to decipher them. Where should we begin?"

"There are two in particular I'd like to look at," said Abby.

"Wherever you want to begin, Abigail. Which two are they?"

"You mentioned the daffodil patches after you visited Charles, and we know Charlotte transplanted daffodil bulbs to cover the graves. Also, we discussed the inheritance."

"Yes."

"Well, one of the needlepoints not only mentions daffodils but has a stand of them stitched over a mound between the scripture and a tree. Another needlepoint mentions an inheritance and depicts three children, two girls playing together and a boy off to one side. I don't think those two are about journal entries. If they are, they don't make sense. Those are the two I'd like to decipher next."

"Let's do so."

"Here's the Collin's version of the one about an inheritance. 'A good man leaveth an inheritance to his children's children: and the wealth of the sinner is laid up for the just. Proverbs 13:22.' Now for the misquoted version on the needlepoint. 'A good man leaveth a letter of inheritance to all of his children: but the wealth of the sinner is sewn up in my inheritance.'

"The needlepoint contains three misquotes. A *letter* of inheritance. To *all* of his children. The wealth of the sinner is *sewn up in my inheritance*. Thoughts anybody?"

"I have a few," said Enid, "but I'd like to hear what Maude thinks first."

"Either I'm channeling Charlotte or I have more of my mind left than everyone would like to believe. The letter of inheritance has to refer to a will. All of his children must include Miriam along with Olivia and Mason. The sinner, noted in both versions, would have to refer to Peter."

"Peter wouldn't have included Miriam in his will."

"Charlotte would have. He was the sinner. She had a will and she sewed up his wealth for all of his children. It's the *sewn up in my inheritance* that throws me. It certainly wasn't in the Bible. Let me think on it while we look at the next one. But before we do, I want to call Lowell Franklin."

"Why?" asked Abby.

"The Franklin Law Firm has represented our family since the early 1800s. If a copy of Charlotte's will exists, it has to be there. Hand me my cell phone. I want to see if he's looked for the old files yet." She dialed his number and pressed speaker.

"Lowell, this is Maude Everly. Have you had any luck locating files for Peter and Charlotte Abbott?"

"Maude, I haven't had a chance to pull those files yet."

"Please do so as soon as possible. It is vitally important."

"How can a century-and-a-half-old document be vitally important?"

"Don't argue with me, please. Just locate their files."

"I'll put Vance on it."

"Thank you."

A loud click signaled the end of the conversation.

"Granny, did he just hang up on you?"

"Sounded like it."

"What's his problem?"

"I'm sure he's just busy." Maude's expression did not match her words. "While I'm thinking on the inheritance and we're waiting for Lowell or Vance to call back and before we read your next choice, I need a small snack."

* * *

"I'm glad you decided to take a break, Maude," said Enid. "I didn't realize I was hungry."

"That apple pie and coffee hit the spot for me, too," said Abby. "I'm reenergized and ready to begin again."

"I hope we figure this one out in its entirety," said Maude. "Abigail, will you again do the honors?"

"Of course." Abby picked up the next needlepoint in the line on the coffee table. "I'm excited about this one. I think I have it figured out. First, the Collins's version. 'The grass withereth, the flower fadeth: but the word of our God shall stand for ever. Isaiah 40:8.'

"Next, the needlepoint version. The grass withereth, but the daffodil does not fade: and the treasure shall lie there for ever."

"My, my," said Maude. "Charlotte certainly took liberties with that scripture. The *daffodil does not fade*. In fact, daffodil blooms last but a short time. The treasure stands *forever*. The word of God is our treasure, but I do not believe that's the treasure to which Charlotte was referring. What's your theory, Abigail?"

"You both have to see it. This must be the needlepoint referenced in journal entry number four. The daffodils cover the graves of the five slaves including Isaac. The treasure—the hidden money—lies there with Isaac and the daffodils forever."

"Abby has to be right," said Enid.

"So we're in agreement. You know what I have to do next."

Abby and Enid glanced at each other and said in unison, "What?"

"I have to make another phone call because I'll be buying Charles Goodwin's property whatever his asking price. I must have legal ownership to be able to retrieve the inheritance and give it to one of Miriam's descendants. No one will lose anything at my death. The property can be sold and divided."

"There were several daffodil patches," said Enid.

"Will you dig them all up?" asked Abby.

"That won't be necessary. I'll have to spend a little money to get it done, but one of those ground penetrating radar machines should help us find the five graves and identify which one is Isaac's. It will be one of the end graves. If we're right, the money should be buried between him and the daffodils."

"Whatever you do, Maude, you must not mention this to anyone—anyone at all."

"Nor should either of you. Not even to Patrick."

"As much as I hate to hide anything from him, I agree," said Enid. She didn't mention their tête-à-tête earlier in the day.

"I'm not about to tell anyone," said Abby. "I'm running on adrenaline now. Let's go ahead and figure out these last two needlepoints."

Before they could begin, Maude's cell phone rang. She answered it and put it on speaker.

"Yes?"

"Maude, this is Lowell Franklin."

"Do you have something to report?"

"Yes and no. I did find Peter's and Charlotte's files. Both made wills when they married, which they updated after Olivia was born. One of the files contains a note about Peter planning to update his again when Mason turned sixteen, but he never got around to doing it. Charlotte did initiate changes in her will, and a copy of those changes is in one of the files, but she never signed the new will. As a result, in both cases, the previous wills had to stand."

"Are you certain there wasn't a signed copy? One she had in her possession?"

"There isn't a signed one in her file, and no one found a signed copy in her possessions after she died. There are notes to that effect in her file."

"Hmm. Lowell, I need…want…to see everything in both files. I need you to bring them to the house, though. I'm not up to coming back to the office. When can you bring them?"

Lowell groaned. "Maude, Maude. You're not my only client. When do you want me to bring them by?"

"In the morning. First thing. I believe you open your office at nine o'clock. You could come by here on your way to the office."

Maude hung up.

"Now for the other two clues and the rest of the story."

CHAPTER TWENTY-FIVE

E nid picked up the two remaining framed needlepoints. "These are not as decorative as the earlier ones."

"I noticed that, too," said Abby. "You can read them and their corresponding verses if you will."

"I'd be happy to. I'll read this one first. I believe, because of Abby's thread color theory, it must be next because it is slightly more decorative than the other one. Both the scripture and the simple border of leaves are stitched with a single-color thread, a dark green. The Collins's version reads, 'Ye shall therefore describe the land into seven parts, and bring the description hither to me, that I may cast lots for you here before the Lord our God. Joshua 18:6.'

"The needlepoint version reads, 'Ye shall therefore sketch the land into a book of seven parts, and bring the description hither to me, that I may cast lots for you here before the Lord our God.' I'm sure you see another reason why I believe this one refers to the next set of journal entries."

"Because of the words *sketch* and *book of seven parts*, it has to refer to Washington Irving's *The Sketch Book*, Charlotte's one remaining book. It was hidden with *The Scarlet Letter*, and it follows that she would use the books until she finished with them."

"How does *seven* play into it?" asked Abby.

"*The Sketch Book* was originally published in seven parts."

Abby reached over into the dower chest and pulled out *The Sketch Book*. She opened it to the front panel and then the back panel.

"Uh-oh. It doesn't have anything glued to either panel."

"Let me see it," said Maude. She ran her fingers down the middle of the front and back of either panel. "I don't feel anything, either. She placed the book in her lap and gently fanned the pages. "Ah, here they are! She placed them inside a muslin pouch, sewed the pouch into the middle of the book, and of course, hid the book. Clever girl. Abigail, you'll need to snip the stitches with even more care this time."

"While I snip, you two can decipher this last needlepoint."

Maude picked it up. Her fingers trembled. "It has no design or border, and the scripture is stitched in black. It must indeed be the last one." Maude's body sagged.

"Do you want me to read it?" asked Enid.

"No, this last one is for me to read but not the actual entries. My voice is too shaky." She skimmed the words and laughed. "How appropriate. It's a partial verse from Kings 22:8. The Collins's version is the longer of the two. It says, 'And Hilkiah the high priest said unto Shaphan the scribe, I have found the book of the law in the house of the Lord.' Charlotte's version says simply, 'And Hilkiah said, I have found the end of the book and it is here.' What do you think, Enid? That maybe the last pages are actually hidden behind this needlepoint?"

Enid ran her fingers down the back. She grinned. "I believe they are."

Abby lifted the journal pages from *The Sketch Book* and placed them on the coffee table. "Shall I snip those before we read?"

Enid and Maude spoke together. "Yes."

When she finished snipping threads and removing the last pages from behind the last needlepoint, Abby placed them to the right of the others.

"I'm sad."

"Why, Abigail?"

"Because after we read these entries, Charlotte's story will be over."

Maude reached out to take Abby's hand in hers. "No, dear, not yet. Charlotte's story will have one last chapter, and we will help write it."

Tears clouded both their eyes. Abby turned to Enid. "You read the first set. I'll get myself together enough to read the last set."

"Will do." Enid picked up the entries removed from *The Sketch Book* and began to read.

* * *

The Journal of Charlotte Abbott Goodwin
A True Record of Daniel's Innocence and Other Events
Entry #9, Friday Evening, September 27th, 1867
Peter's Situation and Searching for Hanna

Five years have passed since Hannah and Miriam left our house on September 26th, 1862. It seems odd that today is a Friday as well. What a draining five years it has been.

Over time, Peter first and then Mason, who turns sixteen this year, began blaming the freeing of the slaves for Peter's own financial ruin. We are not ruined. We do not live as well as we once did, but we are not ruined.

As for blame, no one is to blame but Peter himself. Those men and women who did stay after the war have since left to make a living on their own or with other family members. Whatever they find, it could not be worse than working for Peter Goodwin for ill treatment and meager wages. It is for those same reasons that no one else will hire out to him.

I would leave, too, if I thought I could make my way. However, I have to consider Olivia. We have a roof over our heads and food to eat. As long as we keep his house and prepare his meals, Peter leaves us both alone now. I once held out hope that my presence would help lead to a change in Mason, but the older he gets, the more like his father he becomes.

If I could only hear from Hannah. I have had reason to travel about the counties bordering ours. Mama and I have visited friends who moved a few miles across the state line into Kentucky. Others have traveled through our town, white families and black families looking for a place to settle. Wherever I go, wherever I am, I look into the eyes of every light-skinned black woman I meet to see if they are a reflection of my own—and then hope they are not. Peter swears he will have the warrant for theft served on Daniel if he ever returns. I could not abide that.

The Journal of Charlotte Abbott Goodwin
A True Record of Daniel's Innocence and Other Events
Entry #10, Friday Evening, November 8th, 1867
Events Leading To and Following Peter's Death

Peter has died. Four weeks ago, two weeks after my last entry, he fell into a fit of rage, apparently suffering from apoplexy according to Doctor Huddle. Whatever he suffered, I have no doubt it was a result of his own bitterness and perceived financial downfall and especially his own prejudice.

He grumbled from the time he arose that Saturday morning because of the tools that needed to be repaired. He resented doing business with the local blacksmith, a Negro man named Elias, a former slave of one of our neighbors. On that day, Peter convinced himself that Elias had overcharged him, and he went into what my father called an apoplectic fit. Elias carried Peter to Doctor Huddle's office and then brought him home. Peter never spoke another word. He died on Wednesday. We buried him yesterday. How odd that even now I am recording events on a Friday evening. Nevertheless, I prefer to write when Mason is out of the house. Needless to say, he continues with his father's habits.

I wish I could say I grieved for Peter. I prayed for Peter from the day we married, and I do grieve for his soul, but I cannot say I grieve for him or that I will miss him.

Unfortunately, Mason has tried to assume his father's place in all respects, including taking control of the farm, beginning the day his father took to his bed.

Fortunately, for Olivia and myself, he is not of age and Peter's will left everything to me, if I outlived him, to raise his children. If I did not outlive him, Mason and Olivia were each to receive half of his estate when he or she turned eighteen. Peter meant to make changes when Mason turned sixteen, and Mason knew this. Peter did discuss it with our lawyer, Mr. James Franklin, but he thought he was invincible and had plenty of time. I must say I am thankful for that.

I have thought long and hard on what I should do about this and another matter. Peter continued to keep his money hidden in the house in another metal box. He never trusted banks any more than he trusted individuals. Mason knows this. Peter continued to change his hiding place daily, but he always told Mason where the new place was. He never told me, and he thought I never knew, but I did. He was not that clever, and I always managed to find it. Sometimes I even saw him move it, as I did on the day of his fit.

That last morning, after he hid his money, he meant to tell Mason, but he had to go to town, and he had already sent Mason to the fields. I heard him mumble, "I'll tell him when I return home."

Mason had not returned from the fields when Elias and Doctor Huddle brought Peter home. Before the doctor left, he told me that Peter would likely not improve. I hesitated but a moment after I closed the door behind him. I knew I had to remove the money box from its hiding place before Mason returned home and before I told him of his father's condition so that I could hide it somewhere else it until I could deposit it into my checking account at the bank.

As soon as I informed Mason of his father's condition, he took up his search for the money box. He spent part of every day after that searching for it. After a week or so, he challenged me on it.

"You stole it, didn't you? Where did you hide it?"

I drew myself straight up and fixed my eyes on his. "If I knew where it was, it was as much mine as it was Peter's, and according to his will, removing it would not be stealing. Let me remind you, though, your father never told anyone but you where he hid his money, so perhaps you are the one who stole it."

Anger colored his face crimson. I feared he would fall into a fit the same as his father. After several minutes, he took hold of himself and became defensive. "I did not take it, and I don't know where it is, but I will never stop looking for it. I vow on my father's grave that neither of us will ever sell this house until the money is found."

He has not found it, of course, and in time, he stopped accusing me of taking it. However, not a day passes but what he manages to find fault in something I do or forget to do. It seems any peace I might have had at Peter's passing will never be. I did manage to take the money to the bank on a day soon after our confrontation when Olivia and I went in for supplies while Mason worked in the fields.

At least I have Olivia, and for the most part, Mason leaves us to our own devices. It is as if we have an unspoken agreement. He will continue to work the farm in his father's stead, assuming both the responsibility and to some degree the benefits. I doubt it is out of regard for Olivia or myself but rather because he expects to inherit the farm at my death and so wants to keep it up. For now, he is content with an allowance equal to one-fourth of the farm profits after all expenses, although I suspect that will change as he grows older.

He would prefer that I account for every remaining penny. I have managed to avoid that for the time being. With his knowledge, I deposit an allowance equal to his share into a trust account in Olivia's name at the bank, accessible only by herself when she marries or any time after her twenty-fifth birthday, whichever comes first. He has no knowledge of what I do with the remaining half nor does he have access to it. I am certain he assumes I deposit it all into my own account. I do not. I deposit half of my share to my personal checking account to use for running the farm and the house, but I deposit the other half of my share into a second trust account also in Olivia's name but for Miriam, accessible only by Olivia any time after her twenty-fifth birthday.

Were it not for fear of it being discovered and taken from me, I would deposit what remains of the money I took the night Hannah left. Someday, that money will be part of Miriam's inheritance. Until then, it will remain hidden.

As his father did, Mason makes our lives miserable in other ways as well. A few weeks ago, he broke Olivia's heart. He took off the last of the cats and kittens. We have always had cats and kittens in the barn to control the rats, but Mason hates cats. Not long after Peter died, he decided to get rid of them, all of them. He did. As would be expected, our rat population grew.

Mason thinks he knows everything and refuses to listen to anyone about anything, least of all me, but he must have spoken to someone about the rats because he did manage to get rid of them. I'm not sure to whom he spoke, but it must have been our lawyer, James Franklin. At church last Sunday, Mr. Franklin asked me, "How's your rat problem?" How else would he have known if Mason had not told him?

Whatever Mason did to get rid of them, he lost a couple of his prize pups in the process. A hard lesson learned, but a few days later, he came home with two full-grown barn cats. Olivia spends a few hours of every day trying to make friends with the two cats.

Mason returns. I must leave off for now.

"Abby, you wanted to read the last entries."

"I do." She glanced at Maude. "Should we take another break first though?"

"Yes, dear, I believe so, but I need something more substantial than pie this time. Perhaps a sandwich and some iced tea."

"You lean back and rest while Miss Enid and I get it ready."

"Thank you, Abigail."

In the kitchen, Abby frowned. "Miss Enid, I hate to take so many breaks, but I worry about Granny. She sinks a little more every day. I wish Dr. Finley would call."

"I've asked Patrick to check with the doctor about the lab work. If we don't hear anything by tomorrow, we should take her back in to the office."

"My thoughts, too. Now for food. I can't imagine why after that big piece of pie I ate, but my tummy is growling at me." Abby managed a faint smile before pulling things from the refrigerator.

An hour later, they were ready to begin again.

CHAPTER TWENTY-SIX

Enid fanned the last set of pages from Charlotte's journal. "If these are the last of Charlotte's entries, I wonder if they will say anything about her sickness at the end of her life."

"I do hope so," said Maude. "I don't know if it will help us solve her mystery or ours, but I do hope so." She eased her recliner back. "I'm ready."

Enid handed the pages to Abby and turned sideways on the sofa to face Abby and Maude. "Me, too," she said.

Abby scooted back into her end of the sofa, took a deep breath, and began to read.

The Journal of Charlotte Abbott Goodwin
A True Record of Daniel's Innocence and Other Events
Entry #11, Tuesday Morning, August 10th, 1869
My Decline

I have not written in some time. Almost two years in fact. There has been nothing new to record. I have had no news of or from Hannah and Miriam or Celia. Mason, Olivia, and I have managed to keep part of the farm going and to feed and clothe ourselves though we did have to sell off a few acres at the back.

I believe my fears concerning Mason may have come about. As he approaches his eighteenth birthday, he tries to assert his authority more and more. Worse than this, though, I find myself growing sicker and weaker. At first, my decline was so gradual and general, no one but me noticed it. Even I doubted my suspicions. After some point, my symptoms became more obvious and severe.

My occasional nausea has progressed to vomiting, sometimes with blood and abdominal pain. I have lost weight and experience numbness and tingling in my arms and legs. I have other and odd symptoms as well.

Even though she is barely thirteen years old, I have given Olivia my final instructions and told her of the journal and of the clues.

I have also left instructions for my youngest sister Nancy and her husband Isaiah Kessler to take care of Olivia until she marries or reaches her twenty-fifth birthday.

I am writing for the first time on a day other than Friday, but I feel compelled to write, and I do not have the luxury of expecting any day beyond the present one. I've sent Mason to town for supplies so that I might have this time alone.

I have my suspicions about my decline, but I can find no evidence of it. Nor have I been able to catch Mason at anything as nefarious as what I suspect. Even that I refused to entertain at first. At the beginning, Doctor Huddle suspected I had entered menopause early. Mama calls it either hysteria or change of life, depending on her disposition at the time, because, she says, there is no pause to it. It stops and that's the end of it.

When that proved not to be the case, Doctor Huddle attributed my problems to some kind of stomach disorder. Now he suggests I might have cancer of the stomach or liver or female organs. He offers no hope.

I doubt his diagnosis. The escalation of my symptoms came upon me too suddenly. That and Mason watching me as if to see the moment I take my last breath. I have searched for any sign of poison but have found nothing around the house or in the gardens or outbuildings. I have mentioned my concerns to my sister Nancy but have sworn her to secrecy.

I digress. I am writing now, not so much because I am ill, but because I fear I may not have another chance to write. I fear it so much so that I have recently updated my last will and testament. Mine had read much as Peter's did. I changed it to divide everything equally among Mason, Olivia, and Miriam separate from any monies given to them during my lifetime whether by hand or by trust account. While I did list property, livestock, farming tools, and household items, I did not specify the amount of money I had on hand. I have discussed this with Olivia privately.

I have also explained to her about the two trust accounts, both in her name, one to be kept by her for Miriam. I have cautioned her to keep the purpose of the second account secret form everyone. I do not want Mason to find a way to break or access either of the accounts. Together, we sewed both account books into the doll Olivia received for Christmas last year.

As we have only one lawyer in town, even though he was a friend of Peter's, I had little choice but to go to him to update my will. I met with Mr. James Franklin one week ago on Monday morning. He became quite irate with me when I explained what I wanted.

He slammed a law book against his desk and jumped up. "Peter would not want you to dispose of his property as you plan."

"Peter is dead," I said. "Do you want my business or not? It would not be convenient, but I could travel out of town if you will not honor my wishes."

Mr. Franklin blustered about the room for several minutes and then stopped to gaze out a window. Finally, he turned to me and said, "Fine. I will draw it up and have it ready for you to sign at the end of the week."

I did not like the look in his eyes. I hesitated long enough to consider my health and the difficulty of travel. With some misgiving, I agreed. "Thank you. I will return on Friday. Please have two copies made, both of which I will sign, one of which I will keep." That is what we did when we first drew up our wills, but I did not want there to be any misunderstanding about it.

I should have known he had a plan to prevent me. He spoke to Mason that afternoon and told him everything.

Mason confronted me at dinner that evening. "I'll appeal to the courts."

"Do what you will, Mason. I am within my rights, and I refuse to argue with you."

He stomped out of the house, so like his father. He did not return until after Olivia and I had gone to bed. He was very quiet, but I heard him moving about in the kitchen. I suspected he still hoped to find Peter's money box.

By Friday morning, I had declined even further.

Olivia hovered over me. "Mama, you should see Doctor Huddle while you're in town."

"I'll hitch the horses to the wagon and take you," said Mason. "I can make better time. Olivia can have lunch ready by the time we return so I can go back to work sooner."

I questioned his motives, but I accepted his offer.

The doctor acknowledged my further decline but again asserted his diagnosis of cancer. He gave me pills for stomach distress and for pain. He told me to return if I needed more.

Mason tried to persuade me to return home straightaway and choose another day to sign my will. I thought better of it, though, and insisted he carry me to Mr. Franklin's office.

Mason paced the floor, and Mr. Franklin strummed his fingers against his desktop. If they thought to rush me, it did not work. I read every word of both copies of my last will and testament.

When I finished, I straightened myself in my chair and said, "I'm ready to sign them."

Mason muttered, "It's about time."

I ignored him. I signed both copies. Mason signed them next. After Mr. Franklin signed them, he handed one copy to me.

"I want your secretary to sign as well."

He huffed and said, "That isn't necessary."

"Nevertheless, it is what I want." I did not accept the copy he held out to me.

He and Mason exchanged glances before he complied with my wishes. I did not know at the time what possessed me to do so, but I am glad I did. I thought we should have someone else witness as well, but Mr. Franklin assured me our signatures were sufficient.

After we returned home and finished lunch and Mason left the house, I had Olivia bring my sewing box and my one other inheritance handed down from my grandmother to the living room. I sewed a second cover over the end of my grandmother's gift, placed my copy of the signed will between the two end covers, and stitched the gap closed.

My grandmother had instructed me to take care of her gift. "Its value will increase over time," she said. I am proud to say I have done as she instructed. It is now worth even more to Olivia and Miriam because of its contents. After I finished, I had Olivia return it to its place in her dower chest and gave her the same admonition.

I also had her gather my needlepoints together, especially the ones that give clues to the whereabouts of everything I have hidden, and place them all in her dower chest along with my most precious possessions— my family Bible, my books, my inheritance—underneath the items she has made herself. I will stitch the pages I am writing now behind the needlepoint I finished earlier today. I take it as a sign that I will place them within the last frame Daniel made for me before he left with Hannah and Miriam. As this may be my last entry, I will close with the following words.

Olivia, my precious child, I love you. I pray every day that you will find a good and honest man of your own choosing who loves you and whom you love. Kiss my grandbabies for me. Hang the needlepoints in your home after you marry so that I may continue to be a part of your life and you may be reminded that I have and will always love you. Mama.

The Journal of Charlotte Abbott Goodwin, cont.
A True Record of Daniel's Innocence and Other Events
Entry #12, Tuesday Morning, August 17th, 1869
My Decline, cont.

I hope whoever is reading this can read my handwriting. My hand shakes so I can scarcely read it myself.

One week has passed since I last wrote in my journal. I had Olivia bring me the needlepoint where I hid those pages. I have removed the pages so that I might add a few words before I hide them again. I must stitch them in before my fingers give out, and I do not have long to write. Mason is out tending a sick mare.

Doctor Huddle came to the house today. I slipped him a note asking him to fetch my sister Nancy and her husband Isaiah immediately so that they may take Olivia out of this house now as I continue to decline more rapidly than one would expect, even my doctor.

I outlined in the note what Olivia is to carry with her to my sister's house as her own personal property. The items include every hiding place for my secret journal entries and my will as well as the framed needlepoints that give clues to their whereabouts. I have also listed the items she is to receive when I die. I must remove Olivia from this house before then. I hope we both can leave, but certainly my daughter.

Mason has not left the house this last week but for a few moments at the time. He did not even leave for his Friday night outing with the men. He tends the animals as little as possible and then returns to the house. He will not leave me alone at all with anyone who visits. I slipped the note into Doctor Huddle's hand when I asked him to help me sit up in bed.

I dare not say a word to Mason until Nancy and Isaiah arrive for fear he will finish what he has started and prevent them somehow from carrying out my wishes. I do not know how, but I have convinced myself he is killing me. Nothing else explains my decline unless I believe my doctor. I am not convinced that he believes himself.

I have given Olivia instructions to put the needlepoint containing my last entries in her dower chest as soon as I finish. I cannot do it myself because I do not have the strength to carry it across the room. All but this last needlepoint and the hidden money are already packed. I have no way to access the money, but Mason will never find it. No one will ever find it without the clue in the needlepoint.

I left my final note to Olivia in the last entry. I end this entry with the following note.

Dearest Hannah, I accept that I will never see you this side of eternity, but I look for that future day with joy. I hope you, Miriam, and Daniel have a blessed life. With my undying love, Charlotte.

Abby stopped reading and stared at the next page.

She moaned. "No." Tears streamed down her face.

Maude raised her head. "What's wrong, Abigail?"

Enid reached for the pages in Abby's hands. "I can read if you need to stop."

"No, I can read. I have to."

* * *

The Journal of Charlotte Abbott Goodwin
Continued by Olivia Abbott after Mother's Death
A True Record of Daniel's Innocence and Other Events
Entry #13, Sunday Morning, August 18th, 1872
Mother's Death, the Inquest, and the Days that Followed

To whomever may find and read these words, especially our Dearest Hannah.

Mother died three years ago today on August 18th, 1869, one day after she wrote her last journal entry. At least she died peacefully at the home of my aunt and uncle with Aunt Nancy and me on either side of her bed.

I will remove the stitches that hide her last words, add this entry to hers, and then put everything away until and unless Hannah, Miriam, and Daniel return. Only then do I dare reveal what I know.

I must not continue my endeavors to convince my family of the truth. I am afraid if I do so, they will send me away. They consider my "ramblings" a sign of some mental deficiency. When I was a little child, they almost had me believing the lies they told me. Now they would have my beloved Terrence questioning my sanity as well. I must convince them otherwise so that I might marry Terrence, receive my inheritance and my trust account, and leave this all behind me. I will never stop looking for Hannah and Miriam, though.

So many problems and issues arose during the days after Mama's passing. I was only thirteen. A child. Old enough to remember, though, even the things they tried to make me forget. Had it not been for Aunt Nancy, I might truly have lost my mind. Even she, too, insisted I put it all behind me—for my sake and hers.

One of the issues concerned Mama's will. I knew Mama had changed her will and signed it, but Mr. Franklin insisted she had not signed it. Just knowing the contents caused an uproar in the family. My insisting she had signed it brought their wrath down upon me.

"Olivia," said my Uncle Isaiah with an uncharacteristic firmness, "you must let this go. If Charlotte had signed her last will, your family would work to have it overturned, saying she was not in her right mind at the end, but she did not sign the last will. We've seen it. Mr. Franklin and his secretary confirm that Mason is telling the truth. You are mistaken. She meant to sign it, but she did not."

I told Aunt Nancy I knew Mama had and I knew where the will was, but she advised me not to say anything about it or tell anyone, even her, because of the uproar it had already caused. She said when I was a grown woman, I could decide what to do then.

"We were fortunate," she told me, "to have Charlotte's note delivered to us by Doctor Huddle expressing your mama's final wishes that Isaiah and I have custody and care of you, that we be allotted an amount to do so, and that we hold your inheritance in trust for you until you come of age. You are fortunate that the court awarded you half of her estate under her last known signed will, including half of the property. I know your father was abusive. I know Mason was abusive. Isaiah and I also know that's why Charlotte sent for us before she died, to prevent Mason from taking control of you, your belongings, and your inheritance. However, even though I know Charlotte acted with the best of intentions, Hannah was a slave. Miriam was a slave. The law may have freed them, but they were born slaves. As such, at least in this family's way of thinking, Miriam was not due an inheritance, and you must forget this and let it be at least until you're older. Do you understand?"

I did not understand then. However, I was a child. I did not think I had a choice. I did think I could take care of it when I became a woman, especially as the provisions of the will concerning Miriam could not be honored until I found her. Therefore, I decided to wait until I did find her to pursue it further or to make known the whereabouts of the signed copy of Mama's will.

I am older now, perhaps not grown up, but old enough to be married, and I still do not understand any better than when I was thirteen. However, I do understand how little say I have in anything and how easily one can be declared incompetent, so I have reaffirmed my decision to wait concerning the will. I have also decided not to tell anyone, including Terrence, the purpose of the second trust account in my name. Perhaps by the time I turn twenty-five, I can trust him with Mama's secret.

As soon as I am married, I will remove both trust account books from my doll, even the one intended for me from which I will transfer funds to my checking account, and I will place them in one of these new bank safe boxes to be kept in the bank's vault. As I will have sufficient funds in my account, this new service will cost me nothing, but it will provide me with a measure of security. It will allow me access but no one else. In the event I am never able to make the will known, I will continue to add to the second account until I have added enough to make up for what I received from my mother's estate that should have gone to Miriam.

If I do not find Miriam by my twenty-fifth birthday, I will transfer the second trust fund's balance into an interest-bearing savings account in my name. If I do not find her in my lifetime, I will transfer the balance of that account into an interest-bearing savings account for one of my own descendants, perhaps a child or grandchild, the one whom I can trust to carry on our search, the one to whom I will bequeath my dower chest with all its secrets.

Another issue—one more important than money or property—concerns how Mama died. At the last, she told me she thought someone was poisoning her. She did not accuse anyone, but I thought then and I think now that it must have been Mason. Aunt Nancy agreed. Mama had discussed it with her, too. What I told her later convinced her Mama had been right.

I made my discovery quite by accident. A few days after Mama died, Aunt Nancy and Uncle Isaiah helped me retrieve the remaining items due me. As I collected Mother's last needlepoint from the mantle over the fireplace, I remembered the new litter of puppies. They were old enough to wean and Mason had reluctantly promised me I could take one of them with me. I told Aunt Nancy where I was going and raced out of the house to the back of the barn where Mason kept the pups.

I knew which one I wanted. I picked her up and cuddled her soft, furry body beneath my chin. As I did so, I noticed a pretty blue bottle sitting on a shelf. Curious, I pulled it off the shelf thinking I would carry it with me to use as a flower vase. As I drew it close, I saw an imprint on one side and a label on the other. The imprint read "poison." The label read "arsenic." I did not know what arsenic was, but I did know what poison was. I dropped the bottle into the straw.

At that moment, I heard footsteps. I turned to see Mason entering the barn. When he saw me, he looked toward the shelf behind me. I pushed the bottle with my foot back into the straw and ran toward the door.

As I passed Mason, he grabbed my shoulder and stopped me. He glared at me for a moment before whispering, "Mama isn't here to protect you anymore. You'd better remember that."

He did not admit guilt, and I did not accuse him. An empty bottle did not signify guilt. Nevertheless, he terrified me.

On the way to my new home, I sat in the back of the wagon with my pup. I held my tongue. Who would believe me? Everyone had already dismissed my insistence that Mother had signed her last will changing the list of those who were to inherit from her estate. They would never believe I had seen a mysterious bottle much less that someone had used its contents to poison Mama.

Several weeks after Mama's funeral, I did get up the courage to approach my aunt, although my voice trembled when I did.

"Aunt Nancy, what does the word arsenic mean?" I asked.

"Why do you ask?"

"I saw it on a bottle." I told her about the bottle in the barn.

She said, more to herself than to me, "I suspected as much. Charlotte was right after all."

Aunt Nancy argued with herself and me all morning then went to see the sheriff that afternoon. He called together a group of townsmen, and they went to the farm to search for the arsenic bottle.

By then, Mason must have gotten rid of the bottle. The sheriff's men searched the house, the barn and other outbuildings, and the slave quarters, but they never found that pretty blue bottle.

At the inquest, the county coroner questioned Mama's doctor first. Doctor Huddle twitched about in his chair before answering as if he took offense at being asked anything. "Humph," he said. "I told Charlotte I was certain it was some kind of cancer, most likely stomach or female. I saw no reason to consider any kind of poisoning."

Next, the coroner questioned my brother. Mason looked around the room with his usual smirk and air of condescension. "I have never had arsenic on the farm," he declared. "Daddy never kept it, either. You have to understand that Olivia has a vivid imagination." He glared at me with a fierce hatred in his eyes. "Where she learned of arsenic," he said, "I do not know." He then turned his attention to Aunt Nancy. Through clenched teeth and with narrowed eyes, he added, "Perhaps she had some tutoring in the matter."

Finally, the coroner questioned Aunt Nancy. She looked small and frightened sitting up there in front of all those men. I jumped up to run to her side, but Grandma grabbed my arm. Aunt Nancy smiled at me and then held her head up and told the jurors what she knew.

"Charlotte suspected she was being poisoned," said Aunt Nancy. "She said her full sickness came on too fast and progressed too quickly. I agreed with her on that. After she died and Olivia found the bottle labeled arsenic, I knew in my heart Charlotte had been right." She never said Mason's name, but she held his eye while she testified.

No one ever called on me. Grandma Mary insisted I was too young to be questioned.

In the end, the jurors dismissed our claims. Without the bottle labeled arsenic, they had nothing to support what Aunt Nancy and I said. They agreed with the doctor's suspicion that cancer most likely explained Mama's death.

My assertions and Aunt Nancy's visit to the sheriff infuriated my grandparents and my other aunts and uncles. Grandpa Abraham chastised Aunt Nancy for believing the words of a child. Grandma Mary threatened me with punishment if I didn't stop imagining things and telling tales.

Uncle Isaiah told Aunt Nancy and me to give it up. "There is nothing more that can be done about it," he said, "regardless of the cause of Charlotte's death. Nothing except to keep Olivia safe and that we will do."

Grandma Mary even forbade me to mention my baby doll sister.

"You must remember," she said. "We told you often enough when you were little. You lost a doll when you were a child, and you convinced yourself it was your baby sister. You never had a baby sister or brother, either, for that matter. Now I don't want to hear any more about it."

I continued to argue with her, and she and I had a great row. It is with great difficulty that we have attempted to be civil toward each other during the years since.

Now if some future descendant of mine is reading this, you know not only part of Daniel and Hannah and Miriam's story but Mama's story as well. I have no idea how Miriam's or my stories will end, but I will never stop searching for Hannah and Miriam in the faces I see or asking those who might have known them if they have had any word. Perhaps someday someone will find a better way to search for a missing person.

I will end this journal with my own last note to Hannah and Miriam. I hope that someday you or one of your descendants will learn that Mama and I never forgot you and never stopped loving you.

Your niece and sister,

Olivia Goodwin, soon to be Olivia Woodson

* * *

As Abby finished reading, Enid watched Maude closely, uncertain if her expression was one of anger or physical distress. Maude might be firm and candid, even sharp tongued, but Enid had never known her to react with anger or to lose her temper. Now, with her teeth clenched and nostrils flared, her fists opening and closing, and her breath coming in sharp bursts, she looked as if she could do both.

"Maude?"

"This makes me so mad I could spit tenpenny nails as Granny used to say. Charlotte did sign her changed will. Then she was murdered. Mason killed her. Mason killed his own mother, my granny's mother. Granny Olivia was a child when he took her mother away from her. Olivia knew what he had done. No one except her aunt believed anything she said. If Mason Goodwin weren't dead, I'd kill him myself."

"Granny," said Abby. "Please. You're scaring me."

Maude took a deep breath. She held it for the longest moment and then let it go slowly. "I'm all right, Abigail. I'm angry, but I'm all right. Children and old people. No one thinks they have any sense at all. No one listens to them."

"I listen, Granny."

"Because you're still a child at heart, Abigail. Please don't ever change."

"I won't. I promise."

Enid watched the exchange without interrupting, giving Abby a chance to calm Maude before something did happen.

"Thank you for your promise, Abigail. I'd like to take a nap now, but I wish I could see what's in the file Lowell Franklin has, and I still need to figure out what the inheritance is in which Charlotte hid her will. What was the one other inheritance handed down from her grandmother? It must be here. I'm also very curious as to whether or not Olivia's *safe box* is still held at the bank. I do not recall any mention of it when she died, but I was so young. Could it be?"

"Could what be, Granny?"

"The last thing Granny Olivia tried to tell me. The last word she said was *account*. Could she have meant the savings account? Could she have put it in my name?"

"We need to find out."

"Indeed."

Enid chewed her lip. "We can't go to the bank today. However, I agree that the inheritance where she hid her will must be here. Charlotte wrote that she was going to sew the will into the end of her inheritance from her grandmother. The Bible was an inheritance. She doesn't say the books were an inheritance. So there must have been something else she inherited."

"Inheritance…. Other than the Bible…. The bobbin lace pillow! The only thing Charlotte had from her grandmother other than the family Bible. I removed it from the dower chest years ago and placed it in a glass box to protect and preserve it. It's in the bedroom on the left upstairs."

"I'll get it!" Abby jumped up and ran out of the room. She returned still at a run and out of breath. "Here it is, Granny."

She handed the glass box to Maude, who opened it and lifted the blue bolster pillow, taking care not to rearrange the wooden bobbins. Maude held it up for Enid to see.

"Such a practical tool and yet so beautiful," said Enid.

"The pillow is pretty, Granny, but it's shaped differently than I would have expected, and for the life of me, I do not see the function."

"See the white lace on it?"

Abby touched the delicate needlework and nodded her head.

"It's called a bobbin lace pillow because it was used to create lace with the threads on the bobbins. This one is a bolster pillow. There are other styles, like ring and block, and the pillows can also be in different sizes."

"These little wooden things are the bobbins?"

"Yes. I can only suppose the lace on the pillow is the last lace Charlotte worked before she died."

Maude ran her fingers over the lace and the threads. She lifted a bobbin and traced the thread from it.

"So where is the will?" asked Abby.

"I would expect it to be in one of the ends between the inner muslin liner and the outer cotton cover. Wait. Charlotte said she added a second cover piece to one end." Maude rubbed the cloth at both ends. "Here. This end. See the extra stitches? And the color is a shade different from the rest of the pillow. The will is between the two layers of cotton. More stitches to remove. Each time needing more care in the removal. Abigail?"

"Let me catch my breath first." She took a few deep breaths before placing the pillow in her lap. Then one snip at a time, she removed the stitches holding the false cotton cover. She removed the cover and exposed the hidden pages. "Here they are." She lifted the pages and held them out to Maude. Maude stared at the pages for several minutes, her hands trembling and her eyes filling up with tears.

"You read it, Abigail. Neither my voice nor my eyes are up to the task."

Abby read the will aloud and then handed it to Maude.

"Granny, it says everything that Charlotte's journal entry recorded. She changed her will to divide her estate equally among Mason, Olivia, and Miriam except for any money given to them during her lifetime or left to them in trust. She must have listed everything from the property and livestock down to the spoons and quilts. More to the point, she signed it. 'Charlotte Abbott Goodwin' in her own handwriting the same as on the front page of her journal entries."

Maude scanned the pages again herself.

"This is signed not only by Charlotte but by James Franklin, Mason Goodwin, and the secretary as Charlotte wrote, and it does not match the probate records we found. The copy for the lawyer's file must be missing, but Charlotte said her lawyer made a second copy for his files and each of them had signed it, too. I don't understand. I have to call Lowell Franklin back."

"Granny, he's coming tomorrow. Why not wait until then?"

"I'm being impatient, aren't I? But I must tell him."

Abby dialed. Someone answered.

"Granny, he's out of the office."

"Give them a message for him. Tell him I've found the signed will."

Abby left the message and hung up.

No one spoke.

Enid broke their silence.

"Speaking of the property, what happened to Olivia's part of the land?"

"I haven't thought about that in years. My great-grandfather, Terrence Woodson, had property when they married. Olivia sold her part of her parents' property because it adjoined Mason's. She and Terrence took the money from the sale and purchased another tract of land that adjoined Terrence's property."

Maude's cell phone rang. She handed it to Abby who answered it. Abby covered the mouthpiece before relaying the message.

"Granny, it's your cousin, Arthur Goodwin. He wants to come over and have a talk. He doesn't sound happy."

"Whew! I'm not sure I'm up for it, but I do want to talk to him, too. Charles must have told him about our visit. Tell him to come on over. I'll rest right here while we wait."

Abby conveyed the message and hung up, shrugging her shoulders as she glanced from Maude to Enid. Maude was already napping, tiny snores punctuating her shallow breathing.

Enid and Abby quietly collected and put away the dower chest and its treasures in preparation for Arthur's visit.

CHAPTER TWENTY-SEVEN

Before Arthur could knock on the front door, Enid opened it and shushed him.

"Arthur," she said, "do come in but please try not to upset Maude. Her health, as I'm sure you are aware, is not good."

Arthur entered the hallway. "Happens to the best of us. We get old before we mean to, and it's downhill from there. I'll try not to upset her, but she and I do need to talk."

"Come on into the living room."

Enid led the way and stepped aside for Arthur to enter the room first. Maude attempted to stand.

"Keep your seat, Maude. No need for niceties. We've known each other too long for that."

"We have known each other all our lives, but I can't recollect the last time you visited. You must have something important to say."

"I do at that."

"Have a seat then. You wouldn't have a problem with Abigail and Enid hearing whatever you have to say, would you?"

"Not Abigail. She's family. I suspect Enid knows everything by now anyway. She's the one been helping you dig into the past, right?

"Yes."

"So I guess they can both hear what I've got to say. I heard your musings at the family reunion. Then Charles called me and told me about your visit with him. He and I both know all our family's secrets or at least we think we do. I know my great-great-grandfather Peter Goodwin supposedly fathered a slave child or two. I also know his son Mason blamed Peter's behavior at the last and his subsequent death on the theft of his money and the freeing of the slaves at the end of the war. I know all that, but I'm not eager for folks outside the family to know about that or about Mason's problems, for which he held his mother responsible, especially the loss of his share of the money in the second trust account in Olivia's name that he never could figure out how to access."

"You knew about that account?"

"Every male descendant knew about it. Mason hoped someone would finally be able to break it, but he died before Olivia did, and no one ever tried to break it after his death. I don't even know what Olivia ended up doing with it. It was a story handed down, and that's all it was.

"Mason also suspected his mother had helped the three slaves escape and helped them steal his daddy's first money box. Because of that, he held her at least partly responsible for Peter's untimely death. Those stories got passed down through the sons, too, along with their anger and hatred of anyone with skin darker than theirs. I'm not concerned about the money. I've done all right for myself. I am concerned about anyone learning I may have black cousins. Some of my friends and business acquaintances might take issue with it. I'm running for county road superintendent and many of my most ardent supporters are—"

"Prejudiced."

"Your word, not mine."

"Arthur, are you aware of the inquest after Charlotte's death and of the missing will?"

"I've heard the stories. No proof of either one. More reason not to dig too deep, Maude. This doesn't concern only you. What you find will affect the rest of us, too. Maybe more than you can imagine."

"You're not trying to frighten me or threaten me, are you Arthur?"

"If I thought it would do any good, I might, but I know you better than that, Maude Everly. No, I'm trying to appeal to your good sense and family pride. Whatever you uncover, I hope you'll keep it in the family, better yet, to yourself. I certainly hope you won't add it to that file cabinet Enid has in the genealogy room."

"I can't promise that."

"I didn't expect you to, but I did have to try to persuade you. I don't even mind if Charles sells you the farm. I got no need of it. I would appreciate a little sensitivity on the matter. Well, I've said my piece. I'll be going now. I can find my way to the door."

Arthur nodded at each of the women in turn and left. After she heard the door close, Enid went to make sure it was locked. When she returned to the living room, Abby was wringing her hands.

"Miss Enid, Granny has had enough for one day. I want us to let her go to bed early."

"It has been a long day. We can discuss suspects tomorrow after Lowell Franklin brings the old files by. Does that meet with your approval, Maude?"

"Yes, especially the going to bed early part." Maude did not smile. She leaned back and closed her eyes. "I'll sit here while you turn the bedcovers down and get my gown out. Call me when you're ready."

CHAPTER TWENTY-EIGHT

Wednesday, August 10, 2011

Before Enid could get out of bed the next morning, she heard Abby stirring around. She squinted at the clock on the bedside table and groaned.

No way I can fall back to sleep in fifteen minutes. I might as well get up.

By the time her alarm rang, she had finished with her morning routine and slipped into her bathrobe. She turned off the alarm and shuffled into the hallway.

A thump-thump on the stairs startled her. She grabbed at her chest and breathed a sigh of relief when she saw Abby. Her relief ended with another sigh when she saw the wheelchair Abby drug behind her.

Enid went up a few steps and said, "Here, let me help you with that."

"Thanks."

Together, they got the wheelchair down and opened.

"What's wrong, Abby?"

"Granny is weaker this morning. It was all she could do to make it into the bathroom and back. She's afraid to try to walk to the kitchen or the living room. She sent me upstairs for Gramps' old wheelchair."

"Let's wipe it off first. It's covered with dust and cobwebs."

After wiping the wheelchair down, they rolled Maude to the kitchen for breakfast and back to her bedroom after breakfast to get dressed for the day. Enid left them to do the same.

Later, she followed Maude and Abby into the living room. She inhaled the floral scent of Maude's powder.

A little stronger than usual but still such a pleasant scent. I'll always associate it with Maude. Stop it! You're talking as if she's already gone!

Soon after they got Maude settled in the living room on the sofa, they heard a knock at the front door. Enid went to let Lowell in and found Vance with him. She led them to the living room.

When she saw them both, Maude snapped at Lowell. "You didn't have to bring Vance with you. I'm sure he has work to do at the office."

Lowell glowered at Maude. "And I don't?"

Maude pinched her lower lip with the upper one and didn't respond.

Lowell sat in the chair closest to Maude and set his upright briefcase on the opposite side of the chair. He opened it enough to remove two file folders and then snapped it closed again.

"Everyone waits until the last minute, and everyone wants everything done when they want it done. When we leave here, we're going to see another client who needs to sign papers, and I need Vance to witness them."

"You don't have to explain, but I do hope you have time to take care of my concerns before you leave. Lowell, we have found Charlotte's copy of her last will and testament, not the one recorded with the probate records. The one with her last changes. Charlotte did sign it. Her lawyer must have made a copy, and he certainly would have known about it because he signed it, too. I don't understand."

Maude pulled the signed will Charlotte had hidden in the bobbin lace pillow from the envelope in her lap. She glanced at it and then handed it to Lowell.

"Read this and note the signatures at the bottom. They include James Franklin's signature."

Lowell opened and closed his mouth. The color drained from his face. He shifted in his seat and dropped one of the file folders, its contents fanning out across the floor. As he leaned over to push the papers back into the folder and pick it up, he glanced at Enid out of the corner of his eye before turning his attention back to Maude.

"I don't understand," said Lowell, his voice rising as he continued. I assure you that Charlotte did not sign the copy of the new will in her file. I have no way of knowing whether or not she may have taken a copy home to read, signed it, and failed to return it before she died. Here are hers and Peter's files. Look through them yourself."

Maude snatched the files from him. "I'll look through them, but that makes no sense because James Franklin's, Mason Goodwin's, and the secretary's signatures are all on the will."

Enid watched Lowell and Vance while Maude and Abby spent several minutes examining every paper in both files. She could not help but notice Vance's frown as he observed his employer. When he caught Enid watching him, his frown gave way to an impassive stare.

Maude finished reviewing the files and passed them on to Enid before turning her attention back to Lowell.

"Lowell, what possible reason could she have had for hiding the only copy?"

"She was sick at the time. Perhaps she was too weak or wasn't thinking straight."

Abby whispered, "How would he know that?"

Maude continued. "No, she would have made sure her lawyer had a signed copy as well. You keep looking, Lowell. You keep looking."

Lowell blustered. "I have living clients to attend to, Maude."

"Yes, and I'm one of them."

"I'll see what I can find."

"Thank you." He reached to take the file folders from Enid.

"I'd hoped you would make a copy of the contents for me to keep," said Maude with a huff.

"Maude Everly!" He stopped, mumbled under his breath, and continued. "I'll have my secretary make copies when I get back to the office. You or Abby can pick them up at your convenience."

"Thank you." Maude's response was equally curt.

"I'm leaving now," said Lowell, "after I use the men's room, that is if you don't mind. Vance, you can go on out to the car."

"Sure, Mr. Franklin, after I make a quick phone call."

Lowell scowled at Vance but did not comment. He slipped the files into his briefcase, closed it, picked it up, and left the room.

When Lowell was out of hearing distance, Vance spoke.

"I don't need to make a phone call, Miss Maude. I do need to tell you some things, though, about the will, the accounts, and...about me. I won't have time now. May I come back later?"

"Yes, of course."

"I...I must ask you not ever to reveal what I tell you, any of it. If you do, I could lose my job."

"I will not tell anyone the name of my source. Come back when you can."

"I will. Before I leave, let me tell you this much. If you've done much research, you must have discovered that Peter and Charlotte had slaves. One of those slaves was a young woman named Hannah. I'm a descendant of Hannah's half brother. Celia was their mother, but...they didn't have the same father."

Maude reached out to Vance. He took her hand in his.

"Vance," said Lowell from the doorway, "aren't you ready to go yet?"

"Yes, sir. I was saying goodbye. I'm on my way." He nodded at Maude before following Lowell out.

Enid locked the door behind them and returned to the living room.

"Enid," said Maude, "maybe he can help us."

"Maybe so. He did seem puzzled by Lowell's comments and actions."

Maude chuckled.

"What's funny, Granny?"

"I'm sorry. My mind jumps nowadays more than I care for it to. This time to Lowell and his *men's room*. He did the same thing the last time he and Lucille were here. 'Maude,' he said, 'would you mind if I visit the men's room?' I told him, 'I don't have a men's room, but you're welcome to use the facilities.'

When he returned, I teased him and said, 'That didn't take long.' Lucille snickered and said, 'Men never take long.' Lowell makes up for it, though, by going more often. I shouldn't poke fun. He could have…what is it…a prostate or bladder problem. I'm sorry. I needed to talk about someone other than myself for a minute. That said, I do wish Dr. Finley would call. Abby, where's the wheelchair? I want to lie down in the bed for a short while."

"I put it in the hallway, Granny. I'll get it."

When Abby turned to leave, Maude leaned forward and whispered. "Enid, I'm on my way out of this world."

"We need to call Dr. Finley again."

"I want to die at home."

"What if it isn't time for you to die?"

"He hasn't called with the test results. The hospital may not have them yet."

"Will you let us call him and be sure?"

"If you think it will help."

As Abby pushed the wheelchair through the doorway, Maude's cell phone rang. She checked it.

"It's about time Dr. Finley called me back. I do hope he has the test results."

So do I, Maude, so do I, thought Enid as she pressed her hands together and offered up a silent prayer.

CHAPTER TWENTY-NINE

"Maude," said Enid. "If you don't mind, put it on speaker, so Abby and I can hear what he says."

Maude nodded and tapped speaker before answering. "Dr. Finley, it's about time you called me back. Have you heard from my blood and urine tests?"

"Maude, is Abby with you?"

"Yes. Why?"

"Is she listening?"

"Yes. Tell me! Why?"

"Abby," said the doctor, "take Maude to the emergency room now."

Abby took the phone.

"Dr. Finley, I'm not sure we can get her in and out of the car this morning."

"I'll send an ambulance. Stay with her until they get there. Then come with her to the hospital."

Maude took the phone back and yelled into it. "Dr. Finley, what is wrong with me?"

"Maude, please calm down. The tests do show evidence of arsenic in your system. I'll meet you at the hospital and explain it all then. Hang up now so I can call an ambulance."

Maude closed her phone. Her hands trembled and the color drained from her face. "I knew it. I tossed and turned last night, worrying all of this business in my poor old head. When I did drift off to sleep, I dreamed about my last conversation with Granny Olivia. I don't know if I remembered more of our last day or if I added to it, but in the dream, I heard Granny whispering, telling me I must set things right before I died. Telling me I must give her sister's descendants their birthright and their heritage. Now I'm dying and being threatened if I don't keep quiet, and I cannot imagine who would threaten me or want to kill me to prevent me from exposing something that happened one hundred and fifty years ago." She took Abby by the hand and pulled her to the sofa beside her. "I'm afraid to put the burden on you, Abigail, but what else can I do?"

Enid sat in the chair next to Maude. "Whatever happens, we will continue to search. I will search myself when you're unable to come to the library, and if you...leave us before we find the answers, I'll help Abby search. Patrick and I will work together to keep her safe."

"Thank you, Enid. Thank you, Abigail, for believing in me when no one else did."

Tears flooded Abby's eyes. "I'm going to go unlock the door." She jumped up and ran to the front door.

When she returned, she had wiped the tears away. She sat beside her granny and held her hand.

They soon heard the sound of the siren getting closer and closer until it stopped.

"They're here. I'll bring them to you." Abby again ran out of the living room. This time she returned with the EMTs.

"Mrs. Everly, we have instructions to carry you straight to the ER. We're going to do what we need to do on the way."

Maude worked her way to the edge of the sofa.

"Don't stand up. Instead, lie back so we can slide you off the sofa." Maude's eyes darted from the EMT to Abby and back again. "Don't be frightened, Mrs. Everly." When they had her situated and covered, they strapped her onto the gurney and headed out with her.

"I'm going to ride with you, Granny."

"I'm sorry, ma'am, but we can't allow anyone to ride along. You should go on and meet us at the ER."

"Granny?"

"It's all right, Abigail. This is the way they do things. I don't like it, either, but I'll be in good hands. You let Enid bring you to the hospital."

Enid placed her hand on Abby's shoulder. "Get Maude's and your handbags and be sure her insurance cards are in hers. I'll get mine, and we'll leave right behind the ambulance."

Abby raced up the stairs to her bedroom first then down the stairs to Maude's bedroom. Enid met her at the front door.

As they pulled away from the house behind the ambulance, Abby sat frozen, her face a mask of heartbreak and fear.

"Granny made me promise what she promised her great-grandmother when she was nine. I'm twice that age, but I'm scared. What if she's dying? I am a responsible person, but I need help."

"You're going to continue the search then even if something happens to Maude, even if…if she dies?"

"I am."

"You don't need to stay in Maude's house alone."

"I don't want to, either. Under the circumstances, would you consider staying with me? For a few nights at least? We don't have to tell anyone else."

"Except Patrick."

"Chief Mulhaney?"

"Yes. In fact, he needs to know more than that, and he needs to search the house. We'll call him when we know something more about Maude. For now, Abby, have you been feeling ill in any way?"

"No, not at all. Why?"

"Maude said the two of you searched for poisons after you moved in."

"We did. Kitchen and garden shed first. Then the other rooms. We didn't find anything labeled or unlabeled that we thought might be harmful. Granny has always been careful about such things for as long as I can remember. I do agree with the doctor on one thing. I don't know how she could have been exposed to arsenic naturally or accidentally especially without me feeling any effects."

"I searched, too, and I'm of the same mind. We can't rule out anything yet, though. Do you and Maude eat and drink any of the same things? Do you use any of the same soaps and detergents?"

"Hmm. Let me think. Detergents, yes. Bath soaps, no. We don't even use the same bathrooms. As to food and drink, yes and no. Granny is a tea drinker. I'm more of a coffee drinker. We both drink water, but Granny drinks tap water, and I drink bottled water. Food, though, is pretty much the same, although Granny picks at her food while I eat as if every meal will be my last. As I'm not sick, I doubt anything could have been in our food."

"If you don't mind, Abby, until we can rule out poison, promise me not to eat, drink, or use anything Maude has that you haven't. In fact, maybe we should restock what we'll need for a week or so and put what's at the house away until after Patrick can check everything."

"I'm good with that. I'm also good with carryout and pickup meals. You don't have to prepare them!" Abby glanced sideways at Enid managing a ghost of a crooked smile for the first time since Dr. Finley's call.

* * *

Enid and Abby entered Maude's cubicle minutes after the EMT rolled her into the ER. Everyone who entered the cubicle after them wore personal protective equipment, including Dr. Finley.

"Am I a danger to you?" asked Maude.

"Probably not," said the doctor. "We know we're dealing with arsenic poisoning. However, I suspect it was introduced through your skin. If so, you could have traces on your skin now, so we're going to follow protocol. First, we're going to take blood and urine samples to confirm the original tests. Then, we're going to decontaminate you and your clothing."

"As in give me a bath?"

"More or less. Then we'll do an abdominal x-ray and an EKG. After that, we'll start treatment. Later, we'll do a nerve conduction study. Afterwards, we'll discuss at greater length those symptoms you've been trying to tell Isabel and me about. As we move forward, I'll keep an eye on your urine levels and kidney and liver function. If Patrick thinks I need to test your hair to determine when the arsenic first entered your system, I will. I may put you on oxygen for the night. Just to take away any breathing distress you might have."

In what seemed to Enid to take forever but actually took only a couple of hours, the ER staff had Maude hooked up to some kind of medication and ready for transfer to ICU. Dr. Finley had overseen everything, declining to provide Abby and Enid any details while he worked. All he would tell them was that Maude's vital signs were stable and he was giving her something to counteract the arsenic. All they could do was reassure Maude that they were with her.

As one of the nurses left with Maude for the ICU, Dr. Finley approached them.

"I will tell you upfront before you have a chance to point it out, I almost made a fatal error. If she had not insisted…but she did, and I'm hopeful we've started treatment in time."

"Treatment long overdue," said Enid. She was so furious she didn't trust herself to say more. Abby was crying too hard to ask any questions.

"Yes, you are right, but I cannot imagine how she came in contact with that much arsenic."

Enid and Abby stared at him with open mouths, neither of them able to speak.

Finally, Abby blurted out, "I knew it! Granny knew it! Nobody would listen to her!"

The doctor cleared his throat. "Abby, you need to call your grandmother immediately and get her up here."

Abby breathed several deep breaths before responding. "Don't tell me to do anything immediately, Dr. Finley. If you had listened to us, Granny wouldn't be fighting for her life right now. I will call Grandma but because that is what I would have done anyway, not because you told me to." Her eyes narrowed and she stared him down, as if challenging him to contradict her.

Enid stepped closer. "While Abby calls Isabel, I'll call Chief Mulhaney."

The doctor's eyes widened. "Why would you do that?"

"You know as well as we do that this was not an accidental poisoning."

"We don't know that."

"Chief Mulhaney will make that determination."

Both women walked away from the doctor to make their calls. Enid heard his footsteps as he hurried down the hall in the direction the nurse had taken Maude.

* * *

In the hallway outside the intensive care unit, Enid tapped the cell phone in her hand for the third time as she paced the floor and waited for Patrick to answer. She gave Abby, who stood nearby, a quick nod as she heard his familiar greeting.

"Enid?"

"Yes, Patrick. We need you to come to the hospital."

"Whose we? When and why? Are you all right?"

"We are Maude, Abby, and myself. When is now. I'm fine. Abby's shook up but otherwise fine. Maude is not so great right now although she is finally getting the help she needs."

Enid bit her lip as she waited through Patrick's pause.

"I do have a job."

"This comes under that heading. Someone has poisoned Maude with arsenic." Again, Enid waited out the pause.

"Arsenic? The doctor confirmed this?"

"He confirmed the exposure. He's reluctant to say it was intentional."

"He hasn't returned my latest calls."

"I suspect he didn't want to. He didn't want me to call you."

"So what happened?"

"Maude called him yesterday, but he wasn't in the office. She insisted that the receptionist have him return her call this morning. He must have gotten the message because he finally read the reports and called for Maude to come to the emergency room."

"I'm leaving the station now."

"Good. We're outside the ICU."

* * *

Fifteen minutes later, Enid watched as Patrick strode down the hall toward them. When he reached her side, he touched her arm. She nodded to him.

"I'm fine."

Patrick turned his attention to Abby.

"Abby, I understand from Enid that you have the authority to make decisions for Maude."

"I do."

"Are you prepared to go head-to-head with your grandmother?"

"Yes. Why?"

"She pulled into the parking lot as I got onto the elevator."

The two women drew simultaneous breaths before he continued.

Patrick raised an eyebrow at Enid. "I thought Maude and her research were to provide a pleasant distraction."

"So did I. They did for a time. Not so much now."

Patrick cleared his throat and pulled out his notebook.

"Abby, I need to know if you will grant me permission to have my men search the house for anything that might contain arsenic."

"By all means. Granny and I did search several weeks ago. Miss Enid searched, too. None of us found any kind of poison. Obviously, we missed it."

"Do you know of anyone who might have poisoned her intentionally?"

"We've talked around this for several days now, but we haven't really identified a guilty person, a suspect. That was at the top of our to-do list for today. We ended up here instead. When Granny is better, we'll come up with a list."

"I may need to know before then."

The three of them turned as one when they heard Isabel's voice and her clacking heels from the other end of the hall. Enid recognized the man with her as her brother Barton.

"We'll probably have to finish this later. I want to talk to Dr. Finley and have my officers search the house. I'll stick around a few minutes in case I need to put out a fire here."

Isabel and Barton reached the ICU. Isabel pierced the group with a threatening scowl before addressing Abby.

"What's all this about? Why didn't you call me before you brought Mama to the hospital? What's Enid doing here? This isn't her business." She frowned at Patrick but didn't ask about his presence.

"Grandma, I'm responsible for Granny's welfare. We didn't have time to call you before we came. Miss Enid happened to be at the house and was good enough to drive me here."

"You're too young for this much responsibility. This is something her children should do." Isabel stepped toward her granddaughter.

Abby stiffened. "Grandma, I'm eighteen. I'm the responsible party. I acted responsibly, something the rest of you have not done."

Barton opened his mouth to speak. Patrick interrupted. He and Isabel listened in stunned silence.

"Before either of you continues," said Patrick, "I'm here because of Dr. Finley's findings from the recent lab work, which do confirm that Maude is suffering from arsenic poisoning. It appears that neither Maude's children nor her doctor acted responsibly or quickly enough. I will have more questions for each of you in the near future."

Isabel snapped her mouth closed, dismissing him as she spun around to face Abby again. Abby pulled up straight and held her grandmother's glare with one of her own.

Enid started to speak but stopped when Patrick caught her eye with a slight headshake.

Isabel harrumphed and said, "When can I see my mother?"

"At the next visiting hour," said Abby. "I'll see her first. Then you can go in. But if you upset her, I will prevent you from seeing her again."

With a grunt, Isabel and Barton left them and entered the waiting room across the hall.

Patrick waited for the door to close behind them before continuing. "Do either of you have any thoughts as to where Maude had contact with the arsenic?"

"None at all," said Enid.

"Abby, have you felt ill?"

"No, sir."

The three of them stopped talking when Dr. Finley pushed through the ICU doors. He glanced from them to Isabel and Barton who stood in the waiting room with their backs to them.

"I see everyone is here. I was about to have a talk with Maude, but she wants Abby and Enid in the room to hear everything. No doubt you'll want to come along, too, Chief Mulhaney. I would like to slip back in before Isabel and Barton see us. I'll update them later."

He whirled around to push open the ICU doors.

"I suppose he expects us to follow him," said Enid.

* * *

Enid shuddered as they walked into the sterile, machine-filled room. She had not had occasion to be in the ICU since Bryce's first heart attack some fifteen years ago. As much as she appreciated the care he had received, she was thankful when they released him to a regular room, more thankful for their return home and the five additional years they had together. She hoped Maude's stay would be short and followed by a swift recovery.

The four of them gathered around Maude's bed, she and Patrick on one side, Abby and Dr. Finley on the other side. The beeping monitors punctuated their words.

"I thought I could have only two visitors at a time."

Dr. Finley cleared his throat. "I can be here whenever I want to be. Patrick can be, too. So technically, you have only two visitors, Abby and Enid. Besides, I want them to hear what I have to tell you. I know I'll have to repeat it for Isabel and Barton, but twice is enough."

"So tell me."

"It does look like you have arseniasis."

"English, please."

"Chronic arsenic poisoning. I have to say I never suspected it because you never presented with any gastrointestinal or breathing disorders, no cardiovascular disorders. You had neurological symptoms common to aging, symptoms that could have been the result of any number of other conditions including dementia, stroke, or just simple decline."

"But they weren't. And you didn't check for any of those conditions."

"No, they weren't. And no, I didn't. While I could be wrong—"

"Again?"

"Again. While I could be wrong, your symptoms and your level of decline make me think your exposure was by dermal absorption—through the skin—of an inorganic compound rather than by ingestion or inhalation. Do you have anything in your house or shed that you might use as an insecticide or wood treatment or even a prescribed topical cream to which you might have exposed yourself?"

"No. A thousand times, no. You would know if I had a prescription containing arsenic."

Maude jerked the white sheets up and crossed her arms over them. Dr. Finley continued as if he hadn't noticed.

"No seafood lately?"

"No."

"I also think your exposure was limited to a small but constant amount. Constant enough to maintain and maybe increase toxicity but small enough to prevent your symptoms from being more pronounced sooner. The level of arsenic in your urine is consistent with chronic exposure. However, the abdominal x-ray looked okay, and the EKG detected only a slight cardiac arrhythmia, which I hope will correct itself. Truth be told, I wouldn't have thought symptoms would have appeared so soon, and you first reported them a week after you think the poisoning started."

"I am ninety years old. It doesn't take as long or as much of anything to affect me anymore."

"I know."

"What treatment will we do? Will I live through it?"

"It may take a while for recovery, and you may not get over all the effects, but I'd say you will probably live. You've managed to survive arsenic poisoning better than I would have expected."

"I've always been healthy."

"You have."

"Which is why you should have listened to me."

"Are you going to remind me of that the rest of your life?"

"I expect so. Now. What treatment?"

"As your symptoms don't suggest the need, we're going to hold off on any decisions concerning kidney dialysis, blood transfusion, or bowel irrigation. If we have to do them, we will. I want to do all we need to do, but I don't want to do anything we don't need to do and overtax your system. The first line of defense is to remove you from the source and observe you, so you're going to be here a few days. The second thing is to remove what arsenic we can from your body. We're already doing that with a chelating agent, which will bind with the arsenic and accelerate its removal from your body through your urine. That's another reason to keep a check on your urine flow. I do have to tell you the agents are toxic. We need to monitor you closely. This is not something you can do at home."

"I could die without this chelating agent removal process?"

"You could. It had progressed to the point I was afraid you would."

"I could die from the treatment."

"You could. I don't think you will."

"I expect you to be careful."

"I will. I—"

"What?"

"If this didn't occur accidentally, it was done by someone with knowledge and access."

"Because…."

Dr. Finley glanced at Patrick. "Because arsenic preparations are different. Individual absorption rates are different. Effects in the body are different. The poisoner has to have the knowledge to determine or adjust the dose and the access to change the item containing the arsenic if he does adjust the dose. As I've already said, you had to have repetitive exposure. One incident would not do this."

"So what now?"

"We identified the dermal effects when you were in my office last Friday. We know from your blood tests you're a bit anemic. We can check the levels remaining in your hair and skin if necessary. You do not appear to have any damage to your liver or kidneys, but we will monitor them. You could have some permanent neurological deficits, but you could fully recover. We'll continue to keep an eye out for any other damage that might still show up."

"I suppose things could have been worse."

"They would have if you hadn't butted heads with everyone, including me. You could have had seizures or gone into shock or a coma."

"I could have died. I didn't. I will die. We all will. But I could have died sooner than I was supposed to and may still because of this. We both know that, but I'd prefer to dwell on what is rather than what might have been."

"Good. Now, Chief Mulhaney, I'm supposing you have questions."

"You've answered most of my questions. One thing I do want to confirm. You're convinced the exposure was through the skin?"

"I didn't say convinced. I said I suspected dermal exposure. Maude has always had a strong constitution, and that could explain her lack of gastrointestinal problems, but at her age, I wouldn't think she could have avoided some stomach distress if she ingested the arsenic. Of course, I obviously could be wrong. If you're asking me whether or not you should look for an ingestible source, I'd say look for any source."

"That was my inclination. Maude, Abby has given me permission to have my officers collect items from your house for testing."

"That's perfectly fine with me. The sooner, the better."

"We should allow Maude some time to rest," said Enid. "Perhaps we could discuss other matters somewhere else."

"Rest would be good," said Dr. Finley. "Abby, leave your cell number at the nurse's station so we can reach you if we need to."

"I will."

Patrick and Dr. Finley left the room together.

"Granny, I've told Grandma and Uncle Barton that they can come in during the next visitation time, but I'll be close by."

"I know you will, Abigail." Maude turned to Enid. Her lips quivered as she spoke. "You take care of her, Enid."

"I will. We'll take care of each other. I'll go on out and give you two a minute alone."

Enid joined Patrick in the hallway outside the ICU and waited for Abby.

* * *

"Patrick, instead of joining Isabel and Barton in the waiting room, let's see if the chapel is empty. If it is, it would be more private. If someone does come in, we can leave."

"That's fine with me."

"Abby, do you want to join your grandmother and uncle in the waiting room?"

"No, Dr. Finley is telling them everything he told us, and I don't want to deal with them right now anyway."

"Good. You can help me fill in the details for Patrick."

Once they were settled in the chapel, Patrick wrote without looking up as Enid rattled off the reasons for Maude's research and the events of the last few weeks—the note, the intrusions at Maude's house, the threatening phone calls, the close calls for herself and Abby, and Maude's steady and rapid decline. Both Patrick and Abby frowned when she mentioned her own threatening phone call.

"Enid—"

"I know. I should have told you both. Next time, I will."

"Of course, you will." When he finished writing, he looked up and asked Abby, "When did Maude first see Dr. Finley because of her decline?"

"The reunion was seven and a half weeks ago. Granny started feeling poorly a week and a half after the reunion. She saw Dr. Finley a week later. That would have been five weeks ago. He told her he couldn't find anything wrong other than the natural decline due to her age. Grandma insisted it was all in Granny's head. It wasn't until last Friday, at Granny's insistence, that Dr. Finley finally did lab work—blood and urine tests."

"Did you accompany Maude on her office visits?"

"Not the one five weeks ago. Grandma went with her, but Granny always told me everything that was said and done, including how Grandma insisted that Granny was imagining most of it and that she was more concerned about dementia. Grandma about convinced Dr. Finley of it, too. I did go with Granny and Miss Enid last Friday, though."

"So neither your grandmother nor Dr. Finley suspected foul play?"

"No, but Granny and I did." Abby bristled.

"I know, but I need to get all this written down. For the record again, you do have durable power of attorney for both financial and medical decisions, right?"

"Yes." Abby clipped her response.

"Anything more than that?"

"I'm responsible for everything. I'm also her executrix."

"Any reason Maude didn't want one of her children to handle arrangements?"

"Granny had grown quite irritated with them for thinking she was senile and needed to be in a nursing home. Whatever they or anyone else thinks, her mind is fine. And so was her body until shortly after the reunion."

"Can her lawyer confirm she was in her right mind when she made her last legal decisions?"

"Of course. Miss Enid was there. Granny made him say it back to her before she told him her changes."

"I realize the three of you set yourselves the tasks of solving several mysteries—Charlotte's secrets, her murder, and the whereabouts of Miriam's descendants along with the identity of the person threatening and poisoning Maude. I, on the other hand, have one mystery to solve—the identity of Maude's would-be killer, who also happens to be targeting the two of you. Enid, for Abby's and your sake, you two need to heed my instructions."

"Are you sure you don't mean heed your warnings?"

"Take it however you want to. You will anyway. The point is if someone tried to murder Maude because of her family history research, then you are both, but especially Abby, in danger as well. I'm asking you, if you must do something, confine it to your research into the past. Let me worry about the present. Perhaps that will keep you both safe."

"Safe? Patrick, it was her research into the past that led to all of this!"

"Actually, we don't know that. However and on second thought, maybe you should discontinue all of your research until I've *dug* a little deeper myself. In the meantime, the two of you could have been exposed. You need to be tested. I'm going to instruct Dr. Finley to arrange for that to be done before you leave the hospital.

"As soon as I leave the hospital, I'm going to have a couple of my officers meet me at Maude's house. We'll remove everything and anything that's been opened from edible and drinkable items to cleaners and such. We'll send the most likely sources to the Crime Lab run by the Tennessee Bureau of Investigation to be tested for arsenic. I'll ask our district attorney to ask the Tennessee Bureau of Investigation to push the items to the front. If they will, we can get the results within about five days instead of two or three months.

"In the meantime, because we don't know the exposure route, dermal or oral, the house needs to be cleaned and the clothes need to be washed. You could have someone do it or you two could do it, but I want you to wear something you can throw away and use gloves, masks, and maybe even safety glasses with side shields. When you've finished the laundry, you need to run one of those cleaning cycles in the washer."

"So we don't have to throw clothes away?"

"No, none except those you clean in, but you do need to launder them. Of course, you'll also have to get all new supplies except for anything not opened already. Why the frown?"

"I'm upset on so many levels. Abby's left with an impossible situation. Another dear friend may leave us. If she does, it will not be by natural causes but by intent, and it will be before she can complete her last mission for herself and her great-grandmother. The worst part is that none of this was necessary. This kind of thing happens to old people all the time."

"Murder?"

"Not necessarily murder, but as Maude says often, no one listens to old people. No one takes them seriously. If they say or do anything out of the ordinary, it's because of their mental decline. No one believes them. They're imagining things, acting like a child, or making it all up. I've seen elderly friends *decline* for years before someone realized their problems were because of side effects from some medication they never needed in the first place or because of the combined effects of two medications or because they needed a different medication altogether. That's just three possibilities."

"You don't think you're overreacting a little?"

"So now I'm suffering from some form of dementia or other mental decline, too?"

"I didn't say that. I didn't mean that."

"You might as well have. I know sometimes it is what it appears to be, but sometimes it is not. Nothing should be dismissed out of hand. I didn't mean to snap at you, Patrick. But this happens to be one of my soapbox issues."

"I do understand. Now we're both on the case. We will resolve it."

"Thank you."

"Anytime. Now, let's get your tests scheduled. Then I'm off to collect suspicious items from the house. I'll call you when we're done. By the way, I do need the three of you to come up with that suspect list tomorrow." Enid nodded. "And one other thing. No arguments. I'll have a guard stationed outside Maude's room in ICU and a patrol car parked outside her house." He raised an eyebrow.

"I'm not arguing," said Enid.

"Me, either," said Abby.

"Good. Let's move."

By noon, Enid and Abby had been tested for arsenic levels. Both were within acceptable limits.

Together, they made a list of cleaning and laundry supplies and purchased them. As they put the last bag in the trunk of the car, both of their cell phones rang.

Enid stepped away and answered her phone.

"Patrick?"

"Yes. Have you finished shopping for cleaners and such?"

"We have."

"Our timing is perfect. My officers and I have collected every opened container in the house, and you and Abby are free to return home whenever you're ready."

"Good. I'll talk to you tomorrow."

Enid slid into the driver's seat and told Abby the news.

"Good. Grandma called. She and Granny have agreed that she can stay at the hospital in the waiting room overnight. Also, Granny's guard is already on duty. I confirmed both points with Granny. So we're free to clean!"

"Double good. Abby, after we get laundry collected, the washing machine going, and the kitchen cleaned, why don't you go to the grocery store for food items? I'll continue cleaning and doing laundry. Whatever I lack, we can finish together after we eat."

"Sounds like a plan to me."

At midnight, they bagged up their work clothes, showered, and dressed for bed.

"I'm exhausted," said Abby.

"Me, too, but I'm glad we finished. The house will be ready for Maude whenever they release her. You go on up to bed. I'll check the doors."

"Did you notice the patrol car parked outside?"

"I did."

"I'll sleep quite well tonight knowing they are out there."

"I hope we both do. We need to be fresh in the morning so we can produce that suspect list for Patrick."

As the two headed for their bedrooms, Enid shook her head.

We need the suspect list, but how can Patrick act on it without the TBI results? I cannot imagine which of the items taken might contain the arsenic. And what happens when Maude returns home from the hospital?

CHAPTER THIRTY

Thursday, August 11, 2011

The next morning found Enid pacing an empty hospital room waiting for someone to bring Maude from the ICU. Abby sat in a corner chair, popping up and down every time anyone passed the open door. Finally, a nurse rolled Maude in and asked them to step into the hallway while she transferred her from the gurney to the bed.

"You can go in now," said the nurse as she left.

Maude was sitting up in bed.

"So, what's next?"

"Granny?"

"Yes, Abigail, I do feel better. I don't feel like jumping on a trampoline, but I feel more like ninety and alive than ninety and half dead." She extended both arms toward Abby and wrapped her in an embrace. "I'll be okay, dear."

Tears filled Abby's eyes. "I hope so, Granny."

"Me, too. Now. No need to waste time. What's next? Is the house ready for me to return home?"

They all laughed.

"Yes, Granny, ready and waiting. Clean, clean, and clean. Mostly thanks to Enid."

"Abby did her share."

"New groceries in the refrigerator and cabinets?"

"All new and none opened yet. We're doing takeout for now."

"The next thing we need to do," said Enid, "is develop a suspect list. I'm sure we've all been thinking about who our suspects could be, but we've been a little too preoccupied to discuss them, not to mention having trouble believing someone really was out to stop us by whatever means necessary. We're all past that now, though, and the suspect discussion is way overdue."

"We can't forget our first mysteries, though. We know who killed Charlotte even if we can't prove it. We've uncovered most of her secrets, but several need follow-through. We think we know where Miriam's descendants live, but we need to make contact."

"All true, Granny, but if we don't figure out who tried to poison you, he could try something else—with even more success—and in the process prevent us from solving our other mysteries."

"We can concentrate on Maude's would-be killer," said Enid, "but we can keep our other mysteries in the back of our minds. We must do that because the other mysteries have to be the reason the killer is trying so hard to stop Maude's efforts."

"Which means he or she may already know the solutions to our other mysteries."

"Exactly."

"Which means our culprit must be someone in my family," said Maude.

"Or closely associated with your family."

"That doesn't narrow the field much," said Abby. "Sometimes I think everyone in town is descended from either Mason or Olivia."

A knock on the closed door interrupted their conversation.

"Come in," said Maude.

Vance Abbott opened the door.

"Hello, ladies. Miss Maude, we heard they were letting you out of ICU this morning. I decided to come by and ask if you were up for a visit."

"I am, Vance. Please do come in. Abigail, sit beside me on the bed and let Vance sit in your chair."

"I can stand."

"Nonsense," said Abby. "I've been sitting on the side of Granny's bed all my life. Sit. Please."

"Thank you both."

Vance sat in the chair.

Enid moved the corner chair closer to the bed.

"First, let me say that everyone at the office said to tell you they were praying for your quick recovery and return home. Your sudden hospitalization came as a shock to all of us. We hope it's nothing serious."

"Thank everyone for their well wishes and prayers. Thank you for your concern. I—"

Enid caught Maude's attention and gave her a slight shake of the head.

"We hope it's nothing serious, too. I'm already out of ICU. I may go home tomorrow."

"I'm pleased to hear that. As I had no idea how long you might be here, I thought it best to come by as soon as I could to finish my story."

"I'm glad you did. We're all curious. Please. Go on."

"I must remind you to keep my involvement in your learning of this confidential."

"Of course," said Maude.

"You know Lowell Franklin is a direct descendant of James Franklin, Peter and Charlotte's lawyer?"

"Yes. He's also married to Lucille, one of my distant cousins. That connection is why I stayed with the Franklin Law Firm after Lowell's father died, certainly not because of Lowell's winning personality."

Vance laughed. "I can understand that. You also know James Franklin prepared Peter and Charlotte's original wills and Charlotte's last will, which would have given one-third of everything to Miriam, the child of the slave Hannah."

"I do," said Maude.

"As I told you earlier, I'm a descendant of Hannah's half brother, Noah. Their mother, Celia, and Noah's father, George, and all of their children were slaves owned by Abraham and Mary Abbott, Charlotte's parents."

"Yes, I am aware of that. I was not aware before you told us that you were descended from Celia. I thought Celia and her husband left this area after they were freed."

"They did along with their youngest daughter and her husband. George took Abbott for his surname before he left, as did each of his sons. Most of his and Celia's children moved on. However, their son Noah, my ancestor, remained in Bakersville after being granted freedom at the end of the war. He had married, and his wife's family chose to stay here. He and his wife were expecting their first child, and she was near her time, so they stayed to be near her mother.

"He found work wherever he could. He eventually saved enough to buy a farm and became quite successful. As you are probably also aware, the Abbotts taught all of their slaves to read and write. Noah insisted that all of his children not only be taught the same but that they be educated in every way.

"He and his wife had to do much of that educating themselves until a school for black children was finally established close by. His children and grandchildren followed his lead, for which I am quite thankful. Some of his descendants chose to remain farmers and did well, but many of us chose professional careers.

"I myself hope to pass the bar soon. Lowell's father hired me during the summers while I was in college and law school. He encouraged me. He insisted Lowell do so, too. I like to think he would have done so anyway, but some days I have my doubts. I just wanted you to know our connection before I told you what I've learned over the last few years."

"I'm actually pleased to know your history. It adds another chapter to my own family research. Go on with what you've learned."

"Of course, I knew Hannah and Miriam's story handed down by Celia to her other children, but I knew nothing about Charlotte's last will or of a possible account set up for Miriam. Not until a little over two years ago, that is. Lowell is very technologically inclined and a little...OCD is what his wife calls it. His father was neither. This was a source of contention between them. In spite of his father's inclinations, Lowell had set up a database for their current clients. When his father died and Lowell became the senior partner, he asked me to help him develop a database for the firm's past clients. I was to go through all of the old files and record names, dates, and file contents in the database.

"He even mentioned providing a copy for you, Miss Enid, for use in the genealogy room. Not out of good will, I'm sure, but rather because people were frequently asking him about old cases and files of ancestors. If you had the information, he wouldn't have to deal with the researchers.

"While compiling these records, I recognized many names that were familiar to me for one reason or another, including the names of Peter and Charlotte Goodwin. When I went through Peter and Charlotte's files, I read Charlotte's unsigned will and learned of the account, possibly more than one.

"In one of the file cabinets, I also found a sealed box marked confidential. I showed it to Lowell. He opened it. The only item in it was an old rolodex. I asked him if he wanted me to record the information on the cards. He said maybe later, but it was several days before he brought it back to me. On many of the cards were mysterious even cryptic notes. On the card for Peter and Charlotte Goodwin was a note referencing an envelope labeled *Contingent* that was taped underneath the file drawer containing their files. I looked underneath every old file drawer we had but never found that envelope. I don't know if it had long since disappeared or if Lowell found it. If he did, he never mentioned it.

"While I knew Charlotte's unsigned will would have been essentially invalid, it did provide evidence that she tried to leave an inheritance for Miriam, Hannah's daughter, and it did make reference to *any accounts* set up by Charlotte.

"On a hunch, I went to the bank and asked for any account set up during or after the Civil War by Charlotte Goodwin for a slave named Miriam. I had no idea if it would still be there even if it had existed or if it could be accessed by any other family member. I was told no such account existed, and I didn't pursue it. However, the attendant who assisted me acted strangely. There may not have been any such account, but I thought you might want to consider looking into it yourself."

Maude glanced at Enid, and again, Enid gave her a slight shake of the head.

"I am glad you shared this. I do think the possibility is a reasonable one to consider, especially given the wording of Charlotte's intended last will. Given the attendant's behavior, I may follow up with the bank manager. He and I are good friends. Enid knows him well, too. He's an amateur genealogist himself."

"As no one knows what happened to Daniel, Hannah, or Miriam—even whether or not they lived—do you think if any money was due them, rather than leaving it in the bank, he would allow me to access it as I'm the only known relative living in the area?"

"I have no idea," said Maude. "I would think you would know more about that than I would."

"I can think of no legal precedent, especially considering the lapse of time, and I don't want to ask Lowell. However, the bank might leave the decision up to you as one of Charlotte's descendants."

Enid cleared her throat. When she had everyone's attention, she spoke. "The first order of business would be to ascertain whether or not there had ever been such an account. If so and it had been closed out, its existence would probably not have been recorded when the bank went from paper to electronic records."

"Enid, you and Abigail should go to the bank this afternoon and check on that. I'll stay here. I need to rest."

"Granny, I don't want to leave you alone."

Before Maude could speak, a voice from the doorway broke in.

"I don't know what your bank business is as it's no longer any of my business, but I'm sure I can sit with my mother for a few hours." Isabel looked only at her mother when she spoke.

"I'm sure you can, too," said Maude. "That's an excellent idea." She turned to Vance. "Thank you so much for coming by to check on me and for sharing your information with us. We will be talking again, I'm sure."

Vance stood. "You're welcome, Miss Maude. I hope you're
home soon and up and about." Before he left, he dipped his
head toward Abby and Enid but not toward Isabel.

Maude waved her hand toward the door. "Off with you
Abigail. Ask for the bank manager. Take Enid with you in case
he needs any persuasion. Enid, follow up on that other matter
as well. That box matter that Granny Olivia mentioned in her
last note."

"Box? Oh, box! Yes, by all means."

"Good. Now. Be gone."

"We're off, Granny. Grandma, call me if either of you needs
me."

"I will call," said Isabel. She gave Abby a kiss on the cheek
but kept her back to Enid.

Enid winked at Maude as she stood and followed Abby out
the door.

CHAPTER THIRTY-ONE

Enid led Abby across the slick tile floor, the clicking of their heels alerting the manager's assistant to their approach. The young woman looked up when they were halfway to her desk.

When Enid reached the curved front of the shiny walnut desk, she came to a stop, glanced at the nameplate, and spoke with authority.

"Miss Harper—"

"Mrs. Harper." The smug young woman sat straight in her chair. "How may I help you?"

"Mrs. Harper," said Enid with a slight nod of her head, "I am Mrs. Enid Gilchrist. This is Miss Abigail Croft. We need to speak with Mr. Saul Bolton."

Mrs. Harper's narrowed eyes foreshadowed her response.

"Mr. Bolton is busy at the moment. Do you have an appointment? If not, I would be happy to make one for you. Perhaps you could come back tomorrow."

"No, I don't think so. We need to see him today." Enid turned sideways so she was facing both Abby and the assistant. She pulled her cell phone from her handbag and dialed. "Saul, this is Enid. …. I'm fine, thank you. And you? …. Good. I suppose you've heard about Maude Everly. …. Yes, she is some better today but still in the hospital. I'm outside your office with her great-granddaughter, Abigail Croft. We need to speak with you on Maude's behalf."

As Enid spoke, Mrs. Harper's eyes opened wider and wider. Abby bit her lower lip, distorting the grin that threatened to break through at any moment. Enid crossed her eyes at Abby, making it even more difficult for the younger woman to keep a straight face.

"Yes, sir, we'll wait right here for you." Enid snapped her phone closed. "He said he would be out in a few minutes, Abby."

Abby took a deep breath before she answered. "Good. I'm glad he could see us today."

Neither of them gave Mrs. Harper another glance.

Two men walked out of Saul Bolton's office. One left. The other walked over to Enid and Abby. He shook hands with both women.

"Enid. Abigail. Won't you both follow me?"

Saul Bolton nodded to his assistant and led Enid and Abby back into his spacious, elegant, and orderly office. Every piece of the matching cherry furnishings was polished to a shine. Every item visible—on and within the executive desk, credenza and hutch, lateral file cabinets, and small tables scattered about the room—was placed precisely.

Abby touched Enid's arm and mouthed, "OCD," but with a look of admiration and awe.

Saul closed the door behind them, walked around to his side of the desk, and sat down. He motioned for them to sit also. They did.

"Now what can I do for you—or rather for Maude?"

"Maude is researching her family history," said Enid.

"She's been doing that for years."

"Yes, she has. However, she has uncovered some interesting new information, and some of it concerns the bank."

"I can't give out personal information on anyone to anyone other than that person."

"I'm Granny's responsible person, medical and financial," said Abby. "Besides, this concerns ancestors, not living relatives."

"I don't understand. Are you wanting to know if an ancestor had an account?"

"No, sir. We already know that."

Abby explained about the two trust accounts that Charlotte had set up in 1867.

Saul thought for a moment before speaking. "If they were trust accounts, and Olivia withdrew the money from the original accounts, I doubt I could find any kind of record on them. Banks are not required to keep records for that length of time. If she did not withdraw the money, after a time it might be considered a dormant account. If the trust terms allowed it and based on the rule against perpetuities, the account might remain active for Olivia's lifetime plus twenty-one years, but at some point, the account would be closed, and that money would most likely go to the state."

"How long might that take?"

"Say we allowed her a life expectancy of ninety years and we added the twenty-one years, we might have held the account as late as the early 1970s."

"What if she withdrew it and put it into another account, say a savings account in Granny Maude's name?"

"One that Maude doesn't know about?"

"Didn't know about. Some information has come to our attention that suggests the account should be there, but we were informed by an interested third party that no such account ever existed. At least not in anyone else's name. The third party didn't know to check for Granny Maude's name."

"I see."

"Could you check?"

"Yes. That I can do. Do you have the paperwork to show your rights as Maude's representative?"

"I do." Abby showed him copies of the paperwork.

"Everything appears to be in order. Let me check." Saul turned to his computer and began entering keystrokes. "You say the records have been searched but for another name?"

"Yes."

"Let's try that name first."

"That would be Miriam, no last name. Other names besides Granny's would be Charlotte Abbott Goodwin and Olivia Goodwin Woodson."

"Hmm. No accounts in any of those names since we've converted to electronic recordkeeping. Now we'll check for Maude's name."

"You should probably try under her maiden name, Baker."

"Huh!"

"What is it?"

"There was a savings account set up for Maude Baker in 1928 by Olivia G. Woodson. But—"

"But what?"

"Over a period of a year beginning two years ago, Maude regularly transferred sums from the savings account into a checking account, also in her maiden name, until the savings account was empty, at which time she closed the savings account. Then she systematically made cash withdrawals from the checking account over the next six months until it was empty, at which time she closed the checking account."

"Sir, that's impossible. Granny didn't know anything about it until recently. Besides which, she would not have set up an account in her maiden name."

"Saul," said Enid, "you keep saying *transferred*. If Maude didn't have anything to do with it, you mean that money was embezzled, don't you?"

"I…suspect so."

No one said anything for several moments.

"I need to ask one of our internal bank auditors to look into this."

"How much was in the original savings account?" asked Abby.

"Over ten thousand dollars."

"Someone stole ten thousand dollars? How is that possible?"

"As I said, I need to get one of our auditors to review this. I don't suppose you have the account book, do you?"

Enid nodded. "Yes, we think we do. We got so caught up in the loss that we almost forgot about the account books. According to what we have discovered, Olivia originally put the two trust account books in a *safe box* back in 1872."

"Let me check." His fingers flew over the keyboard. When he stopped, his face drained of color. "Olivia did request a safe box in 1872. At that time, our bank did not charge wealthier customers for that service, and no fee has ever been charged or collected since. She transferred that safe box to Maude in 1928. Hmm. I cannot imagine how this has gone unnoticed. No notations have been made since 1928."

"Two years before Olivia died."

"Did the family not know of the existence of the account?"

"No."

Enid frowned. "Apparently someone discovered it."

"It would appear so. I can assure you that we will determine who that someone was."

"Enid," said Abby. "Do you think the person who helped Vance could be the embezzler?"

"Who is Vance? What person helped him? Do you have information about this, too?"

"Perhaps we do, Saul. You have your accountant look into it, and we'll see what we can find out. We'll get back to you."

"Please do."

"If you learn anything, please call us."

"I will."

The three of them arose at the same time, grim lines creasing all their faces.

Outside the bank, Enid turned to Abby. "We need to get Vance to point out the person he spoke with."

"Agreed. How? When?"

"As soon as possible." Enid had her cell phone out and the lawyer's office number dialed by the time they got to her Subaru. "Hello. Could I speak with Vance, please? .... When do you expect him back? .... I see. .... No, no message. I'll call back tomorrow. .... Thank you."

"No luck?"

"He's out of the office until in the morning."

"So we'll have to wait."

"Hurry up and wait. That's all we're doing."

"We need to check on Granny anyway. Dr. Finley promised to come by today. I hope I don't miss him. I hope he doesn't come while Grandma is there, but I need to go to class, which means I need Granny's Town Car."

"Hop in. We'll hurry to your house and then back to the hospital."

* * *

When Enid and Abby entered Maude's room, Isabel remained sitting beside her mother. Neither woman looked comfortable. Maude had turned onto her side away from Isabel. Isabel sat sideways to the bed, a book in her hand.

Before anyone could say anything, Dr. Finley entered the room. He scrutinized the faces of each of the four women before settling his gaze on Maude.

Enid choked back a chuckle.

A meek little man faced with four strong women. At least you chose the right one this time.

"Maude, I want you to stay at least one more night and most of tomorrow. Chelation can be dangerous, so I don't want to overdo it, but I do think it would be wise to do a second infusion while you're in the hospital so we can monitor your responses. We'll do it tonight. That would make it twenty-four hours after the first one. If you have no negative reactions to the treatment by noon tomorrow, the arsenic levels in your urine have decreased sufficiently, and everything else appears stable, I'll let you go home midafternoon. I do hope you will be agreeable to this."

"I certainly don't want to be agreeable to any of it, but I'm not an ignorant old woman. I'll stay if I can get something other than gelatin to eat."

"I'll see what I can do about that."

"Good."

"One other thing, Maude." The doctor dropped his gaze to the floor and cleared his throat. "I cannot say this enough. Had your neurological problems been more severe or if you had had gastrointestinal problems, I might have considered more tests sooner, but they weren't and you didn't, which still puzzles me. Nevertheless, I...I hope you will accept my apology for not taking your concerns seriously enough." The doctor glanced at Isabel but didn't address her.

Maude addressed them both. "I do accept your apology but only because you did as I asked at the end. I hope you and Isabel both remember this for a very long time."

"Yes, ma'am," he said as he nodded and backed out of the room, pink tinging his cheeks.

Isabel grunted as red raced up her face. "Mama, don't be disrespectful."

"Practice what you preach, Isabel," said Maude. "I'm not the one being disrespectful." She winked at Abby and leaned back into her pillow. "Now I need to rest again. I don't want to delay my dismissal, and we need to prepare a suspect list for Chief Mulhaney." She closed her eyes.

Isabel scowled at Enid and Abby. "I'll no doubt be at the top of that list. Whether or no, it seems I'm no longer needed today, so I'll leave. Abby, if you need me tomorrow, you will call me, won't you?"

"Yes, Grandma, I will."

As Isabel came around the end of the bed, Abby reached out to give her grandmother a quick hug.

When the door closed behind Isabel, Maude opened her eyes.

"Abigail, you need to leave for class. Can Robbie take you?"

"No. He's already on campus, but I have the Lincoln. As much as I hate to drive it, no one would know I was driving it today. My book bag is in the car, so I can drive straight to class and straight back."

Maude frowned and popped her knuckles. "All right. But drive carefully and keep your doors locked."

"I will." Abby kissed her granny on the forehead and left. Maude closed her eyes and lay back on her pillow. The frown remained on her face until she fell asleep.

Enid closed her eyes, too, not to rest but to concentrate on the mental mugshots of potential suspects clicking across her mind's eye.

CHAPTER THIRTY-TWO

Enid tapped her forefinger against the edge of the mystery novel she held. She had read five pages in the last hour. She couldn't concentrate on the story because the real-life mystery they faced wouldn't leave her be. She checked her watch.

It's almost three thirty. Abby should return soon. I know Maude needs to rest, but we need to figure this out or we may be right back up here with worse results than this time.

A rustle of the sheets brought her out of her musing. Maude raised her head and looked around the room.

"Enid, such a frown. Has something else happened?"

"No, thank goodness. However, our failure to discover either the identity of your nemesis or the source of the arsenic frustrates and worries me. How much more can you take? What are we missing? What more can we do?"

"We can develop that suspect list that keeps getting pushed aside. You asked me to think about who had been in my house after my last doctor's visit as we did for the week after the reunion. The task shouldn't be too difficult. We're talking about only five days, Friday through Tuesday."

"The last time we considered your activities, contacts, and visitors. We should do that again for the recent five days. We should wait for Abby, though."

"No waiting necessary. I'm here!" Abby closed the door behind her and dropped her book bag to the floor. "The professor reviewed the material for the final and dismissed us early." She grinned and did a double eye-raise. "Because my grades are so high, I'm exempt from the final. I'm finished!"

"That's my Abigail."

"Congratulations, Abby."

"Thank you both. Now let's do this."

"Arm yourself with paper and pen. I'll fire up my old brain."

With Enid on one side of her bed and Abby on the other, Maude ticked off items for the list.

"I'm afraid part of our discussion is going to be a rehash of our previous one with maybe a few differences from those after the reunion. For example, I saw Dr. Finley again but this time I also saw Lowell and Timothy. And keep in mind that one or both of you accompanied me on each visit. I saw Dr. Finley about my health on Friday but not again until today. I met with Lowell and Vance twice concerning my will, on Friday in Lowell's office and on Monday at my house. Also on Friday, I visited Timothy Foster at the funeral home to confirm my final arrangements.

"I didn't attend church services this past Sunday. On Monday morning, I went to Charles Goodwin's house to question him and to determine the locations of the daffodil patches. I was unaware of it at the time, but someone left Enid a threatening message Friday evening and attacked her Monday evening. I've no doubt he was the same person who left threatening messages for Abigail and myself the previous week.

"As to actual visitors, I'd say pretty much all of the folks who visited me after the reunion did so again *out of concern* for me after they heard about *my situation* from Isabel. Dr. Finley had called her and told her about everything after Friday's office visit, including my insistence on the tests and my trip to Lowell's office. Lowell informed her of my trip to the funeral home. Isabel repeated everything to everyone she saw. Of course, she added her own spin to everything, bemoaning my declining mental capacity, the police department's interference, and your interference, Enid.

"So Saturday and Sunday, which were supposed to be restful days, weren't restful at all. No one stayed long, of course, but one person after the other dropped by ostensibly to tell me of his or her concern. In truth, they wanted details about my health, my will, my funeral, and the intruder.

"I don't think any of them expected me to die, but I do think most of them thought my mind was well on its way out. The meddlers included my children, grandchildren, and cousins. Arthur came by on Tuesday, not so much to meddle as to encourage me to cease and desist."

Abby sat forward. "We need to write some of this down. Maybe make two lists. One with everyone you saw. One whittled down to include only those whom we suspect, who have a motive, or who had access to your house."

"Abigail. I don't suspect anyone."

"Granny."

"I realize someone has to be responsible, but I…. You're right. Make your first list, and then we'll narrow it down."

"We need to include anyone suspicious that any of us have had contact with since the reunion about related matters," said Enid, "regardless of whether or not we think they had access. For example, the bank teller to whom Vance talked. We can figure out access later."

"I agree," said Abby.

"Before we do, I need to tell you both about a decision I've made. From everything anyone has said, not one person suspects that the money taken from Peter's first money box was hidden on his property. If I reveal its existence, either Charles or one of his sons will dig the place up now, and Miriam's descendants will never see the money Charlotte kept for them. I've decided to buy Charles's place."

"That's a big purchase, Granny."

"Yes, it is, and I will consider it another day or two, but I can't delay my decision too long. I hope you both understand, but especially you, Abigail."

"I do, Granny. I will abide by your decision, whatever it is."

"My thoughts are not relevant," said Enid. "However, if I were you, I suspect I would be entertaining the same notion."

"Good. Now back to our lists."

After a good thirty minutes of talking and writing, Abby had compiled the first list along with the details of the contacts.

"Now for those with a motive or access," said Enid.

"You two talk," said Abby. "I'll write. When we finish, I'll organize the short list and read it back."

They spent fifteen minutes more developing the short list.

"This gives us nine possible suspects," said Abby. "Rest a minute, Granny, while I organize and rewrite."

Ten minutes later, Abby held up the new list.

"Here goes. The first three—Charles, Arthur, and Jedidiah—descended from Mason Goodwin. Charles Goodwin knows Mason's stories, owns the Goodwin farm, searched for the lost money, and knew about the hidden key under the flowerpot. Money could be a motive. Arthur Goodwin also knows Mason's stories, is running for public office, is openly prejudiced, and knew about the hidden key. He's overly concerned with public opinion and politically motivated. Jedidiah Goodwin, Granny's handyman, had access but no known motive.

"The next three—Julian, Lawson, and Janet—descended from Olivia Goodwin Woodson. Julian Matthews is always in financial straits, has searched the Goodwin farm for the lost money, and had access to Granny's house. Money would be her only motive. Lawson Baker knows Mason's stories, is prejudiced, and had access. His motive would have to be public opinion. Janet Baker, Granny's personal on-call nurse, had access but no known motive.

"The last three—Lowell, Vance, and the bank teller—are not related by blood to either Mason or Olivia. Lowell Franklin, Granny's lawyer and the husband of Cousin Lucille, is a descendant of James Franklin, Charlotte's lawyer. He had a key to Granny's house, so he had access. If anything about the will or the bank accounts reflects on the integrity of the firm, that could be a motive. Otherwise, we can think of no motive.

"Vance Abbott, one of Lowell's employees, is a descendant of Hannah's half brother. He works in the Franklin law firm, looked into the possibility of an account in Miriam's name, and had access to Lowell's key to Granny's house. His only known motive would be his interest in claiming Miriam's inheritance.

The unknown bank teller who assisted Vance acted suspiciously but had no known access to the house. If he did embezzle the money from the savings account Olivia set up for Granny, avoiding detection or capture could be a motive, but what would that have to do with Granny's research, and how would he know about it anyway?

Maude shook her head. "Charles is at the bottom of my list. He doesn't care what people think, he's too old to climb a ladder, and he doesn't need the money."

"Aunt Julian is at the bottom of mine," said Abby. "She needs the money, and she has searched for the second money box, but we don't think she knows enough about the family to be concerned about what else you might discover, right?"

"Not likely. She's the baby. She's always been the problem child in the family. My husband spoiled her royally, which is probably why she's never been wise about money. She and her husband Richard have recently had even more serious financial difficulties than usual."

"According to Charles," said Enid, "she did try to find the *lost money* herself, which she heard about at the reunion, but she agreed to split it with him if she found it."

"She called me after our visit with Charles. He must have told her about it. She didn't want me to tell anyone how dire their situation is. She said, 'We need the money, Mama. It's unclaimed money. Whoever finds it, it's theirs. Right?' What could I say?"

"Needing money doesn't make her a killer."

"Of course not, Abigail. Certainly not her own mother. She's never expressed concern about public opinion or shown any interest in the family stories. I used to have to bribe her to get her to go to the reunions."

Maude picked at the sheet covering her.

"My youngest brother Lawson Baker, on the other hand, has always attended the reunions, knows the stories, including the one about Peter fathering slaves, and in spite of Mama's best efforts, took after the Mason side as far as prejudice is concerned. He's never disputed the stories about Peter and Mason ill-treating Charlotte and Olivia or their slaves, but he's so prejudiced he insists Peter never would have fathered a slave's child for any reason. He also insists that if Peter did father a slave child, those descendants would be nothing to him, and he wouldn't want anyone to know about them.

"Nevertheless, to my knowledge, Lawson has never acted on his prejudice, and I don't think he'd kill anyone for any reason. It's not in his nature, and besides, he's never approached me about it. Then there's the age factor and climbing the ladder. He is seventy-five years old, although he wouldn't be the first seventy-five-year-old who did that and more. All things considered, his spending time with Charles and Arthur at the reunion recounting old stories about Peter and Mason isn't enough for me to seriously suspect him."

"Which brings us to Arthur," said Enid. "He isn't my family, of course, and I hate to accuse anyone, but I don't think we can eliminate him, not after his visit on Tuesday. You did say he hadn't been in your house for some time, but he did know about the hidden key. Regardless, we can't accuse anyone without something more substantial than being concerned about public opinion. Unless being elected as road superintendent has more value to him than I can imagine. The truth is we don't have enough to accuse anyone on our list."

"Including Jedidiah and Janet. They have complete access and could have done anything anytime if they were able. They're not as old as I am, but they're on up in years. I can't see either of them on a ladder, and I can't imagine them being guilty of anything anymore than I can Charles. Constant and unquestioned access is all we have for them."

"That leaves Lowell, Vance, and the bank employee."

"Lowell Franklin has all kinds of connections," said Enid. "He's your lawyer and the husband of a distant cousin. He's a descendant of James Franklin. He has—had—a key to your house so he had access to your property not to mention all of your legal and financial information. However, he denies knowing about the unsigned will or any possible accounts until they dug into the old files. On the other hand, he resisted telling you anything about the old files. He still insists he didn't know anything about the signed copy of the will. Motive is a little iffy unless those files contain something that might damage the firm's reputation."

"Lowell would act to protect the firm," said Maude, "but murder? I can't imagine Vance being loyal enough to the firm to kill anyone, but he is a descendant of Hannah's half brother. He did look into the possibility of an account in Miriam's name after discovering the unsigned will, but he insists he had no knowledge of the signed will. What other motive could he have? He might have wanted access to Miriam's account, but when he discovered it didn't exist, he would have no reason to stop my attempts to find her descendants."

"I'm inclined to put the bank teller at the top of my list," said Abby. "He acted suspiciously when Vance asked him about the account. The money disappeared after that."

"If no one had accessed an account that old and he found it…. I'm sure people have been tempted by less. But what would the account have to do with me?" asked Maude. "It was in my maiden name, so I doubt he associated it with me. Granted, avoiding detection or capture could be a motive, but what would his capture have to do with my research, and how would he know about it anyway?"

Before anyone could answer Maude's question, Enid's cell phone rang.

"Hmm. It's Vance. Hello, Vance. I'm at the hospital with Maude and Abby, and I have you on speaker. Do you have anything new to report?"

"Yes. I stopped at the bank today ostensibly to cash a check but more to see if I could learn the name of the teller who looked up the account information for me. I was in luck. He was working a window. His name is Jonathan Smyth. The information may not be helpful, but I couldn't let it go."

"Thank you, Vance. Perhaps it will be helpful. We'll tell you if we learn anything more."

"Good. How is Miss Maude doing today?"

"She's much better, thank you. Still in the hospital but better."

"I hope she gets to go home soon."

"So do we."

"I hear Lowell. I'd best get back to work now."

"Thank you for calling."

Enid hung up and stared at her phone for a moment.

"I'm going to call Saul to give him the name."

"I hate to get anyone in trouble."

"There will be no trouble if the audit does not connect him to the account."

"Speaker again, please."

Enid nodded and dialed. Saul Bolton answered.

"Hello?"

"Saul, this is Enid. We've learned the name of the teller who said the savings account we asked about did not exist."

"Good. I'm glad you called. Is Maude with you?"

"Yes, Abby and I are in her hospital room, and I do have you on speaker."

"Maude, I'm embarrassed to admit we didn't know about the old account in your name set up by your great-grandmother and even more embarrassed we didn't know someone transferred the funds from the old account into a new account in your name and then withdrew the funds. My auditor confirmed my own findings about the account and the transfer."

"No need to be embarrassed," said Maude from across the room.

"I should have known."

"Can your auditor determine who transferred the funds?" asked Enid.

"Possibly with a deeper audit. It might take some time. However, if you have a name—"

"We have a name, but it doesn't mean this person is guilty of embezzling the money. He's the person who told Vance no such account existed."

"I understand. We will be discreet and certain of our facts before we accuse anyone."

"The name Vance gave us is Jonathan Smyth."

"I hate to hear that. He's a very bright young man. Huh. Maude, if I remember correctly, I believe he's a distant relative of Arthur Goodwin."

Maude threw her head back against her pillow. "That's all I need. Another family member to suspect."

"I'm so sorry, Maude. I won't breathe a word of this without proof."

"Thank you."

"Enid?"

"Yes?"

"As Maude is still in the hospital, when we do figure this out, I'll call your number if that's all right."

Maude nodded at Enid.

"That will be fine. Thank you."

Enid snapped her phone shut and gave Abby a questioning glance.

"I've added the name and the relationship to the list. Mr. Bolton also answered our question about how Jonathan might have heard about Granny's research. If he or one of his family attended the reunion, he's bound to have heard about Granny's inquiries." Abby's eyes widened. "Patrick, when did you arrive?"

"Just now. Would I be correct in assuming you are holding a suspect list?" He glanced from Abby to Enid.

"You would be," answered Enid, "but none of us is ready to accuse anyone on the list. This is more of a list of who might have a motive or access."

"Please, Patrick," said Maude, "don't use our list to go sniffing around and upsetting my relatives."

"Isabel isn't on the list, is she?" Patrick extended both hands palms up when all three women laughed at him. "I'm serious here, but I do hope she isn't on your list."

"No, Chief Mulhaney." Abby struggled to control her giggles. "None of us even considered adding Grandma Isabel to the list. She's cantankerous as all get out, and she will lash you to death with her tongue, but she would never intentionally harm anyone physically."

"Good. I'd rather not have to interview her. However, Maude, if you have some serious suspects, I do need to interview them."

"Could you at least wait until we solidify our suspicions?"

"Maude, you could die before then."

"I'm better, and you have a guard outside my door. Isn't there something else you can be doing for a day or so? I mean we don't have any real evidence that anyone intentionally exposed me to arsenic."

"I thought you believed you were being poisoned."

"I did. I do. But believing it and accusing someone are two different things."

"Good thing you're not the police chief."

Patrick spoke with humor in his eyes and his voice, but Enid knew how seriously he took his job and his responsibilities. She breathed with relief when Maude changed the subject.

"I understand your officers searched the house."

"They did."

"Did they find anything?"

"Nothing definitive. We took everything that had been opened. We sent the most likely sources to the Crime Lab run by the TBI to be analyzed along with water samples from the kitchen and the bathrooms, although I doubt your water is the source as neither Abby nor Enid has shown any signs of poisoning and Dr. Finley believes the arsenic was introduced dermally. Of course, we dusted each of the items we took for prints." Patrick shrugged his shoulders. "Now we have to wait. We've asked TBI to put a rush on the reports, but it could take them close to a week."

"Patrick," said Enid, "where do we go from here?"

"We?"

"We. Abby and I have to help in any way we can."

"I won't have either of you putting yourself or Maude in any more danger."

"We'll be careful."

"Fine, but you will follow my lead and listen to reason, right?"

"We'll do our best."

"Enid." Patrick threw up his hands in exasperation and dropped them in resignation. "Right. You'll do your best. At this point, we need to have two main agendas. One, we need to keep the three of you safe. Two, I need to review your list of suspects, especially their motives and opportunity. Tell me what you have."

While Enid brought Patrick up to date on their list, Abby rewrote the list so he could take a copy with him. Maude fell asleep.

"I tend to agree our suspect is most likely a family member. I also agree we have a lot of supposition and not much factual evidence to go on."

"Not enough to make accusations," said Enid.

"No," said Patrick. "However, under the circumstances, it is enough to interview family members whether they're on your list or not. Maude's decline began after the reunion, and the perpetrator has to be someone who had access to Maude's house. I'll interview her siblings, children, friends, and business acquaintances under the guise of asking them if they overheard anything suspicious at the reunion or since. If the person is on your list, I'll pay closer attention to his or her responses. By the time I finish the first round of interviews, something else may have turned up in the other areas of our investigation. I definitely want to know when Saul Bolton has anything concrete on the savings account situation."

"On one hand," said Enid, "I would like to accompany you on the interviews. On the other hand, I have no desire to accompany you on the interviews. Regardless, Abby and I have our hands full."

"It would be more prudent to keep all three of you away from my investigation. Besides, you need rest." Abby shook her head vigorously. "Abby, don't pull an Enid on me." Enid pressed her lips together. "You, either, Enid. I'm not insensitive to your concerns or desires to help, but I am worried about your health and welfare. I doubt any of us would be comfortable with only a family member staying with Maude, so I'm going to keep an officer at her door while she's in the hospital. This will allow you two time to accomplish what you need to and time to rest without worrying about Maude's safety. Can you work with me on this?"

"Reluctantly, yes," said Enid. "If it suits everyone, I'll stay with Abby at Maude's house."

"That suits me," said Abby.

"Me, too," said Maude as she roused and pulled herself up in the bed.

"Granny, I thought you were asleep."

"I was. I woke up. Soon enough to hear about the officer remaining on duty. Thank you, Patrick, for the officer. Thank you, Enid, for staying with Abigail."

Both nodded.

"Chief Mulhaney, here's a copy of our list." Abby handed him the sheet of paper.

"Update me whenever any of you have something or someone to add to it."

"We will," said Granny. "It's almost dinner time. It's been a long day. Abby, you and Enid need to be on your way, too."

"Granny—"

"No arguments. I want you rested and back up here early in the morning." Maude smiled and reached out to take Abby's hand.

"Granny, I'm telling the nurses to call me if anything weird happens. If it does, I'll be right back up here."

"I know."

Abby leaned over and gave Maude a kiss on the cheek. She blinked back tears.

"I'm fine, Abigail."

"I know, Granny. I know."

"One last thing before you leave. Call Charles the minute you get home. Tell him I want him to come to the house as soon as I'm home, hopefully tomorrow afternoon, and to come prepared with a fair price on the Goodwin property."

"Will do."

Enid and Abby said their goodbyes and followed Patrick out of the hospital.

"I am so tired," said Abby.

"We have nothing to do but rest when we get home." Enid had no sooner said the words than the pit of her stomach suggested otherwise.

CHAPTER THIRTY-THREE

As Enid locked the Subaru and headed toward the house, her cell phone rang. Abby turned around, fear in her eyes. Enid exhaled when she saw the caller's name and shook her head at Abby.

"It's not the hospital. It's Saul Bolton."

Abby's lip quivered, but she sighed with relief and came around the car, motioning for Enid to use speaker.

"Hello, Saul," said Enid, "do you have news?"

"Yes, I do. Are you where you can come to the bank now?"

"You're closed."

"I'll let you in. I also need to call Chief Mulhaney. Who tampered with Maude's account is no longer a mystery."

"Abby and I will come straightaway. Maude is still in the hospital."

"I'll watch for you."

Neither Enid nor Abby said a word until Enid had backed out into the street. Abby spoke first.

"Someone stole Miriam's money. That must be the reason for trying to stop Granny's research and prevent her from finding the account, the theft, and ultimately the thief. The theft, Granny's search, and her poisoning cannot be coincidence."

"Maybe. Let's wait until we hear the facts."

As Enid parked in front of the bank, Patrick pulled his vehicle in beside hers. The three of them walked to the bank together. Saul met them at the door.

"Thank you all for coming. Thanks to Enid and Abby's diligence, my auditor managed to trace the transactions concerning Maude's old savings account to Jonathan Smyth. Please come into my office."

Inside Saul's office, five chairs formed a semicircle in front of his desk. Two were occupied. Saul extended a hand toward the three empty chairs.

"Please sit." They did. He made his way around his desk and sat in his own chair. He pointed to the man nearest him on his left.

"This is Hiram Austin. He's one of my best auditors. He teased out the twists and turns taken with this account. I'll let him explain."

"Thank you, sir. My search mostly confirms what you already know. It involved two parts. The safe box and the actual accounts. I started with the safe box. Olivia Goodwin Woodson requested the safe box in 1872. When I opened it, I found four account books inside. Two were for trust accounts set up by Charlotte Abbott Goodwin in Olivia Goodwin's name in 1867. Two were for savings accounts, one for Olivia and one for Maude. Both trust account books contained deposit entries made first by Charlotte and later by Olivia, one up until 1881. I'm not sure why Olivia left the account books in the safe box after 1881 because she had closed both of the trust accounts by then, and the books were of no further use to her.

"However, those books and the subsequent savings account books certainly helped us determine the full history. Olivia closed one of the trust accounts in 1872 and transferred the balance to her checking account. She closed the second trust account in 1881 and transferred its balance into a savings account in her name. Then in 1928, she closed that savings account and set up another one in Miss Maude's maiden name, Maude Baker. She also put the safe box in Maude's name."

"Granny was seven years old at the time," said Abby.

"Hmm. No other activity occurred on the remaining savings account except for periodic interest deposits until two years ago. At that time, it appears that Maude Baker transferred the money in the savings account into a regular checking account, also in her name, after which she closed the savings account. Then she systematically made cash withdrawals until the checking account was empty. The checking account was closed three months later."

"Then you lost track of the money."

"Yes and no. I searched for accounts that might have received similar deposits on the days money was withdrawn. I had identified three accounts with deposits matching two of the withdrawal dates, but before I could search further, the call to Mr. Bolton confirmed which of those names I should follow. In every case, he made a cash deposit to his personal account within one hour of the withdrawal from Maude's account all from the same computer station."

Hiram and Saul both turned to the other man in the room, who had not moved or spoken during Hiram's entire explanation. Saul spoke next.

"Allow me to introduce to you Jonathan Smyth, against whom we would like you, Chief Mulhaney, to bring embezzlement charges."

The man, now flushed and fidgeting, stuttered as he tried to speak.

"Mr. Smyth," said Patrick, "I would advise you not to speak as I am placing you under arrest." Patrick finished the Miranda Warning and had handcuffs on the man before anyone could say another word. "Enid, if you and Abby could move one seat over, I'll sit here next to my prisoner. We have a few more matters to cover before I take him in. Mr. Bolton, what about the stolen money. Can you recover it?"

"Only a small portion of it is still in his account. Of course, you can freeze his account, but it would take some time before we could access the money. However, that won't affect Maude. The full amount embezzled was covered by FDIC. It will be replaced as soon as we can process the paperwork."

"That's one piece of good news. Now Mr. Smyth, for the other charges."

"What other charges? I didn't do anything else." He puffed up as if he'd been insulted.

"Right. You haven't been trying to poison Maude Everly with arsenic for the last six weeks? You didn't leave threatening voicemail messages? You didn't tamper with Abby's brakes? And you didn't try to poison Enid with carbon monoxide?"

"No! No! No! And no! I didn't do any of that."

Jonathan jumped up, his eyes wide with fear.

Patrick jumped up beside him.

"Sit back down, Mr. Smyth."

"I'm telling you. I don't know anything about arsenic or carbon monoxide or auto mechanics. I would never kill anyone. I…I…yes, I embezzled the money—"

"Mr. Smyth, you do remember that I recited your Miranda Rights."

"Yes, yes, I do. I'll admit to the embezzlement charge, but I didn't try to murder anyone. I don't know about the other events, but as for the night Enid's little incident occurred, I was out of town."

"Mr. Smyth," said Enid, "as you're so insistent on speaking your piece, may I ask you a question? Did you attend the Goodwin and Abbott family reunion?"

"Don't lie," said Abby. "I have relatives with photographic memories for faces."

"Yes, I was there. I brought my mother, but we stayed for only an hour or two."

"Did you hear Maude's request for family history information?"

"Yes, but what does that have to do with anything? Besides, I've only ever known her as Maude Everly. I never knew her as Maude Baker."

"I have a question, too," said Abby. "How did you come to the whole idea of stealing the money in the first place?"

"Vance Abbott asked about an old account opened or closed between 1865 and 1930 in the name of Miriam. I assumed it was genealogy related. So many people in town are into that sort of thing. I told him I doubted there was a record of it if it had been closed. If it had not been closed, it might have been moved to dormant accounts. I discovered a transfer in 1928 from a savings account in Olivia Woodson's name to a savings account in Maude Baker's name. I saw where the only activity on the account since 1928 was the addition of interest accrued."

"But you didn't tell Vance."

"No. He asked for an account in the name of Miriam, last name unknown. Why would I tell him I saw an account in someone else's name? I froze for a moment when I realized what an opportunity I'd found. Vance asked me what was wrong, and I gathered my wits and told him I could find no account with the first name Miriam on it. I pondered the matter for several days. I didn't see how anyone would ever figure it out, so I stopped thinking and began acting, setting up false accounts and transferring then withdrawing the funds. Now I have a question. How did anyone ever get wise to this?"

"As Chief Mulhaney told you," said Abby, "because someone has been trying to poison my granny. One thing led to another, which eventually led to the account, which then led to you."

Patrick stood and pulled Jonathan up beside him. Everyone else stood as well. "We need to leave now for the station where we'll take your official statement. Mr. Bolton and Mr. Austin, thank you for resolving this. We'll follow up on Mr. Smyth's one alibi and search his home before we charge him with attempted murder."

"I'm thankful we could resolve our part of it," said Saul. "Please keep me apprised of the details of Mr. Smyth's case."

"I will."

Enid and Abby shook hands with Saul and Hiram before they left.

In the car, Abby spoke first. "At least when I call Granny tonight, I can confirm the news about the account and tell her the FDIC will cover the loss. That will relieve one of her concerns."

Unfortunately, thought Enid, *it may not do anything for her other concerns. The arsenic is being removed from Maude's body, and she is improving, but if Jonathan Smyth did not try to kill her, then someone else did, and that someone is still out there. Someone who does know about arsenic, carbon monoxide, and auto mechanics.*

CHAPTER THIRTY-FOUR

Friday, August 12, 2011

Early the next morning, Enid busied herself in the kitchen preparing breakfast. She heard Abby's footsteps on the stairs.

"Up already?"

"Yes. I smelled coffee and bacon, two things I cannot resist. I couldn't stay in bed any longer." She entered the kitchen with eyes closed, inhaling the scents that had drawn her.

"Here. Sit."

They sat on opposite sides of the kitchen table, said grace, and began eating.

"I had a thought this morning," said Enid.

"Something else we can follow up on?"

"Sort of. Something I've been meaning to do since Monday. I'm glad we have a bit of good news for Maude concerning the money. I would love to have a little more good news on our efforts to find Miriam's descendants. As Maude has a guard at the door and I know you will want to see her this morning—and talk to the doctor—I thought I might spend a little time at the library. I believe I have enough information to trace Hannah through 1930 and maybe beyond."

"The last available census?"

"Yes. In 1930, Miriam would have been seventy years old. If they stayed in Michigan and I can find them in the census records from 1900 through 1930, I should also be able to find marriages, births, and deaths, maybe even employment records of her descendants."

"That would be excellent." Abby's grin turned quickly into a frown. "Even if Granny survives this, and I believe she will, she is still ninety years old. I do want to give her at least this one last gift." Her face lit up again. "So I am in agreement with your idea. Here's to a great day!" She lifted her coffee cup.

"The sun is going to shine all day, too."

"A good sign!"

"Don't tell Maude what I'm doing, though. I want it to be a surprise."

* * *

After Abby left for the hospital, Enid left for the library.

When she arrived, she greeted everyone with a smile, especially her assistant who had already unlocked the door to the genealogy room. The bounce had returned to her step.

"Ellen, if no one comes in, I would like to be your patron this morning."

"By all means. Mary has kept me current with all that's been happening with you and Maude and Abby. I'll do anything I can to help."

"I was hoping Mary would keep you informed. I've had scarcely a few minutes before falling asleep at night to call her and tell her the latest. I haven't talked to anyone else but Patrick all week."

"Mary needed you to call her."

"I know. She is a worrywart, especially where her family and her employees are concerned."

"So where do we begin?"

"Here are the names I have from the 1880 census. I would like for you to search for them in births, deaths, and marriages. I'm going to search for them in the census records from 1900 to 1930 and in any directories I can find. Whoever finishes first can help the other one."

By noon, Enid had a folder bulging with record copies.

"Thank you so much, Ellen. Maude will be ecstatic."

"I'm ecstatic, and it isn't even my family! There is something to be said for staying in one place. I cannot imagine the difficulties genealogists will have a hundred and fifty years from now with the way people move around not just from city to city or state to state but country to country as well."

"All the more reason for family researchers today to dig out all they can and keep everything from now forward. Unfortunately, most families don't give it a thought until their older members pass on."

"We've done our part for this family—down to the youngest first daughter!"

"Yes, we have, and on that positive note, I need to do a little more grocery shopping before Maude comes home."

* * *

By two o'clock, Enid was standing in the middle of the kitchen waiting for the timer to sound when her cell phone rang.

"Hello?"

"Hey, Miss Enid. Granny and I are headed home. I wanted to make sure you were at the house so you could help me get her in."

"I am here, and I can. How is Maude feeling?"

"So much better and more than ready to leave here."

"I can imagine. I'll be watching for you. Abby, before you go, I have to tell you—but don't let on to Maude—I have good news from the search this morning."

Enid removed the pan of lasagna from the oven and went to sit on the front porch swing while she waited for Maude and Abby to arrive. She didn't have long to wait. She met them at the driveway with the wheelchair.

"Abby, did you fly?"

"No, but I didn't let anyone get in my way, either." She beamed as she opened the passenger door.

"Home again, home again, Granny."

"Thank goodness. I could walk, but I'd better not push it." Abby raised an eyebrow at Enid as Maude shifted from the Town Car to the wheelchair with greater ease than she had in weeks.

"You could have ridden home in an ambulance. It would have been easier on you."

Maude looked askance. "You have ridden in one of those things, haven't you?"

"Point taken. Let's get you into the house."

They soon had her settled on the sofa.

"Now that I'm home, I want something decent to eat. I smell lasagna. Is it wishful thinking, or do you have some baked?"

"Baked and ready to eat. After we set up TV trays."

"I'm glad to be home, but the arsenic has taken its toll on me. I may still die sooner than I would have if I hadn't been poisoned, but at least I have some time left to work on keeping my promise."

An hour later, Abby helped Maude lie down on the sofa and Enid took the TV trays to the kitchen.

When Enid returned, Maude was sitting up again.

"Charles called," said Maude. "He said Abby had called him to tell him I wanted to talk to him about his property. He wanted to ask if I'd changed my mind before he made the trip to town. He's on his way over."

* * *

Enid met Charles at the door and escorted him to the living room. He had dressed for the occasion in khakis and a light blue short-sleeved shirt. He jumped straight to the point of their visit.

"Maude, I'm guessing you want to do this while you're still here to do it."

"You would be right, Charles. My little trip to the hospital opened my eyes. I hope you're coming to me with a reasonable offer. I may not have time to haggle."

He grunted. "You'd make time, Maude Everly, but I don't see the need for haggling. If any of my boys or even my brother wanted the farm, it would be a different matter. I wouldn't be here talking about it. I do want to make it so that my sons won't think you've cheated their old man. I've printed out the latest listing for the property value and added twenty thousand to that." He showed her the printout. "What do you think?"

"I think if I sold it, I could get that much for it and maybe more, but that's all I would want. Lowell handles your business, too, doesn't he?"

"He does."

"Do whatever needs to be done to have the papers drawn up, and I'll sign them." Maude laughed. "Lowell will get his drawers all in a twist because this will mean I'll need to make more changes to my will. It will be worth the extra twenty thousand to see him squirm."

"Gettin' spry in your old age, aren't you?"

"Spryer today than yesterday."

"A spry day is a good day!" They both laughed. "I'll go straight from here to Lowell's office to begin the paperwork. I can include the part about my boys having first option if and when the property is sold, whether it's by you or your'n, right?"

"Yes, by all means."

"Good. Done and done." Charles stood. "I'll call you when the paperwork is ready."

"I'll be waiting."

* * *

Enid stood by as Maude again stretched out on the sofa.

"How are you feeling, Maude?"

"I feel great for an old woman recuperating from arsenic poisoning. This is a good day. Jonathan Smyth has been arrested and the FDIC will cover my losses. I'm home from the hospital, I've eaten lasagna, and I've bought land I'll never lay a plow to." Her eyes crinkled and she chuckled.

"There's more news, Granny." Abby clapped her hands and rocked back and forth from heel to toe.

"What on earth? Only one thing could make this day any better. I don't mean catching my would-be poisoner, either, if Mr. Smyth is indeed innocent of that. I'm not sure I even want to know who it is if he would leave me alone. However, I would like to know one more thing."

Abby grinned at Enid. "I've no doubt Miss Enid's news is exactly what you want to hear."

"You two sit down and tell me."

Abby sat at the end of the sofa facing Maude, her knees drawn up to her chest. Enid sat in the armchair to Abby's right.

"Your faces tell me this is major." Maude held a hand to her chest.

"Breathe, Granny."

"Give me the end of the story first, and then you can tell the details."

"We found them," said Enid.

Maude's chin trembled, and tears spilled from her eyes down her cheeks. Abby grabbed a box of tissues and handed it to her granny.

"Whew!" said Maude as she blew out a breath. "Now on with the details."

"I limited myself to tracing through the oldest daughters for time's sake and for inheritance purposes beginning with Hannah. With Ellen's help, we traced the marriages, births, deaths, and census records of the oldest daughters. I have it all written down and documents copied, so for now I'll give you highlights.

"Hannah did marry Daniel Jacobson in Detroit, Michigan, in 1863. They had several more children. They died months apart at eighty-five and eighty-six in 1920.

"Miriam Jacobson married David Michaels at seventeen in 1877 in Lansing, Michigan. Their first child and oldest daughter, Lydia Michaels Jones was born in 1878. Miriam died at eighty-eight in 1948.

"The census records helped us confirm two more generations, Lydia's oldest daughter, Ida Jones Ethridge, and Ida's oldest daughter, Hallie Ethridge Beale. Hallie was nine years old in the 1930 census.

"After the 1930 census records, we had to rely on birth, marriage, and death records along with directories. We searched until we found Hallie Ethridge's marriage to Emory Beale in 1946 when she was twenty-five. Hallie died in 2009. She was eighty-eight."

"I missed her by two years."

"Yes, but not her descendants. Her obituary listed her children and grandchildren. Her oldest daughter was Zora Beale Maston. Zora's only daughter was Marian Maston Ross. We found both of their marriage announcements in a Lansing, Michigan, newspaper. We also found Marian by her employment. Then we found Marian's oldest daughter, Alexa Irene Ross through both her birth announcement and the announcement of her graduation, at which she gave the valedictory address."

Maude took Abby's hand. "Looks like brains run in the female side of this family. Let's see now. Alexa would be Hallie's great-granddaughter and Hannah's five great's granddaughter."

"Yes."

"They survived, and they thrived," said Maude. "Lord, thank you from us for us and for Charlotte and Olivia." Once again, the tears flowed down her cheeks. "Have you tried to contact them?"

"No. We knew you would want to be the one who did that."

"I'm so glad I lived to know this. What if you hadn't thought of Michigan?"

"What if they hadn't stayed in Michigan all these years? We might still be searching."

"They found their home. They didn't leave it. I want to hear the rest of their story. I want to live to see them. We must ask them to come here. I'll pay for the trips. I can do that."

"Do you think they will come?" asked Abby.

"We can certainly hope so. Enid, you said you found an employment record for Marian."

"Yes. She works with the FBI."

CHAPTER THIRTY-FIVE

Later that evening, as she was searching her bags for a clean pair of pajamas, Enid received two telephone calls back to back. Both made her realize how tired she was. That made her more concerned about Maude. She dreaded telling her about either of the calls.

No need to postpone the inevitable. I can find my pajamas later.

She left her bag on the bed and returned to the living room.

"Enid, did I hear your phone ring?"

"You did."

"Anything new?"

"Yes and no."

"Always is, isn't it?"

Enid managed a tired smile and related the gist of the calls to Maude and Abby.

"The first was from Patrick. He's managed to speak to each of your children and siblings and several of your cousins, including Charles and Arthur. I'm glad I wasn't able to go with him."

"We're they all hateful?"

"Somewhat abrasive were the words Patrick used. Except for Charles. He's as happy as a lark with everyone and everything."

"He always did like the ring of coins when we were growing up. Did Patrick get anything from any of them to suggest their complicity?"

"Nothing substantial. Mostly agitation at having the family's laundry, past and present, aired in public."

"We always have been a secretive bunch. What about Jonathan Smyth?"

"He can find nothing to connect him to your poisoning. They searched his property and found no poisons at all. He would not have had access to your house, and on the evening I was attacked as well as on the evening Abby and I chased the intruder out of the attic, Jonathan attended concerts in Nashville with his girlfriend and another couple."

"At least we uncovered his embezzlement. What will Patrick do next?"

"Keep tabs on us and wait for the lab reports."

"And the other call? Unless it's none of my business, of course."

"Actually, it was your business, too. Of all things, Lowell Franklin called me to discuss your purchase of Charles's property. He said he was sworn to confidentiality by Charles, but Charles had mentioned that both Abby and I were present when the two of you discussed the terms, so he didn't feel as if he were breaking confidentiality by calling me."

"Why didn't he call me?" asked Abby.

"Because he wanted me to try and persuade Maude not to go through with the purchase. He's afraid of repercussions from the rest of the family, afraid he'll lose clients. He probably figured you agreed with Maude. Although I can't imagine why he would think I would try to dissuade either of you."

"He's desperate," said Maude. "His concern about losing clients is justified. A large number of his clients are members of our family, and we do tend to react as one when any of our number is wronged. If my children or Charles's children got it in their heads that he took advantage of either of us or didn't protect our interests, it would not be surprising if they took their business elsewhere."

"It makes sense in a twisted sort of way."

"So what did you tell him?"

"That his efforts were an exercise in futility. He grunted, and he swore. Then he said, 'Fine. Tell Maude that Charles and I will come to her house at noon on Monday with the papers to be signed.' Then he hung up without even a goodbye."

Before Maude could respond, her cell phone rang.

"You'd think we were operating an old-fashioned telephone switchboard. Hmm. It's an unknown number."

"Put it on speaker, Granny."

"Hello?"

A high-pitched, robot-like voice responded.

Maude Everly, you're no longer behind guarded doors. Neither is your great-granddaughter. You and Enid better leave off with this digging into the past or the bones being dug up will be your own.

Maude stared at the phone.

"Granny, he hung up."

Maude held the phone out to Abby, who took it and snapped it shut.

"Enid, do you think he knows what you uncovered today?"

"How could he?"

"Someone at the library might have told him."

"I doubt it. He's most likely trying to scare you again now that you're home."

Enid wasn't as convinced as she wanted Maude to believe. Mentally, she fast-forwarded through the events of the morning. Three patrons had come in. All three had needed only a little assistance, and Ellen had provided that. Enid knew only one of them by name, and he came from out of town. She had seen the other two before but could not recall their names.

I must remember to ask Ellen.

"Enid, what are you thinking?"

"Looking back over my day. Didn't see anything suspicious."

"This annoys me to no end. I was hoping my nemesis would give up after I went to the hospital and got better. Isn't it ever going to end?"

"Yes, it is," said Enid. "We will discover the identity of your nemesis as you call him and put an end to this. Maybe when Patrick gets the test results back, he will have something to help us."

"At least it wasn't Lowell," said Abby. "He's more concerned with his losing business than your digging up bones."

CHAPTER THIRTY-SIX

Monday, August 15, 2011

After a welcome uneventful weekend and a slow morning, Enid was almost eager to gather her bags and leave the library for Maude's house. Maude and Abby had insisted she be present for Lowell and Charles's visit. She stopped to tell Mary her plans.

"How did Maude make it this weekend?" asked Mary.

"She did quite well considering all she's been through. Sunday morning, she insisted on attending church service. She did use her walker and was more tired than she expected to be but otherwise managed the service without any trouble. This morning when I left, she was getting around again using only her cane. I'd be tempted to go back home if we could identify the person who keeps threatening her."

After a few more moments of idle chitchat, Enid left.

The slow morning had at least given her time to quiz Ellen about the identities of the other two patrons from Friday. One was a gentleman from Texas researching an ancestor who had migrated to Texas from West Tennessee after the Civil War. He had no known connection to the Goodwin family. The other one was a granddaughter of Charles Goodwin. Ellen had mentioned to her that Enid was researching for a Goodwin relative of hers but the line the young woman was researching was on the other side of her family.

She could have talked to Charles...or her mother...or even Arthur, thought Enid. *But we've already passed on Charles as a suspect.* She strummed the steering wheel.

She shook her head in defeat as she pulled into Maude's driveway and parked behind Maude's Lincoln. *She could have talked to anyone. This whole thing is getting out of hand.*

When she exited her Subaru, Charles, Lowell, and Vance pulled up and parked their vehicles at the street. She waited for them.

Charles stepped down out of his white pickup looking as dapper as he had on Friday, this time in khakis and a pale-yellow dress shirt. Lowell and Vance slid out of Lowell's silver Mercury and followed Charles up the walk. Vance looked and acted the part of a lawyer. Lowell, however, even in his dark, professional suit and tie, did not appear as poised and self-confident as either Vance or Charles.

No time to worry about it now, thought Enid. *We have work to do.*

* * *

At Maude's instruction, Enid added the leaf to the kitchen table while Abby made coffee.

Vance slipped into the kitchen while they worked. He leaned against the door facing.

"Enid, I didn't want to say anything in front of Lowell or Charles, but I wanted to ask what you'd found out about the account."

Abby jumped in. "Vance, thanks to you, the bank auditor followed the account trail, Patrick arrested Jonathan for embezzling, and the FDIC will reimburse Granny for the money he stole. We are both so appreciative."

"So the account was in Miss Maude's name and not Miriam's."

"Yes, but Granny knows Charlotte intended the money for a direct descendant of Hannah and Miriam."

"Are you still looking for them?"

"Yes, we—"

"Yes," interrupted Enid, "but searches like this sometimes take years. If we do find them and Maude is able to pass on the inheritance Charlotte meant for them to have, it will be thanks to you."

"I am glad for that. I'm also glad Patrick arrested the scoundrel."

"So are we. The coffee and the table are ready. We should call the others in."

Soon, they were all seated around the table with cups of coffee and stacks of papers.

Lowell scowled throughout the process.

"I want you both to know I consider this a mistake one or the other of you will regret. I've tried to talk sense into both of you without success. If I could declare either of you mentally incompetent, I would, especially you, Maude. According to Charles's granddaughter, you're still digging into the past."

"How do you know that?"

Charles cleared his throat. "Sorry about that, Maude. My granddaughter called while I was in Lowell's office drawing up the papers on Friday. She mentioned hers and Enid's research from that morning. I mentioned it to Lowell. I should've known better."

"Sometimes it's hard to know when to speak and when not to speak. Don't worry about it. Lowell, you've said your piece and you've explained all of this. Let's finish it."

"Fine. One more thing. Don't expect me to drop everything to do something like this again. If you're too old to wait a day or two, you're too old to do it anyway. That includes changing your will again, which I've no doubt you will want to do."

Enid and Abby fought back laughter. Maude waved a finger at them. Charles winked at them. Lowell never looked up.

"That I will," said Maude. "In fact, I plan to come to your office tomorrow. I'm sure you can squeeze me in. I also want to examine the old files again and collect the copies, which I hope you have already made for me. I also hope you and Vance will continue to keep your eyes open for any other paperwork for Peter and Charlotte Goodwin, especially Charlotte."

Lowell grumbled and turned back to the papers in front of him. After Charles and Maude had signed them and Abby, Enid, and Vance had witnessed them, Maude handed over two checks, one to Charles for the farm and one to Lowell for the fee. Charles put his check into his wallet. Lowell put his check and all of the papers into his briefcase then stood to leave.

"I'll hand this off to Vance to process at the courthouse and make copies, which I hope you can pick up tomorrow when you come for the others. I didn't notice either of you discussing Charles's vacating the premises, but that's not my concern."

"That's right," said Maude, a twinkle in her eye. "Before you leave, I suppose you want to use the *men's room*, don't you?"

Lowell's scowl returned. "Yes, I do." He marched off toward Maude's bedroom after setting his briefcase by the door.

When he left the room, Maude turned to Charles.

"You don't have to vacate the premises, now or anytime, Charles. I do want to have access to the property."

"Ha! I may not have to, but I'm going to. I'm not ready for a nursing home by any stretch, but I'm gettin' tired of trying to keep the yard mowed, the bushes trimmed, and the house cleaned in case someone comes to visit once in a blue moon. When I leave here, I'm going straight to that new apartment complex for seniors only. They have everything anybody could want plus an activities center and a workout center. I'm fortunate I can afford it. Other places for seniors are too much like hospitals or nursing homes for my liking. I figure I'll meet some nice ladies at this place. And if they can afford to live there, they won't have no need to be after my money."

"Why, Charles. I never would have thought it."

"Me, either. I still miss my wife every hour of every day, and I do not want to remarry, but what man wouldn't like a little pleasant female company from time to time? Talking about fishing lures and newfangled tractors is fine for a spell, but I'd like to look at something besides another grizzled old face upon occasion. Besides...well, you know, kids have their own lives to lead. This way, I can have a life in between their visits."

Maude held her arms out, and she and Charles embraced.

"When I get everything out, I'll bring you the keys."

"No hurry."

Charles nodded to everyone else just as Lowell returned and picked up his briefcase. The three men left together.

Enid walked them to the front door and watched them get into their cars and drive off, wondering at the differences in the three men. When she turned around, Maude stood in the hallway.

"I need to rest," said Maude. "When I get up, I'd like to go through the dower chest again. Speaking of which, where is it?"

"It's in my room," said Enid. "Hidden from outside prying eyes."

"Good." Maude walked to her bedroom with the cane but with less dependence on it.

At least that, thought Enid. *I hope nothing worse happens.*

* * *

Later than evening, Enid pulled the dower chest into the living room. After a nostalgic reviewing of all of its contents, Abby brought them back to the present.

"We're no closer to knowing who tried to kill Granny than we were. I don't think we need to call Miriam's descendants and ask them to visit until we resolve this."

"What if we don't resolve it?" asked Maude. "I don't have forever."

"I know, Granny."

"Why not wait," said Enid, "at least until after the police have received the test results and Vance has filed the deed so you can search the grounds for the graves and the buried money box?"

"That sounds reasonable," said Maude. "I want to think about the suspects again. In my mind, I've reduced the list to Arthur, Lowell, Vance, and Jonathan."

"Of those four," said Enid, "Arthur has the most concern about appearances. Lowell thinks the entire family research idea is crazy and says he didn't know about the signed copy of the will. He and Vance knew about the old account, and Vance would have claimed it, but I can't say as I would criticize him for that, and now that's resolved although not to his benefit. Jonathan has an alibi for at least one of the intruder entries and my incident."

"As for relationship," said Abby, "Arthur is the closest relative of the four. Jonathan is next though distant. Lowell is related by marriage only. Vance is related to Hannah but not to Granny."

"Consider this," said Enid. "If we eliminate Arthur and Jonathan, we're left with Lowell and Vance. What if one or both of them knows more about Peter and Charlotte's business than they've said so far?"

"That makes more sense than anything else, but not much," said Maude. "If there is something more that could benefit— or harm—either of them, it could explain Lowell's insistence that I give up this futile and possibly harmful project of mine, but Vance hasn't overtly called us on any of it. Rather, he has been more than helpful."

"Which could be a front," said Abby. "Of course, the person could also be someone we haven't even considered. Miss Enid, which one are you thinking it is?"

"I agree with Maude that Vance has been more helpful than Lowell, certainly less hateful, but I also agree with you that appearances can be deceiving. That said, I'd rather wait until Patrick has the results of the tests back to say one way or the other. I do hope we've thwarted the person enough that in spite of his last threat, he doesn't try anything else."

Later, Enid pulled the dower chest back into the closet in her bedroom away from home and prepared for bed.

As she lay there wide-awake, she pondered the thoughts she had kept to herself. *I do have concerns about Vance. Why didn't he tell Maude about the will and the account when he first learned about them? Confidentiality? Maybe. Accessing the account himself? More likely. This threat to Maude probably has nothing at all to do with accessing family money and all to do with hiding one of the other family secrets. Whoever her tormentor is and whatever is driving him, I doubt he's finished with any of us.*

CHAPTER THIRTY-SEVEN

That night, Enid twisted restlessly at the edge of sleep, not quite out but not quite awake, worrying the idea that the intruder had not given up like an old dog gnawing a bone. She sensed something was wrong, but she couldn't decide what it was. Was the intruder back in the house? Was her car running? No. She heard something, but it wasn't footsteps or a car motor. She smelled something, too, but she was too sleepy, too exhausted, to crawl out of bed to see what it was.

With a jolt, she jerked out of her fog. She realized within a moment what she heard and what she smelled. She jumped out of bed and grabbed her cell phone. By the time she dialed 9-1-1, grabbed her robe, and slid into her slippers, the smoke alarm went off. She raced to the hallway and saw Abby at the top of the stairs, barefooted and wearing her gown.

"Go to Maude. Get her out of the house. Where is the fire extinguisher?"

"It's in the kitchen inside the hallway door on the counter, but you need to get out, too."

"Save your breath and save Maude. Go!"

Enid could see the fire was still small inside the house, but on the back porch, orange and yellow flames leaped high. She felt for the fire extinguisher, grabbed it, and sprayed the flames inside. She brought those flames under control, but she could do nothing to extinguish the outside blaze or prevent it from reaching inside again. When the cacophony of approaching wails and horns came to a screeching stop at the front of the house, she turned and raced to the front door.

"The fire is at the back on the outside," she yelled.

Several firefighters raced around the side of the house, pulling a hose behind them. Two firefighters wheeled Maude away from the house, Abby close behind them. Enid followed.

"Abby, how did you manage to get the wheelchair so quickly?"

"I left it out and unfolded. I don't know why I did. I had this gut thing that told me to leave it in case we needed it. How did you know? You were up before the alarm went off."

"I couldn't sleep. Worrying about what ifs." They reached the front sidewalk. "Maude, are you all right?"

"Yes. The smoke had just reached my room when Abby raced in. She didn't give me time to question her or to get my robe. I feel exposed!"

"Here, ma'am, wrap this around you." One of the EMTs handed Maude and Abby each a blanket. He offered one to Enid.

"Thank you," said Abby.

"I don't need one, but thank you," said Enid.

The women turned toward the house. From the front, nothing at all looked wrong.

A short time later, the firefighters had put the fire out and were rolling up the hose.

As the EMTs examined Maude and Abby for signs of burns and smoke inhalation, Enid watched Patrick and one of the firefighters talking and gesticulating at the side of the house. When they stopped, they turned and walked toward the women. The firefighter removed her helmet and squatted in front of Maude.

"Ma'am, I'm Fire Chief Lana McIntyre. You should go to the ER for further evaluation. We'll take care of everything here."

"I probably should, but these young folks—" She pointed to the EMTs. "They can check us out here. I'm confident we got out before any damage could occur."

"Ma'am—"

"I'll see my doctor in the morning. I'm not going to the ER."

Enid didn't say anything, but she did fold her arms across her chest and shake her head at Patrick.

He rubbed his hands together and said, "I didn't say a word."

The fire chief stood and shrugged her shoulders at Patrick. "Any suggestions?"

"Chief McIntyre, we'll let the EMTs check them all out, and I'll stay with them tonight. I understand the damage is mostly at the back of the house."

"Yes. It had broken in under the back door, but the fire extinguisher prevented it from burning farther although I would not advise anyone taking that action in the future with a fire of that size. You were all lucky this time. The interior damage is minimal. but the back porch is a loss. I'll take a closer look in the morning, but from what I saw tonight, I believe someone started the fire in a flowerpot on the back porch with a little help from a cigarette and some crumpled paper. Burned edges of paper are scattered across the steps." The fire chief turned her attention from Patrick to the women. "I don't suppose any of you smoke."

"Indeed, we don't," said Maude.

"In that case, it looks suspicious to me."

"In light of recent events," said Patrick, "I suspect you're right."

"How can that be?" asked Maude.

"I suspect someone lit a cigarette and left it and the crumpled paper in the pot," said the fire chief. "The fire spread to the door and then to the walls on either side. It would have continued into the kitchen and utility room if you hadn't smelled the smoke."

"But how would a few sheets of crumpled paper ignite a house fire?"

"Do you use potting soil or dirt?"

"Potting soil, of course."

"That's what I figured. Potting soil is flammable. It isn't that uncommon for someone to cause a fire by putting out a cigarette in a pot filled with potting soil. It's just not usually intentional."

"I pulled off the officer too soon," said Patrick.

"You are not responsible for this," said Enid. "We all did everything we could, and besides, Abby and I were both here."

"Thank goodness you were," said Maude.

"This calls for further interviews with each of the suspects. Anyone who does not have an alibi for tonight comes in for questioning."

"We narrowed the field ourselves tonight."

"Based on what?"

"What we know and suspect. And maybe a little intuition."

"I cannot base my decisions on intuition," said Patrick, "but I will consider your conclusions."

"Lowell or Vance or both but maybe Arthur."

"Chief Mulhaney." Maude took hold of his hand and pulled him closer to her wheelchair. "Please, humor an old woman and wait about reinterviewing Lowell or Vance until after my deed has been registered and my will has been changed. Please?"

"Maude, I'm afraid I cannot do that. I will approach them the same way I do everyone else. I'll tell them I'm reinterviewing and asking for alibis because of tonight's event. Unless something conclusive pops up, I won't arrest anyone, but if it does, I will."

"You will be discreet, then."

"I will."

"Thank you."

"Yes, ma'am."

"Enid, why are you chewing your lip?"

"I...you haven't heard anything from TBI yet?"

"Not yet. I called today. After this, I plan to give them another call in the morning."

"Good. I can't help but think we have most of the information we need to solve this, but we must be missing some little key piece. I do hope, after your next round of interviews, we can figure out what the missing piece is."

CHAPTER THIRTY-EIGHT

Tuesday, August 16, 2011

The next morning, Enid made her way to the kitchen in spite of half-closed eyes and brain fog from sleep deprivation. Even with Patrick asleep on the sofa, she had tossed and turned the rest of the night.

She met Abby at the end of the stairs.

"Miss Enid, you don't look any more awake than I feel."

"I'm not, but we need to get a move on. Patrick needs to go home to shower and change for work. Maude needs to see her lawyer and maybe her doctor. Perhaps we can take a long nap this afternoon."

"I like the last part."

"Let's try to muddle our way through a real breakfast. We all need it."

Maude and Patrick soon joined them at the kitchen table, drawn by the mixed aromas of crispy bacon, scrambled eggs, old-fashioned hash browns, buttered toast, orange juice, and strong coffee. At Maude's request, Patrick said grace.

"Thank you, Patrick. Now I hope I can keep my eyes open long enough to enjoy this good breakfast. By the way, when did you say you expect to hear from the TBI?"

"I'm hoping to hear something this morning. When I called yesterday, they had begun working on the items from your house. If I don't hear by noon, I'm going to call again. When I do hear from them, I'll get search warrants. I hope something in the TBI's findings will narrow the suspect list because I can't get blanket warrants for everyone on the list. I'll call you when I hear from them."

An hour after Patrick left, the women were ready to leave the house.

Enid chuckled when they came together in the living room. "I see we're of the same mind today."

"How so?" asked Maude.

"Abby dressed in black jeans and black T-shirt. You and I dressed in black slacks and tops. Power colors in preparation for our visits to self-designated powerful men. The only thing feminine about any of us is the scent of Maude's lovely bath powder."

"I try not to get carried away, but I do love it. I never buy anything else, and I never run out. Besides the boxes of powder that I buy for myself, I always receive extra boxes at Christmas from at least one of my cousins. It's not too much, is it?"

"Never too much. Always pleasant and refreshing. Perhaps it will have a calming effect on the men as well." Enid winked at Maude and Abby.

"We need all the help we can get with Lowell Franklin and Dr. Finley," said Abby. "Granny, are you going to change your appointment time with Lowell?"

"No. I'm just going to show up. If I call him, he'll insist he doesn't have time before noon and might even try to postpone the meeting altogether. I want to get my will changed today, see those old files again, and get copies of everything. Will you bring me my purse?"

"Will do."

Enid opened the wheelchair while she and Maude waited for Abby.

"I don't need that," said Maude.

"I know you don't," said Enid, "but I thought it might help conserve your strength after last night's ordeal."

"It would help us move a little faster, which would help us get home sooner."

"Agreed."

Abby returned and they left for the doctor's office.

Enid followed Maude and Abby down the ramp, halfway dreading the day. *I hope Maude's fragrance does calm both Dr.*

Finley and Lowell Franklin, she thought. *None of us needs disagreeableness today.*

* * *

"Would you rather I waited for you out here?" asked Enid when the nurse came to take Maude back to the exam room.

"No," said Maude. "I rather like having my entourage with me. That way I don't have to do all of the arguing."

When he was satisfied Maude had suffered no ill effects from the fire, Dr. Finley sat at his mobile computer table and recorded his notes.

"Maude, if I weren't older myself, I would be tempted to give you a tongue lashing for not going to the ER. However, I probably wouldn't have gone myself if I'd been through what you have these last several weeks. I won't fuss because you weren't exposed to the smoke for very long. A few minutes longer, though, I might be chastising you anyway."

"But I'm fine, right?"

"Yes, as fine as you can be considering."

"Good. I have another appointment to keep."

"Before you all leave, Abby, do you plan to continue to stay with your granny for a while?"

"I'm living with her—period."

"I hoped someone would stay with her. It's your business, Maude, but you could have lingering effects from the arsenic, and I'd prefer you didn't stay alone."

"For once, we are in agreement. I do appreciate your concern. I'm also pleased to be back on good terms. You've been my doctor most of my life. I'd prefer you be the one who sees me out of this world."

"Not anytime soon."

"Not today anyway."

"I want you to return in one month, sooner if you need to."

"I'll see you then."

Maude circled her finger for Abby to roll her out of the exam room.

* * *

Enid soon pulled into a space in front of the Franklin Law Firm, well before Maude's appointment.

Maude chose to use her cane instead of the wheelchair to walk inside.

"I need to appear stronger with Lowell," she explained.

Neither Enid nor Abby argued with her.

When the receptionist ushered them into Lowell's office, they found him standing at the window, staring outside and strumming his fingertips against each other. He jumped when his receptionist spoke.

He jerked around and managed to say "What—" before his jaw dropped and the color drained from his face. He stood speechless until his receptionist spoke again.

"Sir, Miss Maude said she was in town and hoped you could go ahead and see her now instead of her having to wait."

Lowell's eyes narrowed. "I…uh…yes…of course. Please be seated. All of you. Please." He stretched his hand toward the guest chairs and the sofa.

They sat, the receptionist left, and Vance entered the room before anyone could say anything else. Vance spoke first.

"Miss Maude, all of your property paperwork is finished and copied, and I've recorded the deed. The property is yours." He handed her a very large and thick envelope.

"Thank you, Vance. I have things I want to do on the property. Now I can begin doing them."

Lowell cleared his throat. "Whatever could you possibly have to do on that property at your age?"

"That isn't any of your business, is it, Lowell?" Maude stared him down. "Now I'm ready to give you the information for the codicil to my will. Abby has written it all down for me." Abby handed Lowell a sheet of paper. "There's really not that much to do, is there? At my passing, sell the property and divide the proceeds according to the original distribution instructions.

"No, not as much as I expected."

"So we can take the rest of our time together to discuss Charlotte's will."

Lowell's face again changed color, this time to a lobster red. "Vance, perhaps you could take this and prepare the codicil while Maude is here so we can finish with both wills and Maude won't have to make this trip again."

"Yes, sir. It won't take long. Before I leave, I did want to ask if Chief Mulhaney had made any headway on finding the source of the arsenic."

"No," said Enid, "but we…he does have a list of suspects. He's interviewing family members and friends, and he'll be getting search warrants soon."

"Vance…."

"I'm leaving, sir."

"Now, Maude, how can I help you put this question of Charlotte's will to bed?"

"You've seen Charlotte's original signed will that I found. I want to see Charlotte's and Peter's files again to make sure we didn't miss something that might explain why James Franklin did not have a copy of it."

"Maude! This is the third time!"

"You have a problem with that?"

"Yes, I do, but if it will help close this matter, I'll submit to your annoying demands. Nevertheless, there is nothing in those files to explain it and I cannot explain it. According to everything in Charlotte's file, no one ever signed or witnessed this will."

Lowell yelled for his receptionist. They could hear her rushing toward the open door.

"Yes, sir?"

"Have you returned those old files of Peter and Charlotte Goodwin to the basement?"

"No, sir, I'm sorry, not yet."

"That's a good thing this time. Would you bring them in here please?"

"Yes, sir."

No one said a word until the young woman returned.

"Here you are, sir."

"Thank you."

She left. Lowell flipped through the files.

"I see nothing in either file relevant to anything today. I see nothing to suggest Charlotte ever signed her final will."

Without a word, Maude held out her hand.

Lowell slapped both files down on the outer side of his desk.

"Search away. I'm going to the men's room." Lowell jumped up and left the room.

"Him and his bladder," whispered Maude.

"It is a good excuse to leave," said Abby.

Enid bit her lip to keep from laughing.

Page by page, the three of them flipped through the contents of the two files again. As Maude placed the closed folders on the desk, Lowell returned.

"You didn't find anything in them to suggest Charlotte signed her final will, either, did you?"

"No. I won't waste your time about it anymore, but I would still like to have copies of the contents. I would also like to ask one last question."

Vance walked in before she could ask it.

"All done and ready to sign," he said.

"Good. Maude, you sign. Abby, you and Enid witness. Then Vance and I will sign." Vance passed the sheet of paper around. "Done," said Lowell. "Vance, make a copy for our files and bring the original back to Maude. Also, make copies of everything in these two files." He handed him the old files of Charlotte and Peter.

Lowell twiddled his thumbs but again said nothing until Vance returned and handed the envelopes containing Maude's original codicil and the copies from the old files to Maude.

"Ah, here they are," said Lowell. "This business is finished. Now, you said one last question. I would be thankful if you asked one last question."

"Don't be flippant, Lowell. I want to ask you about the rolodex note and the envelope labeled *contingent?*"

Lowell jumped up, surprise bordering on shock frozen on his face. "How did you— Vance, did you tell her about that?

You must have. No one else knew. If my father hadn't made me promise to keep you in my employ, you would be out of here today." He turned to Maude. "Yes, there was a note on the rolodex card similar to notes on many of the cards. However, I found no envelope. Now. Our business is done. I have other clients. Vance, would you show these ladies to the door? I'm going to lunch early today. I...I have some business of my own to take care of. You can take your lunch break when I get back."

Maude gritted her teeth and clenched her fists, but she didn't respond. She stood, straight and head held back. Enid and Abby followed her out of the office and out of the building.

On the sidewalk, she turned to Vance, who held the door open for them. "I am sorry if I have gotten you into trouble."

Vance brushed it off with a wave of his hand. "Don't worry about it, Miss Maude. I can handle Lowell. I've been doing so for a long time now."

Maude nodded, and Abby helped her into the Subaru. Enid caught Vance's eye but could not read the expression on his face. When he closed the door, she got into the car, too, and drove them home.

After a quick lunch of sandwiches and tea, the three women rested, mostly for Maude's sake. Maude went to her bedroom. Abby stretched out on the sofa, and Enid took the recliner.

Abby tapped her fingers together, her frown wrinkling her face from chin to eyebrows. "Lowell's reaction to Granny's question about the contingent envelope shot way over the top."

"I agree," said Enid. "He knows more than he's telling. I hope Patrick hears from the TBI soon, so he can issue search warrants and put an end to this."

* * *

Enid's cell phone woke her from a not so peaceful repose. "Patrick?"

"Yes. I'm headed to Maude's house. I thought I'd check first to see if all three of you were there."

"We are. Have you heard from TBI?"

"I have."

"I'll wake Maude."

"I'll tell you everything when I arrive."

Ten minutes later, Patrick joined the women in Maude's living room. He sat in the armchair, leaned forward, and fidgeted with his hat.

"Tell us every detail," said Maude.

"They identified the kind and source of arsenic. It's called trivalent arsenic, a powdered sodium arsenate. He mixed it with your body powder, Mrs. Everly."

"So that's why Abigail wasn't affected. It wasn't in any of our foodstuffs or cleaning and laundry supplies."

"Exactly. I take it no one but you uses your powder."

"Not me," said Abby, "I love it on Granny. I always have. But I do not love it on me."

"Thank goodness for that," said Maude.

"He most likely replaced the powder more than once. If he had used the same amount all along as was in the box we had tested, your symptoms would have progressed more rapidly. Whoever did this knew what he was doing."

"Enid, I know that frown. What are you thinking?"

"Two things actually. Except I can't get a handle on the first one. It's more like a nudge toward something I already know, but I can't quite see what it is."

"The second one?"

"Fingerprints. What about fingerprints on the powder box?"

"Not one print inside or out other than Maude's."

"So did he wipe his prints off or use gloves or what?"

"I have no doubt he used gloves. He would have used them when mixing the arsenic in with the powder and probably also used them when he got into the house and left the tainted box in the bathroom. As the box we tested was over half full, I suspect he replaced it every time he broke into the house. Of course, technically, he didn't break in. He entered through an unlocked attic window. He did enter unlawfully, though. I…uh…wanted to tell you that before something else became public knowledge."

"You know who it was?" Maude clasped her hands together.

"We think so. Only one person, Vance Abbott, tried to access the account at the bank, is young enough to climb a ladder without any effort, and had access to a key to your house. Circumstantial and weak but stronger than anything else I had. So I requested my first search warrant for his home and the outbuildings. If we didn't find anything, I planned to move on to the next most likely suspect. But we did. We found powdered sodium arsenate in a shed near the house, properly stored in double containers but not marked as such. We found no fingerprints on either of the containers, further supporting his use of gloves."

"Can anybody purchase arsenic?" asked Abby.

"It isn't as easy to acquire as it used to be, and we don't know where he purchased it, but it still has a number of uses, and it can be ordered online."

Maude shook her head. "No. I cannot believe it. What could he gain from it? Have you arrested him?"

"We have. He, of course, said the arsenate was not his, and he had no idea where it came from or how to use it. He swore he did not try to harm you, would not kill anyone, especially an elderly person, for any reason. He asked what motive he could possibly have. He insisted he did nothing but go to the bank and ask about an old account mentioned in a copy of an unsigned will. When he was told the account didn't exist, he forgot about it and the will until you brought up the idea of a missing signed copy. He also insisted he had no idea the signed copy of the will existed until you found it and showed it to him and Lowell. Enid? If that frown grows any deeper, your face is going to break."

"It's too easy. What background does Vance have in chemical substances? There's that nudge again. Could I know something about him I can't remember?"

"Vance does have a workshop. Besides, you can find most anything, including instructions, on the internet."

"Our attacker has been too careful all along to be so foolish as to leave such a poison out where anyone could find it."

"I did consider that, but it wasn't marked, so without a search, who would have known what it was?"

"But he gave you permission to search?"

"No. We didn't need permission. We had the warrant. Besides, he lives with his parents, so we served the warrant to them while he was at work. Abby, by the look on your face, you don't believe it, either, do you?"

"No. He's been too nice and helpful. But.... Nice, helpful people commit crimes all the time, don't they?"

"They do. If it's of any comfort, I'm not stopping the investigation. I do need to pursue this line while we all keep our eyes and ears open."

"You said you had a next most likely suspect," said Enid. "Who is he?"

"Uh...Lowell."

"I thought as much. Do you think Vance could be complicit with Lowell?"

"How so?"

"What if they did find the contingent envelope and James's signed copy of Charlotte's will was in the contingent envelope, and they are both keeping it secret? But that doesn't make sense, either, does it?"

"I don't understand."

"Because," said Maude, "Vance is the one who has been giving us hints and information about the files."

"Hmm. That might tie in with something Vance said."

"What?"

"He said I should talk to Lowell Franklin. He said Lowell had more motive and access and relevant knowledge than he did. When I asked him to elaborate, he said, 'Never mind. It's probably nothing.'"

"Enid?"

"Unless we've left the perpetrator off the list totally, I am more suspicious of Lowell than I am of anyone else."

"Why?"

Maude leaned forward. "I agree with Enid."

"But why?"

"I agree, too," said Abby. "He has been an ornery old cuss about everything, but I thought he was just that way."

"That's all any of you have? He's ornery?"

"No, he has not been as forthcoming about things as he could have been. He's been defensive."

"But listen to yourselves. You said he was an ornery old cuss. Old. Remember the ladder? The person running across the back yard? Someone knowledgeable enough to know about or find out about and use the kind of arsenic this person used?"

"Lowell is physically fit. He always has been."

"He also needed to know about Granny's penchant for her particular body powder."

"My, my," said Maude. "It's been right there all along."

"Again...what?"

"The body powder. Lucille and Lowell give me a box or two of it every Christmas."

"And Lowell has been in your bathroom every time he's been in your house."

"Okay, but that's still circumstantial. There's still the would-be killer accessing the attic. And a knowledge of arsenic. And what about a motive? What would Lowell's motive be? I need something more for a second warrant to search for arsenic on his property when I have a suspect who had arsenic in his possession."

Enid jumped up and shouted. "My nudge! I know what my brain's been trying to show me. Lowell. The diplomas on his wall. His first degree was a Bachelor of Science. If I'm not mistaken, his major was chemistry. That isn't circumstantial. It could tie him and Vance together or point to Lowell alone. We told Lowell you were close to issuing warrants and he left early for lunch, before Vance left. He could have planted the arsenic at Vance's house. Patrick, if you can't get another warrant on the arsenic, could you get one for a missing paper that might incriminate either Vance or Lowell or both of them?"

"Not without cause. And what paper?"

"One concerning Peter and Charlotte."

"From a hundred and fifty years ago? You're kidding, right?"

"To repeat Patrick's question, what paper?" asked Maude. "We have copies of everything that was in their files, don't we?"

"We don't have what was in the contingent envelope, the one he says he couldn't find. I'm thinking Patrick would need a lot more evidence than what we have." Enid sat silent and chewing her lip. "We have to get to that envelope and its contents."

"What is this contingent envelope and what do you think is in it?"

"We only learned about it recently, but Lowell found a note about it at least two years ago. He says he never found the actual envelope. Whatever was in it was important enough for his ancestor to hide it. We know Maude's family history search started this whole fiasco. That envelope could hold something relevant. He did get agitated over it. Even if you could get a warrant, by the time you had it, the contents could be destroyed—if they aren't already. What time is it?"

Abby checked her watch. "It's four thirty."

"When does Lowell close the office, Maude?"

"Five o'clock on the dot."

"Patrick, humor me on this. I need to return to Lowell's office before he leaves for the day."

"Not alone."

"I'll take Abby with me. You and Maude can follow us. We need to go." Enid jumped up. "There's no time to talk! Now! Leave everything where it is. Abby come on."

Enid raced out of the house and to her Subaru without giving anyone time to argue. Ten minutes later, she pulled into the parking place in front of the law office. She raced inside with Abby right behind her.

She yelled at the receptionist. "I need to see Lowell. Right this minute."

"Haven't you all caused enough trouble today? Chief Mulhaney arrested Vance Abbott this afternoon. Of all people to arrest!"

"Where is Lowell?"

"He's in the basement."

"Which way?"

"The stairs are at the end of the hall, but you can't go down there."

Enid and Abby ran to the stairwell. The receptionist ran after them.

"Stop! Stop! I'll call the police!"

Enid yelled back, "They're on their way." To Abby, she whispered, "I hope they're on their way."

At the bottom of the stairs, they stopped and peered through the room, a single bulb casting shadows across its contents. The smell of dust and mold and ages gone by assaulted their nostrils.

Enid called out. "Lowell, where are you?"

"Enid Gilchrist!" he yelled back. "What are you doing down here? You have no right to be in this room."

"I need to see you, Lowell."

He stepped out from behind a filing cabinet near the back wall. "Here I am."

Abby sniffed the air. "I smell smoke."

"So do I," said Enid. "Lowell, what are you doing?"

"None of your business."

"Stay here, Abby." Enid pushed through old boxes to make her way toward the old filing cabinet where Lowell stood. She pushed him away and looked beside the cabinet. Something smoldered in a wastebasket. She scoured the walls for a fire extinguisher, but it hung on the opposite side of the room. She pulled a file containing an envelope out of the wastebasket and threw it on the floor. She jerked off her jacket and threw it over the file. When she began stomping on the jacket and file, Lowell grabbed her and tried to pull her away.

"Miss Enid? Are you all right?"

"Yes, Abby!"

Enid pushed at Lowell with one hand as she bent down to pick up the file. Lowell reached for it.

"Give me that," cried Lowell. "You have no right to see anything in this building."

"Maybe not," said Patrick descending the stairs two at a time, "but I do. Bring me the file, Enid. Lowell Franklin, you're coming to the station with me. Everyone upstairs, now."

Enid gave the file and the envelope to Patrick and carried the wastebasket upstairs with them to be sure it didn't have anything left in it that might reignite.

"Abby, check on your granny," said Patrick. "She's in my cruiser half-scared out of her wits. Go!" Abby did as she was told. Patrick removed the envelope from the file folder and withdrew the sheets of old paper from it. He turned them over one at a time. Without a word, he put the papers back into the envelope. "Lowell, you will need to ride to the station with me. If you resist in any way, I will have to handcuff you." He extended an arm for the lawyer to precede him. Lowell dropped his head and walked to the door without a word.

Enid stood on the sidewalk while Patrick settled Lowell into the back seat of his police cruiser. When he turned his attention to her, she drew a deep breath and said, "I can guess what you're going to say."

"Can you now? Enid, I want to scold you, and I want to praise you. What you did was foolhardy, and you and Abby could have been injured or worse, but if you hadn't done what you did, this file would have been lost. And this file contains the motive."

"Maude has a right to know what's in it."

"And you want to know."

"Well, of course, I do. It's of historical value."

"Right. Follow me to the station. I may let you sit in the observation room. I'll decide by the time we get there."

"We're right behind you."

CHAPTER THIRTY-NINE

By the time they reached the station, Enid had prepared a persuasive argument to convince Patrick to allow them to watch his interrogation of Lowell Franklin. She opened her mouth to speak. Patrick threw up his hand to stop her.

"No need for us to argue about it, Enid. Lowell is ready to confess, and he wants you three *busybodies* to hear what he has to say so he doesn't have to repeat it." The twinkle in his eyes softened the harshness of his words. "One condition. Hear implies listen. Listen. Do not speak. Being in the interrogation room is a privilege not a right nor is it common practice. Personally, if anything, I would prefer you all be in the observation room, but Lowell insists I allow him to *face his accusers.*"

Enid held her tongue. Maude answered for the three of them.

"We will listen, Chief Mulhaney. Unless, of course, you or Lowell gives us permission to speak."

Patrick closed his eyes and shook his head. "Fine. We'll give it a try. At any point, I could ask you to leave."

The women followed him into the interrogation room. Enid sat between Maude and Patrick on the side opposite Lowell. Abby sat at the end next to Maude.

"Mr. Franklin," said Patrick, "my questions and your comments are being recorded."

Lowell spoke first to each of them in turn.

"No need to ask questions, Chief Mulhaney. I'm prepared to tell all. So here we are, Maude Everly, one last time. If this story must be told, I want the whole truth told. I want you and your family, especially Mason's descendants, to hear every word of it. Telling them will be your responsibility. I didn't ask for any of this, and I won't take responsibility for what others did before me. However, it seems I have no choice but to accept responsibility for my own actions.

"To begin with, I did not know about the existence of the signed will until we began going through our old files and Lance brought me the box containing James Franklin's rolodex. The note on the Goodwin card led me to the envelope labeled *contingent*. I wanted to destroy it, but my reluctance to destroy anything prevented me. This reluctance has always served me well until today. Now it has served to be my undoing.

"In spite of my reluctance, I couldn't add the document and its information to the digitized files or database for anyone else to see, including Vance Abbott, although until recently, I had no idea he was in any way connected to your family. I never once thought about Charlotte being an Abbott before she married.

"I should not have left the card in the rolodex. I should have hidden it along with the envelope. I found the envelope underneath the file drawer in which the Goodwin files were located. It held an original copy of Charlotte's updated and signed will along with notes made by James Franklin detailing what had happened, including Mason's complicity in insisting James destroy the will and his *gift* of money as payment to do so.

"James did not destroy it. His notes said he thought it best to keep his copy of the signed will in the event anyone ever found Charlotte's copy. He could then plead forgetfulness or criticize his secretary for misfiling it or both.

"If the will had been discovered and James had failed to convince anyone of simple negligence, he would surely have been held responsible, disbarred, and perhaps even prosecuted. I, on the other hand, could not have been held responsible, financially or otherwise, for what he did. However, I feared that if anyone learned of the deception, the knowledge would negatively affect the reputation of the firm. The firm was my father's life, his legacy.

"More to the point for me, loss of the firm's reputation could lead to loss of clients, which would lead to financial loss. Half my employees and half my clients are African American. Many of those clients are quite wealthy. What happened a century and a half ago continues to affect relationships today. I feared they would take their business elsewhere. I doubted the firm could withstand losing half of its business or employees.

"Like my ancestors before me, I would do anything to protect the firm. I gave up my own life, my own career, for the firm, for my father. I had nothing else to fall back on. I had to protect the firm at any cost. I took the envelope and hid it in my father's antique desk, which no one else is allowed to use. I intended to keep it until I could ascertain that Charlotte's signed copy was not among Maude's belongings after her death."

Maude raised her hand.

Lowell slapped the table and snapped at Maude. "What?"

"How did you ever devise such a plan and carry it out?"

"I'll get to that. Don't be so impatient. If Chief Mulhaney has read James's notes, he has no doubt surmised both the why and how. The contingent file held not only the will but also full statements concerning the ruse with the will and the cause of Charlotte's death. The details of her death are what gave me the idea for poisoning you with arsenic, Maude. You see, Mason obtained his arsenic from James Franklin. Mason asked James what to do about a rat problem in his barn. James had no barn and no cats, so he used arsenic to kill rats. He gave Mason what he had on hand, two full bottles. Later, Mason insisted it took all of both bottles to get rid of the rats.

"After Charlotte died and the sheriff scheduled the inquest, James questioned Mason again about the arsenic, at which time Mason reminded him of his complicity in denying Charlotte had signed her last will. He told James he was complicit in her death as well because he knew Mason had more arsenic than he needed, and he knew Charlotte was dying. James considered it a form of blackmail.

"The only questions the sheriff asked James at the inquest were whether or not he thought Charlotte was of sound mind, knew of anyone who held ill will toward her, or knew anything about her death. He answered yes to the first question and no to the other two. He offered no other comments. Apparently, his testimony was believable. He was a lawyer, after all. Afterwards, James recorded his notes and placed them in the envelope with the signed will to protect himself in the event Mason's actions were discovered.

"James never mentioned Mason's method of delivery, but because of Charlotte's symptoms and the borrowed arsenic, I suspected Mason poisoned Charlotte by putting the arsenic in her food or drink. I couldn't figure out a way to get it into Maude's food without also poisoning someone else, especially Abby. However, I knew exposure could also be through the skin. Huh." A wry smile crossed his face. "The only opportunity I ever had to make use of my chemistry degree. I knew Maude had used the same body powder most of her adult life because my wife gives her a couple of boxes of it every Christmas, so I devised a plan to mix the arsenic with the powder. I carried it with me in a large upright soft leather briefcase, which I left in the hallway when Lucille and I went to Maude's house the week after the reunion, Lucille to visit and me ostensibly to update information for Maude's file.

"When I went to use the men's room that day, I retrieved my briefcase from the hallway and slipped into the bathroom connected to Maude's bedroom where I replaced her powder box with the one I had laced with arsenic and brought with me. I placed the old box of powder in my briefcase. I then removed my shoes and slipped up the stairs to the attic where I unfastened the window latch so I could return to replace the powder later, especially if I needed to increase the amount of arsenic, but also to look through the dower chest for the will or anything else incriminating. I had heard Isabel mention the dower chest and Maude's obsession with its contents, but I had no idea how valuable some of the items in it might be. Then I returned to the bathroom, put my shoes on, and flushed. Then I returned to the living room.

"In the beginning, my intent was only to use a sufficient amount of arsenic to make Maude sick enough to halt her search or to make her family think she was unstable and needed to be in a nursing home so they would disregard her talk about her family's history in the event she did find something incriminating. However, I, too, had to plan for contingencies.

"Good thing I did because the initial amount didn't slow her down much less stop her. While her decline did convince her family she was unstable and needed to be in a nursing home, Maude's reaction did nothing to alleviate my fears. She not only remained in her home and continued her research, but she enlisted Enid and Abby's help. I had no choice but to return and to increase the amount of arsenic each time I replaced the powder.

"I also intended to search through the dower chest when I entered through the attic window, but Maude or someone had removed it from the attic. When I came the next time, Enid and Abby almost caught me. The next time, I found the attic window locked. The best I could tell, the lights were out, so I meant to enter through the back door. I had a key at the office, but I also knew where the key was hidden on the back porch. Unfortunately, the lock had been changed.

"I was growing more and more desperate. I had tried to scare Maude and Abby with the phone calls and tampering with Abby's brakes. The chief rescued Abby, and she got another ride to school. I tried to remove Enid's influence by removing her. Who should show up and drag her out of the car but the chief? I became so desperate I felt like a mad man trying to devise solutions. Especially after you found Charlotte's signed will, Maude.

"The Wednesday morning you insisted I come by to see Charlotte's will and bring the old files for you to see, the morning you went to the ER, I brought another box of powder with enough arsenic to end this whole nightmare. It would have, too, if Dr. Finley hadn't admitted you and Chief Mulhaney hadn't removed it from your house for testing. If it hadn't been for the tenacity of you three women, no one would have ever known. If it hadn't been for Mason and James, there would have been nothing to know."

Abby raised her hand but spoke before Lowell could give her permission to speak. "You didn't take your briefcase with you to the bathroom the last time you were at the house, which means you didn't bother Granny's powder box that time, right?"

"What was the point? Chief Mulhaney had removed everything suspicious from Maude's house. It was only a matter of time before he learned the arsenic had been in her powder."

"But the chief found the arsenic at Vance's house," said Abby.

"You do remember informing me this morning that Patrick had plans to request search warrants."

"I do. Was that why you left for lunch early?"

"Precisely. To place the arsenic in Vance's workshop in plain view so the chief could not miss it. Any more questions, Miss Abigail Croft?"

"None."

"I do," said Enid.

"I am not surprised."

"You were surprised when we entered your office this morning."

"Ah, yes. My final attempt had backfired. None of you had suffered any ill effects from the fire. I expected Chief Mulhaney to walk in next. Then you mentioned the search warrants, giving me one last chance to make it all go away. It might have, too, if I hadn't waited until the office closed to burn the file."

Maude placed a hand on the table between Lowell and herself.

"In spite of your efforts, Lowell Franklin, good did come of all that has happened."

Enid touched Maude's arm. "And more good is yet to come."

CHAPTER FORTY

Thursday, August 18, 2011

Three days later just after noon, Enid, Maude, and Abby met Artemis Channing at the Goodwin home place. Maude had hired Artemis to search for the graves of the five slaves.

Abby pulled two folding chairs out of the trunk of Maude's Town Car and set them up near Artemis's truck. Maude sat in the first one but kept her walking cane beside her.

"How does this work?" asked Maude. "I have to admit I'm somewhat skeptical about spending money on something that sees through the ground. It puts me in mind of the old water divining rods."

Artemis laughed and then explained as he pulled his equipment from his truck.

"It is a little more sophisticated than that, ma'am. The GPR—that's Ground Penetrating Radar—sends a tiny pulse of energy into the ground. That computer there records the strength and time required for the signals to reflect back."

"You can tell if it's metal or not?"

"Yep."

"You can tell if it's…a body?"

"Yep. You can map out a whole cemetery, but you can't see skeletons the way they sometimes do on TV shows. It's more like you can see where the grave was dug and the dirt put back. By the way, before I do this, you all need to turn off your cell phones. Their electromagnetic energy could affect the results."

All three women reached into their pockets and turned off their cell phones. Maude grinned at Artemis.

"What, Mrs. Everly?"

"Even a ninety-year-old woman has to learn how to use some modern technology."

"Ain't that the truth? I would not have thought when I was in school that I'd be using something like this today. Truth is, I still wonder at it."

Enid and Maude watched as Abby walked with Artemis to each of the stands of daffodils near the house. It was the last stand he approached, the one near a tall sycamore tree, where they found the graves.

"Granny! They're here!" Abby waved for them to come to her.

"Gingerly," said Enid. "Watch out for the mole hills in the yard."

"We'll have to do something about those holes," said Maude. "In time, of course."

They reached Abby, who was all but jumping up and down.

"Granny, it's here. The burial spot. You tell her, Mr. Artemis."

"Yes, ma'am. We found five spots here. Two are longer, most likely adults. Two are very small. Most likely babies or very young children. One is sized in between. Possibly a small woman or a teenaged person."

"How are they situated?" asked Maude.

"The two adults are on your right. The two babies lie in the middle. And the smaller adult or teenager is on your left, nearest the tree."

Maude clapped her hands together and then wiped tears from her eyes. "Just where we expected them to be. Can you mark them off? I have someone coming later this week to put up headstones."

"I surely can. Anything else I can do for you?"

"Hmm. Yes. Do any of the body sites appear to contain anything else?"

"Now that you mention it, the one nearest the tree appears to have a metal box about halfway between the surface and the body."

"Could you mark that as well?"

"I can. After I finish marking the spots, if you'd like, I can remove the metal box. I have the tools in my truck."

"Actually, I would like that. I'll pay you extra."

"No need for that. I work by the hour. Just whatever the time is."

"Good."

Abby brought the folding chairs closer to the tree and set them up for Maude and Enid. She stood beside her granny. The three women watched Artemis mark the five spots, gently remove some of the daffodils, and dig up the box. He brought the small metal box to Maude.

"I don't suppose you want me to pry it open."

"No, thank you," said Maude. "I know what the box contains. We'll wait until we get back to the house and clean it off."

"As you wish. I'll put those flowers and the dirt back, and I'll be done."

"Abby will give you a check when you leave. Thank you so much for helping us."

"Thank you for the business, ma'am."

Artemis went back to work.

"Enid, you helped make this possible. I am forever indebted to you."

"It was an honor to do so. I am thrilled that you plan to mark each person's spot with a headstone."

"Thanks to Charlotte's entries in the family Bible, Granny can mark them with their names and dates as well."

"You know," said Maude, "I can almost see Charlotte on her knees right where Artemis is, hiding this money box for Hannah and Miriam and replacing those daffodils."

Abby took hold of her granny's hand. No one said another word while Artemis gathered his tools to leave. Abby paid him and they waved goodbye as he pulled out of the drive.

"Granny, are you really going to wait until we get back to the house?"

"I don't think so. Did you bring that file?"

"I'll get it out of the trunk."

Abby returned with the file, a wooden box, and Maude's apron. She handed the apron to Maude and turned the box bottom up on the ground. Maude set the metal box on top of the wooden box, and Abby pried the lid open.

"It's wrapped," said Abby.

Enid ran her finger over the package. "It looks and feels like a piece of canvas covered most likely with tar."

Maude lifted the package out of the metal box and placed it on the apron over her lap. She unwrapped the canvas and revealed another wrapping of unbleached muslin. She carefully unwrapped the muslin. A jumble of coins and ten-dollar bills fell out of the muslin into her apron. "After all these years. Do you think they have value today?"

"Yes. Those coins and paper are all from before the end of 1862, and they are all in mint condition." Enid picked up a couple of the ten-dollar bills. "These bills are national bank notes. Some or all of them could be quite valuable." She swapped the bills for a few of the coins. "These are 1860 Seated Liberty Dollars. You'll want to list and identify every piece of money here. From the looks of what you have, I'd say their real value is not their face value but their numismatic value for collectors and investors. You do not want to tell anyone what you have until you've had it appraised, insured it, and placed it in a secure place."

"Along with the family Bible and other things?"

"I would think that is long overdue."

"Agreed."

"As far as I'm concerned, the only people who need to know that the stolen money has been found are the three of us and the tax collector. The property on which we found it is mine. The clues with which we found it were left to Granny Olivia by my great-great-grandmother Charlotte with instructions to give it to one of Hannah's descendants. Do either of you have a problem with that?"

"Not at all," said Enid. "Too bad you have to pay tax on it as it really is an inheritance although I suspect the contents of this box alone would be over the untaxable limit."

"I thought about that, but I doubt I could make a legal case for it, and it would probably end up costing as much in legal fees even if I could. What about you, Abby?"

"Nope, I have no problem with it, either. However, I do want you to get this done while you're still here because I do not want to deal with my mama or my grandmamma in court over this."

After a hearty laugh and an even heartier picnic on the ground, they said a prayer over the graves and prepared to leave.

In the car, Maude sighed. "Jonathan and Lowell are in jail. Vance has been cleared and released from jail. My family accepts that I knew what I was talking about and is much chagrinned about their doubtfulness. The account, the graves, and the moneybox have been found. I have but two tasks left, after which I can leave this world in peace."

Abby leaned over and hugged her granny's neck. "You can also live out the rest of your days in peace."

"Amen to that," said Enid. "A couple of phone calls should help you take care of the other two tasks."

CHAPTER FORTY-ONE

Friday, August 19, 2011

The next morning after a most restful sleep in her own bed, Enid once again drove to Maude's house. This visit had nothing to do with danger or death.

"Hurry, Miss Enid," said Abby when she opened the front door. "I don't know who's more excited, me or Granny."

Enid followed her into the living room.

"I suspect we're equally excited," said Maude. They all gathered around the coffee table. "Dial the number, Abby, and put it on speaker. Please, please, let it be who we think it is."

Abby dialed and handed the phone to Maude.

"Hello? Who is this?"

"Hello. My name is Maude Baker Everly. I'm a descendant of Charlotte Abbott Goodwin and Olivia Goodwin Woodson, and I have been searching for descendants of Hannah and Miriam Jacobson. My research leads me to believe that Zora Beale Maston may be a descendant of these two women. Would you be Mrs. Zora Beale Maston, and if so, are you indeed one of their descendants?"

"My, my. How in the world? Yes, Mrs. Everly, I am indeed Zora Beale Maston, and I am a direct descendant of Hannah and Miriam, the first daughter of the first daughter all the way down to me, to my daughter Marian Maston Ross, and my granddaughter Alexa Irene Ross. Whatever caused you to undertake such a search?"

"Please call me Maude, and the cause is a long story. Do you know about Charlotte and Olivia?"

"Indeed, I do, Maude. Please call me Zora. Charlotte and Olivia are part of our story."

"I would love to hear your family's story."

"I would love to hear your search story."

"Do you think you could come for a visit? I will gladly pay your travel expenses, and you can stay with me at my house if you will."

"I would love to. Unfortunately, I am unable to travel due to my health. However, if the invitation could extend to my daughter and granddaughter, they might be thrilled to visit. They could videotape me before they leave, and they could videotape their visit with you."

"I would love that. Let me give you my cell phone number, and you can call me after you talk with them and tell me if and when they can come."

"I will do just that. Maude, Charlotte and Olivia are not just a part of our story. As you've undertaken this search, you must know that."

"Yes, Zora, I do. We are family."

"We are, and I am glad you found us. In fact, earlier this year, my granddaughter began her own search. I had often thought about this genealogy thing, but I thought it would be a lovely retirement activity. Then my health took an ugly turn, and retirement became a process of trying to stay alive. My daughter and I talked about it, but her work doesn't allow her much free time, and she spends that with living family members. I am thankful you have had the opportunity to do this research, and I know my granddaughter will be ever so grateful."

"I look forward to meeting them both. I also look forward to sharing a couple of surprises with them."

As Maude closed her phone, her tears once again flowed but they were overshadowed by the radiant smile on her face.

Enid lifted her head in a silent word of thanksgiving.

CHAPTER FORTY-TWO

Wednesday, August 24, 2011

Five days later, Enid locked the genealogy room's door at precisely twelve noon to leave and meet Hannah and Miriam's descendants at Maude's. She stopped by Mary's office on her way out. Mary was going over the library's budget.

"Just the topic I wanted to discuss with you."

"What? You've all but abandoned us the last couple of weeks and you want to ask for a budget increase?"

If Enid hadn't known Mary for as many years as she had, she might have taken offense. She did know her, though, and she was pleased at how her self-confidence had grown since she had assumed Benjamin's position.

"I have been away but not without cause."

"I know. A worthy cause, too. I have no doubt you saved Maude's life. I had meant to suggest that you take some vacation time, but that was not quite how I envisioned you spending it. You have time left, and I still think you need to relax and enjoy life a bit."

"You are right, but the truth is I enjoy every day I'm here. Nevertheless, this has made me aware of how much I need someone to be my second-in-command. Someone I can rely on when I'm away."

"Ellen has done an excellent job."

"She has. I believe her job needs to be made permanent with pay. She could work part time when I'm not...solving mysteries...but full time when I'm out. She'd be worth it."

"I thought about this last week, but I didn't know how you'd feel about it."

"So we're in agreement."

"We usually are."

"Can you fit her salary into the budget?"

"I believe I can trim a little here and there to cover it."

"Good. May I tell her?"

"Of course. After all, she will answer to you. I have enough to do."

"Thank you, Mary. I'll tell her tomorrow."

"Now go. Enjoy this reunion. You deserve to witness it."

The two women hugged, and Enid left the library with a light heart and a thrill of anticipation.

Outside, she lifted her face toward the bright blue sky and basked in the warmth of the sun's rays.

"This is a good day."

* * *

When Enid arrived at Maude's, she found her and Abby sitting on the front porch. Abby stood at the edge of the porch until Enid climbed the steps.

"They're twenty minutes away," said Abby. "I can't sit still."

"That's the truth," said Maude. "She has paced this porch and popped up and down every minute since they crossed into Tennessee. Truth is, if my knees were a little younger, I'd be doing the same thing."

"I've been antsy all morning, too, waiting for them to arrive," said Enid. "But that's a good thing. Miranda begins medical school today. Our excitement has kept my mind off missing her and Rachel. What about your fall classes, Abby?"

"They began Monday. I have all morning classes this semester, but I cut today's classes. Alexa's classes at Michigan State University begin tomorrow, but she received special permission to miss the first day for hers and Marian's trip. Having a mother in the FBI doesn't hurt. Alexa's going to attend my one Thursday class with me tomorrow."

"Maude, can I do anything for this afternoon?"

"Abby has everything ready and waiting."

"Then I will sit and wait, too."

* * *

Enid and Abby stood on either side of Maude as she walked to the steps without aid of any kind to greet the two women making their way up the walk.

When they stepped onto the porch, the younger woman extended her hand and spoke first.

"My name is Alexa Irene Ross. You must be Mrs. Maude Everly."

Maude took Alexa's hand in both of hers. "Yes, I am. Please call me Maude. I'm your cousin many times removed. Cousins should be on a first name basis, don't you think?"

Alexa smiled. "Yes, ma'am. This is my mother Marian Maston Ross."

"I'm so thankful to meet you. May I call you Marian?"

"Yes, you may." Marian grasped Maude's hand in both of hers. "Our families have waited a long time for this day. I'm thankful to be a part of it, too."

"Alexa and Marian, this is my great-granddaughter, Abigail Louisa Croft."

Abigail held out her hand and then embraced first Alexa and then Marian.

"Call me Abby. Granny and I have traveled through a hundred and fifty years these last few weeks. I can scarcely believe you're really here."

"Your research efforts cannot have been easy," said Marian.

Maude glanced at Enid and Abby. "No, at times they were not, but that's a story for another day. As for today, none of us would be here if it were not for the efforts of one of my dearest friends, Enid Gilchrist." Maude took Enid's hand and drew her forward.

"I'm so pleased to finally meet you," said Enid.

"Alexa Irene," said Abby. "That name sounds familiar."

"Mama named me after Alexa Irene Canady. Maybe you've heard of her. She was the first woman and the first African American to become a neurosurgeon in America. She received the American Medical Women's Association President's

Award in 1993, the year before I was born. She was also from my hometown, Lansing, Michigan."

"I have heard of her. Grand shoes to fill."

"I know, right? Originally, the children of our line were given Bible names, but after Miriam's daughter, Lydia, someone decided our firstborn girl babies should be named after strong and successful African American women. My youngest sister says Alexa Irene should have been her name because she wants to be a doctor. I told her it's not what she becomes but who she is. All of our women our strong and successful."

"This old woman needs to sit," said Maude. "Let's go to the living room to continue our visit."

Later, Maude set her glass of lemonade on its coaster on the coffee table and brushed crumbs from her sugar cookies onto her napkin.

"I have to ask. Alexa, how much do you know of Hannah's story?"

"Every generation of our family has grown up hearing the story of Hannah and Miriam and Daniel. They were our inspiration. Hannah herself wrote their story down 'so our descendants will know the truth,' she said. The one thing she did not do was include the last names of the families who owned them or the town or state from which they escaped.

"Hannah wrote, 'As long as there is a chance that Daniel might be captured on the warrant for theft, I cannot record the surnames of the persons or places we left behind. Daniel and I have vowed never to say them aloud to each other or to our precious Miriam. I regret that I will most likely have to carry those names and places with me to the grave.' Mama had Hannah's story printed and copies made for each of their descendants plus several extras. I've brought four copies with me, one for each of you and one for the library."

Alexa held up a copy of the book. The photo of Hannah, Miriam, Charlotte, and Olivia graced the front cover.

Maude accepted her copy with tears in her eyes. She held the book to her chest. "Thank you, Alexa. I am most appreciative of your gift."

"So am I," said Enid.

"Thank you, Alexa," said Abby quietly, "I can hardly wait to read it. We know Charlotte's telling of their story up until their escape but nothing except dates and such after that. Please, would you mind telling us, if only briefly, the rest of their story?"

"Of course not. From the time they left Charlotte's house until they reached the northern edge of Ohio, their story was much like the stories of any of those slaves who escaped and made their way north. They traveled at night and found safe places to rest during the day. Hannah and Daniel often went without food so Miriam could eat. They barely escaped detection more than once. By the time they reached the northern border of Ohio at the end of December in 1862, they were hungry, ragged, and exhausted, but they were alive.

"And they were close to freedom. Of course, Hannah and Miriam had their freedom papers, but Daniel did not. However, on the first day of January in 1863, Lincoln issued his Emancipation Proclamation. They no longer had to fear being captured and sent back as slaves, and they wanted to remain in the United States. They did want to be farther away from the southern borders than Ohio allowed because they were still concerned about the warrant on Daniel for theft. After some discussion and much prayer, instead of crossing Lake Erie into Canada, they crossed to Detroit, Michigan, and settled there for a time.

"Daniel took the surname Jacobson to honor his father Jacob, who had died when Daniel was a small child. Daniel and Hannah married in March of 1863, soon after they arrived in Detroit. In August, partly against Hannah's wishes and partly with her blessing, Daniel volunteered to fight with the North in the First Michigan Colored Infantry Regiment. The regiment was later renamed the 102nd Regiment United States Colored Infantry.

"Hannah and Miriam were on their own from the time the regiment left Detroit in March of 1864 until it returned in October of 1865. Hannah took in laundry and taught local black children to read and write. She and Miriam survived on that and the few dollars Daniel managed to send her from his allotment each month.

"After the war, Daniel moved his family to Lansing, Michigan's capital, where he and Hannah both became civil rights activists and schoolteachers. In both endeavors, they had an advantage over many of the slaves who migrated north because they had been taught to read and write. Not all slave owners allowed this. Many believed an educated slave would be a threat to discipline and order.

"Hannah wrote that even Charlotte's father questioned the wisdom of it, but he consented to the wishes of his wife and daughter. Charlotte insisted that Hannah be educated along beside her. Somehow, Charlotte and her mother convinced her father that education would be an asset to both slaves and master.

"Since that time, every descendant of Hannah and Daniel, of Miriam's line and the lines of her half siblings, has attended school beyond high school, and every generation has had at least one teacher among the siblings of each family." Alexa glanced at her mother and winked. "Of course, our family is no different than other families. We have our aberrations—like Mama."

"Very funny." Marian raised an eyebrow and shrugged her shoulders at Enid and Abigail. "I'm not so much an aberration as Alexa tries to suggest. I'm in law enforcement. I'm on the Michigan Human Trafficking Task Force. Our member agencies are at every level—Federal, State, and Local. Unfortunately, slavery still exists in the U.S. We call it human trafficking, but it is still slavery. Its victims are used for work and sex, and they are beaten and abused in other ways. In the early days of our nation, slavery may have been about race and supposed monetary survival, but historically it was seldom about race, and it isn't today. It is, and I believe always has been, about power over and exploitation of others. Victims can be of any race, age, or gender. Children, women, and men. Citizens and foreign nationals. Anyone can be targeted. The Civil War made slavery illegal, but it did not end slavery in the U.S. It just gave it a new face and made it more difficult to eliminate. Hannah and Daniel did what they could with Charlotte's blessing and help to save and protect their child, Miriam. I'm doing what I can to save and protect all of our children today."

"Okay, Mom, so you're following in Hannah's and Daniel's footsteps, too."

"Alexa," said Abby, "which path will you follow? Education or law enforcement or activism?"

Alexa winked at her mother. "My middle sister has already committed herself to being a teacher. That left me free to choose Criminal justice as my major and activism as my extracurricular focus."

Maude cleared her throat. "Speaking of which, we have something for you that may help in that endeavor or another endeavor if you prefer. We're not even certain of the full value yet, but it was Charlotte's intent to send a certain amount of money to Hannah after she had settled somewhere and to provide another amount as an inheritance for Miriam or one of her descendants. I've decided it should be the last first daughter, you Alexa, who should receive it."

"I'm honored. I do have a full scholarship, though. Hannah wrote of the money Charlotte intended to send her after they settled if they could make contact. I've always thought if that money was found and I received it, I would want to put it toward a transitional home for girls rescued from trafficking if no one objected."

Maude looked from Enid and Abby to Marian and Alexa. "My dear Alexa, the value of the two sums should go a long way toward that transitional home."

"What an awesome memorial. I've thought about what I would name such a home. It should be called the Miriam and Olivia Home for Girls."

"A perfect name. I'll drink to that." Maude lifted her glass of lemonade, and they drank to the name. "Now we have one more bit of news that I want Enid to share. Without her help, none of this would be possible."

"I only followed your lead, Maude, but thank you. Later this afternoon, when it's a little cooler, we have a dedication service planned. Maude found more than the money left behind. She found the graves of Miriam's brothers, Isaac and Joshua, alongside those of two elderly slaves, Giles and Ada, and an infant named Lewis. She has had headstones erected and a wrought iron fence placed around them. Vance Abbott, a descendant of one of Hannah's half brothers, will be attending the service with members of his extended family."

"I'm overwhelmed," said Marian. "Hannah expressed her grief for her boys until the day she died. Now may Hannah and Charlotte, Miriam and Olivia, all rest in peace."

"Indeed," said Maude. "Abby, would you pull the dower chest closer?"

While Enid moved the coffee table, Abby drug the old chest to her granny's side.

"Next," said Maude, "I want to share with you Charlotte's dower chest, all of its contents, and how some of those contents helped us discover Charlotte's secret and all of the related secrets." Maude stroked the daffodils painted on its side. "Even the daffodils contributed to the story."

* * *

That evening, Enid snuggled against Patrick's shoulder as they sat on her front porch swing. He tipped her chin up with his fingers.

"It's been a hard summer. I thought I'd lose you."

"But you didn't lose me, and we did save Maude from Lowell and helped her connect Charlotte's and Hannah's descendants. Not to mention helped Alexa establish her home for young women who have been victims of trafficking."

"Yes, we did."

"We thought we'd be writing the end of Charlotte's and Hannah's stories. Instead, the transitional home will add many more chapters. I can't think of a better ending for the summer we've had."

ABOUT THE AUTHOR

Sylvia A. Nash lives in West Tennessee. She holds a B.A. in Liberal Arts with a major in English and a minor in philosophy. In another life, she taught high school English. Now she spends part of her time wrestling the stories in her head onto paper and part of her time chasing down the stories of her ancestors. To learn more about the author or her books, visit her website at https://sylviaanash.com.

AUTHOR'S NOTE

When I began writing *Mama's Secret*, my intent was to write a decent mystery about murder and promises across generations. As often happens, though, my story took off on its own and became much more.

I hope *Mama's Secret* highlights some of the horrors and results of slavery for all Americans as well as shines a light on the modern-day horrors of human trafficking. As this is a cozy mystery and as I cannot possibly know the depths of pain and suffering for those who experienced or those who are experiencing those atrocities, I can only approach the reality of their lives.

I also hope this story goes beyond what was or is or even what probably will be. Sometimes stories are about what could be, and everything that could be begins with a "what if."

Finally, I hope you enjoyed reading *Mama's Secret*. If you did, I would appreciate a short review on the site where you purchased or read this book. I would also appreciate a recommendation to your friends. All writers depend on the recommendations of their readers. I write for you, and I appreciate your comments.

BOOKS BY SYLVIA A. NASH

ENID GILCHRIST MYSTERY SERIES
BENJAMIN'S GHOSTS
MAMA'S SECRET
MARTHA'S GIFT
WILLIAM'S CRY

MILLICENT ANDERSON MYSTERY SERIES
THE MISSING CALICO
THE BOOK OF SECRETS
THE MISSING MANUSCRIPT

STANDALONE MYSTERIES AND THRILLERS
RX FOR RETRIBUTION

WOMEN'S FICTION
FACING THE PAST

SHORT STORY COLLECTIONS
CHOICES AND CONSEQUENCES
BEYOND THE MIST
*BIG SISTERS WITH LITTLE SISTER WOES AND
WONDERS*

VERSE
MEMORIES, A BOOK OF VERSE

Printed in Great Britain
by Amazon

27905334R00183

THE
CONQUEST
of FOY

MARK MCPHERSON

ISBN: 978-0-6453164-1-4

for Amber

MAIN CAST

Historical figures unless otherwise stated.

The English

King Edward of England (Edward the Confessor)

Harold Godwinson, Earl of Wessex

Tostig Godwinson, Earl of Northumbria; younger brother of Harold

Edith Swanneck of Wessex; wife of Harold Godwinson

Edith, queen consort of England; King Edward's wife; Harold's sister

Caelin of Wessex, thane and personal guard to Harold (fictional character)

Tilian of Northumbria, thane (fictional character)

Morcar, Earl of Mercia and Northumbria

Gyrd Godwinson, Earl of East Anglia; younger brother of Harold

Leofwine Godwinson, Earl of Kent; younger brother of Harold

Stigand, Archbishop of Canterbury

Aldred, Archbishop of York

Edwin, Abbot of Saint Peter's Monastery and Abbey, London

The Witan; a select council of earls and bishops; advisers to the king

Thanes; England's class of noblemen or aristocratic knights, loyal to the king, serving within the peerage of their earl

Huscarls; elite professional soldiers

The fyrd; part-time peasant soldiers; recruited by thanes

The Foreigners

William, Duke of Normandy (William the Conqueror)

King Hardrada (Sigurdsson) of Norway

Odo, Bishop of Bayeux, Normandy

Father Petrus of Bayeux, Normandy (fictional character)

Pope Alexander II

Guy, Count of Ponthieu

Baldwin, Count of Flanders

Eustace, Count of Boulogne

Alan Rufus of Brittany

Brother Michel of Conques (fictional character)

Brother Hugh of Normandy (fictional character)

Knights; Norman aristocratic soldiers, loyal to the Duke of
Normandy

Norse warriors and berserkers; ranks of soldiers loyal to King
Hardrada

"The tyrant dies and their rule is over, the martyr dies and their rule begins."
Soren Kierkegaard

CHAPTER I

JANUARY, AD 1065

Conques, Aquitaine, Frankish Kingdom

T he abbey was empty. Usually, one or two villagers wandered into Saint Foy to join the monks of the local monastery for vespers, but tonight there were only two monks to carry out the service. The cool gentle breeze shifted leaves into the entrance as Brother Michel closed the heavy doors before heading towards the altar.

The abbey walls were lined with shadows of stone columns, cast from candles lining the nave. Michel's sandals scraped on the cold stone floor as he headed to the altar. The sound echoed into the vast darkness in the ceiling above. Arriving at the altar, he opened the large and dusty bound script of psalms and chants at the calendar, checked the liturgical date, turned three pages to the required prayers, and raised his eyes to the crucified Christ above him.

As Michel's plainsong chant echoed through every corner of the abbey, behind the altar and out of sight, Brother Hugh was wedging a knife into the base of an elaborate gold statue: the reliquary of Saint Foy. Hugh stopped every time Michel took a breath. The task of removing the box beneath the reliquary was proving more difficult than he estimated. The gold gilt statue of Saint Foy enthroned was fine craftsmanship, covered with precious stones and standing at waist height to a man. Despite the value of the statue, the box containing the saint's bones was the real treasure. Hugh had never been close enough to determine how the box was secured, let alone be close enough to bless it. He had been waiting years to have uninterrupted access. Tonight, was the God-appointed time.

"Perago!" *Hurry up!* Hugh mouthed silently in Latin through gritted teeth. Sweat dripped down his cheeks as he continued to wedge the knife between the gold and the timber until the box released with an audible crack. With a sigh of relief, the box fell into his hands. He turned to put it aside before replacing it with a similar box containing pig bones from the kitchen.

Michel was well into the second psalm when curiosity got the better of him, causing him to turn and look around the abbey's interior for his novice, Hugh.

Where is he? He's never this quiet, Michel thought.

Hugh usually stood behind Michel for vespers and rocked on his feet to stay awake, causing the timber floor around the altar to creak and echo through the abbey, often louder than the chant. Hugh had entered with Michel, but Michel was alone. Michel continued to sing his chant while looking around the dim and empty interior, ensuring the abbot listening on the other side of the monastery would not notice the break. Without needing to look at the liturgy, Michel chanted the psalm by memory while he paced down the nave and peered into each dark corner of the abbey, looking for Hugh. His pace quickened. His eyes were no longer full of the wonder of Christ but instead squinting with suspicion as he returned the main doors.

Hugh slammed his back against the rear doors and pushed out to the cloisters behind the abbey. With the box held firmly against his chest, he bolted through the cloisters towards the monastery's stables, his bare feet slapping against the cobblestones.

Michel's head snapped back towards the altar as he heard the cloister door burst open. Lifting the length of his habit's tunic, he ran.

Darting out of the cloisters, Hugh headed for the stables and burst in, startling horses. With the one hand he had free, he flicked the reins over the head of a horse he had saddled earlier that day.

In full sprint now, Michel changed his path from the gate to the stable as he heard the horses stir. While trying to be silent, he reached the stable and peered around the entrance. He watched on in repulse as Hugh fixed the reliquary box to a saddle. Michel remained hidden and silent as Hugh finished knots and hastily mounted the horse.

Before Hugh could ride out of the stable, Michel grabbed a nearby whip and burst in front of them with a loud crack. The horse bucked high and screamed at the whip, throwing Hugh and the box violently on the ground.

"Furta Sacra!" *Sacred theft!* Michel cried at the top of his lungs as he threw himself on the injured brother and wrapped the whip around his neck.

"A thief … a Norman thief!" declared Michel as he tightened the whip. "All this time, you served me with Satan in your heart! I know who you are. Do you think I was deaf to your plans, blind to your deceit? Answer me, brother!"

Hugh's legs kicked as he struggled to breathe, clutching at the whip around his neck.

While they struggled, Michel leant down towards Hugh's ear and whispered, "Perhaps I will let you return to Normandy tonight, without Foy. You can tell Duke William … the bastard … that God has deemed him unworthy of such a holy treasure."

Hugh's head was pounding, and the barn around him was becoming darker. Though air was leaving his lungs, he remembered the knife he used earlier and felt it still attached to his leg. He released one hand from the whip and pulled his leg up towards his reach. Before he could give any time to reason, the knife was retrieved and plunged deep into Michel's ribs, and the whip instantly loosened around Hugh's neck.

In shock, Michel looked down under his left arm and slowly pulled the knife out. Blood flowed from the wound like wine as he fell to the ground.

Hugh coughed as he regained his breath and picked himself up off the floor. He turned to check the damage on the reliquary box and was relieved to find it unscathed, or more importantly that none of the precious contents had spilled out. Still coughing, Hugh took a moment to refix the box to the horse's saddle as he kept an eye on Michel bleeding on the stable floor. He then made his way over to his betrayed superior.

"Forgive me, Father. But don't worry, I will look after her," promised Hugh.

Michel said nothing in reply, continuing to breathe faster while he gripped at the wound under his arm and stared into Hugh's eyes.

Hugh slowly leaned in closer while keeping intense eye contact with Michel. He then placed his left foot on Michel's chest, lifted himself, and applied all his body weight to the heart. Michel yelled in agony as blood sprayed out from the wound across the stable floor. The scream echoed through the dark Conques valley.

THORNEY ISLAND, LONDON, ENGLAND

t's quiet here, Caelin thought.

He could hear the watermill behind the palace dipping into the Thames, broken by the occasional ringing of the abbey's bells. For Caelin, this was a welcome break from the town's hustle and noise, even if the bell ringing was unmistakably novice with its irregular timing.

As Caelin sat quietly, he witnessed a typical scene at Thorney Island. It was situated on the River Thames, west and far enough from London's bustle. The island consisted of the halls and residence of the king, which was separated only by a courtyard to a monastery and a recently built abbey. Earls, bishops, and thanes from the shires would arrive daily, eager to see the king and press their cause. But they would spend most of their time waiting, scripts in hand, dressed to impress, and pacing back and forth in frustration. However, on this day, Caelin watched from a distance as most left in a huff shortly after noon, spitting curses under their breath.

The king's morning prayer, usually no more than an hour,

had turned into several hours. The liturgy of the day had progressed into further meditation and chanting. With the king's routine regularly like this, patience had stopped being a virtue and had become a necessity.

Long into the afternoon, Caelin lingered. Seated just inside the entrance of the abbey's interior, he had managed to keep out of sight. He had a perfect view of the traffic coming in and out of the king's private chapel, allowing him to examine the planned and unplanned movement of servants, kitchen hands, monks, and the abbot. Occasionally the movement escalated into a fuss, causing Caelin's eyes to look up from the ground, but no one significant appeared. As the hours progressed late into the afternoon, he waited, hoping that his gamble would pay off and King Edward would surface, allowing Caelin to join the king's escort on the short walk from the abbey back to the palace. It seemed to be the best opportunity to petition him. It was the only time anyone could get a word in. However, there was no sign of movement; the gamble was unlikely to pay off.

Drifting between sleep and boredom, Caelin's head fell back before springing forward again. The light was fading, and Caelin finally resolved that he had waited long enough. He sat up quietly and gathered his pack to leave. Just as he took a step towards the doors of the abbey, he noticed four monks make their way from the king's chapel to a downstairs room near the crypt.

"Finally," he whispered, assuming this sudden scurry of monks meant they were preparing for King Edward's departure. Instead, the monks began rehearsing a chant and seemingly had nothing to do with King Edward's movements. Caelin shook his head in frustration; he'd allowed himself to waste an entire afternoon. As he stood there in the abbey entrance, rubbing his forehead, he was subconsciously humming the plainsong of the monks' chant. He leaned against the doorpost and allowed himself a moment to listen. His Latin was rusty; he could just make out the words as the monks repeated them. He rested his head and closed his eyes. Surprisingly, the chant gave him a moment's peace before heading into town.

"Kyrie eleison, Christe eleison, Kyrie eleison." *Lord have mercy, Christ have mercy, Lord have mercy.*

Caelin picked up his things and headed towards the river.

Edward is no longer the king he used to be, he thought.

The king rarely left the abbey, sometimes spending days within the confines of the building and its cloisters. Ten years ago, his usual entourage consisted of royal guards, thanes, and his queen consort on the odd occasion. Now that the king had become increasingly focused on spiritual devotion, he kept counsel with Edwin, the Abbot of Saint Peter's monastery, more than anyone else in the kingdom. Making Abbot Edwin effectively more powerful than any bishop or noble. However, it wasn't just the king's routine that was causing a stir. It was his health – it was fading, and many believed that he would not last the winter.

A few hours later, the River Thames was drifting a light mist over London's riverside dwellings, and the main timber bridge was still noisy with movement, though last light had long since passed.

Caelin's small trading boat approach just east of the bridge, paddling slowly almost without a sound. From a distance, the lanterns that moved through the town looked as though they were travelling alone, unaccompanied, but as Caelin drew closer he could make out the silhouettes.

He paddled his little boat to the bank and jumped out with rope in hand. He quickly tied the boat to a nearby post as he kept his eye on the lights in the distance. If some of the lights stopped moving, then Caelin had been noticed. Not many people travelled the Thames on a boat since the bridge was built, particularly at night. If you were seen using a boat at night, it was sure that you were scheming something, and there would be talk of it the next day.

Caelin preferred his little boat to walking. London was getting far too crowded. Saxon families from the south, Angles from the north, and even Danes from Northumbria were heading to London. Leaving their villages, abandoning their muddy oxen ploughs and barren soil to seek a trade in London's markets with whatever they could gather in their carts. This once small town was quickly becoming the heartbeat of the Britons, with almost twenty thousand living within the city's borders.

Aside from wanting to avoid being the subject of tomorrow's gossip, Caelin was keen to have his boat still there when he got back. He tied an elaborate knot to his concealed boat, fixed his sword to his belt, threw a pack over his shoulder, and headed for Southwark,. Weaving his way through the traffic of lanterns and market carts, he passed the bridge's south entrance. His belly rumbled as he noticed the unmistakable smell of roasting pig drifting from Southwark's alehouse. His mind wandered between food and his afternoon at Thorney Island. Strangely, he felt somewhat revived by the quiet afternoon of waiting.

Reaching the hall, Caelin stood outside the door in the darkness and took a moment to breathe before joining the ruckus that awaited him inside. He stared at the door while he shifted his tunic and cloak, kicked chunks of mud off his boots and took one last look around before he pulled at the latch. He struggled. The roof's heavy, wet thatching had drooped past the top of the frame. With a little more effort, he opened the door as wide as he could and squeezed himself inside.

Harold Godwinson finished the final remains of his ale and then slammed the pitcher down on the table to complete a long-winded story to his listeners.

"Now *that* is how you keep a bishop in order," he bellowed, with his posture as high as possible, thumping the crest on his chest. The Wyvern, the Golden Dragon of Wessex. Harold's cronies had heard it all before, but they cheered with pitchers held high, nonetheless.

"Ah, Ethelred," cheered Harold.

No one ever called Caelin by his father's name except Harold Godwinson.

"My lord," Caelin responded as he set down his pack and weapons.

Harold beamed a drunken smile, grabbed Caelin's hand tight and pounded him on the back with an embrace.

"Caelin, we've known each other since we were children. You're my most trusted and most faithful thane. You needn't call me that in an alehouse," he beamed with glazed drunken eyes.

"As you wish. My lord," mumbled Caelin.

Harold sat back down and signalled to the house maid to bring Caelin an ale. "Caelin, you've just missed my story about the Bishop of Bath," he laughed. "He certainly won't be praying to that relic anymore. Ha!"

Caelin took a seat and assumed his role as one of Harold's admirers by joining in on the pitcher-charging laughter with the rest. The company of drinkers consisted of a dozen or so men, Wessex and East Anglian thanes, along with some wealthy landowners. There were also a few from Northumbria. It was Caelin's responsibility to know everyone surrounding his earl, whether friend, subject or foe. He knew everyone at the table, except for the Northumbrians. They were new.

As the noise continued, Caelin noticed the familiar sound of the front door resisting. He watched as the door was shaken a little more aggressively, someone clearly in a hurry. The new guest was young and who was dressed well for a Londoner of his age. Unannounced, he rushed past the kitchen and the group of men, directly to Harold's side, and sheepishly attempted to whisper something in his ear.

Harold grabbed the boy's arm. "Who are you? How dare you burst in here and approach me."

"Uh, I'm from the king's palace, my lord. I work in the kitchens," stuttered the boy. "Th-the king sent me himself, while I was serving him. He asks for your presence at once."

Harold relaxed his expression and released the boy's arm.

"I'll come," he announced and gave a gesture towards the door, ordering the boy to leave.

The drinking and laughter carried on despite Harold's sudden lack of participation. Harold stared at his almost empty pitcher for a moment before turning to Caelin. Nothing was said between them, but it was clear to Caelin that Harold had grown tired of a king he despised.

Harold shook his head with disappointment. He reluctantly rose from his chair, attached his gear, drank the last of his ale and headed for the door muttering,

"Let's see what the monk wants."

The door slammed without struggle, followed shortly after by the sound of Harold's horse heading for the bridge.

Caelin stared at the door; his mind quickly moved to analyse the situation. He thought back to his afternoon at the abbey; he noticed some unusual characters. There were the usual overpaid, overdressed and overweight Witan council member, but there were some others. There were two Frankish-clad men. They kept whispering.

Normans, Caelin thought.

Why would Normans be here? Why now?

Most Normans fled the country when the king and Harold's father, Earl Godwin, went head-to-head over ten years ago. Godwin humiliated the king and exiled all Edward's Norman allies, including his appointed Archbishop of Canterbury, replacing him with a local man already in his pocket, Stigand. As expected, the rest of the Normans were exiled back across the channel within a month. Norman officials visiting the ailing King Edward at this point would cause concern for the Godwin family, particularly Harold.

For a moment, Caelin's mind drifted from Normans to daydreaming of warmer climates in Normandy. He had never made the trip across the channel, but he had heard of the milder weather.

Caelin's dreamy travels were interrupted by the delivery of a frothy ale slammed down on the table in front of him.

"So, good man," whispered the uninvited Northumbrian thane beside him.

"I don't believe I've seen you before. Tell me of your family? I overheard Godwinson acknowledge you as 'Ethelred' earlier. Your father's name, eh? He must have served in Wessex with Harold's father back in the reign of King Cnut. Yes, hmm. I see," he mumbled as he stroked his beard and looked down his rosy nose at Caelin.

"So, now?" the Northumbrian continued, interrupting himself, "What is your service with the Godwins? A Wessex thane, aye?"

The unexpected ale and the uninvited questions caught

Caelin off guard, though he was in no mood to be polite. He turned to respond,

"I am the family embroiderer. Y' know, tapestries?"

Caelin returned to the the roast pig on his plate as the Northumbrian scratched his head. He despised the time-wasting discussions that took place at these events. Particularly talk of ancestries, family alliances, battles, and dead kings. Even worse is when that conversation took place with another thane, England's class of aristocratic knights who served under earls. Thanes could command up to one hundred peasant soldiers and were possessed of land and hereditary title.

Even though Caelin was a thane himself, he despised how they obsessed over rank and allegiances.

———— ◆ ————

The night's freezing rain and sleet had increased to a heavy downpour. Harold's horse was often slipping her hooves in the mud as she darted through people and carts. He knew the route from Southwark to the palace only too well, but it was an awkward ride. Once over the bridge, Harold steered his horse blindly into alleys and lanes, knowing exactly when to duck for trade signs and low hanging beams.

He eventually reached the shared road headed south with the Thames towards the king's private road to Thorney Island and the castle. The king's private road was long, about a quarter-mile, wide at the entrance and narrowing toward the gate. Both sides were lined with two dozen large and flourishing ash trees, the king's favourite. In summer, the fragrance was strong enough to be noticed in town.

Upon reaching the cover of the gate's arch, Harold threw back his hood and wiped the rain from his face. The gatemaster recognised the earl and rushed to take the reins as Harold dismounted with a thud on the timber floor.

"My lord, please follow me, as it is required that you leave your—"

"I know, soldier. I know," assured Harold.

Before leaving his horse with the stablehands, Harold took the opportunity to check the strength of his sword's binding, securely fastened to the saddle.

The gatemaster walked ahead, leading Harold to a cabin just inside the gate. He opened the door, walked in, and hung his lantern in the middle of the room. One by one, Harold removed each weapon from his cloak and belt, placing them on the table side by side. The gatemaster fussed over some documents, though he was distracted by Harold's fine weaponry. He couldn't help but admire the craftsmanship and quality of each item. There were several single-edge knives, each with decorative markings from Wessex and Northumbria. The delicate but strong leather handles were branded with the Dragon of Wessex.

"Be sure that my horse is fed, dry and saddled," demanded Harold as he threw his last knife down, removed his wet gloves and headed for the door.

"Yes, my lord."

Closing the heavy door behind him, Harold paused for a moment and looked across the island's moat towards King Edward's immense castle. The shelter of the gatehouse poured water over the earl's head from its thatching, splashing at his boots. It didn't take long before his mind wandered. Harold compared everything he had ever built to the spectacle across the moat. He shook his head and looked back towards the stablehands who were feeding his horse.

King Edward's stone castle, Benedictine monastery and

abbey were only recently completed, peacefully situated away from the increasing crowds of the town. Though lately, it had been drawing attention away from the usual spectacle in the more populated side of London, the cathedral of Saint Paul's.

Edward's vision of both a palace and a large abbey by the River Thames had consumed him for most of his reign. He chose Thorney Island, which was already home to a thriving Benedictine monastery on the banks of the Thames. The castle's construction was urgent and completed at lightning speed compared to other similar structures. Once the king's residence was complete, it allowed resources to be reallocated to the abbey, allowing Edward to oversee its construction, ensuring his design was carefully followed.

A king who fights for nothing can afford such a dwelling. Harold's late father's words often invaded his thoughts when he found himself envying Edward's palace.

Edward's blood may be Saxon English, but his heart is Norman.

Harold closed his eyes and shook his head to silence the echoes of his father.

Opening his eyes again, he looked toward the palace entrance. He could just make out a silhouette, waving Harold in.

Leaving the cover of the gatehouse, Harold dashed out into the rain, across the bridge and down the path leading to the palace. When he arrived at the entrance, he looked up to greet someone unexpected. Not the usual door-keep and definitely not dressed in the usual attire of a royal servant. It took Harold a moment to realise that he was either a priest or monk.

"Greetings, Earl Godwinson," bowed the strangely dressed door-keep. "King Edward awaits your presence in his private dining quarters."

"And who are you?" Harold asked curiously, looking him up and down.

"You know who I am. I'm Edwin, the abbot of the community here. I'm sure I've introduced myself to you at least dozen times, Harold."

Harold, frustrated and flicking his gaze back to the abbey, responded, "An abbot? In the king's residence? The abbey is over there."

"The presence of God is not confined to a box, Lord Godwinson," responded Edwin, in a much lower tone. They exchanged a moment of hostile eye contact before Edwin walked ahead of Harold down the poorly lit hall.

"This way, my lord. Please remember that King Edward is unwell. Another dose of the usual robust conversation may accelerate his already poor condition."

Harold followed sluggishly, barely keeping up and barely paying attention to anything Edwin was saying. After shaking the rain from his hair and tunic, he curiously eyed the collection of relics and shrines that lined the narrow hallway. One particular reliquary caught his attention. He found himself gazing into the eye sockets of a saint's skull, displayed in an elaborately decorated gold box.

"My lord?"

Harold's gaze was interrupted as the abbot waited with his hand on the door lever. Harold's countenance turned swiftly from curiosity to contempt. He left the curious relic and headed towards the door as it was opened before him. He took three strides inside, stopped and waiting for his presence to be announced.

The door closed behind him, and there was silence.

Harold turned back towards the door; his wet hair flicked across his neck.

"Abbot Edwin is not accustomed to shouting in halls, son of Godwin. You will have to forgive him," declared King Edward, as he picked at specks of meat with his wrinkled hands.

The old king sat alone, hunched over at a banquet table in the centre of a room scattered with many candles, which highlight the mess. The food on the table was surrounded by manuscripts and other loose paper, most of which had fallen to the floor to provide room for dinner.

"Edward, you sent for me. I assume it is urgent?"

"My consort, your sister, is well and sends her love to you and your brothers," responded Edward, without any notion of urgency.

Several moments of awkward silence followed. Harold's frustration grew as he rubbed his forehead. "Edward, why am I here?"

"You know, William … Duke William of Normandy stood right where you are standing now about a month ago. He was even dressed like you are now. Although he was *pleased* to see me," said Edward with a smirk.

"Of course, he was!" Harold's volume increased. "The bastard is expecting everything from you. No doubt you were pouring honey in his ears!"

Edward looked up from his food, his voice remaining calm and quiet. "Harold, you concern yourself with insignificant things."

"The succession is no small matter, Edward … Now, I will ask again. Why am I here?"

"No small matter indeed, Harold … And yet, you've never discussed it with me," Edward responded in a more serious tone.

"I need not discuss it with you!" growled Harold through gritted teeth.

"I see." King Edward sat back in his chair and took a moment before continuing. "Harold, I am sending you to York, Northumbria. Your brother is going out of his way to ruin God's peace in the north. Instead of considering his earldom as a gift from God that comes with responsibilities, he bites the hands that feed him. The bishops and thanes of the north have sent me several protests complaining of Tostig's theft and thuggery. I need you to bring Tostig into—"

"What?" interrupted Harold with a laugh of shock. "You don't send me here and there. Call for Edwin."

He walked to the door, opened it and called out sarcastically, "Edwin! Edwin! The king has a duty for you," before he glared back at the king, his anger at boiling point.

"Who are you to order me anywhere? Surely, you've not forgotten how things work around here since you exiled my father?" Harold burned with repulsion.

"I announced your assignment to the Witan two days ago. They know the king's will," revealed Edward.

"The king's will?" Harold's shock and anger were unmistakable. He stormed to the dining table and removed almost all the food and manuscripts on it with a swift arm stroke. Leaning over the table, Harold grabbed the king's cloak with both hands and pulled him out of his chair to his feet.

"Your memory is failing you, Good King! Let me help you," Harold declared sarcastically as he violently dragged the king to the wall.

"It is I who decides what happens in the north. It is I who speaks with the Witan. It is I who governs!" he proclaimed. "While the monk-king keeps to his prayers."

Edward struggled to speak, and his feet almost lifted off the ground with Harold's strength. "Th-this is for your benefit,

Harold. You need this. You need to grow beyond the limits your father set for you. We can move on, work together."

As the two stared at each other, Harold could see that Edward was trying to break the mould of what had become the norm between them over the years, which was nothing but secrecy and conflict. It confused Harold, and he struggled to trust Edward's motives.

Edward had every reason to hate the Godwin family. Over twenty years ago, Harold's father, Earl Godwin, arranged for Edward's safe return to England from a thirty-year exile in Normandy to take the throne after Cnut's death. Still, Edward was quick to discover that Godwin was in control of the kingdom. Stories eventually reached Edward of how Earl Godwin controlled King Cnut like a puppet, and there was evidence to suggest that Godwin was assuming the same control over Edward. Godwin even forced his daughter on Edward as a prospective wife, intending for a royal heir of Godwin blood. Fearing Godwin's power, Edward could do nothing but marry her. Though Harold's father died more than ten years ago, the Godwin family were still virtually co-ruling England. But for the first time in years, Edward was challenging that normality.

Harold released his hold on Edward and headed for the door, letting Edward fall to his knees as he took in some much-needed air. Harold took a final look back at the king before storming out of Edward's sight.

Harold's boots echoed down the hallway as he headed for the exit, he stopped to open the large doors and headed out into the rain.

As the soldier noticed Harold heading towards the gatehouse, he prepared the saddle and straps faster than ever. Harold burst in and gathered his weapons. With frustration, he secured each item in place on his belt with a thrust, grabbed his sword and headed for the stable. As he reached it, he brushed aside the harried soldier who was tightening the last strap on his horse and instead finished the task himself before he leapt on and bolted out into the night without a word.

CHAPTER 3

RIVER THAMES, LONDON

Later that night, Caelin was already preparing for departure. He left the Southwark alehouse shortly after Harold and headed to a riverside barn in a dark, quiet corner of Billingsgate, a storehouse for Harold's Wessex thanes.

"Normandy," he muttered to himself, sitting at a table by candlelight repairing the leather binding on a short blade.

For several reasons, it was clear to Caelin that Normandy would soon be the main topic of discussion amongst Harold Godwinson and his Wessex thanes. The Normans Caelin saw earlier that day at Edward's abbey were likely noticed by the others waiting for the king. Suspicious detail like that usually gets back to Harold.

Why here, why now? He thought. It was Caelin's job to keep two steps ahead of Harold on local matters, like keeping a keen eye on subtle but potentially catastrophic issues surrounding Harold and his problematic relationship with the Witan council. But when it came to matters beyond the kingdom and relations beyond borders, Harold kept details close to his chest, which often made it difficult for Caelin to do his job.

King Edward's recent shift to a life of righteousness meant he was no longer someone with whom alliance could be bought, and for reasons unknown to the Witan or Harold, it seemed that he was rekindling ties with his roots in Normandy.

To Caelin, the facts were simple; King Edward was old, sick and dying. He had no heir, let alone any distant family in the line of succession. Edward must choose a successor, but Harold had done little to convince Edward of his worth in that regard.

Caelin finished repairing the blade's binding and then laid out the rest of his weaponry on the timber table in the light of a large candle. He jumped up and sat on the bench, resting his feet on a chair, and began his routine of repairing and sharpening his weapons before returning them to his pack. As he worked away through the dark early hours of the morning, he thought through his plans for the day ahead.

Caelin knew he'd be accompanying Harold to Normandy as early as the following day if the indicators were clear. The journey south at first light was apparent.

CHAPTER 4

THORNEY ISLAND, LONDON

Abbot Edwin had been sitting patiently outside the king's dining hall for over an hour, and it was well past the middle of the night. He had seen Harold Godwinson exit in a rush sometime earlier, but the abbot decided it best to leave the king alone afterwards.

Edwin was concerned about how quiet it was in the king's quarters and so knocked before making his way into the dining hall to offer more wine.

"My king!" he shouted as he rushed to Edward's motionless body on the floor.

"Help … HELP!" Edwin's voice of fear boomed down the hall.

"Edward! Can you hear me?" Edwin panicked as the sound of his heartbeat pounded in his head. He began tapping the king's cheeks, opening his closed lifeless eyes, then turned Edward onto his back and straightened out his legs on the floor. Edwin paused for a moment to regain his thoughts. He moved back into action awkwardly, looking for blood or a stab wound under the king's robes.

Two monks rushed in from the kitchen to find the king lying on the floor and Edwin kneeling, rummaging his hands across the length of the king's body, pushing away the thick robes to see the flesh of his torso.

"What are you doing, Edwin?" asked one of the novices.

Edwin briefly looked up from his search, frustrated by the question.

"What? What do you think, brother? I found him like this. I'm looking for blood or wounds. Nothing! Make yourself useful and fetch a physician, bishop, servant, ANYONE! Go!"

Before rushing off, the novice quickly asked, "Is he breathing?"

"GO!" Edwin shouted, his command echoing down to the main hall. The young novices rushed off, leaving Edwin alone again with the king.

Breathing! Why didn't I think of that before? Edwin thought.

Placing his ear to the king's mouth and resting his hand on his belly, he could hear and feel life moving through Edward's body. Edwin's hand rose and fell with the king's breath. He let out a long sigh of relief as he sat back from Edward's prone body, taking a moment to catch his breath.

He picked himself up from Edward's side, grabbed a fur from a nearby chair and placed it over his king.

CHAPTER 5

PEASANT FARMING LANDS, NORMANDY, FRANKISH KINGDOM

Under cover of darkness, Brother Hugh had reached a stretch of peasant farming land on the outskirts of Falaise, Normandy. The horse stolen from the monastery was nowhere to be seen. Dozens of wounds and bruises covered his body as he dragged the reliquary box along the road behind him. His eyes were wide open as though he had seen a ghost, muttering prayers and psalms, sounding like a madman.

A stone's throw away, a peasant girl was binding firewood for the night when she spotted Hugh struggling nearby. Recognising the monk's habit and seeing he was injured, she dropped her firewood and ran over to help.

Hugh fell to the earth with the reliquary dropping to the ground with a heavy thud as thought it was full of stones. Hugh's whole body shivered as the peasant girl rushed to his side, checking the gash on his forehead.

Stuttering and shivering, all Hugh could manage to say to the girl was,

"It's ... it's too h-heavy, she will not forgive. She will not forgive!"

CHAPTER 6

WINCHESTER CASTLE, WESSEX, ENGLAND

Sixty miles west of London, Winchester Castle was quiet in the early hours. It was a clear night. A gentle but cold northerly breeze picked up leaves across the courtyard and blew them into Edith Swanneck's window.

Despite her position on the bed or how she shifted the furs, her mind could not rest. The cold weather, together with the window being completely open, made it difficult to sleep. The new heavy window material had not arrived as expected that afternoon, leaving dozens of the castle's windows open to whatever weather the night delivered. The heavier the fabric, the less cold air, rain and debris could enter. Use enough of a suitable material, drape it in a certain way, and you would be none-the-wiser that a window was behind it at all. The nobility of Northumbria had much worse weather to deal with and crafted a method of window draping so effective that it had been adopted by most of the country's inhabited castles.

Earlier that day, Edith was found storming back and forth

from the court to the stables to see if the cartload of material had arrived.

"The wet marshes have probably kept them another day or two, m-lady," was the repeated excuse of the day from the stableboys.

She burst from her bed and headed for a table at the end of the room. Stretching her arms and feeding them through her furs, flicking out her long gold hair before she reached for the urn and poured herself a goblet of red wine.

Walking toward the open hole in the wall, she could hear the distant hustle and smell the fresh bread as the cooks worked in preparation for the return of her husband, Earl Harold Godwinson.

Edith rested against the window opening and sipped her wine. Vacant minded, she stared toward the dark contrast of the courtyard and warmly lit kitchen below as the moonlight reflected down on her fair cheeks and famously long feminine neck.

The kitchens were attached to the main hall but spanned almost the same length, with quarters above and below ground. The food preparation and the delivery of new window material were two of many things that had taken place over the last few days. People all over the castle were busy, including local stonemasons and builders. There had been sections of the castle's construction incomplete for several months. However, no skilled hands were available to finish the work. The vast majority of the region's skilled stonemasons and builders worked on King Edward's palace and abbey on Thorney Island.

As a cloud of worry hit her, Edith closed her eyes, lowered her head and moved her fingers through her hair. Harold would be returning to Winchester within a day or two, though she knew he would not be staying long. He never did.

CHAPTER 7

FALAISE, NORMANDY

Across the channel, the Chateau de Falaise was awash with colour and music. Norman nobility of all ranks were pouring into the chateau for a wedding banquet. The most anticipated wedding of the season as the bride and groom were the heirs of two rival barons in Normandy – the Hauteville and Belesme families. These two families had been at each other's throats for decades over land and borders until Duke William intervened and forced a treaty that included this marriage. William added a sweetener for the two fathers; he would have the local bishop preside, and the day would fall on the feast of Saint Amandus.

The mere mention of Saint Amandus captured the attention of any Norman or Frankish noble. It was believed that this saint bestowed a special blessing on a particular family of vine growers in Bayeux many years earlier. In all they did, this family was devoted to the Flanders saint. Consequently, the soil, drainage, and climate necessary for the healthiest vines, fattest grapes and perfect drop were attributed to this saintly blessing. Strangely, the grapes of all the surrounding vineyards with the same environment produced sour or inferior wine for several seasons. The wine created by the Amandus devotees was hailed as "heavenly" by every baron and duke in the Frankish Kingdom lucky enough to get their hands on it. Since then, the Saint Amandus winemakers have been unable to meet demand every season. In fear of losing this blessing, there were strict rules the family imposed on anyone who attended the vines, such as daily prayers before and after work and donating the first batch of every well-aged crop to the saint's monastery, far north in Flanders.

Earlier that day, vast casks of the Saint Amandus wine had made its way to the chateau in Falaise for the wedding, and Bishop Odo was eager to access it before it was distributed amongst the guests. He made his way down to the cellar and insisted that he bless the wine before the wedding got underway. Michel, the cellarmaster, bowed to the bishop and humbly obliged Odo's request. But Michel knew Odo was using this as an excuse; he was no different to the throng upstairs, desperate to get their hands on the wine.

"Benedicam vinum, in nomine Patris, et Filii, et Spiritus Sancti." *I bless this wine, in the name of the Father, and of the Son, and of the Holy Spirit.*

Odo's chubby hand, raised over the first cask, quivered as he gave his short blessing in the obscure Roman tongue. He then turned to Michel and ordered a goblet in a more recognisable Frankish address.

"Coupe, monsieur!"

As the bishop took a moment to savour the Bayeux wine, Michel stood aside, head bowed. Odo threw back a hefty gulp; he was proud to enjoy the first cup ahead of the unworthy upstairs. As Michel stared at the floor, he licked a remnant of wine left in the corner of his mouth. Immensely pleased with his sample,

Odo slowly carried his hefty weight up the thirty-odd stairs from the cellar to the main hall.

Guests continued to pour in the main entrance, showering praise on the newly wedded couple as they shuffled into the great hall. The Chateau de Falaise's great hall was the largest and most beautiful in Normandy. The new sandstone columns soared with Romanesque arches and blended seamlessly with the Frankish designs of the other buildings within the walls of Duke William's chateau.

Tonight, inside the extravagantly decorated hall, the walls reflected the glow of an abundance of candles and lanterns, broken up by countless delicately painted ornamental shields and banners featured along the length of each wall. The vast timber ceiling, with beams stretched across the columns and arches, seemed almost entirely black as it absorbed light from the candles.

Most men were dressed in linen under wool tunics featuring embroidery, trimmings and braid weaving crafted explicitly for this occasion. The ladies' tunics were longer than the men's, with a mantle fastening on the shoulder; their long hair was covered with a hood held by a band.

As the merriment got underway, older ladies were seen eating and drinking as though stockpiling for the winter. The younger ladies huddled together, giggling as they observed the bride and groom. Men without titles could be seen elbowing their way to prime positions near noble guests. Weddings were the perfect opportunity to promote yourself or your issue to a local noble when they were happier or drunk and consequently in a giving mood. As always, the higher-ranking noble such as a count, marquis or duke, would attract a larger adoring crowd, Duke William being the highest ranked of all. Though gathered crowds could be as pushy as they were adoring, Normans rarely let their respect for nobility get in the way of an opportunity to complain.

"Duke William," enquired a Norman noble to his liege with a subtle bow, "you have all of Normandy in your hands. You've successfully driven out rebel lords who squandered Normandy's wealth. By contrast, you have increased her prestige and prosperity to a level that even Aquitaine would envy. But I understand you are not a man who is easily satisfied. You seek greater things, do you not?"

"I do not seek greater things, brother. I need not. Greater things are the birthright of the Normans. Greater things are already in our grasp," responded William with a smile.

"To what do you aspire, my liege?" the Norman noble enquired further. "The teenage Philip, King of The Franks, has a secure dynasty, of which you have no connection. Do you intend to ascend to a throne elsewhere?"

"Ascend? The English ascension has already been promised to me, brother," asserted William with a smile.

A lull gripped the twenty or so noble men and women surrounding Duke William, who stared at him with astonishment and disbelief.

"Was he drunk?" they whispered. "Has he struck a succession deal with King Edward?"

Such a deal would be lucrative for even the average Norman commoner, let alone the nobles. More men and ladies left their conversation circles and joined the gathering around William as he increased his volume.

"The King of England is not interested in Saxon power and pride. We all know he has not chosen an English noble to succeed him. What does this mean, eh?"

Duke William's question drew nothing but silence now from the dozens standing around him. He looked at each of them, making an effort to lock eyes with those he knew likely to doubt the notion.

"Believe me when I say Edward does not trust his earls. Edward spent many years in exile here in Falaise. His roots remain in Normandy. Consequently, I assure you, the crown of England will come to me."

Most of the group surrounding Duke William did their best to cheer and raise their goblets, while a few others simply stared at William, filled with doubt and suspicion. William grinned back at the sceptics as he sipped his wine.

Sometime later, past midnight, the older guests had left, and the laughter, dancing and spilling of wine had increased. By this time, Bishop Odo had made himself comfortable, slumped and sleepy in a dark corner away from the merriment and frivolity. He had lost count of the number of times he had had his goblet refilled.

With a belly full of roast meat and a head full of the perfect Bayeux wine, he rested against the stone wall behind him and closed his eyes. His drunken vision took him back to happier times in Rome. Pleasant memories of perfect plainchant, majestic stone cathedrals bursting with colour, fine cloth, wealthy pilgrims, and brothels that didn't distinguish between clergy and merchants. However, now in Normandy, in his humble abbey and monastery of Notre Dame de Guibray, the monks sang like sick cows in comparison. There was never enough money to build cathedrals worthy of wonder, the women were old and toothless, and the monks smelt like pigs. Odo often found himself drifting to nostalgic memories of Rome, particularly following a sizeable meal. The holy city. It was the time in Odo's life where he felt he could achieve or get away with anything.

Odo's dream was suddenly interrupted by a firm grip on his arm. He opened his eyes and heard a familiar voice whisper Latin in his ear.

"Pater Odo venit, hoc vos intellegatis," *Father Odo, come, you must see this,* whispered one of his most trusted priests with an unusually urgent tone.

"Petrus. What is it?" Odo asked.

"Come quickly," whispered Petrus, as he threw his hood back over his head and disappeared through a nearby door.

Moments later, Odo and Petrus were heading through the dark away from the chateau's light and noise. Petrus, younger and leaner than Odo, walked with pace. Odo struggled to keep up after his legs had gone numb from sitting too long on the timber chair. Petrus arrived first at the gate of the abbey of Notre Dame de Guibray, grabbed the hanging oil lantern and lit the way ahead of Odo towards the watermill. The mill was just adjacent to the stone church, which was the social centre of the community. It was where the villagers traded with the monastery and found work from landlords. As the two approached, Odo noticed there was already light coming from the barn attached to the mill.

"What is it? What's in the barn?" Odo was out of breath.

As Petrus walked four or five paces ahead, he turned his head back to Odo and explained, "An injured man was brought to the monastery earlier this evening, and the farmers who brought him said he belongs here, but I've never seen him before. I tried talking to him, but he was not making much sense. He does know your name, and he mentioned being a part of your old order before the Holy Father shut it down. Perhaps it was before my time. From what I could understand, he knows too much of this place and your history to be a madman, but he is clearly in a state. Wearing what looks to be the torn remnants of a monk's habit. He was talking about Conques Abbey and—"

"Conques?" interrupted Odo.

They arrived at the barn and entered. Hugh saw Odo's face and recognised him instantly. Odo, still unsure, squatted beside Hugh, lying on a mound of hay. Petrus brought his lamp over to give light to the situation.

"F-Father ... for-forgive me," stuttered Hugh, clearly struggling to breathe.

"Sweet Lord, Brother Hugh," sighed Odo, instantly recognising his old novice. He then placed both hands on Hugh's bleeding head, blessed him, and proceeded to inspect his countless wounds.

"I thought you were dead or moved back to Rome when you stopped writing to me. I sent you to Conques years ago. I can barely remember why. Have you been there all this time?"

"Y ... yes, Father." Brother Hugh was getting weaker.

"What has happened to you? Who did this?" asked Odo.

"Re—" Hugh coughed violently and eventually spat up blood, his body seizing with spasms. Odo and Petrus glanced at each other with little hope to be found in either of their faces.

Hugh gathered his breath and leant back against the hay before speaking quietly. "Returning from Conques, thieves set upon me. I fell heavy from my horse. I woke later to find them still rummaging through my things. They took it all, left me alive, but they couldn't pick up the box. I watched them heave at it, but it was suddenly stuck or too heavy. She didn't want to move, and then I also had trouble moving her. She became heavier and heavier, Father. I could barely bring her home."

"What box? Who is she?" asked Odo in a hurry, more concerned with inspecting Hugh's wounds but interested in keeping him talking. Hugh slowly cast his eyes past Odo to the other side of the barn, where a cloak covered some sort of object, which Odo and Petrus also observed.

Curious, Odo picked himself up and made his way over to object. Removing the cloak caused Odo's expression to change instantly. Eyes wide open, he immediately recognised a box he had venerated hundreds of times. A shiver of pure delight shot up his spine to the back of his head. The barn, Petrus and Hugh's condition faded out of Odo's cares as he fixed his gaze on the box. His eyes filled with water and his sobering head could hear angels sing as though he had stepped into Christ's tomb itself. He slowly fell to his knees and placed his hands gently on the box.

"What is it, Odo?" asked Petrus. Odo could barely speak through his tears, but he needed only to utter one word to convince Petrus of the item's significance.

"Foy."

Father Petrus instantly flipped back his hood, crossed himself and lay face down, prostrate on the floor towards the box.

Hugh spoke softly through his deep breathing. "She has tortured me since I took her from Conques. I have taken a life before. It was my calling for the order, my God-given purpose. But never a brother."

Hugh closed his eyes with visible emotional heartache. "And now I am hell-bound. I have brought a curse upon myself. She will not give me pardon; my prayers are fruitless. Forgive me, Father."

Silence from Odo. He was barely listening to Hugh while still kneeling and staring at the precious box. He couldn't help but think of the wealth, glory and prestige this would bring his position in the church and the region, which had been rejected by every wealthy and noble pilgrim from Canterbury to Rome. Now Rome would come to Normandy.

Odo turned to look back at Hugh and noticed that he was losing consciousness. He picked himself up off the floor and attempted to lift the box with him, though he misjudged its weight. His grip failed, and he lost his balance, falling awkwardly onto nearby tools scattered on the floor. A small but deep cut, an inch long, appeared on his hand from one of the tools. He sucked on the wound and dusted himself off.

"You see, father? She, she is not satisfied. Take care and return her to Conques." With those whispered words, Hugh slipped into unconsciousness. His breathing faded, and his head dropped back. Petrus picked himself off the floor and attended to the dying brother but was powerless to help. He watched on as Hugh's body moved into stillness, with eyes fixed open towards the sky as though his spirit departed through them.

At that moment, just as Petrus was blessing Hugh's body, a sudden gust of wind swept across the barn's floor, picking up dust and extinguishing both lanterns, leaving Odo and Petrus in complete darkness.

"Odo, I don't have a flint for the lantern, stay where you are, and I'll lead you out of the barn."

"I'm not moving," responded Odo.

"But I can hear you walking ..."

Odo's focus on what Petrus was saying faded away as fear of the darkness set in. He could see nothing but black, not even his injured hand in front of his face, but like Petrus, he heard footsteps in the barn. Odo was ambling and moving his arms around to find a wall before he heard a sudden and incoherent whisper in his right ear.

He quickly spun his body to the right, but his hands found nothing. The whisper returned a moment later in his left ear;

this time he felt a breath and heard his name spoken. Odo rubbed his ears, shook his head and walked faster to flee the torment.

He paused, making out a lone figure standing under a small dim light about ten feet away. He could just make out that it was a young girl with her back to him, cloaked with a head covering that reached her toes, wholly white and reflecting light from an unknown source. As Odo approached her, he could see the side of her face. She was young, short with messy hair escaping her head covering; her sad eyes were fixed on the ground.

Odo made his way around to see her face from the front, but she shifted her countenance, only allowing a slight side view of her face.

Odo was not sure what to make of this girl; despite his curiosity, he stopped himself from trying to see her face and remained a few steps back. He remembered that he still had plenty of wine in his belly, but his mind seemed more alert than he expected.

"Are you lost, child?" Odo asked quietly.

"I am not lost, though you seem to be. Your prayers are not reaching the light. They remain here in this world," she responded, barely breathing her words.

"What? Who are you?"

She ignored his question and gazed at the ground before continuing, speaking with otherworldly calm.

"Down here, I can see your prayers, hear them, and so can every demon in hell because you do not speak the language of light, my fellow servant. Your prayers only provide the darkness with insight into your heart; the darkness knows you well."

Odo finally determined that this was no ordinary girl, and this was no ordinary meeting.

"What must I do?"

"Observe your brother Petrus; his voice is almost deafening as it echoes through the halls of light. Because his heart is not dripping with darkness, like some."

After a moment of silence, the girl changed to a more curious tone. "Can you help me?"

"Help you with what, child?"

"With this." The girl turned to Odo, revealing her pale youthful face and the palms of her hands, from which blood trickled down her arms and onto the ground below.

"Unless these wounds are healed, my master will abandon your cause."

Though shocked to see the blood, it was her piercing eyes that shook Odo's entire body, instantly filling him with a painful memory of every act of betrayal, theft, murder and injustice he had committed and failed to confess. Odo fell to his knees and buried his face into his hands. Tears began to well in his eyes though he tried to fight the emotions away. Hoping to distract himself from the painful thoughts, Odo spoke to the girl.

"What are these wounds, dear child?"

"Your faith," she answered.

Her words were calm but louder than any noise Odo had heard in his life. The force of them threw Odo off his knees and violently to the ground.

As he looked back in her direction, he saw nothing but the darkness again. The vision was gone as though he'd awoken from a vivid dream.

Jumping to his feet and dusting off his robe, Odo headed in the direction of the faintest and only light he could see. Bursting out of the barn's side door, he marched as fast as his heavy body would allow back to the light, noise and merriment of the chateau.

Odo saw Petrus at the same door of the chateau that they had slipped out of earlier.

Petrus turned and recognised Odo heading toward him from the direction of the barn.

"Odo, where were you? You left the barn before I could find you. I returned here thinking you'd come back, but now I see you've come from that direction. Wait. Where did you just come from?"

"I was in the barn looking for you."

"Impossible," retorted Petrus, "I lit another lantern; you were gone."

Odo shook his head at the confusion and changed the subject.

"Where is Foy?" he asked.

Petrus said nothing but simply lifted his hands to show that he was carrying the box with little effort. Odo and Petrus stared at each other, evidently confused.

"How are you carrying that? It was as heavy as an ox when I tried to lift it."

"It's just a box. Where did you go, brother?" asked Petrus again.

Odo responded with a mix of frustration and confusion. "I don't know … I got lost. Forget about it."

"Let's get Foy back to the church, and then you can fetch some brothers to prepare Hugh's body for burial."

Odo and Petrus took a moment before walking away from the chateau without a word. Despite Odo's eagerness to be close to the relics, he let Petrus carry them back to the church. In disbelief, he observed the box as they walked along together.

CHAPTER 8

WINCHESTER CASTLE, WESSEX

I t was misty first light as Harold dismounted from his tired horse, removed his gloves and took a moment to look at the home of his ancestors from the view of the stables just inside Winchester Castle's gates. It was home, but it was not as glamorous or celebrated as the king's new palace, a thought that haunted Harold every time he saw his Winchester Castle from the stable. He picked up his feet and headed into the empty courtyard.

"You're not as quiet on your feet as you used to be, brother," said a familiar voice catching Harold off guard.

Harold smiled and changed direction toward his brother. "Tostig ... Don't you have enough work governing Northumbria? What are you doing here?" he asked with a smile.

"We Godwins are so proficient at governing that it can take place without us being there. You should know that by now."

The two embraced with hearty slaps on the back.

"Ah, Tostig, still the same. You smell of wine and still the same futile talk. How about you talk while I eat," suggested Harold.

In the small dining hall of the castle, Tostig was on his feet waving his hands around as he boasted of his fortunes in Northumbria. At the same time, Harold enjoyed food from several different plates, plates that were still being added to by kitchen maids.

"Father would have been proud, Harold," he continued. "You should have seen the naked monks and their abbot fleeing into the snow. They—"

Harold interrupted with a mouthful of food. "What did you do with the monastery and its stock?"

"The stock?" Tostig responded in haste. "The stock made its way to the lands of my men. The monastery was left standing for the monks to return—"

"But empty," Harold interrupted again.

"I don't see your point, brother," responded Tostig with a confused smirk.

"You have now emptied almost every abbey and monastery in the county. Where will you turn now to pay your men? Perhaps if you tax the right people, you wouldn't need to parade around like a Norseman looking for plunder."

Tostig's countenance changed swiftly from jocular to frustration. "I'm not here to listen to your advice. Besides, you're no different here in Wessex, Harold."

"Tostig! I may taunt the abbots and bishops, but I taunt them to keep them under my rule. I allow their monasteries to run to benefit my lands. If you empty monasteries and storehouses, you may lose their ability to keep producing stock and coin, which is detrimental to your income. I'm sure you know that you are losing favour with the northern families, and I may be powerless to protect you if the thanes want to replace you."

"What?" exclaimed Tostig.

"Can't you see? It's not like it was twenty years ago for our father. We no longer have the Witan's support that he had. The Godwin name no longer demands allegiance. If we continue like you are, the thanes and the Witan will grow impatient, overthrow our earldoms, and we will be powerless to stop them."

There was an awkward silence for a moment as Harold returned to his food. "Why are you here anyway, Tostig? Who governs the north in your stead?"

Tostig took a moment to respond; he seemed shaken and proceeded to pace the hall. "Morcar is raising a rebellion against me. You must unite with me. Gather your men. We can head north and destroy Morcar and his alliance before he secures King Edward's support."

Harold looked up from his food. "Brother, Morcar is a member of the Witan council. More than that, he has the rest of the Witan in his pocket. Going against Morcar, I will have little chance of—"

"You will have little chance of what?" interrupted Tostig.

Harold ignored the question and rubbed his forehead in frustration before responding. "Return to the north yourself. I'll join you there in seven days. You need to either restrain yourself or make peace with Morcar before I arrive."

Tostig walked towards Harold's table and poured himself more wine before heading for the door. "You're weak," he mumbled as he passed Harold's chair before disappearing out of the hall.

As Tostig's fading footsteps were heard outside the hall, Harold was left eating alone. Edith Swanneck quietly watched on from the corridor in the shadows and had been there listening to the entire conversation. Edith rarely missed a critical discussion in the castle. Even the servants had trouble keeping their whispers from her. She made an art of it. She knew every hidden corner and doorway and exactly when the shadows would favour a curious observer without being noticed. She would even wear the suitable cloth to blend in with the drapery.

Harold looked towards the door through which Tostig had just left, knowing Edith was in the corridor entrance behind him.

"It is safe. You can come out now," he smiled.

Edith appeared out of the shadows, walked towards the table and started to undress.

"You know me too well, my love," she said as she arrived at Harold's table and stood unashamedly naked.

CHAPTER 9

THORNEY ISLAND, LONDON

The following evening was colder and darker than the several days prior, as a thick blanket of cloud blocked the moon's glow. London's winter had decidedly set in, the coldest and darkest in years. The fog barely lifted until late afternoon, and freezing muddy roads simply would not dry, making life hell for horses, carts and people alike moving through the town.

There was a lot less movement on the grounds of Thorney Island as the king was not making his usual movements to and from the abbey. By contrast, he was lying almost motionless, covered with furs, and sweating from a fever, which had rapidly increased since he was found unconscious by Abbot Edwin some nights prior.

"Archbishop." Edwin acknowledged Stigand, Archbishop of Canterbury, as he entered the room. He walked straight to him, dropped to both knees and kissed a ring on Stigand's hand.

"What news of Edward's condition?" questioned Archbishop Stigand.

Edwin rose from his knees and walked back to Edward's bedside with Stigand and updated him on the situation as they observed the king's pale face.

"Over the past day or so, he has occasionally wakened and was able to speak, but he has mostly slept today," said Edwin. "Seems to be a sweating sickness. We've seen the king resist this before. However, he might not be strong enough to fight this one, considering the winter. If you allow me to be transparent, my prayerful discernment tells me that this is the end for Edward, and the events that follow will be some form of punishment for England, from God."

"What? Punishment for what?" The archbishop's eyes were wide open.

"For its sins, Archbishop. I needn't list them for you, surely," Edwin replied confidently.

"Brother Edwin, as your God-appointed superior on all things spiritual, I order you to stop this mystical nonsense. The king is ill, that is all." The archbishop's response was sharp, to which Edwin humbly bowed his head in his direction, allowing a moment of silence.

"Then how, Archbishop, do you explain the ambiguity around Edward's succession?"

"This is your final warning, Edwin. Enough of your doomy unauthorised foresight. As for the succession, the Witan council will have that problem under control very soon, I'm sure. But that is no concern of yours. Head back to the monastery and order a prayer vigil for the king. That is what the concern of an abbot should be. Peace be with you, my son." Stigand turned and headed for the door.

Edwin bowed his head until the archbishop was gone. With frustration, he ran both hands over his exhausted face before turning away from the king's side and proceeding down the hall.

CHAPTER 10

NEAR THE SOUTH-EAST COAST, ENGLAND

The late afternoon winter sun was casting warm colours across the scattered clouds, despite the freezing gusts of wind. Dozens of horses and riders darted through a peasant village and exited through its muddy trade roads as peasant folk and their carts hastily moved aside to let them through.

"Make way! Make way!" announced a thane as they rode past.

As they progressed through the lanes of the village, Harold picked up the pace, followed by his band of his Wessexer thanes, Harold's personal guard. The sound of hooves pounding the earth, horses breathing, and steel weapons clattering was an alarm for the oblivious peasants in their way. They were clearly in a rush.

As they darted around a bend in the road, they caught view of another rider and horse resting under an oak tree on the roadside, two hundred yards in the distance, also dressed and equipped much like the other thanes. Harold and his men stayed their course with great speed as they headed straight for the lone rider. The rider waited until they were ten yards off before turning his horse with a kick and a yell, quickly picking up enough speed to ride with them. The other Wessex thanes either rode ahead or fell back slightly to allow room for the new arrival, who measured his pace to position his horse next to Harold's.

"Caelin, brother, you don't miss a thing," said Harold as he maintained his speed.

"I figured your meeting with Edward was significant. So I was sure you'd make a move for either Dover or London. So, what is your plan?"

Harold sped ahead of Caelin for a moment to gather enough speed to dart up a crest. Caelin took a drier and faster route to the left of Harold and met him at the top before they all progressed down the hill.

"I have boats prepared at Dover. While Edward and the Witan think I'm heading to Northumbria with my brother, we sail for Normandy. Just a few of us. As fishermen. Unnoticed by locals. You and I will scout the size of William's army and any preparations he's undertaken," explained Harold.

For Caelin, Harold's story was not convincing. Though he trusted everything Harold said, he was confused and needed more information.

"We already know the size of the duchy and William's army. What preparations do you speak of?"

Harold pulled on his reins and slowed his horse to a trot as the others slowed down around him. "Whoa!" Harold stroked his horse's neck as he looked around at the canopy and foliage. "We'll camp here."

Caelin threw orders to three of the other thanes. "Check the area, half a mile."

The thanes duly obeyed and rode in different directions. Though Harold's thanes would have preferred more comfortable lodgings, they knew this movement must go unnoticed, particularly by English nobility. Visiting any one of Harold's estates in the south would cause a stir and a few tongues to wag.

The men took time to secure the horses off the road and out of sight. Even if they were noticed, nothing on the men or horses paraded noble or Wessex livery. Their weaponry had the appearance of typical Saxon craft to the untrained eye, but any blacksmith would recognise the finest steel upon close inspection.

An hour later, the light had faded rapidly, and the bite of the cold had settled. Harold covered himself with a large fur and flipped a hood over his head as he sat on a log by the small fire. Caelin and the twelve others joined him. It was silent apart from the crackling of the fire but not awkward. These Wessexer men were much like their Germanic ancestors, of few words. One attended a leather buckle on his tunic, another shifted an ember from left to right with a stick, while the others sat still and stared into the fire, silent, as though in a trance.

After running through all the possibilities in his head, as he had numerous times throughout the afternoon, Caelin glanced over at Harold, looking for some clarity. He knew they were headed for Normandy, but what then? And what was the objective, the plan, the tactic?

As Harold continued to stare at the fire, a smirk appeared on his face. He knew Caelin well, very well, more than he knew his brothers, and he knew Caelin was looking for answers. Caelin made it his business to understand every campaign detail;

Harold expected that from his thanes. Although Caelin was quite happy to be in the dark when it came to the meaningless information of kings, earls and bishops. He was single-minded and cunning when it came to the safety of his old friend and liege.

Harold broke the silence and began to talk of his plan and give rest to the curiosity of his dear friend Caelin, his most trusted and loyal thane.

"We sail for Normandy at first light. Once we land at Bayeux, we must not be seen by Norman nobility or soldiers. We must try to blend in with common folk. We don't speak Norman, so we must be quick and light on foot. No swords or bows, just knives. We can re-arm once we reach Falaise on the second day. On the eve of the third day, we will surround and penetrate the chateau's walls undetected. Once William is dead, we will head for the coast and not rest, returning under cover of darkness across the channel back to England. We'll aim to land north of the River Thames to avoid detection. We will have horses and supplies waiting for us and will make our way to Northumbria by the sixth day."

There was a pause as the men stared at Harold, mostly in awe of this confident and aggressive move. They could see that Harold had given this plan some thought and was unshaken by the enormous task at hand. Caelin was relieved that the arduous trip across the channel was not merely to observe the Normans.

"Are you with me, brothers of Wessex?" asked Harold.

The men said nothing. They sat up from their previously slouched positions, placed their right clenched fists on their chests and dropped their heads.

More than one set of footsteps were heard in the distance. The men stood and reached for their fastened knives. Caelin darted off into the bushes, almost without a sound, making his way around to his horse to fetch a bow before scaling a nearby tree.

"My lord?" spoke an unidentified figure approaching the campfire.

Caelin watched from the tree, hidden by the shadow of the large trunk. One of Harold's thanes returned from scouting the area, but it wasn't his footsteps that alarmed Caelin and the men. They expected the sound of a horse. The Wessex thane had returned without a horse and with an entourage of several people.

Well-dressed Mercians? Ah yes, I recognise that overweight useless piece of meat under that robe. Morcar. Caelin thought.

Morcar removed his hood on his elaborate scarlet robe and scanned the men around the fire to find Harold himself. "Good evening, Lord Godwinson. Your scout stumbled across my travelling party and was too suspicious for us to ignore. We wouldn't have bothered to care so much if I hadn't recognised his pretty face."

Harold began to speak as his men stepped aside. "Where are you off to, and from where have you come?"

Morcar laughed. "Godwinson ... I'm sure if I asked you those questions, your answers would be far more interesting than mine. I expected you to be a day's ride ahead of me to Northumbria by now. Did not our king send you there to sort out your brother's mess? Why do I find you near the sea, southeast instead of north?"

Harold was unmoved, though Morcar continued with his laughter. "Are you really surprised to see me here, Morcar? Don't waste our time with your banter. Let's speak plainly, shall we?"

Morcar responded with a smile. "I'm more than happy to, Harold."

"The king is old and dying," proceeded Harold as he walked casually around the fire, rubbing his beard. "And we have observed over the past few months he has again sought counsel with Normans as he did years ago. Unless we want to see a Norman on the throne, we must unite. While we squabble over land and titles like children, foreigners will land on our shores and take power before we notice. It happened before with Cnut. Never again will we let a foreigner rule our people, lands and customs of which they are ignorant."

Morcar stopped Harold and stepped in sharply. "Harold, stop wasting my time with this rhetoric. If Edward has not already announced a successor amongst our ranks, perhaps it is because he has already chosen a successor from his old alliances in Normandy. If he has and informs the Witan council accordingly, we will honour it. Perhaps Edward will announce a successor within our ranks yet? If that is your plan, Harold, remember that you will not only need to win his heart, which will be difficult in his current state, it will need to be witnessed by the Witan council. I can maintain the confidence of the Witan if you can obtain Edward's blessing."

Harold responded with silence.

"Let's come back to that later and return to why you are here, Harold. It is obvious that you intend to remove the ... Norman risk, am I right? Perhaps that is why you are here?"

Harold rubbed his bearded chin and looked deep into Morcar's eyes. His mind fixed on the enormous tasks of assassinating William and winning Edward's heart. It would take the emptying of all Harold's pride to ask Edward for anything, let alone for succession to his throne. He preferred to assume it after Edward had died, but the Witan may oppose Harold's claim if Edward failed to select Harold as his heir. Harold knew he must win Edward's heart, but it would prove difficult after all that had taken place between them to this point.

For the first time, a Godwin would be forced to ask for something rather than taking it, and everyone knew that would not come easily.

Harold turned his back on Morcar and headed to the campfire. "Leave Edward to me," he said casually. "You worry about the Witan council. I'll see you in the north in seven days. Tostig will return to methods more fitting to his role. I promise you that."

Morcar's eyebrows lifted in shock as he glanced sideways at Harold. "You misunderstand me. No, no, you misunderstand the king. Edward did not send you to Northumbria to simply rebuke and restore your brother. He sent you there to remove him as earl."

"What?" Harold turned sharply back to Morcar, lunging for him and grabbing his cloak with both hands. All present, including Morcar's guards and Harold's men, drew swords and knives at each other.

"Men of the north! Lower your weapons! … Now!" shouted Caelin from the pitch-black trees above. Morcar's guards looked up at the black leafy silhouettes in the starry sky, trying to make out Caelin's position.

Morcar looked down at Harold's hands, grabbing his precious robe, and with an insolent grin, spoke quietly. "Harold, think about what you're doing. You need me for your prize. I want Northumbria. Your brother is lost, but if you support him, you will be alone. You need to let him go, and you need to let me go."

Harold slowly released his grip and signalled for his men to stand down with a nod. "We shall see. Seven days," he conceded, waving his hand at Morcar's party to send them off as he resumed his position by the fire. The Mercian and Wessexer men, who were at each other's throats a moment prior, exchanged final glances of watchful uneasiness before Morcar's party disappeared into the darkness, northbound.

CHAPTER II

FALAISE, NORMANDY

The morning breeze shifted the drapery away from the window, bringing unwanted light into Duke William's bedchamber. The light pushed like a weight on his brow, which was already burdened with pain.

"Trop de vin," *Too much wine,* he mumbled to himself.

Blocking the sunlight with his hand, William struggled to open his eyes enough to see the cleaning activity taking place around him. Several household maids were busy gathering up the mess left from the wedding feast the night before. He struggled to remember much of the night, let alone how the chaos progressed into his bedchamber—an unusual amount of ribbons, goblets, food scraps, tunics and a wheeled food cart.

"What is that doing in here?" William mumbled his question to the nearest servant as he pointed at the food cart before remembering being pushed around the halls of the chateau in the cart just a few hours ago.

"Oh yes, the food cart. I forgot about that. Amusing." Rather than dismissing the busy maidservants, he simply threw his face back into the softness of his feather bed and furs and returned to sleep within a moment.

A few hours later, midday approached, and the noise of the servants had disappeared. The sunlight shifted from William's bed, reflecting off the dust lifted during the cleaning hustle and now settling slowly toward the rugs.

William's deep sleep lifted to a light daze, allowing his dreams to become more vivid. His world drifted to a river and a bridge of stone, fields of lush green rolling hills in the background, though standing in front of him was a faceless figure. Although William recognised the man as a Norseman, only a helmet and clothing gave that indication. The unidentified warrior removed his battle helmet and dropped it on the ground. As it fell from his hands, it was replaced with a gold crown.

The Norseman fell to his knees and lifted the crown to William, offering it to him freely. As William reluctantly reached for it, the Norseman looked up to reveal his face. A dry human skull.

Instantly waking from this macabre and confusing experience, William opened his eyes. The dream was still vivid in his mind, as though he'd been there. He lay still and pondered what he'd seen. The lush grass, impressive stone bridge and the crown of gold, the details were strangely more vivid than the identification of the Norseman.

"But why a Norseman, and why was he dead?" William asked himself.

He rubbed his eyes and ran his fingers through his short dark hair to dismiss the peculiar dream. He sighed as he rid himself of the anxiety and attempted to return to a restful state. However, he was now unavoidably awake. He lifted his head to survey the room, now impeccably clean, and saw Bishop

Odo waiting by the window. William threw his head back into the bed.

"Surely, you have more important matters to attend to than pester me?" sighed William.

"There has been endless discussion amongst the local nobles this morning about your drunken talk of claiming the English crown last night," reported Odo.

"Is there? What of it?" responded William with little interest.

"William, do you really want to take Normandy down this path?" asked Odo. "Normandy needs realistic campaigns to flock to. This talk of England is ... impossible."

"Impossible?" interrupted William as he burst himself into a sitting position on the bed. "The English succession is promised to me! Edward has told me himself. It is not a campaign. It is a principle."

"But where it is it written?" responded Odo, growing visibly tired of William's optimism. "In what pages is this truth made law, William? Nowhere! You have no proof, and if you continue to say it is so, without proof, you will lose the confidence of Normandy herself."

There was a moment of silence as William and Odo stared each other down before William spoke in a quieter tone. "Odo, I have men in London this very day, asking Edward to put his promise, which he has already given, in writing. His sickness is delaying the outcome."

"Take control of your ambitions," advised Odo, as he rubbed his forehead in frustration. "You needn't care for English glory. We will soon have what you desire here and more. I assure you our lands are soon to be overrun with the powerful and faithful from near and far. From now on, the English will desire Norman splendour."

"What are you referring to?" asked William.

Odo turned to the door and signalled for someone to enter the room. A novice monk slowly entered, holding a timber box. He carefully placed it on a table near William, bowed, crossed himself and walked backwards to exit the room.

"The relics of blessed Saint Foy of Agen," announced Odo, with great pride beaming from his breast. "Stolen from Conques Abbey not five days ago by one of our novices. This precious and holy relic has captured the imagination and hearts of the faithful throughout the Empire. I have written to His Holiness to inform him that Foy has taken residence here, and once he acknowledges her to be here, multitudes will come with hearts and coin bags full. Local and English pilgrims on route to Rome, Santiago or the Holy Land will almost surely pass through here to venerate this saint. Romanesque glory is at our door, my liege."

There was a quiet pause from William as he slid out from his bed and limped his sleepy body over towards the box. Staring at it, he rubbed his chin. "Isn't this the saint who was brutally martyred in Agen seven hundred years ago and now is famed for driving pilgrims mad with visions and apparitions?"

"Uh, yes. A young virgin martyred in Agen in the early fourth century during the Great Persecution under Emperor Diocletian. In Aquitaine and Normandy, devotion to Saint Foy is rivalled only by the Virgin Mary herself. Incredibly popular saint. But yes, while there are countless reports of miracles attributed to these relics, there are also stories of strange visions and torments. As though Saint Foy is making a fool of certain people."

"Hmm, I see. Isn't this box supposed to be underneath some sort of awe-inspiring gold and jewel-encrusted reliquary?" continued William, with his hands waving around, describing what he was hoping to see.

"Yes, but that would not have been so easy to steal. Once Abbot Etienne at Conques realises that we have the box, he'll simply send us the bust reliquary," responded Odo with confidence.

William turned to Odo with a somewhat confused expression. "What? Just like that?"

"Yes. It is Conques Abbey's interest to preserve and grow the cult of Foy, even if it is with us here in Normandy," revealed Odo.

"Why?" asked William, still confused.

Odo took a deep breath before giving his tuition. "Having two churches that claim to have Foy will only damage her popularity, so Conques will not take that path. Keeping her authenticity and mystery intact is important, no matter where she is. They will soon conclude that the relic will benefit from increased traffic in Normandy and send us the bust. And once they steal her back, they'll benefit from her increased popularity."

"Steal her back?"

Odo started to walk the room. "Yes, they know how to play this game better than most. They stole Foy from Agen two hundred years ago. Conques realised they were on the path to the popular pilgrimage site of Saint James at Santiago de Compostela, but the pilgrims were not stopping at Conques. They were stopping at Agen because Agen had Foy. Conques needed a relic of their own, and not some pathetic relic attempt blessed by an unknown bishop fifty years ago; they needed an ancient saint. A saint powerful enough to mop up the wealth these pilgrims were carrying on route to Saint James. So, they cunningly dispatched a monk to disguise himself as a novice and live among the brothers at the monastery in Agen. After living undercover for ten years, their monk managed to steal the relic and bring her to Conques. Soon after, pilgrims were flocking to Conques on their way to Saint James. Some pilgrims were so absorbed by Saint Foy that they abandoned their plans see Saint James in Santiago altogether and returned home. The theft plan at Agen was perfect, so we copied it, as have many other monasteries around the empire. The common practice is known as *Furta Sacra*. We dispatched our monk to Conques to acquire Foy four years ago, and now we have her. So, I expect Conques Abbey will not let Foy go so easily. They will soon send us the reliquary bust, but they'll start work on an equally cunning but more aggressive move."

"But we won't let that happen, will we?" stated William as he took in the significance of the relic.

"I would hope not, but that is up to you, my liege. Along with some improvements to the building to cater for this increased popularity, the church of Notre Dame de Guibray could do with some improvements. Perhaps some increased security," replied Odo with a smile.

"Granted."

CHAPTER 12

HASTINGS, SOUTH-EAST COAST, ENGLAND

The northerly wind on the channel was picking up and blowing in the right direction for their passage. Harold, deep in thought, looked south at the horizon towards Normandy, the wind throwing his long hair across his face. The channel was uneven, changing and unpredictable, not ideal for a sail south. However, there were three small fishing boats in the distance pulling in nets. That was a good sign. Harold estimated the conditions would cause them to arrive shortly after the last light, ideal for remaining undetected.

Harold turned his thoughts elsewhere as he walked across the sand. The undeniably risky task ahead was causing his mind to consider all the possible outcomes, hoping he would be mentally superior. His Wessexer thanes were skilful, trained and experienced in almost every military tactic. They could lead armies to victory on a battlefield, but an untraceable assassination on enemy turf was another skill. Harold and his men must avoid or outwit every Norman that stood between them and Duke William, a risk indeed. Harold must also not be recognised. There are members of the Norman duchy that could make out Harold's face on close inspection. They spend enough time in King Edward's court to know that Harold was just as powerful as Edward himself.

Harold turned from his thoughts and headed across the sand to the boats as his plain black tunic flowed behind him in the wind. "Are we ready?" he quietly queried Caelin.

Caelin was ready with his report. "We're as light as we can be. We've removed some of the weapons and all the bows. We also found knives among the gear with Wessex branding on the leather, which was fortunate to discover. I added a fishing net in each of the boats, and we'll pick up a small catch on the way for cover if we need it tonight. What do you think about this wind?"

Harold rubbed his bearded chin. "I'm not sure, but we have no choice. We must leave now if we are to arrive before first light."

Caelin nodded to Harold and turned to order the men to embark. They started pushing the two longboats out into the water as Harold jumped on board one, causing it to rock in the shallow shore waves. The assassins were on their way.

CHAPTER 13

THORNEY ISLAND, LONDON

The night brought a southerly wind through the ash trees that led to London's Thorney Island. From the castle's ramparts, high above the ground, the soldiers watched a storm develop as it flashed lightning across huge billowing clouds far in the south.

Across the courtyard in the abbey, oblivious to the storm, a priest led twenty clergy and novices in a *processiones extraordinariae, a* two-by-two-line procession carried out in times of need such as famine, plague, or war. The procession was slow and mostly silent, in almost complete darkness apart from the candles scattered throughout the abbey. With heads bowed and in prayerful meditation, the brothers moved slowly in single file through a course that would take them through the castle, cloisters, and then into the abbey. Once inside, they would approach the altar and proceed up a particularly narrow spiral staircase on the north transept, then move high over the altar and down the equally narrow stairs at the south transept before returning down the nave. The procession was to be repeated throughout the night until first light.

At least half of the men in the community had begged to be given a vocation in the monastery to avoid a threat of some sort, such as starvation, famine, or to escape creditors. A procession like this was a small price to pay for their vocation, and perhaps some considered it a chore. But for the truly humble and penitent of the community, this was an opportunity to be savoured. To experience communion with God and his saints while the rest of the world slept was a rare delight. It was an opportunity to empty the heart of worldly distractions inflicted in the day and dive deep into the stillness found in the arms of the holy, more satisfying than a royal feast.

But there were fewer still who hungered for more. There were whispers amongst the community that some who had taken part in recent *processiones extraordinariaes* experienced some sort of spiritual ecstasy. Some had seen angels walking amongst the procession; one brother claimed to have seen a statue of Christ weep as he passed by.

"Mis-er-ere. Mis-er-ere. Mis-er-ere. Mis-er-ere," echoed the repeated chant of *Mercy* as they proceeded through the abbey and then remained in silent prayer through the courtyard and palace, in the hope of dragging the presence of God from the altar into the castle and more specifically to where King Edward rested.

The king's condition was declining. The physicians and apothecaries had moved their focus from curing Edward to relieving his suffering. Between the coughing fits and hallucinations, he remained in bed. There were roughly a dozen men gathered around Edward's bed, discussing various topics relating to Edward's condition or his imminent passing. There were clergy discussing potential changes to the monastery, apothecaries debating the next course of tonics, thanes and members of the Witan council discussing royal succession and whether their land and titles would be secure. Edwin and his local bishop stood silent, staring at Edward's suffering state.

"Edwin, Edwin." Edward suddenly awoke, alarmed, his eyes wide open as he signalled for Edwin.

"Yes, Good King. I am here," responded Edwin, who quickly knelt beside Edward and grabbed his hand.

Edward took a moment to regain his breath and strength to talk, but his eyes remained fixed on the dark ceiling above him. "I had a strange dream. Very strange," Edward started.

"I'm listening, Edward," said Edwin.

"A monk drew near to my bed and said that because of her sins, God had given England over to evil spirits. Of course, I asked, 'Will God not have mercy?' and he replied, 'Only when a tree cleft in two by a lightning storm will come together of its own accord and grow green again. Only then will there be pardon.'"

As Edwin stared at Edward in shock at what he had just heard, Edward took a moment to pause and closed his eyes.

"Who was this monk, Edward?"

"I'm not sure, brother. Though, he spoke to me in the Norman language. It is not important. We must pray, Edwin."

Edwin's eyes were wide open. He was fascinated but confused. Edward's dream wasn't exactly clear, but it wasn't wholly ridiculous like most of the hallucinations he had had over the last few days. Edwin turned to the bishop hoping that he might be able to make sense of it, but he simply shook his head as if to suggest it was the usual nonsense talk from the fading king. Edwin was not so convinced. This was the first few words of sense he'd heard from the king since Harold visited.

"Harold," Edwin said to himself. Thoughts about Edward's

dream were swiftly diverted by the realisation that Harold visited Edward before he found him passed out four days ago. *What had taken place?*

Across the courtyard, the procession continued slowly around its path. As the brothers prayed through the cloisters, one particular monk had trouble concentrating on his chants and prayers. His mind was not distracted by trivial matters but rather by strange visions that were not like his usual distractions. Though he had never been at sea in his life, all he could see in his mind were huge waves tossing around tiny longboats filled with men screaming for their lives. For the previous hour of the procession, he could not erase the scene from his mind, no matter what he tried. As he reached the abbey, he drew breath to start the chant with his brothers but instead, he simply exhaled "Christe eleison," *Christ have mercy.*

CHAPTER 14

THE ENGLISH CHANNEL

"OSRIC!" screamed Harold through the deafening wind, as one of his men was thrown into the sea by a monstrous wave that swept violently across their boat. He had been attempting to remove a square sail from the mast. Harold, who steered and clung to the rear of the longboat, could only watch on helplessly.

The two Wessex longboats were tossed around the channel like toys. In complete darkness contrasted by flashes of lightning, huge waves from the raging storm would slam into them with little or no warning, causing the boats to roll and taking lives indiscriminately.

It wasn't until more than half the men had been lost before Harold and the remaining men abandoned one of the longboats and combined what was left of the cargo. Which wasn't easy as the boats crashed into each other, leaving one with considerable damage to its keel.

At the moment the remaining boat was headed in the right direction, lightning flashed around them, providing momentary light to their situation. But what the men saw struck fear deep into their hearts. Behind them was an impending and terrifying swell of water towering like an enormous sea monster about to devour their feeble boat. The men embraced the secure timbers as the wall of water fell and engulfed them. Blackness and the deafening roar of the sea consumed everything around Caelin and Harold.

Moments later, they surfaced amongst the waves and rain with desperate gulps of air. Relieved to find each other, they quickly discovered a large piece of the boat's timber, big enough to accommodate them. They swam to it and held on while calling out the names of their companions. As they floated using boat planks and struggled to keep their heads out of the water, they concluded the other men were either out of audible range or gone.

CHAPTER 15

BERCK-SUR-MER, FLANDERS, FRANKISH COAST

A gentle early morning breeze swept across the sands of the Frankish coast of Berck-sur-Mer, a small village of little consequence, though populated with some of the most skilled fishermen in the Frankish kingdom. Some of the men had headed out onto the sand to get a closer look at the conditions before planning the day's movements. Although the day was favourable for fishing, the motionless bodies of two men on the beach caught their attention, along with scattered pieces of wreckage. As the fishermen made their way to the two bodies, they argued in Frankish over what conditions during the night could have caused such a severe shipwreck while they slept. Most of the men were sure the night was utterly calm. Two had said they heard distant thunder across the channel, to which the others concluded that they must have been dreaming.

One of the fishermen, who considered himself a boat construction expert, wandered off to inspect the wreckage while the others dragged the two bodies away from the shore, rolled them over and noticed that they were both still breathing.

"Vivant … pas pêcheurs," *Alive, but not fisherman,* concluded one of the men, from the look of their clothes.

Further down the beach, the boat expert was still curiously inspecting two large pieces of wreckage held together by iron rivets. "Ceci est integer … Saxon," he yelled to his compatriots. He was eager to point out that the boat was Saxon made.

The group still standing around the two bodies looked over to see him holding up the timber and pointing at a particular rivet, which was by no means a Frankish longboat building method.

At that point, Caelin opened his eyes to a blinding vision of sunlight beaming around silhouettes of men standing above him but looking away. He looked around for a moment to gather in as much as he could before closing his eyes again to avoid drawing attention to the fact that he had awoken. With his eyes closed, Caelin listened to the men talk amongst themselves with increasing volume. He could gather from his rusty Frankish that the fishermen concluded that Caelin and Harold were alive, Saxon, not fishermen, and possibly spies. Although relieved to hear Harold was alive, there was still plenty of damage done. They'd been seen and identified as Saxon and assumed military. Not ideal. Caelin was considering options, but he wasn't ready to give up on the mission's objective, not yet.

He managed a comatose performance as the fishermen attempted to wake them before dragging them further away from the shore. With little care and a heavy thud, Caelin and Harold were thrown onto a cart by men swinging at each end of them, as they would for a large catch. Caelin listened as the group delegated one of the men to wheel it away while the rest carried on back to the shore.

Moments later, the bodies of Harold and Caelin were warming in the sun and bouncing gently as the cart made its way toward the village. Still recovering from a night of terror and survival, Caelin felt strength slowly seep back into his body as the morning sun warmed him. The Frankish weather was just as he had hoped. Perhaps not as warm as further south in Iberia, but anywhere the sun shined more than it does in London was ideal.

After several minutes, Caelin opened his eyes and visually checked the state of Harold, who at this point was quietly mumbling the names of his men who were lost at sea during the night. With Harold's condition improving, Caelin switched his thoughts to a way out of the situation. However, escaping without leaving any evidence of it would prove difficult. It was clear that the fisherman would likely hand them over to a local count or duke, no doubt to secure favour or coin in return. Caelin knew that time was running out.

Confident that the fisherman was busy pulling the heavy cart, Caelin popped up and quickly surveyed the area before returning his head to the timber. He had seen a village in the distance, no more than a mile away. Even if the fisherman did not hand them over, with a town full of people to witness the fisherman's catch of two Saxon men, there would be whispers spreading, fast enough to reach the ears of the local nobles. Caelin had no idea where on the Frankish coast they had landed and, more importantly, how close to Normandy they were. There was little time. Caelin needed to act fast if he was going to rescue Harold and salvage something from the disaster the mission had become.

With little thought, Caelin leapt forward from the cart bed, launching over the fisherman and landing directly in his path as if he had dropped from the sky. He left only enough time to see the shocked expression on the fisherman's face before he struck his jaw, which sent him directly to the muddy trail with a splash. With no one holding the cart, it flipped up on its two wheels while a senseless and mumbling Harold rolled out the back. Unfortunately, Caelin was so focused on the fishermen when he leapt from the cart that he had ignored his surroundings.

"Arrêter!" yelled a deep hoarse voice from behind him.

Caelin turned to see several Frankish soldiers on horseback, armed to the teeth, some of whom had already drawn bows.

"Qu'est-ce que votre entreprise ici?" continued the husky soldier in the middle of the legion, who was more decorated than the rest.

Caelin could understand a few words, but considering the situation, it was clear he was being asked what he was doing. He said nothing and stared back at the soldier; there was no use removing all doubt that he was a foreigner by trying to communicate with his basic Frankish. By this time, the mounted soldiers had surrounded Caelin, the cart and the mumbling Harold behind the cart.

"Réponse!" yelled the lead Frankish soldier, his patience wearing thin.

He and Caelin continued to stare each other down while a groggy and muddy fisherman lay moaning at Calin's feet.

The soldier signalled to his men, who gladly dismounted, approached Caelin and swiftly sent him to the ground with numerous blows to his face and belly. They bound Caelin's hands with rope and then fastened it to the back of a horse; two other men picked up Harold. Caelin was soon jogging behind a horse towed by his bound hands, with blood dripping from his mouth and nose.

As he watched Harold's oblivious head bob up and down on the back of a foreign soldier's horse, he could be forgiven for thinking the mission was over.

CHAPTER 16

FALAISE, NORMANDY

In the grand hall of the Chateau de Falaise, Duke William was seated on an oversized decorated chair adorned with blue silk and gold embroidery. The attention of his court was fixed on William's expression, his eyes wide open with excitement portraying a mind full of unrepentant optimism as he stared in wonder at the message he just heard. The messenger stood silent but proud in front of him.

"Read it again," demanded William.

Going along with Duke William's excitement, the messenger proudly unrolled the message and projected his voice once again. "My liege, Duke William. I, Guy, Count of Ponthieu, hold the Briton Harold Godwinson, Earl of Wessex, and his unidentified companion at Beaurain. They were captured at the coastal village of Berck-sur-Mer, where they were found shipwrecked three days ago. I understand this noble Briton is of value to you. I will transport the two men to you immediately if you agree to compensate accordingly. Otherwise, I will release them unharmed and see that they are transported safely back to England. Please see that my messenger returns safely with instruction."

"Compensate accordingly?" asked William.

"The count assured me that you would know the price," responded the messenger with his eyebrows raised, curious as to whether the duke would acknowledge Count Guy's claim.

"Ah yes, how could I forget?" William declared to the few flatterers around, who seemed to smile at whatever he said. "Certain profitable borderlands between us and five seasons of Saint Amandus wine. It's the price Guy has used for anything I have asked of him. I am his liege lord, though there is a price for everything. Until now, I have avoided paying this compensation, but now I believe my subject deserves a reward in response to this gift."

After an awkward pause, William's brow dropped before he turned to the messenger. "How is Count Guy so sure that his prisoner is the real Harold Godwinson?"

"Godwinson identified himself to Guy in an attempt to secure a safe release. We were not easily convinced, but Guy has local bishops who frequently visit London and speak fluent English. They recognised him. Godwinson made a poor effort to alarm Guy. He warned that he should avoid conflict with the King of England by holding his earl prisoner," declared the messenger with a sly grin.

The messenger noticed William was also grinning. Confident he pleased the duke, he then asked, "Shall I return to Ponthieu with your orders to transport them here, monsieur?"

William, unable to hide his excitement, still paused for a moment before responding. "Yes. I'll send you with men to ensure your safe return to Ponthieu. They are to return with Harold. Guy will have his compensation."

"And what of Harold's nameless companion, monsieur?" asked the messenger.

William rolled his eyes and waved his hand as though dismissing a mosquito. The court immediately burst into action, with charters and other documents dragged out to note the official decisions.

YORK, NORTHUMBRIA, ENGLAND

The roofs and lanes of York were blanketed in crystal-white snow reflecting the dim morning light. The morning's snowfall was light compared to the night before, but the air was still thick with fog. It was the heavy snowfall that allowed Morcar to slip past watchtowers unnoticed upon early evening. Morcar and his entourage of scholarly men and leisurely ladies were not a common sight in the expanding town of York, especially while the city was under the watchful eye of its nervous, hot-headed but cunning earl. Tostig Godwinson, like all Godwins, was ruled by fear. He had well-paid scouts in almost every town, village and monastery in Northumbria, with a reward system for reporting swiftly. With easy money to be made, it was unlikely that Morcar's presence went unnoticed.

On a small mount, two miles north, Tostig looked down on the fog that blanketed the town of York. His horse was jittery, moving backward, left and right, perhaps nervous about the steep downhill gallop inevitably about to take place.

"My lord, do you think Morcar intended for us to be informed of his presence? He could have a trap planned," asked one of the three men accompanying Tostig, dragged along on this visit with a moment's notice.

"You underestimate the pig," responded Tostig casually. "He may not be the most cunning pig in the pen, but he's no fool. What possible trap could he set up in my town that could bring me danger? Still, he is foolish enough to come here at all. His efforts to rally support and supplant me ends today."

With that, Tostig kicked his horse into action and headed down the rocky hillside.

A short time later, he and his fellow riders slowly entered York through the main watchtowers. The horses flicked their tails and shot frost out of their nostrils as they caught their breath. Tostig took his time passing by all the main gathering spots, and it was easy for him to see that something was different. The local farmers and merchants would generally be out and about on the roads and lanes, making every effort to look busy as Tostig rode past, but not this time. It was morning, one of the busiest times of the day, but York was quiet. The only people moving about were children.

Tostig's concern increased rapidly. He spun his horse around, stretched his neck and squinted his eyes, looking down laneways in the hope of finding a large group of people gathered to explain the quieter main roads through the town. Tostig found nothing that gave him the suggestion that this was a typical day in York. He glanced at his three men with an unspoken order to be on guard. With that, they picked up speed and headed toward the food store barn to the south, the most extensive timber construction in the town.

As they approached the barn, the noise increased; there was a commotion inside. Whatever was happening, clearly order was lost; men and women were shouting with no lead or direction. Tostig and his men exchanged looks of confusion before dismounting and gathered outside the barn's colossal timber doors. They had not been noticed by anyone inside. The commotion allowed Tostig to approach and lean in to try to make sense of it, still undetected.

"We should leave and return with more men," suggested one of his men.

"These are townsfolk, you fool, not Norse warriors," smiled Tostig.

"But what of Morcar, where is he?" another asked.

"They have no leader, and they will be dispersed in a moment. You watch," insisted Tostig.

And with that wager, Tostig mounted his horse, drew his sword and ordered his men to open the doors. One drew a two-handed axe and swung it twice before landing it heavily between the two doors, smashing the timber bar inside. The doors were burst open by the other two men and the commotion reduced to silence as the crowd of people stared in shock. Tostig slowly moved his horse amidst the group of farmers, marketers, and blacksmiths, but not a soldier to be seen. They all stared at Earl Tostig without a word. He looked around with a confident grin. All doubt removed. Whatever this gathering was about, it was feeble.

Just before he opened his mouth to question the gathering, a loud voice from the back of the hall shouted, "Tostig! Your time has come."

"Who speaks?" Tostig moved his horse around on the spot, outraged by the audacity as he looked across the crowd to see the unidentified voice. There was a moment's silence before a figure at the rear of the group climbed a wine cast and turned to be seen.

"Morcar. There you are! Leave York now, and I will spare your life," threatened Tostig.

Morcar held his belly and laughed. Wiping his eyes and catching his breath, he responded. "Oh, my dear Tostig. Today your confidence is unfounded. Archers!"

Morcar's order caused a dozen archers to appear from the barn's upper level, aiming straight at Tostig and his three men.

"A trap, just as I feared. We've been lured here like prey," said one of Tostig's men.

As the townsfolk gasped in shock at the turn of events before them, Morcar took control. "You are no longer under the king's favour, Earl Tostig. Relinquish your evil stronghold over Northumbria and renounce your rule. Here and now, and I will spare *your* life."

"Treason!" barked Tostig at Morcar, but Morcar was unamused.

"No, I am here with the full support of King Edward. Oh, of course, I almost forgot, and your brother Harold."

"Impossible," whispered Tostig in disbelief. "THESE ARE LIES!" He tried to assure the onlookers, but it seemed too late.

Anger and shock pounded like a heartbeat in Tostig's head. Outwitted and outnumbered, he knew he had little time to act before he would be captured. With a snap decision, he swung the massive rear of his horse around, knocking over several people, including two of his men, and charged for the barn doors. Arrows flew through the air, missing Tostig altogether and allowing him to flee into the fog and snow.

Morcar stood calm, confident and silent as the commotion recommenced, with numerous questions thrown at him from the confused locals, who now realised they were pawns in Morcar's seemingly failed plan.

As Tostig charged his horse through the empty town, he

could make out movement on the watchtowers; the towers that were empty on their way in, now filled with archers, ready for his approach. Tostig pulled hard on the reins to turn back, but before his horse managed the turn, an arrow pierced Tostig's leather boot and progressed through his leg and into the horse's belly.

Tostig fell to the earth with his leg pinned under the horse. As concussion set in and the daylight faded in his eyes, Tostig could see his men in the distance, killed by the archers or being put to the sword by Morcar's men as they also tried to escape.

CHAPTER 18

BEAURAIN, PONTHIEU

Caelin shook his head and forced his eyelids open. He had been drifting in and out of sleep as he sat on the cold, wet and rocky ground. Crouched with his knees against his chest and his iron-bound hands resting on his feet, it was the best he could manage to stay warm through the night. He stretched his stiff neck by rolling around his head and then stared at the opposite stone wall. It was wet from a fair amount of moisture dripping from broken masonry work at the top, which reflected a tiny amount of moonlight peeking through a gap in the wall.

Caelin's thirst was strong enough to cause him to wonder whether he would consume water by licking the stone wall. He concluded it would soon be inevitable.

He took a moment to stand and stretch his legs. Though his movement was restricted, a chain connected the iron around his wrists to the wall. He was, however, able to move his head far enough to look outside his cell through the bars. He could see that there were no soldiers standing guard outside the cells and that there was a single set of stairs at the end of the short corridor, which seemed to be the only entry and exit. He assumed that the top of the stairs was likely to be guarded.

"You're awake, Caelin?" asked Harold in a groggy voice from the next cell.

"I don't think it is possible to sleep in here," answered Caelin as he continued to inspect his surroundings. "It seems we're alone," he continued. "I'm pretty sure these locks were improved by a blacksmith recently, which doesn't help. There's only one exit."

"You're looking for escape options? I'm pretty sure we're stuck in here, for now," assured Harold.

There was a pause for a few moments, and Caelin could be heard moving around. On the other hand, Harold was immovable on the floor of his cell. He had been awake for a few hours, although his mind was burdened with grief.

"That monstrous storm ruined everything," started Harold.

"It certainly did," considered Caelin as he stopped to continue the conversation with his liege, even though he preferred not to bring those events to memory.

"I've never seen anything like that on the channel near the Frankish coast. It was like a curse." Harold paused again, helpless to fight off the guilt and shame that had played havoc in his mind since he regained consciousness two days earlier. He closed his eyes and shook his head.

"We lost good men, brother. Such good men." breathed Harold through his grief.

Caelin sat back down on the cold stone floor, closer to the bars so that he could hear Harold better. "This is not over, Harold," he assured.

"Caelin, look where we are and who we are without."

"I'll grant you, being in here is not good. But we must read the signs and watch for an opportunity. You told me yourself that Guy's liege lord is Duke William, so I assume Guy will send us to Normandy, probably soon. Once we're in Normandy, William will not be foolish enough to bring us any harm if he wants to keep favour with King Edward. And we're unlikely to be in a position to kill William, but we may have the opportunity to outwit him and get home safely. No doubt William will take every opportunity to break your will; remember that. Our mission is unchanged, Harold. The only difference is that we will be using very different tactics and weaponry than what we planned. We just need to be ready."

Harold smiled a little. "You are right, brother. It is a good thing I have you here. We should be on the move soon. Let's try to stay together."

Harold took a few moments to let Caelin's encouragement sink in and bring him out of despair, which allowed his mind to drift back to trivial matters.

"I forgot to ask you something earlier," said Harold. "One of the men mentioned seeing you leave Thorney Island alone a few days ago. The same day I saw you at the Southwark alehouse at night. Why were you at the palace? Did Edward summon you?"

Almost embarrassed, Caelin responded sheepishly, "If he did summon me, you would be the first to know. No, it was something different. You need not worry. It was nothing secret or of any importance. Usually, I make an effort to be unseen, but my mind was otherwise engaged that day. I had some spare time, so I wanted to see Edward about a matter, spiritual."

"Oh," Harold said quietly. "I had no idea that you... Do you still hold to faith?" he asked quietly.

Caelin exhaled and gathered his thoughts before answering. "I ask myself the same question many times. I don't want to hold to faith, but I feel I do not have a choice."

"No choice? Oh wait, I understand." Harold paused for a

moment as it all became clear. "Caelin, if it were anyone else, I would be mocking. But I understand now. Was it about your sister?"

"Yes," responded Caelin slowly, as though the very thought of the subject pained him. "They say she can only be in hell because of what she did. I'm haunted by dreams of her surrounded by darkness and screaming in terror. I need to know if it is true, and if so, can I release her somehow? I've heard that the king understands these matters or knows someone who knows. I hope to speak with him soon. Because of her, it seems that faith has chosen me, brother. Not the other way around. I assure you, Harold, I am faith's most reluctant servant."

"Caelin, you'll never gain access to Edward waiting around Thorney Island with the rest. Go by your normal means. The way you know best," advised Harold.

Caelin smiled and nodded. "I will certainly give that a try, brother."

The conversation was brought to a sudden end as footsteps descended the narrow stairs down toward Caelin and Harold's cells. A fat guard appeared and stopped for a moment to catch his breath, coughing up to spit on the ground.

He eventually turned to the two cells with his burning torch and inspected the prisoners as he continued to breathe heavily. He then hung his torch on the nearby wall and unlocked the iron doors of Caelin's cell.

"Hey, you Englisc. You oot! You go!" The oversized guard abruptly brought Caelin to his feet, released the chain attached to Caelin's bound hands and pushed him out of the cell.

Harold jumped to his feet as swiftly as he could with his hands also chained to the wall. Yelling at the top of his voice, he said, "Frankish bastard! Where are you taking him? He stays with me, do you understand?"

The guard ignored him as he shuffled Caelin up the stairs until their footsteps faded away.

An hour or two had passed without a sound from the stairs or anywhere else. Although the cell was still completely dark, an exhausted Harold could gather morning had dawned as he made out a small amount of sunlight peering through a gap in the wall.

Where did they take Caelin, and what have they done to him?

After thinking through all the possibilities, he considered it very likely that their captor, Guy, had struck a deal with Duke William, which did not include anyone other than Harold, and therefore Caelin was dead.

If he's dead, there'll be hell to pay when I get out of here. He thought as he buried his head in his palms.

His mind slipped back to their earlier conversation of Caelin's sister. Harold could remember Caelin utterly overcome with grief after his sister took her own life. It was days before Caelin would take food and a few weeks before he was fit enough for service. For Harold, the grief of losing his father seemed to roll off his shoulders after a relatively short amount of time, like rain off a leaf. So, he was a little unprepared to see Caelin so wounded in the wake of his sister's death.

He must have truly loved his sister, Harold thought. *Like no other.* She was the person Caelin wanted to protect from this world.

Her death was my failure. Harold remembered Caelin's words, though he felt Caelin was not to blame. Caelin's sister was tormented by the omens, relics and mysteries fed to her by zealous priests. The superstitions drove her so mad that she eventually threw herself off the cliffs at Dover to escape all that she feared. Caelin vowed never to trust clerics, let alone have any faith.

Though he may despise clerics, it seems his faith has remained.

Harold's thoughts drifted back to their mission. Contrary to the optimism Caelin advocated, this mission had progressed from bad to complete disaster. Though it was a struggle for a Godwinson that prided himself on precision military tactics, Harold was determined not to let the feelings of failure overwhelm him.

There, alone in his prison cell far from Wessex, he still held to an unwavering sense that the throne was rightfully his.

This is not over, he thought. *I must get through this. There is so much to do. I must get home soon enough to deal with Tostig and Morcar before Edward dies.*

Harold's troubled and weary mind continued to spin with struggles as he drifted into a fitful slumber.

Count Guy headed down the narrow winding stairs towards Harold's dark cell, along with an English-speaking bishop and two guards. As they arrived, the footsteps and clanking of armour woke Harold, and he slowly sat up.

Guy instructed the bishop and guards in a calm but direct tone before the bishop interpreted. As the bishop spoke, the guards opened the iron door and released Harold's bound hands.

"You are a popular captive, Monsieur Godwinson. You are to be escorted to Normandy immediately. Duke William will be your new host. I believe you know of him?"

In the dim light of the torches, Harold stared past the bishop directly into Guy's eyes as the bonds on his hands were released. The stare drew a sly grin from Guy. Harold was not so amused.

"What of my soldier, what did you do with him?" asked Harold as he looked away from Guy's gaze.

"He has been sent back to the coast, unharmed. He will remain unharmed and shipped back to England once we receive word that you have reached Normandy. Go in peace."

Harold was led up the stairs and outside to the sunrise peering over distant mountains. Two stablehands stood in the courtyard with four horses, prepared for the journey southwest to Normandy.

Harold and three soldiers mounted their assigned horses, and as the stablehands adjusted the bindings, the bishop approached Harold.

"You will ride with these three men and remain in their sight at all times. Tonight, you will be hosted at a monastery in Bec before you continue to Normandy. Again, I assure you, no harm will come to you or your companion if you arrive safely in Normandy."

Harold said nothing in response, although he could think of nothing but returning with enough men to raze the place, leaving nothing but a spike displaying Guy's head. He resisted the temptation to threaten the bishop and led his horse out of the courtyard.

Harold rode on slightly ahead of the three heavily armed soldiers. His hands and feet were not bound, but he was dressed lightly and without any supplies. He needed to protect Caelin, and their route was far from any villages or the coast. It seemed Harold's only choice was to submit to Guy's requests, for now.

As the day progressed, Harold trotted over the beautiful

scenery of lush green hills and farmland. Still, he stared blankly into the horizon. His vulnerable situation played havoc on his mind. Being a prisoner in the hands of the Franks was a stark contrast from the praise and expectations draped on him from his youth. With only his thoughts to consult, feelings of failure had progressed to frustration and anger in this silent journey. Harold went through lists of candidates and situations that could be blamed for not only this but a whole range of failures that fell short of the Godwin standard.

After several hours, Harold stopped his spiralling thoughts as he noticed a pattern emerging. Most of the struggles he had experienced over the past decade were with the church itself, clerics, or seriously devout individuals. The church's laws, the wealth of the monasteries, the stubbornness of bishops, the idleness of the faithful. Blame, built up in Harold's mind as the hours of travelling passed, was falling in the direction of the church. Inevitably his mind seemed to snap with the realisation that the responsibility of his problems landed in the lap of one person: an angry god, a god who seemed bent on limiting every ambition Harold ever had. The existence of God was not the question now; it was more convincing now that Harold could see a pattern of his family's misfortunes, following his family's treatment of the church along with anyone who believed.

My family has been cursed, he concluded. What was more, the curse would see its final blow with Harold's end in Normandy. God, it would seem, would have his vengeance.

The culmination of these thoughts over several hours left Harold tired, powerless, but the anger remained. His head slumped and bobbed around with every trot.

CHAPTER 19

BEC ABBEY, ON ROUTE TO NORMANDY

As the monk looked out into the distance from the walls, he could recognise Ponthieu soldiers approaching and called to those below to open the monastery gates.

The awe-inspiring stone-built monastery of Bec Abbey sat in the middle of the village Le Bec-Hellouin, where most of the peasants avoided slavery or serfdom by keeping regular trade with the abbey. Rather than being cleansed of worldly power and wealth, large monasteries all over Christendom had increasingly become economic strongholds, carefully protected by powerful patrons and local nobility. Their communities boasted masters in almost every trade and produce, from watermills to pig farming and woodwork. Bec Abbey was no exception.

Like many other large monasteries, Bec Abbey not only transformed and controlled the economy of its surrounding towns and villages, but it had also developed an unchallenged control over the minds and imagination of the locals. The nobles and peasants around Bec were renowned for holding fast to faith and the teachings upheld by the church, which included the belief that their ancestors relied on them for prayers and acts that would bring or speed up their repose. This strong belief bound the faithful to their local abbey, priest or monastery. It was the only way to blessing in this life and the next.

Harold slowly trotted through the gates into the confines of the abbey and looked around the various stone buildings within its walls. The first thing he noticed was the vast difference in architecture. While recent constructions of the English were built to survive attacks of invaders and the weather, Norman architecture seemed to focus on beauty and inspiring awe. Arches and columns soared, colours flourished.

The riders reached the stables and were unloading their horses when a smiling brother approached them with hands raised in welcome. Harold noticed he was a little less filthy than the others around the courtyard.

"Bienvenue messieurs. Venez manger, boire, se reposer, prier." *Welcome gentlemen. Come eat, drink, rest, pray.*

"Prieur Lanfranc," responded one of the guards. "Nous avons besoin de la sécurité pour l'Anglais." *Prior Lanfranc. We require security for the Englishman.*

Lanfranc turned to Harold. "Anglais? Oh yes, I remember. I heard of your capture in Flanders. I am Lanfranc, a prior and teacher within this community. I bid you welcome on behalf of Hellouin, the Abbot of Bec Abbey."

"You speak English?" asked Harold.

"Of course. I am a great admirer of the scholarly work that flows from London and Canterbury. It seems that their work over the last twenty years has rivalled work found in Rome and Paris. So, my curiosity has led me to Canterbury. I try to learn from the masters, wherever they are. I need to keep Bec Abbey and my mind, how would you say, up to date," smiled Lanfranc.

Though he had trouble understanding much of what

Lanfranc said through his thick Frankish pronunciation, Harold responded with a nod.

"Come," motioned Lanfranc.

Harold followed Lanfranc ahead of the three guards towards the large refectory hall, where brothers together with locals and pilgrims gathered to eat.

Lanfranc ordered a novice to lead the men to a table before disappearing to the kitchens.

As he followed along, Harold looked around curiously; he found himself uncommonly interested in the place. At how organised everything was, how quietly the brothers shuffled in, single file and separated from the pilgrims. How calm and sincere everyone seemed, how clean the hall was. The experience was new for Harold, as he had never taken the time to notice such things at English monasteries.

Harold and the three guards were directed to a table where they all gladly sat with sighs of relief following their journey. As the guards spoke amongst themselves in Frankish, Harold continued to observe the busy refectory around him. Several groups were sitting together; pilgrims were respectful but loud compared to the almost silent monks. Harold noticed that one young and somewhat awkward monk moved away from the others and headed towards where the guests and pilgrims were set. He stopped and sat directly across from Harold even though there were plenty of seats elsewhere. The young brother kept his face down, occasionally scratched his head and did not acknowledge anyone.

As the food arrived, the guards wasted no time in being courteous. Harold hesitated and looked down at his simple serving of game stew, bread and wine, which was significantly more extravagant than the vegetables, bread and water the monks were served. At first, Harold was a little cautious about the possibility of being poisoned, but his exhaustion and hunger took over. It was his first tolerable food in two days.

"Latine ou Franque?" *Latin or Frank?* The quiet brother spoke to Harold without looking up.

"Anglais," answered Harold with the only Frankish word he knew.

"English? But these men with you, they speak—"

"I am their prisoner," Harold responded with a partial smile.

"The four of you seemed so comfortable. I assumed— forgive me." Harold and the monk continued eating, but Harold anticipated more questions.

"You travel to—?" the monk asked.

"Falaise."

"I see. I will pray for you. What is your name?"

"I am Harold Godwinson, Earl of Wessex."

"A noble? Forgive me, monsieur. I am not familiar with nobles outside of the kingdom of the Franks. I am sure most others would recognise you."

"No need. I must ask, why will you pray for me? I am an alien in this kingdom."

"I will pray for anyone. You are no alien, monsieur. We are all equal under God," assured the monk.

"Thank you, but I find it hard to understand how you believe that you can change anything by praying?" Harold said as he ate his food.

"I do not always believe I can change much."

"Then why pray?"

"Good question, monsieur. I'll try to explain in English, let me think, hmm. Let's say I have a little faith in God, very tiny. But that is enough to make me seek more. So, I pray."

"I don't understand." Harold was amused as he pushed the

brother further. "Why don't you seek first and then believe when you find?"

"My dear friend, then I will most certainly find nothing," continued the monk. "God requires faith, even if it is little faith, before he can be found. So, I do not seek to find so that I may believe; but I believe so that I may find and understand. Unless I believe first, I shall not understand. It is the same with you, is it not? You will not have knowledge of God and truth unless you first believe. Perhaps you have faith already, hmm? A little will suffice."

Harold laughed. "I certainly have no faith if you have only a little."

The monk and Harold exchanged a brief smile before the two continued with their food. The topic continued to eat away at Harold's curiosity in what he considered blind and foolish faith. As his thoughts got away from him, he suddenly leaned in to enquire further about his new friend.

"Another thing I don't understand is how people travel hundreds of miles just to lay their eyes on the bones of a saint? When they arrive, they find nothing but death and bones in a manufactured box. But still, they continue to believe it was a worthy experience. I find this faith madness. So, I suppose I will continue to find nothing with this ..."

Harold paused mid-sentence as the monk listened with undivided attention and waited for him to continue.

"Ah, I've grown tired of this church. I have seen too much suffering and confusion for me to believe in this silent God of yours. You need not waste your time with me," Harold concluded as the monk listened silently. Harold raised an eyebrow and returned to his food, but the monk seemed curious about Harold's questions.

"What is your name, friend?" asked Harold, without looking up.

"I am Anselm."

"Are you a monk here, Anselm?"

"I was. But now, I am part of a smaller community in Caen. I am here to see my teacher, Lanfranc."

"I see. I met your teacher when we arrived," Harold said.

"He is a very wise and learned teacher, and I am fortunate to be his student. I will follow wherever he goes."

"You mentioned that you're currently at Caen? That's not far from Falaise. What do you know of Falaise and Duke William?"

"A little, I don't listen to much talk outside the walls of my monastery, but I have heard of their recently acquired holy relic. It was exciting news in my community, but probably not so interesting for you."

"You're right, probably not. But why was it exciting?"

"This particular relic is popular amongst the devoted in the Frankish Kingdom and beyond. Some travel from as far as Rome just to venerate this saint. Popularity is growing. There have been stories of powerful signs on those who draw near the relics, good and bad. Healings and curses." explained Anselm.

"Are the stories true?"

"We shall see. I've not had a chance to venerate her relics in person yet. I plan to visit as soon as—"

"Her? This saint was a woman?" laughed Harold as he interrupted.

"Not a woman. A young girl, The Blessed Saint Foy. She was martyred for her faith during the Great Persecution, almost seven hundred years ago. Her name is the Frankish word for Faith."

Harold raised his eyebrows, but his expression of disinterest was clear.

"You may laugh, my noble friend," responded Anselm, "but perhaps God has brought you and Foy here for a reason. Maybe to help your faith, no?"

"That I doubt, my friend," responded Harold as he returned to his food.

CHAPTER 20

THORNEY ISLAND, LONDON

Abbot Edwin burst into his bedchamber, closed the old heavy timber door behind him and fell to his knees. His head bowed to the floor, the dust from the timber entering his mouth as he breathed heavily.

"Almighty Father," he prayed. "I don't know how, but I feel the pain of your pending wrath against this land. It's like a weight on my soul. Stay your hand, I beg. Your servant Edward will soon be at your side. I can see now – yes – it is clear. Edward's death leaves a void that will release your judgement. Have mercy. Blessed Peter, pray for us now."

Approaching footsteps could be heard down the hall, which Edwin initially ignored as he prayed.

"Father Edwin? Are you here?" echoed a woman's voice.

Edwin sat up as he recognised the voice. He rose quickly to peer out his door.

"My lady, why are you here? You know a woman is not permitted," Edwin pressed.

"I know, Father, and I beg your forgiveness. I needed to

speak to someone I trust, and ..." The lady's voice started to break. "You are the only one I trust in this whole place."

As quietly as she could, she began to cry as Edwin watched on with compassion. The lady, aged just over forty, was well dressed in a glowing long white tunic of the finest silk covered by a delicately decorated long red robe lined with silk and fur.

"Bless you, child, come this way." Edwin made the sign of the cross over her before leading her away from the brothers' quarters in the least conspicuous path towards the abbey.

As the two made their way down the poorly lit nave, the lady attempted to talk several times, but Edwin kept her quiet until he was sure they would not be seen or heard.

"Sit, sit," he instructed.

The two sat in a dark corner in one of the abbey's transepts on the east side facing the River Thames, furthest away from any entrances. Though empty at this time, this transept was particularly popular as it featured one of the most beautiful stone sculptures in Christendom. The life-size Blessed Virgin statue looked down upon Edwin and the weeping lady like a caring mother in the dim light.

As the lady wiped her tears, she opened to Edwin. "Father, I know you are pained. I've seen you at Edward's side. Your face shows the same fear I have."

"My lady, I don't understand? Why should you fear? You are King Edward's wife, his royal consort, and you are a Godwin. The prize daughter of that powerful family, what could—"

"Father Edwin, please, I am no fool," Edith insisted as she stared him down with a stern expression. "If you will permit, we should talk plainly."

"Go on then, child."

"My husband will soon be dead. Soon after, this nation will be at war," she insisted.

"How can you know that, Edith?"

"Surely you know of what I speak, Father Edwin. We both know things that we have not shared. But the reason I have come to you, I feel that the bloodshed that is coming will be on my hands," said Edith as she dabbed a delicate cloth at her tears.

"Edith – no. Why would this be?"

"If Edward and I had a child, if we had a son, you and I would not be weighed down with fear like we are now. If I had only ..." Edith paused as she attended to her tears again.

"What, child? Go on," pushed Edwin.

"Years ago," she started, "when my father and the king were at war, like dogs, before my father's exile, Edward looked to me for love. He felt alone. Far from any family or alliances, there was no one he could trust. You would think, as his wife, that I would love and support my husband in his time of suffering and pain. But no, I was young and foolish. I withdrew myself from his presence, and I distanced myself from him. I do not know why, perhaps to support my family or maybe I lost respect for him. Nevertheless, I was selfish and foolish. Sometime later, there was pressure on me to produce an heir. You may remember the time. But as everyone waited for me to fall pregnant, I could not. It seemed that after all those years of my selfishness and rejection, he no longer wanted me. I had broken any bond that we had. No matter how I tried to love him or invite him to my bedchamber, he never arrived. The love he sought, he found in the church, not in me. It was too late. The damage had been done."

"Dear child," Edwin assured, "if this darkness is God's will, no one's foolish decisions will change anything. Your failure to produce an heir is not the problem now. It is your husband's failure to elect a successor that is causing anxiety amongst the nobles. This is the problem that will cause the conflict, I'm sure of it."

"But Father, I thought the king had elected a successor years ago?"

"No, there is no record of any such decision."

"You mean, there is no English record, Father?"

"What?" questioned Edwin before moving closer to her. "What or who are you referring to?"

CHAPTER 21

FALAISE, NORMANDY

The warmth of the midday sun was thawing the morning's winter frost as a light easterly breeze scattered leaves across the gardens of Chateau de Falaise. The tranquil sound of swooping red kite birds was broken by slow trots, blows and nickers from the horses of four approaching riders, which had not escaped the notice of the Norman soldiers on watch at the gate.

Harold and his horse rode a few strides ahead of the three Ponthieu guards as they appeared at the crest of the approach to the chateau gate. His unguarded and aloof disposition matched his defeated riding posture. He had resolved that he could not improve this situation by forcing his will but also knew full well that William could not afford to kill him under this situation.

One of the Ponthieu soldiers shouted in Frankish towards the chateau gate, announcing their arrival and that the captive was not bound. The announcement was unnecessary; at least a dozen Norman soldiers had had their bows aimed at Harold since he was first sighted at various watchtowers leading to the chateau. His arrival and subsequent incarceration were too important for anything to go wrong.

"He mustn't be harmed, and he mustn't escape!" were the orders barked around the ramparts of the chateau hours before the arrival.

"Godwinson. Dismount horse," yelled a Norman soldier from the wall.

Harold dismounted from his tired horse with a thud and looked up at the wall. He raised his open hands and slowly turned around to show he was unarmed. At this point, the chateau's gate began to open, revealing the feet of at least two dozen heavily armed soldiers led by a decorated Duke William, dressed in dark furs and leather. As the gate was raised high enough, William approached with his soldiers in tow and stopped short of Harold by a few yards. For a tense few moments, nothing was said. William and Harold faced each other in silence. Their eyes squinted from the bright midday sun as the weight of grievances and injustices between their two kingdoms over the last fifty years were brought to the forefront of their minds. In their stares alone, it was as if there was a war of immense proportions taking place in another world in their honour.

"I am Duke William. You are Harold Godwinson of Wessex, are you not?" William broke the ice with his thick Norman pronunciation.

"I am."

"I see. You and a companion were captured some days ago on the Flanders coast," stated William as they continued to stare each other down. "So, why did you cross the channel, Harold? Am I to prepare for an invasion of Britons?"

"We were shipwrecked in a storm on our way to visit my kinsman here in Normandy and so ended up far north at

Flanders," responded Harold, breaking the stare and looking into the distance.

William laughed. "No, no. I do not believe this, this, story."

Harold said nothing as he stood with confidence, almost ignoring William as he surveyed the horizon, while William began to pace around Harold's position confidently.

"Do you think I am a fool, son of Godwin? I think you came here to watch us without being recognised. Why else would you be found free from any clothing or weaponry baring the Wessex dragon seal? Why would any English earl, no — why would a Godwinson do that?" laughed William.

William stopped his pacing and leaned into Harold's ear.

"Never have I observed a family so proud of their own house as yours."

Harold remained still, staring at the horizon as William moved away and continued. "So! It is clear to me why you have come. Very clear. But it is not so clear why you let yourself be delivered here with such little fight, no resistance at all."

William stopped circling and stood in front of Harold again, waiting for him to respond. Harold remained silent and glanced away, leaving William feeling uncomfortable and not in control of the situation.

After a moment of silence, William raised his hands, smiled and lightened his tone. "Argh, it is not important what was yesterday. You are here now. You are my, how you say, dis-tinguished guest, hmm? You should stay a while," William announced loud enough so that those around could hear and lower their guard. "Let us make the most of this um— oppor-tunity, huh?"

William slapped Harold on the back and led him into the chateau courtyard as the Norman soldiers followed. A court official remained behind to formally dismiss the three Ponthieu escorts, who subsequently turned their horses to leave. They were happy but shocked. They had carried out one of the most critical but most straightforward escorts they had ever under-taken, successfully delivering the most powerful English noble to their liege lord without spilling a single drop of blood.

CHAPTER 22

SOUTH-EAST COAST, ENGLAND

The English coastal swell was making it difficult for the small boat to beach safely. The Flanders fishermen, ordered by Count Guy to sail Caelin across the channel to the English shore, feared that their precious vessel would be dashed against the rocks if they ventured much closer. The boat was no more than half a mile from the coast, and it was safe for their captive to swim. But the fishermen considered that releasing the bonds on Caelin's feet and wrists could prove risky. He could turn violent and steal their boat, or he would drown as he swam to shore, which would eventually cost them once their liege lord was informed.

As the fishermen argued amongst themselves on how to fulfil Guy's order without losing their source of income, Caelin listened to their animated Frankish discussion and could quickly determine the dilemma they faced.

The fisherman wanted to release Caelin at this point but feared the risks. Confident in his ability to swim the half-mile distance, Caelin spared the fishermen the pain of indecision. As they watched on in horror, Caelin unravelled the bonds on his hands and feet, which he had severed during the voyage. He bundled up the ropes and threw them casually at the terrified fishermen before diving into the cold, rough sea.

The men on the boat were shocked and relieved as they watched Caelin comfortably navigate the swell and swim for shore.

CHAPTER 23

NORTHAMPTON, ENGLAND

A slap on the jaw quickly brought Tostig Godwinson into consciousness. His blurred vision and pounding head limited his ability to recognise the numerous faces around him.

"Godwinson. Where is your brother, Harold? He was meant to be here to witness," asked one of Morcar's.

Tostig 's vision cleared up quickly as the weight of the situation came flooding back. "Bastards. You'll pay. I am the earl here, you fool," he yelled but unable to move from his bounds.

"Not anymore, not anymore," laughed the man. "Well, certainly not here anyway. We're in Northampton."

"Northampton?" asked a shocked Tostig.

"Yes. For the king's council," said the nameless man as he casually walked around the room and looked out of the door as though expecting someone.

"And now that you're awake, Morcar will have words," he said as he quickly exited the room and called out, "My lord? He's up."

As Tostig stretched his neck and spat blood from his mouth, he could hear the footsteps of at least four men approaching. Morcar entered, followed by several men, all with crafty grins.

"Ah yes, finally," bellowed Morcar. "This is long overdue. We, along with everyone in the north, have been waiting for this for a long time. Now, all we need is to wait for your brother. He can witness the abdication, and we can get on. But you, on the other hand, will probably want to hide under a rock somewhere."

"You've lost your mind, Morcar," laughed Tostig. "Harold won't agree to this, I assure you. Now, release me."

"No. I think I'll keep you here. This room, that chair, it suits you better. It's good for, well, everyone." Morcar and his men shared a laugh before leaving the room.

"Morcar! ... MORCAR!"

As the threats from Tostig faded behind the closed door, Morcar turned to his men. "Stay here with Tostig. Make sure he's not rescued or killed. I'll head to London to ensure Harold is directed here to Northampton upon his return from the channel, not north to York."

CHAPTER 24

FALAISE, NORMANDY

"You must forgive me for my poor English, Harold. But come, let us sit and discuss your purpose."

William led Harold into a large court within the chateau, where his voice echoed under the timber roof. The walls were decked with Norman arms, weapons and crests, and it was clear to Harold that his tour of the chateau was meant to intimidate.

"My purpose?" asked Harold.

"Ah yes, my English, terrible. I have purpose and duties for you here in Normandy," responded William as they took seats by a large table.

"I don't understand. I have duties in Wessex, not here. Surely, William, you must release me now as the king is unaware of my presence here," stated Harold with a confused expression.

"Exactly!" yelled William with a cunning smile as he launched from his chair to pace around. "The king does not know you are here, which is no surprise to me. If you stay and do my duties, we keep this quiet. Easy. But I understand that you may wish to escape or disobey my orders. If you do, all of England will know that you were found here."

"What?" Harold's eyes widened. His expression was now less cordial. "Do you think it matters that England knows I was here? Even if I were spying on Normandy, it would be praised in the shires. This is not a secret I need to keep."

William swiftly launched at the seated Harold, drew his sword and edged its tip into the soft flesh of Harold's jugular notch. The two stood with eyes wide, though William's friendly smile had remained, which at this point made Harold question his sanity.

"Hommes!" *Men!* announced William towards the court's grand entrance. "Préparer Harold pour le service." *Prepare Harold for service.*

"You will look much better in Norman blue, don't you think?" insisted William while maintaining the position of his sword.

Harold said nothing in reply. His thoughts were a mess of confusion and anger; shock outweighed any rational response.

William was still smiling and lowered his sword as his men arrived. "We ride south. For Brittany. Now." His announcement echoed off the walls.

Two large and armed Norman knights approached Harold and led him away, one on each arm. Harold went quietly, resisting the urge to fight off William's men and attack William with his bare hands. Harold turned back with a glare as William continued to smile.

Harold was swiftly escorted into a nearby armoury across the courtyard from the chateau's great hall. As they entered the cold dark room, one of the knights headed toward some old timber storage chests tucked away in a corner. After spending a few moments rummaging around, he emerged with helmets, chainmail, swords, boots and tunics with the bright Norman blue livery. The knight dropped it all on the floor in front of Harold, pointed at the pile, gave Harold a nod, slapped him on the back and proceeded to change his own gear to something more suitable for riding.

As a dozen more knights entered the armoury and made their preparations, the subsequent clanking of steel wasn't loud enough to dull the noise in Harold's head. He couldn't remember a time where he had been so humiliated. Not only under the duress of a foreigner but forced to wear their armour and livery as one of them. William was right; Godwinsons wore only their own suits, the shining Dragon of Wessex seal blazing proudly on almost everything they owned. Being forced to wear Norman armour was shaming. Harold dawdled in his corner of the armoury as he watched the Norman knights prepare.

One of the knights caught on and noticed Harold stalling.

"On! On!" said the knight as he pointed to the stack of spare gear on the floor.

Concluding that this was not the time to resist, Harold started reviewing the weapons and armour. *The most useless sword I've ever seen, blunt as stone,* he thought, but reluctantly proceeded to dress. Contrary to his attitude, Harold made an effort to find equipment most useful for riding and prepared, nonetheless.

Moments later, a dozen Norman knights in riding armour emerged from the armoury and headed for the stables. Harold, barely recognisable, trod closely behind.

CHAPTER 25

WINCHESTER CASTLE, WESSEX

The eyes of Caelin's black horse were wide open as it galloped hard toward Winchester Castle under an ominous sky. The last several hours for Caelin were a blur. It had all happened so fast. After he jumped from the Norman boat and reached the beach, he found the nearest coastal village, seized a horse from its stable and headed west, picking up supplies as he went. There were several secret Wessex stores between the east and west coasts, well-hidden and known only to Harold and his thanes.

For Caelin, the new mission was clear: skirt London, head to Wessex, gather as many men as possible possible, mount a swift rescue across the channel.

Potential suicide, Caelin thought. But he wouldn't let doubt slow him down.

"This cannot be!" said Edith Swanneck, as she buried her face into her palms and rested against a column in the Wessex Castle courtyard.

"Why did he dare such a feat? It was a mad plan, even by Harold's standards." Edith paused for a moment to gather her thoughts as she breathed heavily with frustration. Caelin stood still as he watched Edith respond to the news of Harold while he kept an eye on the castle gates.

"He listens to you, Caelin. Why did you not advise him away from this?"

"I trust him, Edith. The plan was bold, I'll grant you that, but it wasn't madness. We've accomplished missions with greater complexity than this. It seemed achievable. He inspired the men and me to want it as much as he did. If only it weren't for that storm. We could not; he could not have foreseen it." Caelin paused as he remembered the men lost that night. The battle between loyalty to Harold and the cost of Harold's decisions was beginning to weigh, but he didn't want Edith to know it.

"Edith, I must go back to Normandy and pull Harold out of there. Who knows how long William will keep him?"

"Why do you trust Harold, as you said?" Edith moved away from the column and approached Caelin, lowering her voice. "Why do you always trust him, Caelin? You have more faith in him than any of his family. You give almost every waking hour of your life to his service when you could walk away whenever you wanted. A man of your talents could disappear and be untraceable, but you stay and serve. Why?"

Edith stood before Caelin and looked up from the cobblestones to his lonely green eyes with a childlike but somewhat flirtatious curiosity.

"Edith ... yes, Harold can be ruthless and even unwise at times. But he has trusted and believed in me when no one else has. I feel I owe it to him. I owe him my service. Now that Harold is determined to succeed Edward as king, I do not believe he will succeed without my help. Besides, what would I do? Where would I go? I have no life to escape to."

"Set up a home? Marry? Watch the seasons roll over?" suggested Edith.

"You know that is not my way, Edith." smiled Caelin.

"Well, tell me, what do you think about Harold's ambition. Be honest with me; I will not tell. What should he do, Caelin? What should he do with his royal ambitions?"

"I think … he should abandon this pursuit for the throne; it is nothing more than a dream of his father. It could be his end."

"If only there were a Godwinson with your wisdom, Caelin," smiled Edith as she leaned back against the stone column. "I would surely follow such a man."

The two took a moment to catch each other's warm gaze.

For a moment, Caelin then felt unusually uncomfortable. Without noticing his actions as they talked, Caelin was staring at Edith. As she leaned back on the column, he caught a glimpse of her long slim neck, the white marble skin reflecting the afternoon light as it plunged toward the press of her firm breasts under her decorated red tunic. He had never taken the time to notice and appreciate her feminine appeal.

Edith was amused to watch Caelin's gaze move slowly from her face to her chest. Usually, seeing the eyes of a man lower to her breasts made her uncomfortable too, but with Caelin and his usual steely disposition, the gesture was a compliment. She felt as though she had achieved something. But before awkwardness set in, she stepped forward and raised his chin with her delicate index finger.

"Take a dozen men, Caelin. Rescue your liege," she ordered.

Caelin smiled. He knew that there was a connection between

them and that it was safe. He slowly turned toward the gates to leave.

"Oh, Caelin. One more thing," called Edith. "If you manage to rescue Harold, take him to Northampton as soon as he returns."

"I was planning to escort him further north, to York. Why Northampton?"

"Morcar has captured his brother Tostig and taken him there. That is all I know. No doubt they are waiting for Harold to settle something."

Caelin nodded to Edith before turning back toward the gates. He rustled the back of his long hair as he walked, thinking through the possibilities that awaited Harold.

Northampton was a wise move from Morcar, he thought. *Far enough from Tostig's men in York and close enough to London.*

CHAPTER 26

THORNEY ISLAND, LONDON

"Who is it?"

The queen consort hesitated to respond as Edwin peered out of the chapel and checked the abbey's nave to ensure they were still alone. Until now, the queen consort had thought that the nobles just ignored her information, but now she could see it was simply unknown. Its unravelling would be the spark to start a merciless fire of war.

"Do you remember Robert of Jumieges?" Edith asked.

"Of course, it was ten or so years ago," assured Edwin. "The Norman that your husband made Archbishop of Canterbury. Until that is, Harold's father, *your* father, had him exiled and replaced by Stigand."

"Well, when the king first installed Robert at Canterbury, he sent him to Rome so that the Holy Father might confirm his position. But on his way to Rome, Robert was ordered to visit Normandy."

"Yes, go on," pushed Edwin, rolling his hand around in Edith's direction.

"You still don't understand, do you, Edwin?" Edith covered her mouth in disbelief.

"Wait," said Edwin as he turned to gather his thoughts. "Child, are you suggesting Duke William, wait ... that Edward sent Robert to Normandy to inform William that he is to succeed Edward as king? But that is impossible— Why would your husband do that without telling anyone in England?"

Edith, still seated and unmoved by the notion, looked deep into Edwin's eyes. "Father, do you think the king would have any peace if he had informed the Witan or anyone else in England? People seem to forget he was in Normandy and the guest of Duke William's father for many years while in exile before he returned to become king. Edward's ties with Normandy remained strong long after his return. I'm not sure where his loyalty lies now, but ten years ago, his heart was still in Falaise."

Abbot Edwin scratched his head as he stared wide-eyed down the nave of the dark and empty abbey, digesting what he had just heard.

"Edward's affections for Normandy are known, Edith," he assured. "But no one in England would suspect for a moment that he would go so far as to choose a Norman successor to the English throne. No one would expect that he would dare to make such a move. But, as you say, perhaps this is why he has kept the matter silent. Your brother, Harold, would be outraged to know of this. This must remain unspoken; no one can know of this."

"I agree, Father. I will tell no one," assured the queen consort.

Abbot Edwin turned to Edith and made the sign of the cross over her. "I absolve you of your sins, my child. Remain here and pray awhile. I must return to my quarters."

"Father, you mustn't tell ...," insisted Edith.

"I know, child. I know."

CHAPTER 27

FALAISE, NORMANDY

William stepped out of the chateau into the sunlit courtyard, dressed like a Roman emperor going into battle. His iron and gold helmet, which still showed his face, was crafted with lighter materials for a long journey into a battlefield, not the battle itself. His horse, held by two stablehands, was also dressed elaborately in a long deep blue and gold caparison. William mounted and casually trotted over to inspect the formed line of his guard of knights, erect on their horses with Harold at the end.

"Monsieur Harold, ride with me. My knights will flank us," he instructed.

Harold proceeded forward from the line of knights and took a moment to skilfully assert his power over his somewhat disobedient Norman horse, moving it hard left then right. As the horse duly gave Harold control, he then slowly trotted to William's side.

"What are we doing in Brittany?" asked Harold through his heavy helmet.

William steadied his horse and grinned. "A regular

assessment of my land along the borders with Brittany," he explained. "You may have heard of Le Mont Saint-Michel? I understand there is a small mob of rebels threatening bishops and terrorising pilgrims. We stop them, yes?"

"But do you know the size of the mob? We may need more men."

"Perhaps," responded William. "We have a post near Mont Saint-Michel with thirty men, but I think we will be sufficient."

William then turned to lead the thirteen knights out of the confines of the chateau and through the south of the walled Falaise city. Harold kept a keen eye on his surroundings as people throughout the town bowed as they noticed their Duke pass.

Outside the walls to the south of the chateau, William led his men past a small stone abbey, Notre Dame de Guibray, before picking up speed, leaving a trail of dust.

As William and his entourage disappeared into the horizon, a more contemplative occasion was taking place inside the church. Bishop Odo was carrying out the Roman rite ordained for the installation of a new relic. The vast gold reliquary of the Blessed Saint Foy took a large and prominent place just a couple of steps to the left of the high altar. The brothers of Notre Dame had never sounded so good as they chanted the psalms, their praises echoing off the stone walls louder than ever.

As Odo predicted, the monastery at Conques Abbey delivered the bust soon after they realised the bones were stolen by a Norman monk disguised as one of their own. The priest from Conques abbey left Falaise without a word after handing the reliquary bust to Odo personally; his face and posture communicated the defeat well enough.

Work immediately got underway to improve Notre Dame in preparation for the arrival of the new relic. New art and tapestries from Rome, sculpture repairs, exterior and interior stonemasonry improvements, large beeswax candles, but most importantly, the church was under the watch of three Norman soldiers at all hours.

Under his episcopal robes, Odo's whole body dripped with sweat. The fear of God gripped every fibre of his being as he gazed in awe at Foy's reliquary. He could not forget the vision of Foy he had experienced not so long before. For Odo, it was now unmistakably clear that the spirit of Foy was not to be taken lightly. Nevertheless, he was determined to be the bishop who had the relic that everyone was talking about. For Odo, the glory of Foy was the key to bring his church and bishopric the recognition it deserved. But deep in his heart, he knew that he was ignoring two crucial things: the instruction to return the relics, given by the monk Hugh before his death, and the warning he received during his haunting apparition of Saint Foy herself. Odo knew he was chasing the dream with a powerful and dangerous relic that was unlikely to ignore his motives, but he could not stop. There was too much at stake. This was his time.

Odo's hands quivered as he raised them heavenward to quote the psalm. "Speret Israel in Domino, ex hoc nunc et usque in saeculum." *Let Israel hope in the Lord, from this time forward and forever.*

With his hands still raised, Odo's gaze locked with the eyes of the gilded reliquary bust of Foy as fear gripped him.

CHAPTER 28

MONT SAINT-MICHEL, BRITTANY

William and Harold's horses came to a stop as they reached the end of a thick forest. A sheer cliff dropped fifty yards or more at their horses' hooves, but it was not the cliff that drew the men to a halt. The view in front of them was astonishing. No words were spoken, though sighs and men crossing themselves was evidence of their deep admiration of the sight. William and his men had seen it several times, but every time it always looked better than they remembered. The roaring Brittany coastline, bone-white sandy plains and the tide lapping at the base of one of the most spectacular sites in Christendom, Mont Saint-Michel.

An abbey, monastery and village built on top of a volcanic rock mount, almost completely covering its surface, overlooking the sea to the west and the plains to the east. Though it was one of the most inaccessible places, it featured some of the empire's most elaborate stone masonry and architecture. Inhabitants, builders and pilgrims could only access the mount by crossing the dangerous sandy plains at low tide. Often, inexperienced pilgrims would miscalculate the tide times and drown.

"Harold. I believe this is the first time you have seen this. What do you think?" asked William.

"Aye, this is the first time. It is worth its fame."

William spun his horse around to face his men and ordered that they head to the pilgrim's road. "Route de pèlerinage."

He then turned to Harold. "We head for the pilgrim's road east. The men will split up and signal to us if they see rebels. You stay close to me."

The eyes of Harold and William met for the shortest moment; it was a stare full of distrust and hate. Both men were biding their time, waiting for the opportune moment to take their complete revenge and hoping it would inflict the most shame. The group of riders headed down the hill with horses gradually gathering speed into a gallop. As the pilgrim's route was just in sight, William's men started to peel off into pairs, off-track, through the scrubs and sandy mangroves bordering the plains. Harold watched the knights take positions and appreciated their formation movements; they were clearly well trained and rehearsed for this type of attack.

The pilgrim road had become suddenly quiet for William and Harold as they brought their horses to a trot as the knights had peeled off. William looked focused as he listened for signals from his men further down the road. Harold kept one eye on the road and the other on William, casually studying his tactics.

A moment later, a short and barely audible whistle was heard, possibly fifty to a hundred yards away. It was all that William needed. He immediately kicked his horse and bolted further down the road, with Harold following closely behind. As they drew nearer, they could hear riders' approach from behind, heading towards the whistle signal. But as William and Harold turned their horses around, they did not see William's men but a league of a dozen unrecognisable riders heading straight for them.

"Rebels," reported William to Harold as he brought his horse to a halt.

"So much for your tactics," said Harold as he bolted past William and headed straight for the pursuing rebels.

"Wait!" William yelled, but it was too late.

He watched as Harold quickly approached the first rider. Harold skilfully ducked to narrowly miss the rebel rider's swing of a sword and quickly turned his horse so he could reach with a counterattack swing, slicing the rebel deep into his back. As Harold watched, the three closest rebels were suddenly hit with a rain of arrow fire, bringing them swiftly to the ground along with their horses.

"Finally," whispered Harold.

Several of the Norman knights appeared out of thick scrub behind the rebel gang, first taking out those still closest to Harold with bows before drawing swords for a full attack on the remaining. William continued to watch from a distance as Harold joined the Norman knights to finish off six unidentified rebel riders before the final member disappeared in a desperate getaway.

As the skirmish finished, William noticed that not all his men had returned to help. "Où sont les autres?" *Where are the others?*

There were no answers. Instead, the men, including Harold, sprang in various directions, leaving William on the road alone. It all happened so fast that William was not entirely sure which direction Harold had taken. After a few moments to gather his thoughts, William's expression changed to anger, his suspicions triggered. Not wanting to be cheated so easily, he wasted no time, drew his sword and charged his horse in pursuit.

* * *

The horses ahead of Harold were kicking up dirt into his face as they turned a sharp bend in the road. Before they could pick up speed, Harold and the Norman knights all drew to a halt as the situation became more apparent. They immediately dismounted.

Just off the road after the bend, two of William's men had fallen into a pit filled with the notorious Mont Saint-Michel quicksand. Such pits were usually found closer to the coast and the monastery island, but there were smaller pools amongst the marshes inland that would often catch travellers off guard.

The two men had taken the bend at great speed, with both horses losing their footing and throwing their riders. The horses were nowhere to be found, either scared off or already swallowed by the sands. There was little time. Both men were resisting the temptation to panic or move. Instead, they started throwing ideas in Frankish at the others on the road.

Rather than attempting to translate the incoherent Frankish debate, Harold started fastening a rope around his waist and through his legs. As he completed the knots, he handed the men on the dry ground the rope and gave the nod. The Norman soldiers quickly understood what he had in mind. Four men took a firm grip and leaned back on the rope to ease Harold down the bank. As he reached the mud and sand, he took hold of a thick overhanging tree branch before proceeding into the sand. When he was waist-deep, he raised both hands above his head, holding fast to the bending branch to reduce his weight. Reaching the two men, Harold stretched out his legs toward them, allowing them to grab his feet. The weight of all three instantly pulled the branch low enough to cause everyone to inhale with fear that it might break. Sweat dripped down Harold's face; the strain of keeping the branch steady with his hands and his legs stretched toward the others was a test of his strength.

With every inch of power left in him, hand over hand, Harold started pulling his way back up the branch toward the bank, pulling the two men out of the thick, heavy sludge with him. The quicksand-covered men were heavier than Harold realised. It was as though the marsh was clawing the men back into its grip. Without warning, the thick overhanging branch gave an enormous crack, lowering Harold into the mire, but somehow the branch remained attached to the trunk. Though he was now waist-deep, and the Norman soldiers were back into their chins, Harold continued to hold fast to the branch over his head. Once again, he proceeded to pull the men by his feet toward the bank. Before he could manage both hands on the branch, it gave a final crack and ripped away from the trunk. All three men slipped back into the quicksand.

As the soldiers watched helplessly from the bank, bubbles could be seen rising to the surface as all three men were enveloped in stillness.

Not far away, William used his sword to cut through low hanging branches while his horse pushed through the scratching twigs and thistles. He spun his horse in every direction but still no sign of his men or Harold. William wanted to keep quiet, preferring to catch an escaping Harold by surprise, but his frustration escalated. He had little clue as to which direction he should take.

"Harold!" William yelled.

"William," was the muffled response from one of his men in the distance to the south.

William kicked his horse and bolted south down the pilgrim trail; he couldn't help but think the worst had happened. Harold had fought off one or more of his Norman knights before escaping, injuring or even killing them. Even worse, Harold could be dead. For William, that would be a disaster. Harold's disappearance or death would be disastrous to William's plans. If Harold were killed, it would be near impossible to keep England from invading Normandy. If Harold had escaped, William had missed the opportunity to manipulate and break him.

As William approached the scene, he came across a very different story from what he imagined. He remained on his horse, sheathed his sword and watched on in astonishment and confusion. He never imagined he would find Harold rescuing two Norman men who had fallen off their horses into a deceptively small quicksand swamp.

CHAPTER 29

MONT SAINT-MICHEL, BRITTANY

As they sat around a campfire at the base of Mont Saint-Michel, the mood was quiet amongst the men, though Harold found it amusing. He was pleased with himself that the Normans were uneasy and awkward. They talked amongst themselves in Frankish as Harold stared at the fire and picked at his small plate of food. The Normans were grateful to Harold for his undeniably heroic rescue of the two sinking knights but confused with how they should respond. It was only the day before that Harold was the captive they mocked and forced to wear their armour. Now they didn't know what to think.

William stood up from the circle of his soldiers, wandered over to Harold and sat beside him. "The men told me what happened before I arrived. They say you fell under the quicksand and that you but burst out of it, as though it were water. With one man under your arm, the other on your back."

Harold turned to face the duke and smiled subtly. "I did my duty."

"But the men want to know how you managed to get out."

"I pointed my feet down as we fell. Then I found something stable and strong. It must have been a large rock or an old tree stump. I grabbed who I could before I pushed up."

William listened and paused, in awe of Harold's strength to manage such a feat. "The men wish to thank you, but they know no English."

Harold looked over at the circle of confused Norman knights. They looked back, placed their hands on their chests and nodded. It was awkward, but Harold could sense it was genuine.

William kept a steady eye on Harold's composure as he nodded back to the soldiers. "Shall we walk?"

Harold reluctantly rose from his tree stump seat and followed the duke towards the beach and the setting sun. As they walked, William sighed and stared into the horizon. "My knights, not only thank you, Harold. They nod to acknowledge you," he explained.

"Acknowledge? I don't understand."

"You have become their equal. You are no longer their joke."

The earl and duke exchanged smiles, although they silently kept their guard up.

"Let us ride north to Falaise tonight, and then tomorrow I will arrange for you to be escorted to England," insisted William.

"Arrange for me? William, I think you misunderstand. I am here because I choose to be. I will leave when it suits me," responded Harold sharply while maintaining his smile.

Harold knew that the knights, only yards away, were watching but could not understand the English conversation. William was also aware that his soldiers if alarmed, could kill Harold in an instant. They both kept their tone and expressions moderate.

"You English are all the same. I think you misunderstand the situation you are in," warned William through his smile.

"Amuse me, William. What is my situation?"

"You were found spying on my land. You are my captive. I can do with you what I will. Release you, keep you or kill you."

"Do it. Do it now. End this here. Or perhaps you are not willing to take that risk?" taunted Harold.

Their two pairs of eyes burned with rage as they met through seemingly pleasant expressions. But neither of them were willing to break the act. William broke eye contact and headed for the campfire, giving Frankish orders to his men to pack up and prepare to ride.

Harold released his hold on the knife fastened to his thigh.

CHAPTER 30

FALAISE, NORMANDY

T he first light of morning was only hours away, but there
was much activity at Chateau de Falaise. As soon as
William and his men passed through the gates, he ordered to fire up the kitchens, wake up Bishop Odo and prepare
the great hall for ceremony.

Not since an unexpected visit from Philip, King of the
Franks, two years prior had the chateau seen such commotion
in the middle of the night, but at least on that occasion, the
purpose was clear. This night was an exception; not a single
servant in Falaise knew what was going on or what was about
to happen. "Je ne sais pas" *I don't know,* could be heard again
and again through the chateau's corridors as the curious whispers spread.

The group of riders entered the courtyard and dismounted
from their horses. William quickly disappeared into the dark
of the chateau without a word, while Harold found himself directed to the enormous hall by the two knights he had saved
from the quicksand. They had orders and were cordial but
firm. It seemed that his new solidarity with the knights had

somewhat dwindled during the ride home. Like the others, Harold was tired, but he decided not a good time to fight. He had already worked out what William had planned; he would release Harold but with strict conditions. Harold, however, had other plans.

He entered the almost empty grand hall, which was dimly lit by several flaming torches. Toward the middle of the hall, there was what seemed to be a large, low table draped with an abundance of scarlet silk that flowed onto the floor.

"S'agenouiller," *Kneel,* ordered one of the knights, pointing to the small pillow on the floor at the base of the table.

Harold hesitated. He looked past the knights and around the hall. "Where is William?"

"KNEEL!" was the response he received, with a heavy kick to the back of the legs from the knight's armoured shin, sending Harold's knees directly onto the pillow.

He quickly rose, grabbed the closest knight's tunic and swiftly threw him crashing to the hall's timber floor. As he turned to the other knight, who had already unsheathed his sword, there was a resounding order to stop from the hall's dark side entrance.

"Arrêter!"

The knight slowly returned his sword to his side as the other picked himself off the floor. The three of them glanced into the dark corner from where the unidentified figure emerged. The tall hat gave away his position before his face could be seen.

"Earl Godwinson. I am Bishop Odo."

"Why do we need a bishop? I have terms to discuss with your liege, not a common cleric." Harold's strong voice echoed through the hall.

"I assure you, Monsieur Godwinson, I am very much needed here. This is *Sacramentum,*" said Odo calmly.

William burst into the hall, followed by several armed knights. Harold's escorts resumed their task of having Harold kneel before the silk draped table. Though he resisted, Harold's wrists were strapped and forced down with palms open on the table as though he was about to receive something. As it became apparent what was about to take place, Harold protested with groans and struggled to rise and release his bound hands. Two knights forced their weight down on each of Harold's shoulders, while two others ensured his hands did not move.

"Dishonour! This is not binding," Harold protested, but was not heeded.

Bishop Odo commenced a Latin chant and proceeded to walk around the table as William approached and brought forward a sword. He rested its handle in Harold's right hand and the blade in the other. Harold's shaking hands changed colour as the blood flow was constrained.

"In English, so you can understand ...," started William. He then closed his eyes and looked heavenward. "Almighty God. Bless this sword which your servant, Harold Godwinson, will bind to his side, that it may defend the weak, protect the humble, punish the heretic, and serve his ... earthly master," he sneered, looking down at Harold's appalled face.

"Harold Godwinson of Wessex," William continued. "Will you promise to fear God, protect the church and her saints, fight for the honour and prosperity of Normandy?"

"Are you mad? I am an English lord, you fool!" echoed Harold's protest throughout the dark hall.

"An English lord *and* a Norman knight. It is possible, Harold. You served Normandy well these last few days. I am determined to honour you with this, brother," assured William.

The sweat dripped down Harold's face as the two stared

each other down. Both of their heads pounded with fear and adrenaline, though William smiled and continued his rhetoric.

"Fight for the honour and prosperity of Normandy with loyalty of mouth and hands?" asked William as Harold's head was forced to bow in response.

"Harold Godwinson, I name you Harold of the Blessed Faith. To serve Normandy and her Lord, throughout the world," proclaimed William.

Harold slowly raised his eyes back to William. "Throughout the world? Are you mad?" he growled through gritted teeth.

William ignored the question and ordered that Harold's hands be released. As the bonds were untied, William removed the sword from Harold's hands and turned to pass it to Bishop Odo. With calm, he turned back toward the table, but with a swift change, he violently removed the scarlet silk covering, revealing a large oak chest. Harold, still kneeling, was confused, oblivious as to why William had removed the silk or the significance of the chest.

"Harold of the Blessed Faith, or *Foy* in Frankish. Have you heard of the beloved Saint Foy?" asked William.

"You said 'throughout the world' in the oath," said Harold, ignoring William's diversion. "A Norman knight's oath is limited to Frankish borders. My loyalty and protection of Normandy, and your protection of me, is not binding beyond these shores. Do you understand?"

"Do you understand?" Harold yelled when he noticed William ignoring him.

"Saint Foy," repeated William as he gestured to the chest in front of Harold's bent knees.

With that, Bishop Odo stooped in front of Harold, unlocked the chest and opened it wide before Harold's eyes. Odo stepped away in fear. Harold looked down and observed a bright and decorated gilded box. His mind flashed back to the conversation with the awkward and inquisitive monk, Anselm, at Bec Abbey.

There have been stories of powerful signs on those who draw near the relics, good and bad. Healings and curses. Anselm's words echoed in Harold's head as his vision became clouded with scenes of almost forgotten acts of theft and shame against the church in England, carried out by Harold and his father over the last half-century.

Eager to ignore the foolish belief that the relics could have any effect on his mental state, Harold shook his head, rubbed his eyes and forced his consciousness back into the present moment. "What is this?" he asked flatly.

"Our precious Saint Foy. You have heard of her, I am sure. Such blessing she has brought our province since she arrived. Tell me, Harold, have you ever heard of a knight's oath taken over a reliquary of a saint of the church that is limited to borders? I have not. May the blessed Foy guide you as you search your heart," smiled William.

Harold suddenly pulled down on the knights' arms that held his shoulders, causing them both to lose balance and fall behind him. He quickly broke free, rose and slammed down the oak chest with his foot. Then he launched over the oak chest in William's direction with an unarmed attack before being struck down with a heavy blow to the back of the head.

Harold landed flat on the ground at William's feet. The shock of the blow was more from the impact than the blow itself. He was quickly picked up off the floor and dragged back to his position behind the timber box by William's men. He then realised who and what he had underestimated. With his solid episcopal staff, the fat Bishop Odo was a threat he failed to account for when he planned the attack.

"Thank you, Odo," acknowledged William.

Odo closed his eyes and nodded to his liege before reopening the chest. Harold breathed heavily and stared at William as though fire burned in his eyes. The weight of the two knights continued to push down his shoulders, and the weight of the situation pounded in his head. Harold knew that William would use this oath as binding and felt as though he'd been outwitted. William had won the tiresome three-day battle of mental strength.

As the day's first light could be seen peering through the doors, William raised his voice to announce an order for his new knight.

"Harold of the Blessed Faith. I bid that you return to England and inform King Edward that I will accept his request to succeed him as king," boomed William. He then proceeded to announce it again in Frankish so that the whole chateau could hear his proclamation.

William turned to his men and ordered that Harold be escorted to the coast and returned safely to England. Harold's head slumped as he was picked up off the floor and taken back to the stables.

William turned to Bishop Odo and the other witnesses. Although exhausted, his face shone with rapture. His triumph was complete.

"You see, Odo? Have I not convinced you? England will be mine. It seems your beloved Foy has brought more blessing than I expected. Let it be known that Normandy will soon extend its borders beyond the sea," he declared as he walked past Odo toward the corridors of the chateau.

Odo gave a token smile, bowed his head and said nothing. Concluding that his services were no longer required, he then called for the two monks waiting outside and ordered that they safely transport the reliquary back to the abbey. Odo was not willing to touch the box himself, let alone attempt to carry it again.

CHAPTER 31

PEASANT FARMLANDS, NORMANDY

Hours later, Harold once again found himself trotting ahead of three Frankish guards as though it were a recurring dream. As they headed north, the events of the last few days blurred. With each step of his horse, his head drooped and bobbed side to side. The constant horseback journeying and lack of sleep played havoc on his grip on reality, and he could almost believe it was all a dream. Harold struggled to remember why he had travelled across the channel to Normandy in the first place or why he chose to comply with William's demands. There was a strategy to it all, he assured himself, but he could barely remember it.

"Save Caelin, yes ... I did that," he murmured to himself like a drunkard.

"Saved some other Norman bastards in those bloody sands. Killed William? No. I didn't have a chance, and surely I did ..." Harold's incoherent murmurs continued as they headed north to the coast, where a waiting Norman longboat would take him across to England.

Suddenly, Harold stopped as his mind darted back to the oath sworn to William earlier that day before sunrise. Recalling what had taken place, he was overwhelmed. "There was a reliquary," he remembered, "and I foolishly swore a knight's oath over the bones of a saint."

A flood of fear, anger and confusion came over him as he recalled whispered tales of those who betrayed sacred oaths, particularly those witnessed by holy relics. Harold shook his head. *Surely this superstition was for the weak,* he thought. But despite the effort to be logical, the fear in his head remained.

"Curse after curse ... How can I ...," he murmured.

His abstract and darting thoughts were thrown back to days earlier, when while journeying from Ponthieu to Bec Abbey and Falaise, he concluded that God himself cursed his family.

"Ah yes, of course. There are powers against me. Against my family. How can I be expected to flourish under such an angry hand? Nevertheless, I still breathe. I am not destroyed. This bastard god is blocking my every move, and yet he has not destroyed me. Am I a toy for his pleasure?" he asked himself.

Despite the battle raging in his mind, Harold sensed something ahead and looked up. A lone figure in the distance caught his attention. As he trotted on, he could make out a black monk's habit standing in the field about two hundred yards away. The monk's face was covered by a large hood but not moving.

Here is my chance for vengeance. Harold thought that if God wanted to mock him with curses, then God would have consequences, concluding that no clergy or devout would ever be safe in his presence again. His eyes squinted with rage at the monk in the distance, as though the monk embodied all that the Christian god was, and it was standing in Harold's way.

You can watch me suffer under your hand, but you will also watch your servants suffer. Starting with this faceless sacrifice. Let's see you stop me, he silently threatened.

Harold kicked both feet into the sides of his horse and yelled a loud cry for speed, "YAAHHH!!!"

The three guards were caught by surprise. For a moment, they watched in shock with jaws open as Harold bolted ahead, achieving a reasonable distance between them within a few moments. Fumbling at their bows and carelessly rousing their horses to sprint after him, their horses instead turned and bucked, only eventually speeding off in pursuit.

Harold's direction and rage were unchanged, heading straight for the unmoving monk as he roared loud curses at him. He intended to simply run him down under his horses' feet and return to finish him off with the only weapons he had available—his bare hands. But just as he was twenty yards away, the monk looked up at Harold from under his hood with eyes of fire that silenced his cursing and pierced through his very being. The monk instantly began to change, transform and increase in size rapidly as Harold watched in disbelief and slowed his horse.

An arrow pierced Harold's shoulder from the pursuing Norman knights. The arrow's momentum caused Harold to lose balance and fall from his horse to the grassy earth below. He quickly rose to his feet to see the spectacle ahead, as he had barely believed his eyes before the fall. The monk's hood remained, but everything else was different. The once small helpless figure now stood over the humiliated Harold with a height of twenty feet. He was arrayed in full battle armour from the feet to the fingers and wielded a double-edged sword. It was not only the most significant weapon Harold had ever seen, but it also reflected the sun so brightly that it seemed to burn red.

With eyes wide open in shock and oblivious to the pain of the arrow in his shoulder, Harold took a step back. The enormous and otherworldly warrior before him took a battle position as though preparing to attack. As the warrior spread bright white wings on either side of his back with a span longer than he was tall, it was clear to Harold what was taking place. God was done toying with Harold and was about to bring him to an end. As Harold took another step back, the warrior wasted no time. He launched into the air, causing the long grass and Harold himself to fall flat on the ground. With his sword raised above its head, the warrior took flight and headed straight for Harold like a falling mountain.

It was the end, and Harold had no fight left in him. He had surrendered. As Harold watched the warrior head towards him from above, he whispered.

"Who are you?"

A bright light surrounded Harold. He could not only feel the warrior's blade burn across his chest, but he also heard him respond.

"Caprasius."

"AAAAAHHHH ..."

Harold's whole body shook as he yelled and awoke on his slowly trotting horse. His jolt startled the horse a little, which was followed by laughter from the Normans riding behind. As the relief of reality quickly filled his weary head, he noticed something familiar in the distance—a black monk walking on a small hill a hundred yards away. The monk stopped, turned to Harold briefly, and then disappeared.

CHAPTER 32

HASTINGS, SOUTH-EAST COAST, ENGLAND

Small rolling waves lapped onto the smooth stones on the beach. Caelin stopped to watch his men preparing the boat, though his mind was not focused on them; Edith Swanneck dominated his thoughts. Women mostly had little effect on him. It was the first time in a while he had been so captivated by feminine beauty: her glowing skin, her figure, her confidence. But Caelin was somewhat disappointed in his momentary show of weakness; this wasn't just any woman. She was the wife of his liege lord and friend. As his thoughts progressed, Caelin casually kicked stones into the water as he chastised himself.

"Caelin, Caelin! Look. Norman sails," yelled one of the Wessex thanes.

Caelin looked up from the stones to see his men on the shore curiously staring out to sea instead of preparing the boat. He then looked out to sea himself and immediately recognised something unusual.

"That is no fishing boat," he whispered.

"Doesn't look like they're trying to hide. A messenger perhaps?" suggested one of the men as he approached Caelin.

No one knew. The men watched in silence as the boat approached with a good wind behind it.

"Whoever is sailing that craft knows what they're doing," acknowledged Caelin. "Wait. That's Harold on the bow, waving to us. The Normans are releasing him."

"Are you sure, Caelin? How can you see that far?"

"Men, get in, sails down, we'll row out to meet them," Caelin ordered.

Moments later, the two boats met just offshore, on unseasonably calm water. Caelin and the men pulled in their oars while the Normans pulled down sails. Both sides braced for conflict but kept their weapons out of sight.

"Bring your boat closer so that we can receive the earl," said Caelin.

Slowly the boats drifted together, with slight movements of the oars on each, the silence of the calm sea a stark contrast to the potentially dangerous situation. As the boats drew close enough for Harold to jump across, he was given the nod from a Norman soldier and so swiftly made his way over to Caelin.

Eye contact between the Wessex and Norman men on the two boats was quiet but intense. A sudden move could have sparked a melee of arrow fire between them. Instead, the oars of the Wessex boat dipped back into the calm sea and gradually picked up speed to the beach as the Normans returned south across the channel.

"My lord! We were about to cross the channel to get you out

of Normandy," Caelin said with a smile as Harold stood and embraced him.

"What a mess! It's good to see you alive, brother," said Harold, almost choked with emotion.

"We need to get you to Northampton, Harold," insisted Caelin.

"Northampton?"

"Yes. It's Morcar. He has Tostig held there."

"Bastard. He's taken the matter into his own hands. I told him to wait until I returned."

As the men rowed the longboat to shore, Harold stared towards his homeland. The last few days seemed to have broken his spirit, but the air of the north was sobering, reminding him who he was.

"Do you have horses?" he asked.

"In a village, not far."

"Good. We'll ride for London before Northampton."

CHAPTER 33

THORNEY ISLAND, LONDON

Harold and Caelin's ride to London from the south coast village of Hastings was swift considering the conditions. The muddy ground slowed them down, but Caelin often led Harold through his secret trails where the ground was less trodden. Near the middle of the night, they turned their horses into the road leading across to Thorney Island to King Edward's palace gate. The giant ash trees on either side of the quarter-mile road, heavy with rain and sleet, creaked as the wind pushed on the weight.

Caelin and Harold halted under the cover of the gate's arch. Just as he had earlier, the gatemaster recognised the earl and rushed to take the reins.

"I'm sure you remember, my lord, it is required that you leave all weapons here before entering the palace."

"Yes, we know," assured Harold.

The gatemaster walked ahead of Harold and Caelin into the cabin just outside the gate. He hung his lantern as the men laid down the few weapons they had on the table.

"Not so many tonight, my lord?"

Harold gave a half-smile before leaving the cabin ahead of Caelin.

"The horses. Fed, dry and resaddled. We won't be here long," ordered Harold as he continued to walk towards the palace.

"Of course, my lord."

As he did several days prior, Harold paused and looked across the moat and up towards the immense castle before giving a long and audible exhale. Caelin, who was a step behind, took a moment to watch Harold. He was still pleased to see him, sooner than he expected, but he felt something was different with his liege.

"Are you well?" Caelin asked.

"I am, brother," Harold quickly responded, still looking at the fine stonemasonry.

"What happened over there? Guy sent you to Normandy, but that's all I know. Did you cut a deal to secure your release from William?"

"No." Harold swiftly turned to Caelin to squash the notion. "No, I didn't cut a deal. William just couldn't keep me or kill me. So, off I went."

Caelin knew he needed to drop the subject, but he also knew the Normans well enough to know they wouldn't let opportunities like that slip through their hands. There was more to the story, but he wouldn't hear about it tonight.

"Let's get this over with so we can move on to Northampton," ordered Harold as they proceeded to the palace.

Abbot Edwin stood quietly and watched from the dim moonlit shadows within the main doors as Harold and Caelin approached.

"Lord Godwinson. Welcome."

"Ah yes, Abbot Edwin. How could I forget?" said Harold.

"My lord, I pray your visit this time will be more sustaining, for the king's sake."

"What? What are you suggesting?" asked Harold, frustrated by Edwin's insolence.

"The king has been at heaven's gates since you were here last. I found him on the floor unconscious and barely breathing shortly after you left."

"The king has been at your heaven's gates for months, Abbot. Enough of this game. I needn't defend myself to you. Take us to the king, now," demanded Harold.

Edwin turned his displeased expression toward the long hall and proceeded as Harold and Caelin followed.

Moments later, Harold entered the king's bedchamber. The room was dimly lit with candles and a smouldering fire in the corner. The king was motionless on his bed and looked even more pale than usual. Harold was surprised to see so many people in the shadows against the walls. Archbishops, bishops, members of the Witan, earls, even Morcar. A gathering of so many powerful men surrounding the dying king meant only one thing. The whispers that were already filling the room increased upon Harold's entrance. As Harold looked around, noticing he was being observed, it was clear that much talk had already taken place. He could only imagine what alliances and deals had been made and severed around those walls in the past several hours and in his absence.

Harold mentally shook off the pressure that enveloped him and turned his attention to the pale motionless king. He boldly approached and knelt at Edward's side. Caelin slipped into a dark corner to study the faces of those around him.

"Edward. Edward. It's Harold. I'm here," he said gently.

Edward's eyebrows raised as he recognised Harold's voice, which was enough to draw the attention of everyone in the room. Before he dared to continue, Harold took a moment to clear his mind; he knew the next few moments would make or break his bid for the throne as the weight of expectation coming from everyone in the room rested on his shoulders.

Just at that moment, King Edward's consort, Harold's sister Edith, opened the timber door and entered the room. Everyone, including Harold, turned to her as Edith covered her head and knelt with her brother at Edward's side. The two shared a look before Harold turned back to the king, who looked undoubtedly frail. The urgency of the situation was apparent. Harold needed to act fast while Edward could still at least recognise his presence.

"Edward. I know you can hear me," began Harold. "We've been fighting for decades, first, between you and my father. My father brought you here to be king, but he never allowed you to rule, and then I, I haven't been much better. I've never tried to heal the breach between us, even though you stopped fighting years ago. I know now that we could have worked together to bring peace to our subjects. Your subjects."

Harold's countenance dropped to the floor as everyone in the room watched and listened in silence.

"When I saw you days ago," he continued, "you said that I never spoke to you about important things, about who would rule in your place. I know, you were right. I refused to. I was proud and considered you a hindrance to my plans to surpass my father's achievements, even his dreams. But now I can see, you were indeed wise. But your wisdom was only evident to those willing to listen. You also said that I could grow beyond the limits set by my family. Yes, I've been living as though my father were still alive. It stops now."

As silence filled the room, Edith watched on in wonder as her brother slowly melted before her eyes into someone she had never met before. The impenetrable iron shell had fallen away, leaving an unrecognisable underbelly of humility and reason.

What has happened to bring Harold so low? she thought.

After several long moments of reflection, Harold's head sprang up to look at the dying king.

"Edward, after I left you days ago, I headed for Normandy, not York as you had ordered," Harold continued, knowing full well that Edward was not his only audience.

Gasps and whispers increased around the room.

"William, Duke William, he claims to the world that you chose him as successor many years ago, that he will rule England. Is he your chosen successor? Tell us. You must tell us before it's too late, brother," pushed Harold, as his sister's eyes widened with shock at this declaration.

The king's pale, wrinkled hands were crossed on his abdomen. Moments later, Edward's left hand slowly moved across the furs toward Harold's bowed head. Startled by the gasps in the room, Harold looked up to see. The king's hand moved closer and closer until it gently moved across Harold's left hand as it rested on the furs. Though the king said nothing, his hand rested on Harold's. Harold looked up at Morcar. The several members of the Witan instantly began whispering, nodding their heads and pointing to the king's hand.

The silence returned as Morcar turned from his meeting with the Witan, looked over to Harold and subtly nodded. Harold slowly stood, and his hand slid from underneath the king's touch. He quietly headed for the door and proceeded back down the hall with Caelin close behind.

Abbot Edwin stood from his kneeling position on the other side of the bed with his eyes wide open in shock.

"Is this God's mercy or is this judgement?" he asked himself. Fear and confusion flooded his every thought.

"Harold!"

Caelin and Harold turned back down the dark corridor to see Morcar approaching.

"Harold. I must say I am impressed with your little performance back there. I confess I have not seen that side of you. It certainly makes things a little easier for you. The Witan will support your claim, but before I allow them to get carried away, you and I have another issue to address."

"Yes, I know. You've been hasty. Did you forget our agreement a week ago to wait for my return, Morcar?"

"You were headed for Normandy, so I wasn't sure if you'd return at all, Harold. We all know how unpredictable William can be, particularly if you're uninvited."

"We intended to ride for Northampton to see you after visiting Edward, but you're here. Why did you not wait for me there?"

"I anticipated you'd come here first, but that's not important now. So, do we have terms?"

"Terms?"

"Must I spell it out, Harold?" laughed Morcar. "Look, present yourself at Northampton tomorrow and ensure Tostig is stripped of his earldom and banished from this land, not just out of Northumbria. If you can ensure that takes place, I can ensure the Witan consider no other claim when King Edward dies. Hmm?"

Harold squinted and looked down his nose at the shorter Morcar before letting out a long breath of frustration. He knew the terms, but having it so clearly spelt out made him realise how powerless he was. He had become a slave to his quest, and even if he would become king, he would still be subject to the cunning machinations of someone as worthless as Morcar. Harold had already considered the alternatives to the Tostig problem, but without Tostig gone, Morcar would not be satisfied. Morcar had never wished the throne for himself. He was much more interested in getting and spending wealth. Since his governing power now stretched beyond the borders of Mercia into Northumbria, the members of the Witan were increasingly watching and coveting Morcar's wealth and lifestyle. His grip on the Witan's powers of election was at its peak.

"I'll see you in Northampton tomorrow, Morcar." Harold pushed past and headed down the long, narrow and dark corridor.

"Oh no, I won't be there, Harold, I'll be here," announced Morcar. "You need me here. My men will let me know when Tostig has relinquished power and is on a boat to Flanders."

Harold heard but continued his path to the door. Caelin lingered for a moment, staring at Morcar before heading for the door himself.

As Harold and Caelin moved into the night outside, Morcar was left in the dim candlelit hall.

"Gabriel, you can come out now."

From the darkest corner moved a figure who would otherwise have been mistaken for a stone sculpture covered in material.

"Lord Morcar," he whispered.

"Gabriel, come to think of it, I don't believe Harold will cause any more problems for us. He seems to be following the plan. Caelin, on the other hand, is a different case altogether. Someone with his skill and resources needs to be managed. Particularly if his liege lord is soon to be king."

"Leave it with me, my lord."

"Good man." Morcar headed back into the king's bedchamber.

Harold and Caelin stormed back to the gate, where their dried and resaddled horses waited.

"Caelin, I think you should stay here in London and keep watch on Morcar."

"What? Harold, I don't think that's necessary. You don't know what other tricks Morcar has planned for you in Northampton. I'll round up men to—"

"You don't understand, do you?" interrupted Harold. "In the strongest terms without speaking, King Edward just made me heir, the successor to the throne. I can be king, brother! But Morcar can make this opportunity disappear like a puff of smoke if he wants to. I need you here to observe Morcar's movements until I get back."

Caelin gave a long blink and shook his head. "Do you think me ignorant of Morcar's schemes, Harold? I've watched him and everyone else for years, and all this time you've trusted my counsel, almost without question. You're not trusting me now. It's clear your unquenchable thirst for Edward's throne clouds your judgement." Caelin knew he was pushing the boundaries of obedience.

"You're wrong. On the other hand, I can see something else now, clear as ever. You disobey my orders!" Harold's rebuke echoed across the moat and off the castle walls.

Caelin fixed his eyes on the ground below and said nothing in response.

"Gather men and means, do whatever it is you do. But stay here in London. Observe the Witan's movements and report when I return in two days. Is that clear, soldier?"

The two said nothing further as Harold mounted his horse and disappeared down the long road north. Caelin turned and without much effort, struck his fist through the cabin's thin timber wall before fetching his horse. The nearby stablehands and guards came from several positions to investigate the noise, but Caelin had disappeared.

Morcar's hired spy, Gabriel, had been watching Harold and Caelin's argument from a distance, hidden in the shadows of the moonlight. He made haste and approached the gate to get a closer view of Caelin's course.

Not taking orders, hmm? So, where is Harold's most trusted going now? Ah yes. Of course. West. Wessex.

Gabriel turned to the stables to fetch his horse.

CHAPTER 34

NORTHAMPTON, ENGLAND

"Morcar was right. Harold is here."

"What?"

"Get moving. Go!"

The appearance of Harold in Northampton was a welcome sight for the many men in town under Morcar's orders, but not this early. Harold was not expected until late afternoon, and he was not expected to be alone. Two of Morcar's men were already in a state of panic, as their recent assignment to set up and manage the royal courthouse was not as easy as Morcar suggested when he appointed the task to them.

Though the town of Northampton was small, its significance was not due to its local shire court being recently upgraded to a royal court, now used to settle all royal disputes and trials north of London to York and the greater Northumbria. During its time as a shire court, it was famed for its speed to close disputes, not its ability to uphold fairness.

Two days earlier, Morcar had little confidence in the adequacy of his men.

"But this is a shire court, isn't it, Morcar?" they had asked him.

"I'll explain it one last time for you utter donkeys," responded Morcar frustratingly. "This court is now functioning as a royal court for the king and the earls; therefore, it is only active at the king's request. It is no longer dealing with pitiful shire, manor or shire-tithe disputes. So, we need to prepare it suitably. Go to Aldred, Bishop of York, today. Gather all the necessary Northumbrian charters dating back to King Cnut; he'll know which ones. They need to be ready for referencing in the trial. We can't afford any chance of this being thrown out. Wait! Come to think of it. Old Aldred, yes. He may be of more use to us than just his charters."

Harold casually rode through the gates of the small town and watched as the recognition of his face sent dozens into a scurry towards the town's centre.

He took a long frosty breath as the reality and weight of the task ahead bore down heavily. Tostig and Harold rarely saw eye to eye from childhood, which often escalated to bruised faces and grazed knuckles. But they were blood, not just any blood; they were Godwinsons. Sons of the old Wessex line. No childish dispute would ever break such a bond.

But this is different, Harold thought. *He's gone too far.*

As Harold trotted on, he spotted a familiar hooded figure in the distance about a hundred yards away on a hill, at the town's border. He watched it as though he had lived or dreamt this before. Assuming it was the exhaustion of constant travel, he shook his head and blinked his weary eyes heavily to clear them, and when he looked up, the familiar lone hooded monk was gone.

"Just like that monk in Normandy. The same habit and posture, the same look. The one who called himself Caprasius. But that was a dream, wasn't it?"

"Welcome to Northampton, Lord Godwinson. I can take your horse from here," offered the local stableman.

"Yes. Have her fed and brushed. I leave at first light tomorrow," accepted Harold, though a little distracted.

"Very good, my lord."

As Harold watched his horse being led away, he noticed three of Morcar's men approaching from the direction of Northampton's town centre. He casually headed towards them, powder-like snow crunching under his fur and leather boots. With every step, he felt his world changing. Achieving his dream but leaving behind his family. Despite the voices in his head, it was too late to go back.

"Good morning, Lord Godwinson. We will accompany you to the hall."

Harold said nothing and followed their lead.

"You must have passed through London, my lord. Did you see Earl Morcar by chance?" asked one of the men.

"Yes, and yes, I did see Morcar."

"Then our objective for today is clear, or do we need to discuss this before we enter court?" asked the Mercian thane as they walked.

"Whatever my understanding of today's proceedings, you won't be giving orders to me," responded Harold, without looking up from the ground.

Harold and his new hosts reached the courthouse without speaking another word. Upon entering, several townsfolk swiftly finished their cleaning, bowed to Harold and exited.

Harold took his place on the eastern side of the court and was followed shortly after by three Northumbrian royal delegates, who took their places at the head.

Moments later, an elderly priest entered, his long robe shifting dust behind him as he moved slowly across the floor to find his place. He was followed by another elderly cleric, a much less decorated monk. He wheeled in a small makeshift cart full of old parchment and paper charters which he immediately began shuffling as he took his place next to his superior.

As the shuffling carried on, the decorated priest took off his hat and glared at Harold as though he were disappointed to see him. Exhausted from the ride overnight, Harold was in no mood to be belittled by a northerner, let alone a northern clergyman, and simply stared back.

"Bring him in," called the elderly priest.

As the priest's order echoed off the walls, Tostig's complaints about his dishonourable treatment were heard as he was led toward the courtroom. As he reached the stand moments later, his eyes scanned the room, his clothes torn and bloodstained, hands bound behind him with irons. Harold and Tostig's eyes met, and for Harold, it was as though time stood still. Godwin family solidarity would be tested this day and in a public courtroom.

"This is all you, isn't it?" yelled Tostig to Harold. "Morcar and this court, you set all this up!"

The elderly priest rose from his seat and spoke loudly. "Silence, Tostig Godwinson. You may speak only when addressed."

As silence fell over the room, the priest's eyes again found Harold. "Do you know who I am, Harold Godwinson?"

"Earl Godwinson, to you, whoever you are. No," retorted Harold.

"Well, let me enlighten you, Earl Godwinson. I am Aldred,

Archbishop of York. Did you mistake me for an abbot or a humble Northumbrian priest, perhaps? I rarely wear the full episcopal dress of a primate. You may not have remembered me a moment ago, but I do believe, yes. Your face is easier to read than an ale-house sign, Harold. At present, your mind is flipping through vague memories from fifteen to twenty years ago. Yes, that's right. Your father and I were close friends. Even during his time in exile. However, the Godwin family is now but a ruin of what it once was when your father was alive."

Moments earlier, Harold was ready to leap out of his chair in defence, sat back, exhaled and reflected.

"I remember you now," he said with uncharacteristic calm. "You were an unwavering support for my father and our family. For that, I thank you."

Like the rest of those present, Tostig stood silent. His countenance had also changed as the memories of the single most supportive figure in their father's later life came flooding back.

"Harold, before we commence, let us be clear. Today you have an opportunity to bring honour to your family and your father's memory. I'm sure you understand. Let us begin," announced Aldred.

Aldred gave Harold a brief but genuine smile and then turned to Tostig. His expression changed as quickly as he turned.

"Tostig Godwinson … at the king's pleasure, you have been brought here to account for the crimes of a common tyrant. Instead of bringing prosperity and peace to your peerage, your powers as Earl of Northumbria have been used to inflict hardship, injustice, and in some cases, death upon the king's subjects. We have evidence and witnesses who, prior to this court, have given detailed accounts of your sacking of the abbey in Lindisfarne. Upon your orders, certain Northumbrian men entered the abbey, emptied it of all sacramental vessels and other priceless relics. We have been told that the abbot of Lindisfarne happened upon your men as they tried to leave. The abbot was then severely dealt with, and it was said that your men could be heard saying, 'Remember to pay your dues to Godwinson next time.' They left his broken and bloodied body on the abbey floor, and he died within two days. The monks of Lindisfarne have attested to this, and the messenger you sent has also come forward. This, Tostig Godwinson, is one of many other crimes we have on record to bring forward today, spanning back ten years. These acts are sinful, shameful and it stops now. The king's subjects of the north deserve leadership and peace, not tyranny and death. What say you of these charges?"

Tostig glared at Harold before commencing his defence. "I will say this. These charges were all carefully constructed by my brother Harold," he announced to Aldred before turning to Harold. "This unspeakable betrayal of blood is unnatural, after everything we have achieved together, brother. We crushed Welsh rebellions and brought the Welsh king Gruffydd to his knees and look where we are today. Our father would curse you for this abomination. Indeed, he does curse you from the grave. As for these charges, these slanderous stories can be explained, Aldred, when my once-brother confesses that they are nothing but horse dung—conjured up by none other but himself and Morcar, the Earl of Mercia, who is eager to add my earldom to his rank. But also, and this is the best part, that MY head is the price required to guarantee Morcar's support for Harold's bid for the throne of England once Edward is dead. Am I not right, brother?"

The courtroom erupted with accusations from almost every observer and official, but mainly at Tostig or Harold. Harold said nothing, his gaze and countenance unchanged, his head pounding, tempted to burst out of his seat and defend his dear brother but held down to his timber chair by the weight of his vision as though it was a curse. The mayhem around him seemed to be an echo from a distant valley as the consequences of his inaction filled the room. He lifted his eyes to Archbishop Aldred to find him already staring back. Aldred subtly shook his head.

Amongst the commotion, Aldred rose from his seat with his episcopal staff in hand, walked calmly out into the middle of the courtroom and pounded loudly into the court's timber floor while shouting in Latin.

"Pāx! Pāx! Pāx!" *Silence. Silence. Silence.*

Silence fell on the courtroom at once, just as the Archbishop instructed.

"It is too late for these pathetic counteraccusations, Tostig. You are charged with these crimes, and there are countless other charges we could bring forth to convict you, but we have heard enough, and the patience of the king and his subjects has run out. Unless the Earl of Wessex objects?"

The pause was brief but long enough for everyone in the room to turn and find a motionless and Harold.

"In that case, I have the king's authority to bring these proceedings to an end, now. I declare that you, Tostig Godwinson, are banished from this kingdom and this land indefinitely. Your exile will not be reconsidered, annulled or reduced if King Edward should not recover from his illness and die. Longboats await to take you to Frankish lands. May God have mercy on you. This royal court is now closed."

The shouting and echoed noise erupted again as Aldred made his way out of the courtroom with his monk shuffling in behind him. Tostig glared at Harold as he was escorted out of the courtroom towards the stables.

Harold rose and pushed through the crowd of shouting locals to reach the main doors. As he burst into the snow-reflected daylight outside, he looked in all directions in search of Aldred. To the east, a large and elaborate red and gold carriage pulled by two horses was surrounded by at least a dozen various ranked clergy, fussing over the archbishop's ability to ascend the stairs into its interior. Harold swiftly made his way to its side as Aldred took his seat.

"Ah, young Harold," declared Aldred as he adjusted a thick fur covering his lap. "I'm sure you found that very difficult, but you chose correctly. You had the authority to shift Tostig's sentence, and I would have honoured it. You took the difficult but right path. But I suspect you find comfort in knowing that you have put wisdom and your father's wishes before brotherly love? What say you?"

"I hope so," replied Harold. "But Aldred, Tostig will not go quietly. He has allies in Flanders through his wife's family and may have ties with duchy there, and who knows what other alliances may be established if Tostig's temper is not cooled in exile. There's much to consider here."

"No. There's nothing to consider here other than this: you will be king," assured Aldred. "Do you understand what that means, Harold? You will have men one-hundred-fold at your command compared to your current tiny band of Wessex thanes, or whatever you call them. Forget about Tostig. No prince southeast of this island would dare support a Tostig-led invasion. It would be suicide. You best keep your eyes on the Normans instead. Edward's Norman ties may have been quiet these last ten years, but now they seem to have awoken. Who knows what their expectations are following Edward's death?"

"Yes. I, at least, have some wisdom on that front."

"Good. Good. I thought you might. I can't help you any further here, Harold. The Witan and the Archbishop of Canterbury are in Morcar's hands and the Pope, well, let us say I am not his favourite servant."

"Thank you, Aldred. You've been more than enough help so far."

Aldred nodded at Harold before signalling to assistants to move the carriage along.

"Wait, Aldred. Before you go, does not an archbishop bless his flock as he leaves?"

"Harold? You've never cared for God's help in your life," said Aldred as the carriage halted. "You certainly are different today, aren't you, my son? I don't know what has brought on this change, but I will say this, God will either use you or humble you in this. You are not in control."

With that, Aldred made the sign of the cross over Harold and placed his hand on his head.

CHAPTER 35

THORNEY ISLAND, LONDON

It was past midday, but Abbot Edwin was not watching the time. He had not slept in two days and had barely seen any daylight. His eyes had grown weary, drifting between the dying king and the candlelit shadows that danced across the stone walls of Edward's bedchamber. The situation had escalated overnight. Edward had stopped responding and Stigand, Archbishop of Canterbury, authorised the commencement of rites.

No ruler or noble in England had ever made such an impact on Edwin as Edward had. Never had a king of such stature and spiritual devotion graced these corrupt halls. Edwin secretly hoped and prayed that Edward would usher England into a new age of purity, humility, and prayer. But hope, it seemed, was lost. Edwin's prayers nor even King Edward, this vessel of God, could penetrate such evil times during his reign. England, Edwin thought, was lost in its greed and corruption. God's patience had expired, and judgement was imminent.

"Edward. Edward … Edward," called Archbishop Stigand, before placing two fingers under the king's nose.

Stigand's eyes moved to Morcar, then to Abbot Edwin. "The king is not breathing. He is truly dead."

Without much delay or any sign of emotion, Stigand removed the sacred ring from Edward's finger, which was easy, as his fingers were vastly thinner than the rings original size. As soon as the ring was removed, the silence in the room was replaced with movement and murmurings.

Everyone, it seemed, had something to do except for Edwin. Stunned, he slowly slid his back down the tapestry on the wall behind him and slumped to the floor. As though he had been driven through with a sword. He crossed himself slower than ever before and whispered, "Kyrie eleison." *Lord, have mercy.*

An hour had passed, and much had taken place since Stigand's announcement, but Morcar and the Witan had not left the king's bedchamber.

"Patience, patience," assured Morcar. "My envoy will arrive any moment with word of the trial. Oh, here he is now."

Morcar's messenger confidently walked past the bed of the dead king and straight to Morcar's eagerly awaiting ear. The members of the Witan watched on in anticipation as Morcar questioned the messenger for a few moments before turning to his fellow Witan.

"It is settled," he announced. "Before the king died, Archbishop Aldred successfully passed judgement on Tostig without any objections from Harold. They have effectively exiled Tostig."

The members of the Witan all knew that Morcar would take the opportunity to gain as much leverage as possible before the

Witan would be required to elect Edward's successor. But they never expected him to manage this feat.

"Tostig's earldom of Northumbria falls to me. I am now the Earl of Northumbria and Mercia, and I now pass my recommendation to the Witan council that Harold, Earl of Wessex, succeed Edward as king. You all, no doubt, witnessed how Edward touched Harold's hand as he pressed him on the succession and the presumption of the Normans. Are we in agreement, or shall I inform Archbishop Stigand that we have a problem?"

Not one member said a word; they nodded their heads in agreement.

Morcar smiled, left the circle of Witan members and headed for Stigand's ear.

"Harold."

CHAPTER 36

WINCHESTER CASTLE, WESSEX

Caelin's late afternoon entrance into the Wessex Castle's inner courtyard often sent servants into action, as his presence was usually followed by Earl Godwinson an hour or so after.

"No need to panic; the earl is not behind me," Caelin informed the men in the stables. "I'm here alone."

"Very good, sir. I'll let the others know."

Caelin was amused to see how the business of Winchester Castle carried on, oblivious that their master had been held captive in Normandy these last several days.

As always, above the courtyard, Edith watched on through an opening without being seen. She smiled to herself as she watched Caelin dismount and talked amongst the servants before making his way up to the castle's living quarters. She headed to the hall and made herself comfortable.

"Welcome back, Caelin. Did you find Harold?" she enquired as Caelin entered the hall and bowed.

Caelin approached the table, where Edith was sitting with

food and wine. "I did find Harold. By chance, we found him approaching the coast before we set sail. The Normans escorted him back on a small boat, unharmed. So, we—"

Almost ignoring his news, Edith approached Caelin with warmth and touched his arm. "Caelin, you haven't rested since I saw you last? You must be exhausted. Come, sit. There's food and ale."

Caelin was still uneasy and tense from his encounter with Harold the night before, let alone the long ride from London. He stopped talking and took a deep breath. He felt comfortable enough to do away with the formal duties, for now, and followed Edith to the table, which had everything he wanted. As Caelin made himself comfortable and filled his plate with meat, bread and fruit, Edith poured him a pitcher of ale.

"So, the Normans simply dropped him off after almost a week of holding him?"

"We were no less puzzled. Harold looked tired and seemed distracted, but there was not a scratch on him. Then, he and I headed for London."

"That's it? There's got to be more to the story than just 'We then headed to London'. What happened to Harold in Normandy?" Edith pushed, while drawing close to Caelin.

'Well, as we travelled, I asked him about Normandy, but he didn't give me a convincing story. Something about Duke William being unable to keep or kill him, so William was forced to release him to be rid of the risk. It's not like Harold to keep foreign information from me, but I'm not convinced. I do believe there is more to the story than that. Normans would only release such a high-profile prisoner at a price. So, what was that price? I don't know."

"What happened in London?"

"Harold spoke to the king, who is almost dead, if not already.

If only you were there to see it yourself. It was quite a spectacle and strange."

"Why?" pressed Edith.

"Well, I was already suspicious that Harold was hiding something about what happened in Normandy, but his speech to King Edward at his bedside was … well, it was clear that something happened in Flanders and Normandy, something had changed him. He's become humble, almost fearful or superstitious about something, and I'm not sure if it's a good thing or not. As we were leaving King Edward's room, we happened upon Morcar, who pressured Harold to head to Northampton to sort out Tostig's mess. Harold ordered that I stay in London to watch Morcar's movements, but I wanted to come here to update you before I get to work on that," explained Caelin.

"Is that all?"

"Yes, that is all that took place in London," Caelin assured her.

"No, Caelin, I meant, is that the only reason you wanted to come here after Harold left London?"

Their eyes met for a moment that seemed longer than it was.

Caelin responded slowly. "Of course, … also, I, I needed to head back here for supplies."

"Caelin, you have ample supplies in the barn in Billingsgate, which is a stone's throw across the river from Saint Peter's. Winchester is a six-hour ride at your pace. You could have sent a man to us with the latest news."

"There is more at stake here, Edith. Things that a messenger cannot convey. Only you and I know what state your husband is in, in his mind," pressed Caelin, hoping to bring the conversation back from potentially awkward places.

"You're right, Caelin. I would feel completely alone in this if it weren't for you. We both understand Harold and his limitations. But we also understand each other, don't you think?"

Edith gently touched Caelin's cheek, turning his gaze to her. Their lips slowly drew closer and softly met.

Deep in the drapery and shadows of the hall, someone was watching Caelin and Edith, and he was getting more information than he hoped for.

After Morcar noticed Caelin heading west from London the night before, Morcar sent his most trusted assassin, Gabriel, to follow him. But Gabriel, a former Norman faithful who happily became a servant of Mercia and Morcar as soon as he saw how profitable it was, didn't follow Caelin to Winchester to kill.

As Edith and Caelin were momentarily distracted, with skilful quiet, Gabriel slipped out of his shadowy corner and quietly made his way down towards Edith's quarters, avoiding the line of sight of any servants. As soon as he entered Edith's private sleeping quarters, the sound of approaching servant girls forced Gabriel to climb into the roof beams above Edith's bed. He waited and watched from above as the oblivious servant girls stripped Edith's bed linens and replaced them with another set. He could hear them talking but could not make sense of their thick Northumbrian English, as though it were another language altogether. The girls soon left and closed the heavy door. When the footsteps and gossip could be heard far enough down the stairs, Gabriel dropped from the beams with almost no noise. He wasted no time and began searching through chests full of clothes and undergarments.

"Aha, taille parfaite." *Perfect size.* He exclaimed quietly to himself as he emerged from the large chest with a small but intimate piece of Edith's undergarments, something that most men never knew existed.

Caelin pulled himself back from Edith's smooth, soft lips.

"Edith. We can't do this. It won't help."

Edith turned away, sat and buried her face in her hands.

"I don't know how much longer I can do this, Caelin. Being the strong and supportive wife, as though I don't have flesh and blood of my own."

Caelin sat silently as Edith's tears began to flow.

"I'm not strong, Caelin, as you can see for yourself. I'm weak and not fit to go on with this, this disguise."

"You're wrong, Edith. You are strong. You're strong for making it this far into the mess that the Godwin family dishes out. But there's something else. If things went well for Harold in London and Northampton today, then you won't just be the supportive wife of an earl, you'll be consort to the king in a matter of days, and I can't think of a more qualified person to stand by a king than you."

Caelin rested his hand on Edith's shoulder before heading for the door at the other end of the long hall. He turned to smile. "Don't despair, Edith. I'll see you in London."

Caelin's footsteps echoed as he headed down the stairs. Moments later, he swiftly made his way across the courtyard toward the stables, shaking his head and rubbing his brow as though he had just dodged an arrow.

"Is my horse fed?" he asked the stableman.

Gabriel turned in shock to see Caelin standing before him just as he was fixing something inside Caelin's saddle. He was sure Edith would have Caelin entangled in her arms for longer than that.

"Yes, of course, sir," Gabriel responded awkwardly.

"I've not seen you here before. You must be new." Caelin swiftly untied and mounted his horse.

"Yes, I'm new here in the stables. S-stable work," stuttered Gabriel.

As Caelin mounted his horse, he couldn't help but be a little suspicious. For a moment, he could detect a Norman accent but concluded that to be unlikely, and so just smiled and nodded before heading to the gates.

CHAPTER 37

TWENTY MILES NORTH-WEST OF LONDON

The following morning's heavy rain and sleet made for difficult riding, though Harold's quest south to London carried on. There were four riders with him when they left Northampton the previous day, but by the time they passed the monastery of Saint Alban, the riders that surrounded Harold amounted to forty Mercians. Harold expected to be escorted back to London after Tostig's trial, but not by so many.

Something has happened, Harold thought as he noticed the Mercians riding with him, not talking at all. He had time to think over the scenarios that could await him in London, but the travel and lack of sleep since Normandy made it hard to be positive.

A rider drew alongside. "My lord. One of our men from London joined our group in the last hour. He brought news that our King Edward is dead and that we are to escort you directly to Earl Morcar at Saint Peter's."

Harold knew there would be no further information, so he remained silent and focused on avoiding deep mud as he rode further ahead of the group. A few months ago, news like that would have made him laugh or cheer, but as it set in, a completely unexpected response slowly draped over Harold's mind and body, like a heavy yoke placed over a plough ox. Harold's breathing increased, his eyes widened, the usual focus on a precision ride faded away, and he could feel the colour in his face disappear as fear of the unknown gripped him. It wasn't Morcar, the Witan or the days that lay ahead, but the unknowns of Edward. Was Edward now more powerful in death than he ever was alive? With all the unexplainable things Harold had experienced over the past several days, it wasn't difficult for him to believe that the monk that had been haunting Harold was somehow a curse from Edward himself. Or perhaps Edward's ghost was hovering above him at that very moment while he rode, able to unleash vengeance and fury for years of treason and belittling by the entire Godwinson family during Edward's reign? Harold was harbouring more superstitious fear than he ever expected to experience in his lifetime.

As they reached the outskirts of London, the roads became denser with people and carts. As they progressed, Harold noticed an increasing number of people heading in the same direction he was, west toward Saint Peter's monastery on Thorney Island. Markets and stalls which filled London's more populated east were being boarded up, halls and alehouses emptying as the news of Edward's death spread through streets and laneways. The riders around Harold were making noise, clearing the way. In contrast, the multitudes on the road were not making much sound at all. They were quiet and gloomy, and some were even chanting prayers.

It took Harold a few moments to realise that the movement of people and the unusual hush was London in mourning. He had never seen London like this, and he certainly did not expect this response to Edward's death. Edward rarely ventured out to see his subjects, at least not in the last ten years, so it seemed more apparent to Harold that London's devotion to Edward never diminished in his later years while he stayed within the walls of the monastery.

As the riders emerged from the crowd near Thorney Island, the bulk of the Mercians turned off, leaving only six with Harold as they steered sharply onto the quarter-mile road leading to the palace gate. The subtle winter fragrance of Edward's ash trees lining the approach was just another reminder for Harold's already tortured mind.

Upon reaching the cover of the gate's arch, Harold and the Mercians dismounted. Once again, the gatemaster recognised the earl and rushed to take the reins of his horse.

"You need not disarm this time, Lord Godwinson. These horses will be dry and fed. Is there anything else you require, my lord?"

Harold slapped the gatemaster on the shoulder and led the Mercians across the moat to the palace entrance. He looked up, expecting to see Abbot Edwin waiting; instead, Caelin was there and held the door open. As Harold approached, Caelin bowed his head and looked to his own feet. Caelin always bowed his head to nobility, especially to Harold, but he never dropped his gaze lower than the feet of those around him to keep watch for sudden movements. But not this time. It was a full bow. Harold noticed.

Harold turned to his Mercian escorts. "Thank you. I know the way from here."

"But, my lord, we were to escort you directly to Morcar," responded one of the Mercians.

"You will receive your reward, soldier. I'm not going

anywhere." With that, Harold moved inside and proceeded down the hall, while Caelin remained outside with the worried Mercians.

Harold stopped and casually turned towards the open door. "Caelin?"

Moving inside and giving the Mercians a brief nod of assurance, Caelin closed the heavy timber door and followed Harold down the long hall. Passing the numerous shrines and reliquaries, they reached the closed door to Edward's bedchamber to their right. Two monks stood at the door, their whispered prayers in unison, their heads bowed and their hoods hiding their faces. Harold paused; his eyes stared down the hall and beyond, not toward the door and monks to his right.

Caelin also stopped, remaining silent and a few steps behind. He watched on and wondered what had caused Harold to stop suddenly halfway down the hall. Was it the knowledge of Edward's body being prepared for burial to his right or Morcar and the Witan with Harold's fate in their hands down the hall? *Perhaps it was both,* he thought.

The fragrance from the abundant fresh herbs and flowers used in Edward's burial preparation was unavoidable and filled the long dark hall. After a deep breath, Harold moved down to where most of the noise was coming and pushed the door open. The sun beaming through the hall's large windows flashed directly into his eyes, illuminating the silhouettes of the Witan members, who were all immediately silenced as they turned to him.

"Indeed, the sun does rise on you this day, Harold," bellowed Morcar as he approached.

"Enough of your rhetoric, Morcar. I've been riding for three days straight. From Normandy and across the channel, to Northampton and now finally back here. I secured a blessing from Edward before he died, which you all witnessed, and I banished my own brother from these lands. What more could you possibly want? What have you and the Witan decided? Are we still on terms?"

"Yes, Harold. Edward will be buried tomorrow morning, and you crowned as King the following day."

"No!" Harold's protest echoed off the walls. "The same day! I will be crowned after the sun of noon following Edward's funeral in the morning. Heaven knows you won't need more than a few hours to mourn."

"Heaven?" laughed Morcar. "You've certainly changed Harold, becoming more in touch with God. I'll inform Archbishop Stigand. He'll want to know about the new coronation time, but he'll be more interested to hear about your new ... religious fervour. No doubt you'll need Stigand's guidance when you rule as king. Religion was such an enormous benefit for Edward when he was in power."

The Witan members laughed along with Morcar's sarcasm. Harold and Caelin remained unchanged. Harold briefly turned to Caelin, long enough to see him mouth two words. "Stigand. No."

"Aldred, Archbishop of York, will place the crown on my head, not Stigand." The laughter stopped immediately as all eyes turned to Harold.

Like an unstable madman, Morcar's face immediately changed from laughter to rage, and he stepped forward to address Harold.

"I don't care if the Pope's bastard child does it. But you'll need to remember that you don't have a crown on your head yet. I'm the one who—"

"You're the one who what, Morcar? What can you do, exactly? Do you know how to lead an army of pikemen, archers, huscarls and thanes? And who will these men flock to now? The banners of Mercia and Northumbria? No, they'll flock to their king. So, I suggest you let me take it from here. Don't worry; you'll still have your land, servants and castles of luxury."

Harold and Caelin left Morcar and the Witan in the banqueting hall and headed back through the long dark corridor and out into the light of the square overlooking the palace moat.

"Caelin, didn't my father install Stigand as Archbishop of Canterbury? Why did you call that out?"

Caelin shifted swiftly back into his role of key advisor to Harold, as though the argument the night before never took place, although they both felt uneasiness.

"This topic is more political than the counsel I usually give, but five successive popes have excommunicated Stigand over the years since your father installed him and exiled Edward's Norman. He seems to have kept it secret in England all this time, mostly. So, being crowned by Stigand could be used against you in the future."

"Good counsel, brother. Anything to report on Morcar's movements in London while I was north?"

Caelin felt he could get away with accounting for the time he'd lost while he visited Edith in Wessex. He knew Morcar was asleep, and most of his men were up north minding Harold, but he was not so relaxed as he lied. "Nothing to report. He stayed in the palace and consulted only with Witan members. Most of Morcar's men were up north with you."

"Caelin, Morcar has more men at his disposal than you think, and they won't be wearing Mercian colours. He has spies everywhere. He'll want to control me like he did Edward, so we need to be diligent if we're to avoid his puppetry. Are you sure no one was watching you while you were watching Morcar?"

"I'm sure of it. I know his tactics," Caelin assured him.

"Good. Head home to Wessex, bring Edith and some servants back to London for the coronation tomorrow. This has all happened so fast. No doubt she'll be confused."

"Harold, Edith knows that the throne has been your goal for many years."

"Do you think so? We've never spoken of it. Perhaps you understand her more than I do."

At that moment, a novice monk approached.

"My Lord Godwinson, I'm to inform you that quarters have been arranged for you in the palace, with a bedchamber for you to rest from your travels."

Harold nodded at the monk.

"I think not, my lord," Caelin said. "It seems you have a new status in this place already. Perhaps that will be the last time I call you 'my lord'. I ride for Wessex and will return before morning with Edith."

With that, Caelin headed for his horse at the gatehouse, feeling as though he'd betrayed his liege somehow, even though he never would.

CHAPTER 38

BERCK-SUR-MER, FLANDERS

The morning brought gusty onshore winds, unfavourable for the skilled fishermen of Berck-sur-Mer trying to prepare boats and nets for the day ahead.

"Anglais," announced one of the locals as they noticed a Saxon boat approaching the coast. As the local fishermen began to discuss why their small town had been popular lately with Saxon English entering, they observed that one of the men onboard was bound by the hands. Clearly, a prisoner being banished from England. They watched as the prisoner's bonds were cut before he was thrown from the boat into the sea.

"Bastards!" yelled the man, forced to swim ashore.

"We were ordered to take you across the channel. This is close enough, wouldn't you say?" laughed the Mercian soldiers onboard.

The man did his best to navigate the problematic swell and swim to the beach, with the number of Berck-sur-Mer observers increasing along the shoreline, curious as to whether this new foreigner was a criminal.

One local fisherman left his nets and headed down to the shore to check on the saturated foreigner.

"Qui es-tu?" *Who are you?*

"Je suis Tostig de Northumbria, le beau-frère de Baldwin, le comte de Flandre. J'ai besoin d'un cheval."

The local was surprised to hear this Englishman so fluent in the Frankish language. It's usually enough to get by. Instead, this one was eloquent; he even used a slight Flanders accent on certain words. He was clear in expressing his name was Tostig of Northumbria, the brother-in-law of Baldwin, Count of Flanders, and needed a horse.

———

Later that evening, Tostig was dry, dressed like a Flanders noble and drinking fine wine in Bruges Chateau.

"Your wife, my sister, Judith, arrived here three days ago. She was banished by this Morcar fellow shortly before you and was treated a little better than how they treated you when they dropped her off at the coast," revealed Count Baldwin in his thick Frankish accent.

Baldwin often entertained wealthy English guests after they crossed the channel, either on official church business or on pilgrimage to Rome, so he ensured the chateau was well prepared and stocked for such unexpected visits. Most visitors would leave the court after bestowing the Count with a generous gift, so it was a profitable operation regardless.

"How is she?"

"She is fine. I think she is happier here. She can stay for as long as she likes. But I don't imagine you will be staying very long?"

"Your English is as good as it ever was, brother," complimented Tostig, attempting to divert attention away from his plans.

"Yes, many of your bishops and nobles visit on their way to ... but enough of the small talk, let's talk about you, Tostig. What are your plans? Surely you can't sit back and let this betrayal of a brother, your own flesh and blood, go unpunished?"

Tostig stared out the window toward the wintery sunset and took a moment to respond. "Of course not." He turned away from the view and placed his wine goblet on a nearby table. The tone of his voice lowered along with its volume. "But I want Harold completely humiliated, Baldwin, not just defeated. So, I'm going to need more than just Flanders to make it happen."

"What? Flanders? My men? Are you mad?" laughed Baldwin. "There is no way I can send my men with you to London. It would be suicide. And you must remember, Duke William, is my son-in-law."

"Why would Duke William care about such a plan? It has nothing to do with him."

"It seems you northern English all live in caves. Your King Edward promised the succession of the English crown to William many years ago," responded Baldwin with an increasing smile.

"That is madness. Why would an English king do that?" laughed Tostig, amused by the notion.

"English, is he?" Baldwin was now the amused one as Tostig's expression turned puzzled. For Baldwin, or any Frank, a conversation that celebrated the brilliance of the Franks while humiliating the English was something to be savoured. He stood up from his elaborately cushioned chair and proceeded to walk the room to commence his lesson for his unlearned brother-in-law. "Before he was your king, dear brother, Edward spent twenty years in exile in Normandy."

"Yes, I know that." Tostig returned to his wine.

"Well, do you also know that during that time, Edward was one of the men chosen to keep an eye on the young William when his father died on pilgrimage to the Holy Land? So, I'll put it this way, Edward was like a father to Duke William. He returned to England to be king as he had the strongest claim, but his reign was limited by the strict control of your father. Edward only married your sister because he feared your father. He only stayed in England because he was like a prisoner. He had no children with your sister because that would produce an heir of Godwin blood. His childlessness was his revenge on your father, not some religious vow as some would believe. Edward hated everything on that island, and his heart always remained in Normandy."

There was a long pause while Baldwin stared at Tostig with a cheeky smile. "Should I go on, Tostig? Hmm? You have underestimated his Norman influence, or should I dare say, his allegiance. If you seek a useful ally, you should look elsewhere. The Franks have their own battles to fight, and they won't need your English, how you say? ... expertise."

There was another long pause in the conversation as Tostig continued to stare out to the dim moonlight, and Baldwin poured the last half cup of wine remaining in the decanter. He signalled to the servant to fetch more.

Baldwin turned to Tostig with a thought. "There is someone who may be interested in such a plan. But before you see him, you'll need to visit the Scots."

CHAPTER 39

TONSBERG FORTRESS, NORWAY

The night skies above Norway were an immense show of thunder and lightning. A clear indication that the gods were watching the imminent destruction and bloodshed below. The fierce storm sent blinding winds and skin-piercing sleet across the plains below the towering Tonsberg fortress.

Unmoved by the storm, Hardrada, King of Norway, stood elevated on a large rock mound amid his overwhelming army of Norse warriors. With rain splashing off his shoulders like he was of the stone itself, he looked up at the colossal fortress that had eluded him for years, beyond his reach for so long until now. He was taller and heavier than any man in his army of ten thousand. Wearing little more than a full-faced battle helmet crafted to be almost impossible to remove, along with a long fur cape draped over enormous cliff-face shoulders and wolf-skin boots wrapped in leather. Hardrada had been lying low for nearly a year, planning a swift but sure move. Waiting for the opportune moment when the Tonsberg lord, Sweyn, was in residence but with his main army abroad, so Hardrada's men would outnumber the defenders fifty to one.

He turned his massive frame towards the sea of men, swords and axes, raised his sword above his head and let out an explosive roar of bloodthirsty fury. The Norsemen warriors responded with a deafening shout and clash of metal against shields, louder than the raging storm itself, shaking the very foundations of the fortress and its inhabitants.

Hardrada turned and pointed his sword at the fortress, signalling his men to destroy and leave none alive.

"ØDELEGGE LA INGEN ALIVE!"

Hardrada's voice was unlike that of a man, guttural from years of battle cries, now sounding more like the breath of a dragon.

Catapults burst into action, launching iron caged fireballs of immense weight, exposing weaknesses in the fortress walls ahead of the men charging toward the base of the main tower. Above were three or four archers, pitiful compared to the attack of Hardrada's army.

The fire from one of the catapults flew just over Hardrada's head with impeccable accuracy into the fortress base, with a catastrophic smash of stone and fire. As massive stones fell, an opening into the tower revealed itself. Hardrada climbed into the interior, followed closely by the dozen men assigned to stay with their leader. As the bulk of his men poured into the halls, treasuries and supplies, Hardrada began pacing through the corridors of the tower surrounded by his warriors, roaring out the name of his local enemy.

"SWEYN ... SWEYN!"

Sweyn's costly mistake was not joining his men on campaign this once, feeling that his body was growing too old for raids across treacherous seas, now that Hardrada's time had come to overthrow his former trusted ally and combine the armies. The tower's corridors were empty apart from the odd poor brave soldier who attempted to restrict Hardrada and his men from going deeper into the castle. Such attempts were quickly swept aside with the swing of an axe to the belly.

Hardrada's men kicked open doors and gates as they progressed through to the courtyard, where a tall timber-built keep sat at the centre of the stone fortress.

As they exited the tower's corridors, they paused to survey the open courtyard leading to the keep. Hardrada and his men were still in full view of the keep's archers within the keep despite the blinding wind and snow. Hardrada's men glanced toward the upper part of the keep, where archers were spotted readying their bows; an unplanned approach would be costly. Long-range attacks from their position were impossible as the personal guard did not carry bows. The men took glances at the keep and its surroundings, narrowly avoiding arrows from above as they discussed their options before one of the men announced the only remaining option.

"Skjold." *Shields.*

Hardrada's personal guard quickly moved into position. They surrounded their king in a square formation and holding their shields above Hardrada's head and around him, protecting him from the shower of arrows fired from the top of the keep. In this impenetrable formation, they proceeded slowly across the courtyard. Under his temporary hut of shields, Hardrada's walk was almost casual. He approached the keep's entrance, which was promptly kicked down by one of his men. Hardrada exited the protection of his men's shields and charged inside with a swinging sword, skilfully reaching the archers before they could aim, slicing them down where the shoulder meets the neck. A shower of blood sprayed across his face as the others pushed through the pathetic defence on the stairs one by one.

Upon reaching the upper room where Sweyn had taken refuge for the last few hours, Hardrada signalled his men to secure the keep, towers and ramparts. They disappeared as Hardrada himself burst through the doors, wasting no time and lunging towards Sweyn in a ferocious attack. The initial swing of his sword was not well-timed, which allowed Sweyn to crouch, roll and slash Hardrada's legs with a short blade before Hardrada's sword could reach its target.

"AAAARGG!" Hardrada's huge body hit the timber floor hard; he dropped his sword as he gripped at the wounds.

Relieved, Sweyn picked himself up off the floor and slowly walked away from the injured Hardrada, breathing heavily and keeping an eye on his foe in pain on the floor. Knowing he'd already lost his precious Tonsberg Fortress, and Hardrada's army would not join Sweyn if Hardrada were dead, he wanted to savour this moment of personal victory over the great warrior, who now struggled in pain before him. Sweyn took a moment to consider his words and final move. In their mother-tongue, he began his speech.

"Du tankeløse tosk! Gudene har bedratt deg ... Nå vil dø." *You mindless fool! The gods have deceived you ... Now, you will die.*

With a sly grin on his face, he readied his sword and took his first step to attack, but his second step was suddenly halted by two swords bursting through his chest from behind in a V-formation. Before he could look down to see the swords, they were pushed further again, protruding far enough to allow Hardrada's warrior to lift Sweyn's weight off the ground from behind by the blades, before splitting Sweyn's body in two as the swords separated. Sweyn's separated corpse fell on either side of the skilled swordsman, covering him in blood. Hardrada and his warrior exchanged a smile of amusement before Hardrada was helped off the floor.

———◆———

As the morning drew near, the food, wine, treasury and weaponry had been plundered and distributed amongst the victors. Despite the freezing storm, most Hardrada's men gathered in the courtyard to celebrate the victory in the traditional manner, stomping, grunting and slamming their bodies together in a circular motion around a large fire fuelled by timber furniture and corpses. The circular movement of the ritual was steady and relentless, spurred by the constant beating of drums and empty wine casts, causing a circle of mud to appear in the snow around the fire. As more wine was consumed, the circular stomping ritual became more physical and violent. Fists, shoulders and elbows were recklessly thrown into jaws, groins and bellies. A knocked-out tooth resulting from the ceremony was considered good luck, and the tooth was worn around the neck like a trophy.

As the commotion continued in the courtyard, Hardrada and his closest advisers dined in the main hall, surrounded by food from Sweyn's kitchens and stores. The discussion amongst Hardrada's men progressed the concept of a combined army and what it could achieve. Once Sweyn's army returned and was under Hardrada's control, no ruler could withstand their attack. The men further debated and argued about various options and paths across a makeshift map on the large timber table, without a word from Hardrada himself, who was listening but more interested in ripping the last remnants of meat from the bone in his hands.

One of the higher-ranked men raised the possibility of taking a vast fleet of longboats to England. Not to simply plunder another monastery, but to take hold of London itself, especially considering King Edward would soon be dead, if not already, and assume Hardrada's ascension to the throne through his ties to Edward's predecessor King Cnut.

Hardrada's attention was caught as the topic moved to England. He looked up from his plate, eyes burning with anger. Norse rulers had long desired the English throne, and though Cnut managed to claim it years ago, he was considered by the Norse as nothing more than a puppet. Hardrada was no fool. He knew that the Saxon English were the real people in power when Cnut was King of England, and he wasn't about to be the next in line to dishonour his legacy amongst the Norsemen.

Hardrada dropped his bone and slammed his fist on the table, silencing everyone in the room. "NEI! Jeg er ingen marionett av sakserne, og heller ikke er deg! Vår plass er her." *NO! I am no puppet of Saxon, nor are you! Our place is here.*

CHAPTER 40

THORNEY ISLAND, LONDON

It was a short walk from the palace to the Abbey of Saint Peter's, only fifty yards or less. But for Abbott Edwin on this particular morning, it felt like ten miles. Along with seven brothers from the monastery, he carried Edward's coffin slowly behind Stigand, Archbishop of Canterbury, who led the procession. The simple timber coffin, covered with elaborate embroidery and an abundance of winter flowers, was fixed to two twelve-foot iron poles on either side, carried by the eight men—four at the front, four at the rear.

Archbishop Stigand was adorned in the elaborately decorated episcopal gown and mitre, which were crafted specifically for the burial of a monarch. His long bristling white beard moved with the crisp winter morning breeze. As he swung a chain censer, incense smoke billowed around him.

One foot in front of the other, Edwin stared at the snow-dusted ground as he moved along, whispering with the archbishop's slow Latin prayers. Edwin felt as though the prayers were wasted breath, as nothing could soften the wave of wrath coming England's way. But as tears and hope fell from his heart, he reached out into the unknown and continued the prayers.

———————

While the funeral procession continued its solemn pace, elsewhere on Thorney Island in a large armoury room within Edward's palace, Harold Godwinson stood with arms stretched out, wearing only a thin under tunic. He was surrounded by several hurrying royal embroiderers, bladesmiths, and armourers draping, measuring and fitting royal coronation dressings to their soon-to-be king. Harold was quiet, his gaze fixed on the morning light beaming through the small windows facing east, his mind swirling with feelings of pride and fear. Pride in what he had achieved, fear of everything else.

Edith 'Swanneck' Godwinson was in the corner of the same room, also being fitted and adorned, by fewer servants but with many more jewels. Her eyes were fixed on her husband, considering the decades of schemes, bribes and pursuits by Harold and his father to reach this point. She felt both deference and pity for him. She wanted him to say something to her, but instead of prompting him with a question, she waited and watched in silence as the dressing continued.

———————

In the Abbey of Saint Peter's, Archbishop Stigand stood with arms raised to heaven in front of the high altar with the burial opening at his feet. As Abbot Edwin and the seven others approached slowly down the nave, Stigand commenced the Latin Roman rite for blessing a place of burial instituted in England by the first Archbishop of Canterbury, four hundred years earlier.

"God of endless ages. Through disobedience to your law, we fell from grace, and death entered this world. But through the obedience and resurrection of your Son, you revealed to us a new life. In a spirit of repentance, we earnestly ask you to look upon this grave and bless it so that, while we commit to the earth the body of our humble and glorious King Edward, your servant, his soul may be taken into paradise. In nomine Patris, et Filii, et Spiritus Sancti."

"Harold. May your consort ask after her king's health?" Edith Swanneck enquired with a nervous smile, still standing a few feet behind Harold as they continued to be dressed.

Harold felt as though he was just awoken from sleep. His mind was in another time and place. He turned and gave Edith an unconvincing smile.

"You've been staring at nothing and not spoken a word for some time," she ventured. "Caelin told me everything, your capture across the channel, Tostig's trial, Edward touching your hand before he died. It has all happened so fast. Caelin and I only arrived here a few hours ago, so I haven't slept much. But you, you must be exhausted. Are you?"

"I am," was all the response Harold could muster.

The eight monks lowered the two iron poles, allowing the coffin to sit to the right of the burial opening in the abbey's stone floor. The poles were removed and taken away while Edwin and the remaining monks slowly lowered Edward into the burial open-ing by hand. Once finished, they did not rise but remained low on the ground, moving on hands and knees from either side to the base of the opening and lying prostrate with their faces pressed into the cold stone floor. Dozens of monks around the north and south aisles of the abbey began chants.

"Kyrie eleison, Christe eleison, Kyrie eleison."

Following the liturgical calendar, Stigand declared the Latin mass for the feast of the Epiphany and walked around Edward's coffin with his chain censer, allowing the incense to surround Edward and the blessed grave. Most of the mourners present could interpret the Latin.

"Arise, be enlightened, O Jerusalem, for your light is come, and the glory of the Lord has risen upon you. Darkness shall cover the earth and a mist the people, but the Lord shall arise above, and His glory shall be seen. The Gentiles shall walk in your light and kings in the brightness of your rising."

"You really shouldn't read my quietness as anything other than weariness, Edith. Yes, a lot has taken place these last few weeks, and now I have much to celebrate, but I'm exhausted. I also have much to fear. I feel as though I have arrived at this moment empty, disbursed. Early this morning, I spent some time at Edward's side to honour him before the funeral. I'm not sure what good it achieved. I already feel as though Edward is haunting me. I do not have his forgiveness."

Edith persisted, "Harold, instead of worrying about Ed-ward, there is so much you can look forward to. You've achieved something your father only dreamed of."

"At a cost I didn't intend to pay. I think I may have overspent a great deal, and the debt will soon be due." Harold moved his gaze to the cold stone floor.

Edith was stunned at what she saw in Harold.

Caelin was right, she thought. *He has changed. What happened in Normandy?*

Archbishop Stigand commenced the burial rite as Abbott Edwin and the others picked themselves up off the stone floor of Saint Peter's Abbey. Edwin crossed himself and headed for the back, behind the throng of nobility.

"In sure and certain hope of the resurrection, through our Lord Jesus Christ, we commend to Almighty God, Edward, our King, and we commit his body to the ground. Earth to earth, ashes to ashes, dust to dust. The Lord bless him and keep him, the Lord make his face to shine upon him and be gracious to him. The Lord lift up his countenance upon him and give him peace. God of holiness and power, accept our prayers on behalf of your servant Edward. Do not count his deeds against him, for in his heart he desired to do your will. As his faith united him to your holy church on earth, so may your mercy join him to the angels in heaven."

"A cost you didn't intend to pay? Harold, if you're referring to Tostig's trial, he got what he deserved. It was just a matter of time before there would be a rebellion against him in the north," pushed Edith.

"Of course I know that. But to Tostig, it wasn't the rebellion and Morcar's doing. To him, it was all me. He won't just leave this. Don't you see? He won't leave this act of brotherly betrayal. I know him. He won't stop until he's dead." Harold's words echoed off the timber ceiling.

"And there are other things I fear. Other costs," continued Harold.

"Like what? Something in Normandy? What happened over there, Harold?"

"Nothing. Nothing I can't manage. Now that I'm king."

Edith said nothing in response, but it took all her will to stop the two words in her mind from progressing to her lips. *Kings fall.*

<hr />

As Stigand's mass echoed off the abbey's towering stone walls, Abbot Edwin was hiding in a dark corner, his head pounding with the weariness that comes from days without sleep. He bowed his head and closed his eyes. His hands, in a prayerful position, rubbed at his eyes and brow. The vision behind his eyelids was dark, and it had mostly been that way of late, but this time it was more than dark. It was disturbing. His vision showed a large gate being opened by Christ himself. Just as Christ released a legion of evil spirits to a herd of pigs in the gospels, here Christ was releasing an enormous wave of evil spirits on the lands of England, free to roam. Though Edwin was aware that his fears combined with exhaustion were the likely cause of the vision, he remained curious and kept his eyes closed.

The flow from the opened gate was like a thick black mud that formed into evil and grotesque creatures once it reached the lush green hills of the land. The sky turned black, and trees withered. The dark beasts swallowed up the faithful and the heathen alike, and nothing was spared, but there was one small white place on the land where the creatures did not tread nor devour. The flow of black mud and evil creatures moved around the white spot as though they were forbidden. The white place began to move across the land, against the flow and toward the gate. Edwin's dreams and visions were plenty of late, but nothing like this had ever appeared. The white spot was becoming much brighter, drawing closer to Edwin's view of the scene.

It was a child—a young girl, walking, unaffected by the flow of evil around her. Edwin was tempted to open his eyes and almost laugh off this madness as a taunt from the devil, but he could not. He kept his eyes closed and focused on the vision as the young girl finally stood in front of him and spoke.

"I am Faith. I am coming."

Aldred, Archbishop of York, entered the hall where Harold and Edith were still being attended. He placed his hand on Harold's shoulder, saying, "You look a little less miserable than when I last saw you at Tostig's trial."

"Aldred, good to see you. You look more like an archbishop than when I saw you last. Thank you again for your help that day." Harold smiled at Aldred. The first Edith had seen from him all morning.

"I felt as though I did it for your father, Harold." Archbishop Aldred walked toward the light of the windows at the end of the room, moving to avoid the urgent servants. "Tostig couldn't be kept in check; he had to go to make today possible. But we have other matters to consider. Your request to have me conduct the coronation not only has frustrated Archbishop Stigand, but it will also raise an eyebrow of His Holiness Pope Alexander when he hears of it, and he will. Because, as you know, it's supposed to be the Archbishop of Canterbury, not York, to crown English kings. But I will keep my eye on that; you needn't worry about it for now."

"The Pope? There are potential consequences of that, surely?"

"No, no, no." Aldred rested his hand on Harold's shoulder and gave him a somewhat convincing smile.

Abbot Edwin's old leather sandals were slapping on the cobblestones as he shifted his weary and ageing body through the cloisters and out into the courtyard towards the monastery. The funeral mass drew to a close. The mourners rising from their pews blocked the view between Archbishop Stigand and Edwin, making it possible for him to disappear into the cloisters without being seen. Reaching the monastery, he ran upstairs into the empty library and scriptorium. He grabbed a nearby ladder and headed to a large section of the library labelled 'HISTORIA', mumbling as he went.

"Young girl. Faith. From the south. Jerome's *Book of Martyrs*."

After some moments of rummaging through scripts of various sizes, Edwin emerged from the large shelf pulling out a sizeable hand-written script with *MARTYROLOGIUM HIERONYMIANUM* sealed into the cover of its leather binding.

He descended the ladder and slammed the script down on the closest scripting desk before opening to the first page, which was decorated with fine calligraphy, gold leaf and drawings of many celebrated church saints who had been martyred over the centuries. Edwin turned most of the pages and found the calendar month of October, then the sixth day.

"Saint Faith. Fourth-century martyr. Young girl. Foy of Agen, Aquitaine. Frankish," he mumbled as he read.

After reading for some time, Edwin looked up and scanned the dusty and empty scriptorium, rubbing his bearded chin. His eyes pinpointed the area where new deliveries of yet-to-be-copied scripts were stored. He could vaguely remember recently accepting delivery of a dozen or so scripts from a monastery somewhere in Aquitaine. Leaving the desk, Edwin made his way over and started shifting various timber crates and book piles before eventually locating the Frankish scripts. Near the bottom of the pile, Edwin discovered a script he had never seen before. It was loose paper with string ties, the title page denoting only *LIBER MIRACULORUM SANCTA FIDIS*.

"*The Book of Miracles of Saint Foy*. From Conques Abbey," he whispered.

"To more important things, Harold," Archbishop Aldred continued. "The funeral should be concluding soon if it has not already. The transition arrangements will occur, and then shortly after we will be informed that we can move into the abbey and shift our attention onto the living. A few things to note; after the ceremony itself, Edith will be summoned to kneel and pay homage, followed by local bishops, then thanes in your royal personal guard. And finally, we'll emerge from the abbey with you as king."

"No homage from the earls?" asked Harold.

"Yes, of course, but not today. The earls have been summoned to do the same in four days. Everything will run smoothly. Once this is all over, then the real work begins. But Harold, let me say, I believe this is the beginning of a lasting, truly Saxon dynasty. The way it should be."

━━━━━━━ ❖ ━━━━━━━

Edwin had returned to the desk in the scriptorium with the *Book of Miracles of Saint Foy*, from Conques Abbey. Experienced in the practice of scripting, Edwin found the discreet markings within the loosely tied manuscript, denoting that it was copied recently, and the original was compiled forty years prior by a Bernard of Angers. The author Bernard was initially a sceptic but became truly devout as his thorough research led him to discover and confirm many miracles attributed to the relics of Saint Foy.

After spending a few rushed moments flicking through the pages of the manuscript, Edwin drew a long breath to slow his mind before he turned back to the start.

Bound at the beginning of the script of miracles was a Latin copy of the account of Foy's martyrdom in Agen, known as *Passio: The Passion of Sainte-Foy*. As the first few lines drew Edwin in, his mind entered a scene of an imagined fourth-century village of Agen. The tranquil sounds of the nearby River Garonne, the smells of fresh fish being sold at market stalls, the quaint village architecture of Lower Gaul. But, more importantly, he could only imagine how difficult it was for the young church under the persecution of the tyrant Emperor Diocletian.

Edwin remembered his studies on the Great Persecution when he was a novice. Diocletian dispatched his Imperial Prefects to four corners of the Empire. Their sole purpose was to root out followers of a new and growing religious cult, which he believed to be the cause of many problems in the Empire.

The Christians. Unless they renounced their faith and offered sacrifices to the Roman gods, they would be put to death in any creative way the Prefects saw fit. Though some of the furthest regions of the Empire went unchecked, one zealous Roman Prefect did make the long and arduous journey to Lower Gaul. His name was Dacian.

Edwin shifted his mind from the Great Persecution and returned to the tiny fishing village of Agen. He continued to read the account of Foy's martyrdom, her passion. The cumbersome early-church language of the writer, with interludes of rhetoric, made it difficult for Edwin to picture the scene, but he read on and allowed his mind to fill in the gaps of the text.

> The sound of at least twenty Roman soldiers making their way into the small village of Agen was unmistakable. The hundred or so villagers gathered in the village centre had never seen or heard the rumble of so many horses together, let alone horses carrying decorated soldiers. The Romans dismounted and immediately gave orders to several town officials, who seemed to have expected the arrival contrary to the rest of the village. The village officials humbly noted down hospitality needs, eagerly bowing as they listened to each request, which proved to be more than just lodgings and stables.
>
> Curious elderly peasants peered from windows, raggedy children stopped their games and watched from rooftops and trees, rugged fishermen emerged from the nearby River Garonne, all eager to see the spectacle.

One elderly local man, dressed in a beggar's cloak, peered at the scene leaning on a wall of a small nearby house, just a few yards from the commotion. Though his appearance showed otherwise, his mind was sharp and attentive, eyes watching every move from under his hood, ears eager to hear everything spoken between the Romans and the officials. Like the village officials, he seemed to have expected the Roman's arrival but kept a safe distance.

"Have you gathered them?" asked the most decorated of the Romans.

"Yes, Praefectus Dacian. We have them ready for your review in the village courthouse just over there," responded the Agen official as he continued to bow, keeping his posture below his superior.

"Are you sure you have all of them? The Emperor didn't send me here for a demonstration. We're here to remove them. How many have you captured?"

"We have twelve, my liege."

"Twelve? You were supposed to have them all before we arrived. There's more than twelve, surely," insisted the disappointed Dacian.

"Yes, Dacian. The Agen Christians have grown in number, but many scattered to the hills in the north or neighbouring villages shortly after the Emperor's edict. I have locals informing us in those villages. But my liege, you need not be disappointed, I assure you. You will be interested to know that these twelve are the most devout, the influencers. Possibly the leaders. With these gone, it should remove the problem," suggested the official.

"And what makes you so sure these twelve are the leaders?"

"We didn't discover them. They gave themselves over to us. It was quite strange. And, instead of being rattled with fear, the Christians were at peace. Not what we expected at all," revealed the official.

"Hmm, you're obviously new to this. Christians often sacrifice themselves in the hope of diverting attention away from a larger or younger group hiding elsewhere. They're not necessarily leaders, more often just the elderly saving the fleeing young. Nevertheless, I am here for two days, continue with your search. Show me the twelve you have," ordered Dacian.

Dacian followed the obliging official toward the village courthouse, locals bowing as they passed by.

On the other side of the village square, the curious beggar turned swiftly from his position, moving between houses and farming carts to keep out of sight but stopping briefly in the tight lanes between buildings to keep an eye on Prefect Dacian's movements. He was also careful to note the position of the Roman soldiers scattered around the village centre. As Dacian entered the courthouse, the beggar moved to the rear of the building, where he scaled a ladder leading to a heavily thatched roof. With little effort, he shifted a weak and movable section of the thatching and moved inside the shelter while balancing on the beams within. As he closed the thatching behind him, he took a final look to ensure he wasn't seen.

Meanwhile, in the hill region north of the village, a group of thirty Christians hid in a dark cave. The cave entrance could not be seen from the town and was inconspicuous to passers-by, only visible upon close inspection. Once inside, the cave opened to an expanse with shelter enough for a hundred or more. Towering crystal-white stalactites and stalagmites adorned the walls, dimly reflecting the light of a campfire. The group of men, women and children sat around the fire, trying to calm their nerves with the faint singing of psalms and chants.

Just away from the campfire, two young men lay prostrate at the entrance of the cave, keeping watch and keeping themselves out of sight. Their view down to the village was clear, and they were encouraged by what they had just seen.

"Felician, can you believe it? Praises to our Saviour. Caprasius is safely inside the roof of the courthouse, just as we planned," said Primus with a beaming smile as he continued to watch the village.

"I've never seen him move so fast. Surely God is with him. But Primus, it isn't over yet," responded Felician.

"Indeed, brother."

As the two continued to keep a sharp eye on the courthouse and the Romans around the village square, a young woman stood up from the campfire and headed in the direction of the cave entrance. She kept herself low, crawling and eventually shifting her body along the earth next to Felician and Primus as she drew near.

"What news?" she asked.

"The Roman Prefect was ushered into the courthouse, and Father Caprasius successfully made his way into the roof. Nothing more yet," answered Primus.

"Alberta, don't worry. I'm sure they'll release your sister soon. She's a child. The Romans would be more interested in finding our bishop than dealing with children," assured Felician.

Alberta responded with an unconvincing smile; the weight of worry that plagued her was evident.

Inside the village courthouse, Dacian was ushered into the main courtroom. "Bring me a challenge," he insisted as he looked around the room, somewhat unimpressed by the feeble Gaulish architecture and furnishing around him.

"As you wish," responded the official before he exited through another door.

Dacian was left alone for a few moments. The room was dim but lit enough to see the stuffiness floating in the air from a small amount of light that peered through a window. It was the first time he had been alone since he left Rome days before, though oblivious he was being watched by Father Caprasius above through cracks in the ceiling timber.

Dacian unsheathed a broad Roman sword from his side and placed it on the large timber table in front of him before taking a seat at the head of the room. Moments later, three local young maids entered the room from the kitchen, approached Dacian, and placed down water, wine, bread, and other refreshments. Dacian raised his eyebrows, impressed by the quality of the local produce before him. He wasted no time and proceeded to eat and drink as he waited for the village official to reappear with the first Christian captive.

When the official finally entered, Dacian's view was obstructed by the busy ladies waiting on him. "Enough. Enough food. Be gone," he instructed, eager to see the challenge awaiting him.

As the ladies dispersed and headed for the kitchen, the local official exited with them, leaving Dacian alone with his food and the captive before him. Dacian's eyes widened in shock and instantly rose from the table and headed for the door to the kitchen. He opened it and called for his host, the local official.

"No ... Foy," whispered Father Caprasius in shock from the roofbeams as he saw which of his flock was first to front the Roman Prefect.

"Hey. What is this?" Dacian seethed, grabbing the cloak of his host. "I told you to send me a challenge. This is a child, you fool."

"This IS your challenge, my liege." The official smiled wryly at him. "You will see."

Dacian released his hold and pushed the man back into the kitchen before slamming the door. He took a moment to look at his challenge captive from behind. A young girl, no older than twelve. Long dark hair flowing down the back of her soiled clothes. Her bare feet peppered with sores, hands resting by her side, posture high, proud and still. Dacian rubbed his gritty chin and headed back to his table of food and wine, which was more interesting for him as he expected this to be over in a few moments. Without looking up from his food, he proceeded.

"Young girl, what is your name?"

"I am Foy of Agen," she quietly replied.

Foy's calm, gentle voice was like nothing Dacian had ever heard, as though it was untarnished by the world. It unnerved him and caused him to look up and appraise the captive anew.

"You are so young, child. Why are you here?" he asked.

"We heard that Rome was seeking out the followers of Jesus of Nazareth across the Empire, and so we came forward," Foy responded simply.

"So, you are a Christian?"

"With all my heart," she declared.

"Look, child. I have no interest in your heart. You can believe whatever you wish in your heart. All that your Emperor requires of you is that you say that you reject this Jesus and offer a sacrifice to one of our gods, even the goddess Diana if you wish. Diana is one of your sex. It is quite simple. Do this, and you can go free."

"I cannot do this," Foy said.

"But your Emperor demands that you do this," insisted Dacian.

"The Emperor is just a man. Christ, on the other hand, has conquered the world," explained Foy.

"What? Your Christ is dead, child. Why must you persist with this nonsense when it leads to your death? I would much rather send you home," complained Dacian as he rubbed his forehead in frustration.

"Do you offer sacrifices to Diana?" asked Foy.

"Of course, it's simple."

"Simple, you say. But what do you believe in your heart? Do you believe that Diana can help you?"

"Child, we are not here to question my devotion to the gods," snapped Dacian, with his patience waning.

"I can see that you seek truth, truth beyond this material world. There is truth to be found." Foy's voice was still calm.

"Silence, child!" yelled Dacian.

"Your face tells me so much. I can see it all," continued Foy. "You have ordered and witnessed the death of thousands like me, people who believed in something ... with all their heart. But their peace in the face of death has shaken you, softened your heart of stone. Has it not?"

Dacian had heard enough. He burst out of his chair, headed for Foy and grabbed her around the throat with one hand.

"I said silence!" he menaced through his gritted teeth as he released his hold and threw Foy to the ground.

Father Caprasius, who was still quietly watching from the roofbeams, was astounded by Foy's fearlessness but at the same time devastated to witness the dearest child of his flock injured at the hands of this monstrous Roman. But he could only watch on.

"Child, I have the power to end your life now. Just renounce this worthless creed and do what everyone else in the Empire is doing right now. Bow to our gods!" declared Dacian.

"I will not. So, do what you will with me," Foy challenged from the courtroom floor.

With that, Dacian dragged Foy by her hair towards the kitchen door and burst into shocked kitchen maids working over hotpots and benches. One maid was working over a large pot that sat over a red-hot coal pit covered by an iron grate on the ground below. Dacian brushed the maid aside before moving the large pot, exposing the grate below.

"I was going to simply cut off your head, but you clearly have no fear of such an end. Perhaps you will reconsider now?" growled Dacian.

He reached for Foy and dragged her body towards the intense heat of the grate, pushing her face closer with his hands. Those still in the kitchen watched on in horror. As Foy's face drew near to the heat, her previously calm expression was now one of fear and horror. It gave Dacian hope that he had successfully convinced her to renounce. Surely now, he had conquered this challenge.

"Renounce!" yelled Dacian as he pushed Foy's face forward, causing her hair to burn slightly.

"He is my all," she responded. Struggling under Dacian's strength, her eyes rolled back as though she had lost consciousness or entered a trance.

Dacian had heard enough. He reached down and, with little effort, lifted Foy's light frame and carelessly dropped her on the iron grill. Her clothes instantly ignited as Dacian held her down with a stoker. Foy's screams of pain were joined with the maids' cries of horror as they watched on, held back by the village official.

In the roof beams above, Father Caprasius' despair was so overwhelming that he barely held on to the frame above him. The horror of the scene below covered his face with pain and tears. His body convulsed with sweat and spasms of unbearable grief. His mind filled with confusion toward his benevolent God.

Such a dear child, he thought. *So innocent, devoted and kind, and yet to see such an end.* "How can this be?" he appealed to his God.

The noise from the courthouse kitchen alerted the whole village, and dozens gathered outside. Word spread from those peering in the windows through to those gathered. Whispers and shock turned to mourning as it became apparent that the Romans had purged their first Christian in Agen, and it was the young girl, Foy. Everyone knew of her faith, but they never expected this.

Barely able to see through his tears and grief, Caprasius made his way through the roof beams to the thatched opening. He squeezed himself out and into the bright afternoon sunlight, which caused him to misplace his footing. Caprasius didn't have the energy or the care to stop or reduce his fall; he allowed his body to be limp and fell several feet onto his back on a soft pile of hay. Though Caprasius was uninjured from the fall to the haystack, the horror he had just witnessed from the roofbeams gave him more pain and anguish than he had ever known.

"Why, Father, why? Are you not merciful?" he cried to the sky.

As he lay there motionless with arms stretched out on the hay, tears pooling in his eyes as he gazed into the open sky above him, he questioned his purpose and whether his God was merciful at all. Against the temptation to curse his God, he reached deep into his soul and drew from the tiniest remnant of hope that remained, which showed him that the dear young Foy was no longer in pain but in the embrace of her God.

Caprasius blinked his eyes, which caused the pooled tears to fall and his blurred vision to clear. There in the sky above him, he saw the clouds open like curtains, and Foy herself emerged from behind them, draped in a glistening snow-white robe, with Christ himself standing behind her. Before Caprasius could rub his eyes, a pure white dove flew into the scene and placed a delicate gold crown on Foy's head. Christ and the dove disappeared, leaving Caprasius staring into the eyes of heaven's newest arrival.

"My dear child," Caprasius whispered through his wonder and tears, "the crown of martyrdom, of course. Christ has rewarded your faith. Pray for me, Foy."

Foy said nothing in response but smiled at Caprasius with an otherworldly peace and calm.

At that moment, Alberta, Felician and Primus startled Caprasius as they appeared behind the haystack, all three out of breath from running.

"Caprasius! Are you hurt?" they asked as Caprasius sat up in shock.

"I am not hurt. What are you doing here? I thought you were keeping watch from the cave with the others."

"We saw you fall from the roof, so we ... made haste to check ... on ... you," Alberta explained. She noticed from the colour of Caprasius' eyes and face that he had been weeping.

"Where is my sister? Have they released her yet?" asked Alberta.

Caprasius had not the strength nor the words to relate Foy's fate to Alberta, let alone what he witnessed from the roofbeams of the courthouse. Instead, he turned his eyes from Alberta and lifted them to the sky where Foy had appeared to him.

As Alberta, Felician and Primus followed their priest's eyes and turned their attention to the sky, and they too could see Foy as Caprasius did. Glorious and beaming white and with a crown on her head.

All three audibly sighed in complete wonder at what they were witnessing and fell to their knees. Not a word was spoken amongst them as they gazed into the open heavens.

Moments later, Foy's appearance in the sky faded from view, and the four faithful on the earth below remained on their knees. After some time had passed, they turned to each other, smiling and laughing as though sorrow and mourning was the furthest emotion from their joyful hearts. No words were spoken. Nothing they could say would do justice to the strength that the vision had imparted.

Suddenly, Roman soldiers emerged from the trees behind the courthouse. They surrounded Caprasius and the three, with swords drawn in their direction.

"No surprise. I knew there would be some nearby, watching the courthouse," said the village official, who appeared behind the Roman soldiers. "Caprasius, I know who you are. What about these others? No doubt also Christians who refuse to sacrifice to Roman gods?"

"Yes," spoke Alberta. "You may do with us as you will. Your Emperor may conquer Agen today,

but my sister's bones will conquer more than your
Emperor ever will."

The scene dissolved, and, completing his reading of Foy's martyrdom, Abbot Edwin buried his face into his hands and wept
over the manuscript.

"Blessed Foy." Edwin prayed with tears in his eyes. "Indeed,
our great God has glorified you. Crowned you with rewards
that can never be taken away. And now, he has made you a
conqueror, much more than a conqueror. Far greater than any
king or emperor could ever boast. God has decreed that you
should conquer our hearts. Only the foolish will see a Norman
conquest land on our shores, but God has opened my eyes to
your greater conquest. A most noble and holy conquest. Pray
for us. Pray for us."

CHAPTER 41

FALAISE, NORMANDY

T he service for early morning Lauds at the chapel of Notre Dame de Guibray had concluded, and the faithful
were filing out of the abbey into the day's first light.
As the monks headed toward the monastery and the villagers
toward their fields, Bishop Odo stayed behind to fold away his
crisp white vestments behind the altar.

Odo's folding was always perfect, like the old days. He liked
to take his time, ensuring the folds were placed in a way to
make them almost invisible when he wore the vestments next.
But lately, his folding had been less than perfect, his concen-
tration distracted by the reliquary of Saint Foy, which was
installed in a prominent position near the altar. Odo couldn't
look away. Unlike any icon or relic in the Frankish Kingdom
he had seen and venerated, he both loved it and feared it. One
moment he would see at it as a priceless treasure the whole of
Christendom envied, the next as a curse hanging over his head.

He would often think of the night the relics were delivered
to Falaise, the tragic death of his spy monk, Hugh, and the
strange vision of the young girl he experienced. Though he

had studied the countless spiritual visions and even physical manifestations of the mystic saints throughout church history, he never expected to be included in such company. It was an experience unlike any other.

"But what did it all mean?" he asked himself. "Why me? Why now? What am I being asked to do?"

At the rear of the abbey, while a dozen or so monks were still shuffling out, a concerned Father Petrus entered looking for Bishop Odo. He made his way through the doors. His eyes scanned the abbey and found Odo exactly where he expected and so made his way down the nave. Upon reaching the altar, Petrus stopped, dropped to his knees, bowed his head and crossed himself slowly. He then raised his eyes to heaven and picked himself up off the floor.

"What are you doing here, Petrus?" asked Odo as he finished his folding. "I thought you were with the novices today."

"I am. I'll see them after the first meal. But I needed to come and see you first."

"Oh, it sounds serious."

"It is. A young local messenger arrived at the monastery looking for you an hour ago. I took his news, checked his sources and sent him away with orders of silence."

"Sources?" asked Odo.

"Yes, I verified his English and Flanders sources," responded Father Petrus.

"English?"

"I think you should inform Duke William."

"What is it, Petrus?"

Nearby, in the dense hunting grounds of Chateau de Falaise, the fog from earlier that morning was lifting, and the melting frost from the tallest trees was dripping frequently enough that it sounded like light rain.

While Duke William focused on controlled breathing, he could hear footsteps, heavy footsteps, approaching from behind. Though it frustrated William, he couldn't look back; an arrow was already stretching his bow, and its feathers were tickling his fingertips. He had been watching the nearby stag nibble fresh grass shoots for some time, waiting for the perfect shot, but now unavoidably, it was all over as the stag looked up at the sound of the same approaching footsteps and quickly darted away for cover.

William could hear that the heavy and swift steps were working through thick foliage instead of the nearby track, breaking twigs and shifting branches as they went, with the occasional complaint. William dropped the aim of his bow and let out a breath he had been holding for what seemed the last hour.

Eventually, the loud and heavily breathing Bishop Odo arrived within earshot of the Duke. "Duc William. Nouvelles do Londres," he called, leaning on a large tree and catching his breath.

"Yes, yes. News from London. What is it?" barked William as he fixed his bow.

"King Edward is dead." Odo's breathing was heavy, and he was still holding onto the tree. After a slight pause, he added, "And Harold has taken the throne."

There was silence from William, which Odo knew meant that William was waiting for more information.

"They buried Edward and crowned Harold on the same day, two days ago."

William was still staring at the empty patch of grass where the stag once was. *Just like the stag that got away,* he thought, *so will his grip on power in Normandy be when this news is out.* Everything William had boasted about concerning his place in the English succession would now be a common joke.

He immediately drew the arrow that was still in his bow and loosed the string, the arrow whistling in the direction of the stag that got away. He then slammed his bow on the ground before throwing it far into the bushes.

"Oath breaker!" he shouted.

Saying nothing to Odo, William walked past him and headed back towards the chateau. As he walked, he grabbed the leather ties of his mantle and tightened them with frustration before immediately loosening them again, causing the mantle and quiver to drop to the ground. Odo gathered them up as he quietly trailed behind.

CHAPTER 42

THORNEY ISLAND, LONDON

For the first time in over twenty years, the Great Hall on Thorney Island was full of light and colour, decorated with new burning torches, royal and regional standards and packed to capacity. All were eager to witness the king's vassals pay formal homage to their new ruler.

Along with the earls of the realm, the homage ceremony was attended by almost every rank of English nobility, most of whom considered attendance synonymous with being suitably dressed for the occasion, which brought much-needed business for the local tanners and embroiderers across London.

The final years of Edward's rule lacked the courtly show or pomp most English monarchs enjoyed and consequently caused many skilled artists to seek business elsewhere. However, Harold's coronation and homage ceremonies suggested a return to the old Saxon court ways, proving to be a boom for the trades across town as the population swelled with wealthy nobility lavishly spending across the four days. The gloomy atmosphere brought on by Edward's death seemed to disappear as the town's attention now turned to new possibilities with a new king.

The crisp and calm January evening provided the clearest sky seen in months, which saw almost every astronomer in London gathering out in the cold, stretching their necks to the heavens and consulting scholarly texts sourced as far as Arabia. Practically every known star constellation and planet location could be seen, so the opportunity to update tables and records was not missed.

The recent snowstorms leading up to Edward's death caused some of the northern thanes to miss Edward's funeral, and Harold's coronation, which was overlooked by Harold but missing the opportunity to pay homage would not be. More than any Saxon dynasty, the Godwinsons knew only too well that the support of the earls needed to be established early, checked often and never assumed.

The noise of the hundreds packed into the hall was interrupted for a moment as the southern doors burst open, causing everyone to move forward, keen to catch a glimpse of their newly crowned sovereign.

Harold emerged through the doors first, his elaborate scarlet robe drifting behind, followed by a royal guard of six thanes, including Caelin, who were decked in more ceremonial armour and weaponry than they had ever experienced. Archbishops Aldred and Stigand followed shortly after.

Behind the archbishops came a swarm of royal servants, ladies and Edith Swanneck, who also wore a small jewelled crown, hidden mostly by her delicately plaited gold hair, which circled her head before falling down her back. However, it was the much larger gold and colourfully jewelled crown on Harold's head that seemed to catch the gaze of every attendee, as though something sacred or holy had just entered the room.

Harold sat confidently with his scarlet robe gathering on the floor beneath him. The gilded and cushioned throne on which he sat was elevated three feet above the stone floor, with three stairs and ample room for kneeling at its foot. The hall separated into two distinct groups. At the eastern side was the royal household, and those at the western side were either yet to pay homage or other invited nobility.

The crowd had settled to a lull as Archbishop Stigand stepped forward into the empty floor space between them and opened a large illuminated manuscript. To sufficiently fill the Great Hall, Stigand raised his voice.

"Earls of the peerages of England, I present to you Harold Godwinson. Your undoubted King. Wherefore all you who are come this day to do your homage and service. Are you willing to do the same?"

"God save the King!" The earls shouted with one voice.

At the time of the ceremony, the Kingdom of England was divided into six peerages or regions, each with earls. Wessex and Hereford, for which King Harold was still earl. Kent and East Anglia, both earldoms held by younger brothers of Harold, Gyrd, Earl of East Anglia, and Leofwine, Earl of Kent. And Mercia and Northumbria, which were, at this point, under the Earldom of Morcar. Consequently, only three earls were required to pay homage at this ceremony.

"To the peerages of Mercia and Northumbria. The Earl Morcar is summoned to pay homage," called Stigand.

Morcar stepped forward and gave a wry smile to his men in the crowd before heading to the steps. Each raised step towards Harold seemed slower than the last until he reached Harold and their eyes met. Morcar lowered himself to his knees.

"I, Morcar, Earl of Northumbria and Mercia, do this day, become your vassal. Faithful and true. Faith and truth, I will bear unto you our king, and unto your heirs and successors. To live, fight and die against your enemies. So, help me, God."

Morcar lowered his gaze from Harold's. Raising one knee at a time, he picked himself up and turned. Shortly after, as though time stood still, his eyes met Caelin's for a moment before he took his place behind the throne.

As the archbishop stepped forward to announce the Earl of East Anglia, he was interrupted as the large western doors to the hall were opened, followed by noises of commotion or struggle from behind the large crowd.

Someone had entered, and there was incoherent shouting from a stranger who pushed his way through the crowd of people and approached the throne.

"Stop. Stop. Stop," the stranger shouted in an unmistakable foreign accent, confidently waving his hands in the air.

Within a breath, Caelin led his fellow royal thanes from behind Harold and formed a wall in front of the throne, blocking any possible access to King Harold.

"Halt!" all six of the heavily armed thanes shouted as they drew swords.

The stranger, still waving his hands around, stood alone between the crowd and the thanes.

"State your cause, Norman!" shouted Caelin, who had no trouble recognising the attire.

The messenger irreverently gave a smile, mockingly bowed in the direction of Harold, who at this point he could no longer see, and held back a laugh. "I bring word from Duke William of Normandy, my liege," he announced, loud enough for the entire hall to hear and recognised his Frankish accent, which drew a subtle sound of shock from the crowd.

"That's all we need to hear," said Caelin as he approached

the messenger, grabbed him by the tunic at the neck and began dragging him back toward the western doors with one hand.

"Wait!" yelled King Harold. "Let him speak."

Caelin reluctantly released his hold on the man and returned to his position in front of Harold.

The messenger, who still found the humour in it all, maintained his confident smile, straightened his tunic, stood as though he was a great orator and continued his speech. "Duke William declares these ... ceremonies, are not effective, not binding, how you say, false. Harold is not your rightful king. Edward's succession was confirmed to Duke William many years ago by William of Jumieges, your former Archbishop of Canterbury. Harold is not only dishonouring Edward's wishes, but he is also breaking an oath he has with Duke William."

"Lies!" announced Harold, which sent everyone in the hall into a hum of murmurs. "William of Jumieges was a Norman emissary. His word is void. The oath I have with William is binding within Normandy only," continued Harold.

As the noise of murmurs continued, Morcar attempted to approach Harold, hoping to question him about his Norman oath but was stopped by Caelin. Furious but preferring to avoid a scene, he slowly stepped off the rise and back to his position.

"If you believe so," the messenger continued, "Duke William declares that if you will abandon these ceremonies and issue him with an invitation to be your king, he will be gracious. If not, we will see."

"Return to Duke William," replied Harold, "And issue this. Harold is king by the bidding of King Edward himself and the Witan council. William's claim is weak and false. You have overstayed your welcome, Norman." He turned to issue commands. "Away with him! And be sure he is given safe passage to the coast."

The Great Hall burst into movement and gossip as the Norman messenger was escorted out.

The ramifications of an oath between their newly crowned king and a Norman duke sent tongues wagging, filling the hall with a buzz. An angry and somewhat embarrassed Harold turned to Morcar, Aldred and Caelin and, though nothing was said, one thing was clear: the ceremony was no longer of any importance.

After a few moments, Harold rose from his throne, which brought the noise to a minimum. He took a moment to look around at everyone staring back at him, anticipating some sort of explanation. The anticipation of his subjects escalated as they waited for clarity and assurance.

Watching himself being watched, Harold took a moment to reflect. *This is the way it will always be,* he thought. His subjects were looking to him, waiting for him, waiting for the truth. They wanted direction and vision. The reality of his position was now clearer than ever. This moment needed to be seized, not avoided. *The truth,* he thought, *could come later, but these people needed direction now.*

Harold took a step closer toward the crowd gathered at the west end of the Great Hall and spoke in a deep, sober and clear voice. "Normans threaten our lands, our kingdom, our prosperity, my crown." He stepped off the rise and approached the crowd, meeting almost every eye in the hall.

"Let. Them. Come!" Harold shouted, which was met with an enormous roar. The many thanes in the hall raised their swords.

"We will be will ready, but we will not bid them welcome," he added.

Harold turned and headed for the hall's south doors with his entire entourage in tow as the cheers continued behind him.

The doors were promptly opened, allowing Harold, Caelin and the other Wessex thanes to exit into the palace courtyard.

"Harold. Harold," called Morcar.

Harold let out a sigh as he stopped his walk in the middle of the courtyard, which also halted his thanes, and turned to find Morcar leading Archbishop Stigand, Archbishop Aldred and Edith Swanneck.

"Earl Morcar. What is it?"

"Harold. You must explain the particulars of this oath. Or perhaps our new king has misunderstood what he swore to Duke William?"

"On the contrary, Earl Morcar, it is you and Archbishop Stigand who should be explaining. How is it possible that we didn't know Edward sent the last archbishop to Normandy to confirm the succession to William?"

"You seem to forget," continued Morcar, "that it was your father who constantly controlled and humiliated Edward, and it was your father who exiled the former archbishop back to Normandy, replacing him with Stigand. Let's be honest here. It was the way the Godwin family bullied Edward all those years that forced him to continue his allegiance with the Normans."

"Don't be so simple, Morcar. You know there's more to it than that. And you were always involved and benefiting from those times," laughed Harold.

"Enough," interrupted Archbishop Aldred, which everyone obeyed, although Aldred was outranked by almost all in the group gathered in the courtyard. "We've just received an un-ambiguous message that William intends to cross the channel and invade. If we continue with this squabbling, we may as well deliver Harold's crown to Falaise now. There is much to be done. Now, Stigand and I can appeal to Pope Alexander to ensure a Norman campaign will not be authorised, though I confess

I'm not sure how effective that will be. The earls here, Harold included, need to gather thanes, active and inactive. Harold surely needs to take stock of his available huscarl infantry and cavalry. And then there's the fyrd who need to be mobilised too."

"The fyrd?" asked Edith.

"My dear Edith, the fyrd are able-bodied peasant men, scattered across the shires, who are obliged to serve two months every year in the king's service. By that explanation, the fyrd do not sound imposing, but when you combine them all on one battlefield, they are," Aldred responded, leaning on his episcopal staff as Edith smiled and bowed in appreciation for the lesson in military ranks.

"Aldred is right," assured Harold. "We have much to do and little time. Although, I will say this, yes, I did swear an oath to Duke William in Normandy, but it was only to be his knight within Frankish borders."

"Why were you there, Harold? And why did you agree to take an oath?" enquired Aldred.

"Why I was there is not important now," stated Harold. "As for the oath, I was outwitted and tricked into taking it. The requirements were rhetorical Frankish nonsense and ambiguous, and I am certain the oath does not extend beyond Frankish borders. William did have a local cleric and knights witness the event. He also revealed later that I took the oath over the bones of a saint."

"Who was the cleric?" asked Aldred.

"A Norman bishop, from Bayeux, I think. His name was Odo."

"Hmm," responded Aldred, "And the saint's bones? Any idea who?"

"They mentioned the name Foy, which I think means Faith. Why is this important?"

"Forgive me, Harold. It's not important," assured Aldred.

"Well, if we're going to work together," announced Earl Morcar, "I think it's important we start being honest with each other. Harold, since you've started by telling us about your oath across the channel, I'll confess that I have been posting men in Wessex for some time, a practice which I have terminated since your coronation, of course."

"How gracious of you, Morcar," responded Harold.

"But before I reassign my most trusted spy to other Mercian and Northumbrian duties, I will ask that he show you all his final discovery." Morcar signalled to Gabriel, who was approaching the group from the direction of the stables. As he drew closer to the light of fire torches around the courtyard, it was clear that he was leading a horse towards them.

"Morcar, why does your man have my horse?" asked Caelin.

"Gabriel followed you back to Wessex, more specifically to Winchester Castle, two days before Harold's coronation," announced Morcar, through grinning teeth. He turned to Harold. "I believe that you had asked him to stay in London. Isn't that right, Harold? Stay in London, he did not. Flee to Edith's embrace … he did."

"Absolute lies, Morcar," yelled Caelin as he attempted to front Morcar but was stopped by a subtle but effective motion from Harold.

"King Harold, if we're going to work together, as wise old Aldred has implored," Morcar continued, "you need to know the truth about your most trusted thane. He was seen in the arms of your consort, Edith. It was also observed that Edith gave Caelin a tiny intimate piece of her undergarments, which he stowed in his saddle."

At Morcar's notion, Gabriel dug his hands deep into the leather compartments of the saddle of Caelin's horse and emerged with the delicately feminine piece in question, which drew a gasp from Edith herself.

Caelin urgently turned to Harold to assure him but said nothing as he noticed Harold's steely, wide-eyed expression.

Caelin knew he'd lost this fight. Morcar had outwitted him. He had disobeyed Harold, he did see Edith, and it did look like treason. At this point, he recognised Morcar's spy, who acted as a stablehand at Winchester as Caelin picked up his horse that afternoon. Caelin's usual hawk-like ability to sense spies and foreigners had weakened of late, and it had now been exposed. He felt weak and ashamed that he had let himself be bettered. Worse, he had betrayed his liege and friend.

Without much time to think, Caelin moved fast in the direction of Gabriel, who was distracted with pleasing Morcar and struck him to the cobblestones with a fierce blow to his jaw using the handle of his sword.

Caelin grabbed the reins of his horse and swung himself up. His horse bucked, causing everyone to stand back. Caelin then kicked and shifted the rear of his mount, which slammed into Morcar, knocking him to the ground. He bolted for the bridge.

"Treason!" yelled Morcar from the cobblestones in Caelin's direction as his silhouette disappeared into the night.

As Harold watched Caelin ride away, Gabriel and Morcar picked themselves up, with the much larger Morcar taking a little longer. Gabriel dabbed his hand on a bloody lip, bowed in the direction of Harold then headed for the stables.

Harold, still in a rage, turned to Edith with fire in his eyes. "Treason indeed. Lock her up in her quarters, see that she doesn't leave," he ordered his nearby thanes before he stormed off in the direction of the palace leaving only Morcar and the archbishops in the courtyard.

As the drama between Morcar and Caelin unfolded,

archbishops Aldred and Stigand had noticed the homage crowd gathering at the western doors of the Great Hall. They were increasingly interested that the crowd had gathered and stayed just outside the gates instead of moving on, staring into the clear night sky and pointing. By the time Harold had departed and Edith escorted away, the two elderly archbishops were diverted by the strange gathering by the Great Hall.

"What do you suppose they are looking at, Stigand?" asked Archbishop Aldred.

"Star constellations, I gather. I'm curious because I've heard about this kind of behaviour from various priests and bishops. It seems astronomy has captured this crowd along with the rest of the town. People are going mad over it, I'm told."

"Yes," Aldred responded. "I hear the same things. Though, this is the first I've seen of it. Hang on, I need to squint, but I think they're all looking at the same star. Wait. Christ have mercy, is that … ?"

"The hairy star. Yes, I believe you're right," responded Stigand. "That's what the crowd are staring at, and understandably. It's a sight once you notice it. However, I don't think the crowd are only interested in the star's beauty, Aldred. I think they're more interested in its timing."

"Yes, and so am I," Aldred agreed. "This is not a good sign, Stigand. I vaguely remember reading a script that the Celts on the west islands recorded seeing this hairy star seventy to eighty years ago. It proved to be precisely what they had feared, an omen of pure evil. Most definitely not an omen of blessing."

"Yes, that does sound familiar." Stigand sighed.

"Stigand?" enquired Aldred as they both continued to stare in awe at their astronomical discovery. "It's fair to say that we haven't spoken much these last few years, but I'm pretty confident that you weren't the only one to notice Harold's mention of the saint's relics over which he was forced to take an oath?"

"Yes, I did notice. Saint Foy. That, along with this hairy star omen, isn't giving me much comfort, Aldred. I've heard a few things about Foy's miracles, and they were often disturbing."

"Hmm. It seems that God has been using Foy to confuse and punish the wicked. Now it seems she is being used to determine the future of a kingdom, our kingdom. The Normans, Saint Foy and this clear night so we can see the hairy star, these signs are all too apparent. It seems that prayer would be too little, too late. Do you know of any mystics that could offer more spiritual discernment here?"

"Yes." Stigand stroked his beard. "The abbot at the monastery here. His name is Edwin."

CHAPTER 43

FALAISE, NORMANDY

The great hall at the chateau of Falaise was bustling with the noise of gossip and debate as hundreds of decorated men and women representing the span of Frankish regions and nobility poured in at the invitation of Duke William.

William stood alone, slightly elevated by a stage at the head of the hall, covered in Norman standards, weaponry and regalia. Though adorned in his most delicate tunic and robe of striking blue, along with new leather tied shoes, William's posture and countenance portrayed a different story. His eyes were blank, staring off towards the rear of the hall as he bit into his fingernails. Occasionally his eyes would drop to the crowd that moved closer to himself as latecomers pushed in from the back.

He observed that the crowd had separated into groups of likeminded opinions or of similar rank, many of which gave William inconspicuous glances between sarcastic comments and laughter.

Though he was the liege lord of the majority in attendance, their presence as a gathered mass proved terrifying, like a multitude of ants devouring a wild boar. He was certainly more confident presiding over an audience of one or even several rebellious nobles, but this was something altogether new.

Bishop Odo was positioned along the wall behind William with William's wife, Matilda, and William's knights. Odo could see that several bishops had arrived from the neighbouring regions; they also had gathered towards the front in clear sight of Odo.

A standard was raised at the rear of the hall to inform William that all regions were represented. Shortly after, the closing doors echoed throughout, which reduced the crowd noise to a lull. All eyes moved to Duke William, and he took a few steps closer to commence his oration.

"Men and women of Normandy, Brittany, Flanders, Aquitaine and beyond. I'm sure you all know that the crown, lands and titles of England that were promised to me and our region by King Edward himself have been assumed by a deceitful Saxon earl. This shameful man broke an oath, witnessed by some here today, to secure for me the succession of the English throne once King Edward was dead. Instead, he assumed the crown for himself and proved himself unworthy of noble posterity. We must rise and take what is rightfully ours."

William concluded and allowed enough time for the guests to return to their original noise level.

"We don't have the men or resources," yelled one Frankish noble from the crowd. "If we took what we have now and invaded England, it would be a slaughter. We would return empty-handed, weakened and unable to protect our own lands if a counterattack was launched. It will be too expensive and too risky."

"Ah yes, Count Eustace. Let me come a little closer," responded William as he quickly moved into the middle of the room and stood on a large timber dining table. "You have a terrible memory, Eustace. You would have no land, title or the tunic on your back if I did not crush a rebel uprising in your region of Boulogne-sur-Mer years ago." Drawing laughter from the rest of the crowd.

"You all need to remember," continued William, "that the English crown and everything that comes with it is our right. It was promised to us, and we have the means to do this. The problem is that you are unwilling to risk anything. You lack vision, and you lack courage. If you only had faith in our strength, you would see that this victory is more than just possible. It is within our grasp. Imagine English lands and hereditary titles that will make your current stock meaningless."

Instead of the enthusiastic cheer hoped for, the packed chateau hall responded with a hum of gossip and displeasure at William's proposal.

"You don't know the strength or tactics of this English army," protested a knight.

"It's not worth the cost" and "We don't have enough longboats," complained others.

The gripes and objections continued until it was all indistinguishable and loud. William turned to Bishop Odo, and the frustration was evident on both of their faces. William knew that the nobility in Normandy and Flanders needed something more substantial to entice them.

"This is how you respond to your liege lord? Someone who could easily apply a levy or acquire the patronage of Philip, King of the Franks," William shouted.

To which an eruption of laughter was the response from almost every man in the hall.

"Our obligation to you, liege, is limited to Frankish borders, certainly not beyond the shore to England," jeered a nearby knight.

"The teenager king, he will not bother with such expense," laughed another.

Bishop Odo headed to William's side and whispered into his ear. "William, I have another idea."

"I'll take anything. What is it?"

"Harold swore the oath over Saint Foy's relics. It was, *sacramentum*. So, this is God's will. We just need to make it ... *Officialis Sanctus*," responded Odo.

"Odo, my Latin is not as fluent as my Frankish."

"We make this a holy war, William. Authorised by Pope Alexander. Everyone will flock to that."

"I never thought that was possible. Can you make that happen?"

"I would need to draw on old friendships to get an audience with Pope Alexander. But once I get past that problem, I believe Alexander will favour our cause," assured Odo.

"What makes you so sure?"

"I know Alexander better than most, and I know that he particularly hates sacred oath breakers," said Odo, with a smile.

"*Parfait*, Odo. You leave for Rome tomorrow, though you won't be going alone. I'll summon Count Eustace to join you. He needs to be reminded that he's a subject of Normandy."

CHAPTER 44

TONSBERG, NORWAY

Tostig Godwinson jumped off the Flanders boat into the shore of the coldest sea he had ever experienced. Enormous plates of ice peppered the shoreline, and the town of Tonsberg leading up to the fortress was covered in the thickest blanket of fresh snow Tostig had ever seen.

The boat on which Tostig arrived was a Flanders-style longboat provided by his brother-in-law, Count Baldwin. Along with food supplies, furs and leathers, and three Flanders sailors experienced travelling north to Scotia and Norway.

Tostig turned to the Flanders sailors as they disembarked and ordered them to stay with the boat before he fixed a sword to his belt and headed toward the fortress. He managed to locate a recently used trail from the shore, which was ideal to avoid the deep snow which rose past Tostig's knees in some places.

Moments later, Tostig arrived at the Tonsberg fortress, and upon closer view, it looked as though it had recently been sieged. Apart from the many red and black raven flags raised, there were large holes in the outer stone walls, seemingly catapult fire. Holding both hands up, one holding his sword, he signalled to the archers at the entrance wall above, who were already aiming. As instructed by Count Baldwin and after much practise on the voyage, Tostig attempted a Norse greeting.

"Jeg ønsker å se Hardrada. Jeg er Tostig Godwinson. Engelsk." *I wish to see Hardrada. I am Tostig Godwinson of England.*

One of the archers ordered the gatekeepers to open the gate for the English ally.

Though it was somewhat damaged, the dual-gate opened inward, and several Norsemen approached Tostig, who was still raising both hands. He allowed his sword to be seized. The Norsemen proceeded to pat down the leather and fur covering Tostig's body, and when no concealed blades were discovered, the men directed Tostig towards the tower. Surrounded by several Norse warriors, Tostig made his way through the courtyard before reaching and entering a great hall.

"Engelsk edel," *English noble*, announced the more decorated and higher-ranked men surrounding Tostig.

The hall was poorly lit; only a few torches were burning towards the entrance, so it was difficult for Tostig to see anyone at the far end. Slow, heavy footsteps approached, and the sound from the timber flooring gave away that the steps included a limp. As the halting steps drew closer, the enormous frame of Hardrada was revealed by the nearby torches. Tostig looked up and was amazed that all the legends were true. Indeed, Hardrada, King of Norway, was a giant. Tostig no longer doubted the tales he heard of Hardrada's colossal frame and super-human strength.

One of Hardrada's men knew some English and indicated to Tostig that he was able to interpret. "You speak English. I will tell King Hardrada," he instructed.

Tostig placed his right hand on his heart and bowed his head to begin his introduction and plan. "Great King Hardrada. I am Tostig Godwinson of Northumbria, England. I come to offer you a plan that will grant you the throne of England. With my knowledge of English lands and alliance with Malcolm, King of the Scots, we can attack the English from the north and arrive in London victorious. What say you?"

Hardrada took his time to listen to his soldier's interpretation, to whom he asked a question in a barely audible Norse mumble.

His soldier responded with two words. "Ja. Skottland."

Hardrada laughed a little and turned for a moment as he stroked his chin. With lightning speed, he turned and grabbed Tostig by the throat with his right hand and dragged him towards the hall doors, which were swiftly opened for him. Still dragging Tostig, who was powerless to release Hardrada's grip, Hardrada reached the open courtyard and threw Tostig along the muddy cobblestones. Hardrada then signalled to a nearby soldier, who threw him a single-sided battleaxe. He placed his enormous foot on Tostig's head and rested the axe on his throat. Tostig twisted his body and grabbed with his hands to lift Hardrada's foot, but the struggle was useless under Hardrada's weight and strength, and the pressure on his skull increased.

"Hvem er du?" yelled Hardrada with his frightening guttural voice as a hundred men gathered from various parts of the tower to watch the hilarious spectacle.

"He wants to know who you are and why you would be of any use," yelled the interpreter, as the laughter from the men around the tower increased.

Tostig had trouble breathing, and his increasingly squashed face made it difficult to respond. After a few moments of further struggle, Tostig was able to say a few words that could be understood. "I am the King of England's brother."

The interpreter then translated to Hardrada.

"Kongens bror?" asked Hardrada, to which the interpreter nodded. "Edward bror døde for lenge siden," Hardrada continued, still effortlessly holding Tostig down with a single foot.

"Hardrada says that King Edward's brother died many years ago," stated the interpreter.

"Edward is dead. My brother Harold has taken the throne," yelled Tostig through a squashed face.

Tostig's declaration was translated, which caused Hardrada to lift his foot, throw the axe back to the nearby soldier and walk away from the choking and gasping Tostig, who had blood dripping from his nose and mouth. Hardrada then ordered the nearby men to pick up Tostig while the rest should return to their work.

CHAPTER 45

ROME, HOLY ROMAN EMPIRE

Bishop Odo and Count Eustace were the key delegates within the embassy sent by Duke William to Rome, along with several others, including priests, knights and servants. While the others settled into lodgings within the Leonine walls, Odo and Eustace were escorted across the atrium toward the awe-inspiring Saint Peter's Basilica by the Archbishop of Milan, Guido da Velate.

"You are fortunate, Odo, that I was here in Rome when you arrived. Otherwise, your chances of securing an audience with Pope Alexander would have been slim," Archbishop Guido assured him with a sense of pride in his position.

"Once again, Archbishop," responded Odo, "I can't begin to tell you how grateful the Count and I are for your hospitality and kindness. Duke William will also be grateful once he hears of it."

Archbishop Guido felt obliged to accommodate any Norman nobles and clerics, due predominantly to his respect for

Lanfranc, the Abbot of Bec Abbey, widely regarded as one of the greatest minds in the church.

But Archbishop Guido was more interested in ensuring his Norman guests acknowledged the privilege Guido was providing and that they were grateful. They had only been in Rome for several hours, and Odo had already grown tired of the archbishop. He was also not looking forward to being the lowest-ranked cleric in almost every situation he was about to find himself in.

Odo wasn't about to let those feelings get in the way of relishing what he loved more than anything, and that was being under the roof of Rome's Saint Peter's Basilica. Though the basilica had been repaired and improved by several previous popes, the original sections were consecrated by Emperor Constantine in the fourth century.

Odo and Eustace were trailing behind Archbishop Guido in the basilica's atrium when Guido stopped just short of the western entrance, an area known as the narthex. He turned to his Norman guests with a concerned look. "You know how these meetings work, don't you?" he enquired.

"How do you mean?" asked Eustace.

"He means, do we know how to behave in an audience with a pope," assisted Odo. "Eustace, we're about to meet the most powerful man in the Empire, and it is an unscheduled meeting. If I'm not wrong, Archbishop Guido, you'll approach His Holiness and inform him that we have requested an audience. Once he has permitted, you'll then allow us to approach."

"Then we bow?" asked Eustace.

"You bow to people like Duke William, Eustace," continued Odo, "but to His Holiness, we both lie prostrate, face down, arms out. Until he invites us to rise."

"Then we can stand?"

"No," Odo confirmed with a wry smile. "When we are invited to rise, we rise to our knees and stay there. Speak only when addressed. Is that correct, Archbishop?"

"You have done this before," said the archbishop, grateful that this audience would not prove to be an embarrassment.

"I certainly have, and we will not disappoint you, Archbishop," assured Odo.

The relieved Guido proceeded through the narthex and into the basilica's vast expanse as he led Odo and Eustace down the nave. As they reached the high altar, Guido signalled to Odo that they remain there before he continued to the small chapel of Saint Petronilla in the southern wing, where Pope Alexander was known to escape and pray.

"Your Holiness," interrupted Guido as he approached the kneeling Pope at the small chapel altar, behind which was a recently installed statue of the Blessed Mary.

Pope Alexander raised a finger in Guido's direction without turning his gaze from the Virgin, to which Guido dropped his head and patiently waited until Alexander was ready. Alexander's sprawling and elaborately decorated red robe gathered on the floor and over his papal slippers. His white hair was perfectly combed and exhibited a circled kink where the papal helmet-shaped crown rested for most of the day, but as he knelt and prayed, the crown rested by his side. Several young novice monks stood at the rear of the chapel, singing plainchant sequences with their angelic voices echoing softly off the stone walls.

"Isn't she amazing?" asked Pope Alexander, as he continued to kneel and gaze at the sculpture.

"Yes, she is, Your Holiness."

"I've been reading some treatises on our Blessed Mary," continued Alexander, as he continued to stare in wonder. "Some from my former teacher, Lanfranc. Some suggest that Mary, to have been chosen by the Father to conceive our Lord, would have needed to be sinless, immaculate. And not just at the time of the annunciation, Guido, but from her birth. Completely set aside by God from original sin. I have not considered this until recently. This opens the door to so many opportunities in deepening our adoration to Mary. The Theotokos, the Mother of God. Our Mother. Our Lady."

"The church of God will rejoice at these holy revelations, Your Holiness," praised Guido. His words were followed by a lengthy silence in which Alexander resumed his prayers and adoration.

"Your mention of the Norman abbot Lanfranc is testament to your prophetic wisdom, Your Holiness. There are two Norman delegates here in the basilica who wish to have an audience," declared Archbishop Guido. "Shall I permit them?"

"Normans. Yes, I expected they would be here soon enough. Bring them in," replied Alexander, who stayed in his prayerful position.

Guido turned to dismiss the young plainchant singers before he hurried off in the direction of the high altar and signalled to Odo and Eustace, who were distracted looking at various art pieces. Moments later, Odo and Eustace filed into the chapel, which was now silent. Eustace was careful to watch and imitate Odo precisely, which was to face the Pope and lay face down on the cold mosaic tiled floor with his nose and forehead touching the tiles, both arms stretched out.

They assumed the required position, and there was a time of silence before Pope Alexander crossed himself, rose from his kneeling pillow and placed the papal helmet-shaped crown on his crisp white hair. Rather than inviting his guests to rise, he took a moment to straighten his papal robes and enjoy the authority of his position.

"You may rise," he finally declared.

"Allow me to introduce Bishop Odo of Bayeux and Count Eustace of Boulogne, Normandy, Your Holiness," said Guido as the two men rose to kneel.

"Yes, Bishop Odo, I know. You are both welcome. Why are you here?" asked Alexander.

"Your Holiness, we are to ask for your blessing for a campaign," began Odo.

"Brittany, again? Duke William is obsessed with Brittany," insisted Alexander.

"No, Your Holiness. To England," corrected Odo.

"England? I see. I understand King Edward died months ago and that a local noble seized power. Is that right?"

"Correct, Your Holiness," affirmed Odo. "The situation we have here is that the local noble you spoke of broke a sacred oath he swore to Duke William, which was to secure the throne for the duke, the throne which was promised to him more than ten years ago by King Edward. But instead of raising the Norman standard following Edward's death, this noble seized power, as you said."

"You witnessed this oath yourself?"

"Of course, Your Holiness," responded Odo.

"Your situation is like many others I currently have the misfortune of dealing with," responded Alexander. "What we have here, Odo, is a fundamental breakdown in reverence to holy statutes declared by the church. My Holy Roman Emperor, for example, Henry IV. He is tempted to abandon his betrothal, which I blessed, to Bartha of Savoy and marry another woman. Another example. Unlike countless popes before me, I was elected Pope by a council of cardinal bishops here in

Rome, which is the way the apostles themselves established it. But that hasn't stopped this poor excuse of a cleric, Honorius, to claim that he is Pope because a gang of excommunicated Lombard bishops decided it must be so. We also have several princes and kings, right now, in Christendom who claim to have the right of investiture, the right to elect bishops, over the papacy. Have they forgotten Christ and his holy church? Have they forgotten that we are the successors to Saint Peter and that we have the keys to the kingdom?"

"This, Your Holiness, is why we are here," assured Odo.

"So, tell me, Odo, this oath that you witnessed with the English noble, you mentioned it was sacred?"

"Yes, Your Holiness, it was taken over the reliquary of ... Saint Faith of Agen," answered Odo cautiously, as he feared the inevitable follow-on questions.

"Ah, yes, Blessed Saint Foy." Alexander smiled, and his eyes lit up as though the topic shift excited him. "I enjoy reading about these relics, immensely popular in the west. How does the story go again? Um, Conques stole it from Agen two hundred years ago, *Furta Sacra*. Now it seems you have it. *Furta Sacra* again, with the same method. You had a monk secure a vocation in Conques for several years before he could get his hands on it and bring it back to Falaise, yes? Then I assume Conques sent you the gilded bust when they discovered the theft? Am I right, Bishop Odo?"

"Yes, you have assumed correctly, Your Holiness," responded Odo, bracing himself.

"Let's see, where do we start? Were you aware that your monk murdered his superior while he escaped with the relics?" asked Pope Alexander as he slowly walked around Odo and Eustace.

"Yes, but that was not part of my instruction."

"I didn't ask you that, Bishop Odo. Yes or no will suffice. I was informed of the theft, and it was ... amusing, but the murder of a superior demonstrates poor leadership on your part," declared Pope Alexander.

"Forgive me, Your Holiness," begged Odo.

"We'll come back to the relics later. Going back to the oath," continued Alexander, as he made a swift sign of the cross over Odo's head to absolve him. "So, you claim that this English noble swore an oath to secure the throne for William when he returned to England. But why was he in Normandy, and why would this noble swear an oath to secure the throne for William while he evidently had royal ambitions of his own? Perhaps the oath was in Frankish, which no one can understand, or perhaps just ambiguous or taken under duress?" suggested Alexander.

"I don't know why he went against his oath," answered a bolder Odo. "But I can assure you that the oath was clean, in English, and he took it with a sober and sound mind."

"I see," stated Alexander, as he turned away from Odo, somewhat unconvinced.

"Your Holiness, may I ask how things are progressing in Sicily?" Odo diverted.

Alexander turned his head in Odo's direction without looking at him, somewhat impressed by Odo's cunning move at this point in the negotiations. Alexander had forgotten about the Normans in Sicily, and it was something that could not be ignored. Several years prior, Alexander's predecessor, Pope Nicholas II, managed to reclaim Sicily for Christianity away from the Arabs. But this was only possible by way of an alliance with a large Norman army which just so happened to be conveniently situated nearby at Melfi, led by two powerful and notoriously reliable Norman nobles, Robert Guiscard of the Hauteville family and Richard of Capua. The successful campaign saw Robert and Richard formally invested with several regional titles. However, the notable win for the church was that the Sicilian region was brought back into the fold, allowing the church to exercise its full rights again. This all concluded with significant economic and political victories for the church, from which Alexander benefited.

But Sicily was not a Norman conquest; it was Roman. Further, it was an unofficial and unrecorded understanding that the successful alliance could be repeated should a similar Norman-initiated campaign require it. It was clear to Alexander that Odo was bringing this understanding to the table now, and Alexander knew the papacy would struggle to maintain a healthy alliance with the Normans if he failed to honour it now.

Alexander considered another more current benefit. A church-endorsed Norman conquest of England would be an opportunity to bring the unruly English senior clergy back into line, following a string of incidents over the last decade which incurred excommunications.

"Sicily was a good move, Odo," stated Alexander. "And to answer your question, the church in Sicily is progressing very well, thank you. So, let's talk plainly, shall we? You want me to approve a Norman conquest of England. Today. Is that right?"

"Yes, Your Holiness," pushed Odo, as Eustace continued to watch the political spectacle unfold in front of him.

Alexander took his time to respond as he stared down at the kneeling Odo. They both knew that Odo had inexplicably taken a gamble in boldly asserting that Alexander somewhat owed the Normans this blessing.

"Before I grant my blessing, Odo, I have certain requirements."

"Of course, Your Holiness."

"King Edward's tomb is to be given the highest honour in

London's recently built abbey. Also, Duke William is to ensure the English archbishops submit to new papal ordinances or be removed from office and replaced by more suitable candidates."

"I will see to it—"

"I'm not finished, Odo," interrupted Alexander. "I permit William to carry fragments of Saint Foy's relics into battle. However, as penance for the murder, you must return all the relics and reliquary to Conques after successfully installing William as king. With all this, you will be vested an edict, the papal ring and the papal standard. What say you?"

Odo's expression was that of unmistakable disappointment. His prized possession, the relics he had come to love and fear, would be returned to Conques, leaving his abbey without a jewel to draw in recognition and wealth. He desperately wanted to challenge that particular penance, but he reminded himself that he was the one on his knees.

CHAPTER 46

THORNEY ISLAND, LONDON

"Again, how many huscarl soldiers are listed?" Harold sat as his council stood around him.

Harold had taken the liberty to adjust the selected members of the Witan Council. Though pressured to keep Morcar and Stigand on, he replaced a few Morcar's toadies with two brothers, Gyrd and Leofwine, the earls of East Anglia and Kent. Along with Aldred, Archbishop of York.

"About three thousand, my king," responded Morcar.

"About? How is it we don't know the exact number? If Caelin were here, he'd know. So, we will be somewhere between ten thousand to thirteen thousand strong if we combine the huscarl foot and cavalry troops, thane foot and cavalry and the fyrd. Is that right?"

"No, the three thousand huscarls are additional to the ten to thirteen thousand we discussed earlier," added Archbishop Aldred.

Harold covered his face with his palms as he felt the lack of support and expertise he had enjoyed during his time as Earl of Wessex. He lost most of his skilled and trusted men in the storm while sailing across the channel. And he had lost Caelin, whose skill and loyalty was just what Harold needed at this time.

"Gentlemen, we are no longer in Edward's era of prayers and lack-lustre military discipline. I need a complete inventory of ranks and positions, and then I need to station them on the south coast near Hastings. We're running out of time. Go! Aldred and Stigand can remain," ordered Harold.

Morcar and Harold's two brothers headed for the door.

"Morcar!" yelled Harold, as Morcar was just about to exit. "I think it is time you include all of your men for this cause, not just your titled thanes. Unlike Edward, I know your numbers. We need everyone."

Morcar, with seemingly authentic and uncharacteristic humility, closed his eyes and nodded in Harold's direction.

"We stand together now, Morcar," continued Harold. "No more games. My victories are your victories."

Morcar said nothing and closed the door behind him. As disappearing footsteps on timber flooring were heard, the two elderly archbishops drew closer to Harold.

"Archbishops, I have not heard from you in weeks, months. Did you appeal to the Pope?"

"We did," responded Stigand. "But it seems we were too late, Harold. The Pope had already entertained a Norman embassy just a few days before our envoy arrived. They were expecting us, and from what we heard, our letter was accepted but probably never made its way to the Pope himself. Obviously, our envoy was not granted an audience with His Holiness, let alone the details of William's request. But our unofficial sources in Rome indicated that William's embassy did request a blessing for an English conquest, and it was indeed granted. Ring and banner."

"Your loyalty to my father and consequent lack of obedience to Rome over the past decades have proved costly in this situation, Stigand," stated Harold quietly as he stared out of the nearby window.

At that moment, a palace messenger entered the king's council room and bowed. "Good King, your consort, Edith, is here. Shall I permit her?"

Harold nodded to the messenger then turned to Stigand and Aldred. "Stigand, your relationship with Rome is as useless as it ever was. Now it seems that your primate rank is chained to the success or failure of William's attack on this soil. So, I suggest you start preaching in the shires about loyalty to the king. We need more men, now. You're dismissed."

Edith passed the exiting archbishops and entered the council room with her head bowed and eyes to the ground.

Harold rose from his chair and headed over to the west-facing window; rare afternoon sunshine beamed through. "The weather is getting warmer in London. I'm relieved to see the end of that winter," he said.

"Yes," Edith responded after an awkward moment of silence.

"What are you doing here, Edith? Don't you have tapestries to attend to?" Harold continued to stare out into the view towards the courtyard, the abbey and the River Thames.

"It's been weeks, Harold. I'm doing what you asked of me, but you need to hear about what happened, from me, not from some cheap Norman spy from Morcar's ranks," pushed Edith.

"The spy was Norman?" Harold turned to Edith.

"Why do you think he didn't speak?" Edith's voice held a note of urgency.

"What do you mean?"

"That night," Edith continued, "when Morcar accused Caelin and I months ago, the spy in the courtyard. Did you notice that he never spoke? He may have revealed something stolen from my quarters in Winchester. If he had spoken, you would have heard his accent and questioned his allegiance or his motive. Morcar knew the spy was Norman, and so he did all the talking. This spy only witnessed Caelin and I in deep discussion about you, about what you were going through since your capture in Normandy and about how we can support you. And so, the story Morcar declared to you was easily conjured up. Caelin and I had no … intimacy, Harold. You should know your most trusted and faithful thane would never betray you like that, even if I wanted him to."

Harold turned back to the window in frustration, and some moments passed before either of them spoke, but it was clear to Edith that Harold's perspective on the alleged betrayal had changed.

"Harold, take this," said Edith softly as she approached with her head bowed and handed Harold a medallion fastened to a delicate silver neck chain. "I know religious ornaments are not usually found among your ceremonial pieces, but I made this for you. It's a pilgrim's medallion of Saint Edmund the Martyr. You mentioned before your coronation that you had felt almost haunted by King Edward since his death. Saint Edmund was King of East Anglia two hundred years ago. You probably already knew that, but what you may not know is that Edmund is known to assist those who seek peace from spiritual torments. Take your time, but please, my dear Harold, wear this as a sign to me that you believe that I would never betray you in the way Morcar has claimed."

Harold slowly took the medallion and gave Edith a subtle but genuine nod as thanks. His expression towards her was calm and reflective as she bowed and turned to exit the room, leaving Harold alone with her gift and his thoughts.

CHAPTER 47

FALAISE, NORMANDY

"Good Christian men of Normandy, Flanders, Brittany and afar. Come and take refuge in God's blessed army against the English legion of the damned," preached Duke William from a frost-covered grassy hill before a gathered crowd of more than one thousand knights and nobles.

"No doubt you have heard," William continued, "of the blessing. See here, with us now, the papal banner and the ring on my finger. His Holiness, Pope Alexander, the Vicar of Christ himself, has heard, understood and blessed this cause."

"We believe that the blessing you have is real, but my issue is with Bishop Odo, whom you sent to Rome. That cleric is in your pocket," yelled one knight from Brittany. "Who else from the church, apart from Odo, can confirm that the holy office wasn't tricked into this?" A hum of concerned approval went over the crowd.

"This was no trickery on our part, I assure you. His Holiness needed no cunning speech from Odo. The news of Harold's broken sacred oath was enough," William pleaded.

"William is right," responded an unidentified voice from within the crowd. The figure emerged, aided by an episcopal staff. He headed to William's side as the crowd gradually recognised him.

"I am Lanfranc of Bec Abbey. Yes, I was Pope Alexander's superior for many years when he was a novice, and I can assure you that he is not easily tricked. What is more, I advised His Holiness before Bishop Odo arrived in Rome." Lanfranc looked over to a shocked William before continuing. "This is your duty to God. God wills it, and he will not fail you. Put your trust in God and his servant. Your liege, Duke William."

The crowd responded to the abbot's assurance with an enormous cheer as the grateful and relieved William watched on in awe of Lanfranc's presence and authority over the nobles.

"Before you leave to gather men for this cause," Lanfranc continued, "kneel before almighty God and I will bless you for this task."

The entire crowd obeyed the abbot's instruction and humbled themselves to their knees, some with faces to the earth. Abbot Lanfranc raised his right hand. With his fingers, he made the sign of the cross over the crowd and commenced his prayer.

"In nomine Patris, et Filii, et Spiritus Sancti. Amen. Benedicat tibi Dominus, et custodiat te. Ostendat Dominus faciem suam tibi, et misereatur tui. Convertat Dominus vultum suum ad te, et det tibi pacem." *In the name of the Father, and of the Son, and Holy Spirit. Amen. The Lord bless you and keep you. The Lord make his face shine on you, and be gracious to you. The Lord turn his face toward you and give you peace.*

As the crowd rose from the grass and slowly started to disperse, the knight from Brittany who questioned the validity of the blessed campaign approached William with his right hand on his chest.

"Forgive me, Duke William. I was wrong to doubt. May we, together, conquer with the power of God."

"We shall indeed. You are from Brittany, I assume?"

"I am, my liege. Alan Rufus, of Brittany."

"Rufus, you shall lead my left-wing attack line. Gather your men to the River Dives in two weeks. The other nobles will be instructed to do the same."

Rufus nodded in agreement and completed his apology by kissing the papal ring on William's right hand before dismissing himself down the hill to join the other nobles. William was still amazed at how the situation had concluded as he turned to a smiling Abbot Lanfranc.

"Lanfranc, I almost lost them, but you ..." he laughed.

"This Harold visited Bec Abbey," smiled Lanfranc, "as he was being escorted to you some time ago."

"Yes, I was informed. But, how did you?" William asked.

"I observed him as he sat and ate in our refectory, and I recognised a troubled mind. I also concluded that the two of you were after the same thing, so I wrote to Alexander, my old novice, and gave him my thoughts on the subject, knowing that you would approach His Holiness in due course. Alexander knows, as do I that you are no better than Harold, but we agreed that the Saxon dynasty is pulling England further away from Christ's church. I believe God has chosen you to bring England back, but you must acknowledge God and his holy church at every victory. Do you understand?"

Uncharacteristically, William said nothing and nodded at Lanfranc.

"Another thing, William. I heard that you would not only ride with the Pope's ring and banner but also with the relics of

Saint Foy in your armour. This is not something to take lightly. You must not commit any sin to God while in possession of those relics. Be careful not to offend the power that goes with you into England. If you do, who knows what will happen to you or your campaign?"

CHAPTER 48

HASTINGS, ENGLAND

"Make way. Make way for the king!"

Harold arrived at the mile-long army camp stationed along the coastline near the village of Hastings. A large entourage of royal thanes, earls and servants accompanied him. Harold insisted that the group canter along the length of the camp, waving as he went to the cheering soldiers of all ranks before arriving at the royal tent. The large, crisp white tent reflected the mid-autumn sun, while the royal banners and various peerage flags danced in the coastal onshore wind. At the entrance stood two unmoved servants who opened the entrance material, waiting for the king.

Harold dismounted with a thud to the earth. As his horse was taken away, Morcar, Gyrd, and Leofwine dismounted and followed the king into the tent. Inside stood three commanding thanes, all healthy, strong and armed for battle. The three thanes bowed as Harold entered, and the highest-ranked stepped forward to speak.

"Good King, we have ranks—"

"Before we get into the ranks and costs," interrupted Harold as he made himself comfortable on his fur covered chair, "who has found my thane, Caelin?"

"We have reports of various sightings," spoke the high-ranked thane, "from Wessex to London and in the area here on the south coast. As you can appreciate, he is impossible to track, let alone capture, my king."

"What is your name, soldier?"

"Tilian, of Northumbria, my king."

"A northerner. One of your men, Morcar?" Harold glanced over at Morcar before returning to the thane. "Did you serve under Tostig before Morcar?"

The thane, who looked unsure how his answer would fare, also looked to Morcar, who answered instead for his uncertain thane. "He did, Harold. He was loyal to Tostig before he joined my ranks."

"Good." Harold rose from his chair, approached Tilian and slapped him on the shoulder. "Because that shows me you're loyal ..." Harold then turned to Morcar before completing his sentence, "... and local."

"Tilian, I'm not interested in Caelin's capture," indicated Harold as he returned to his chair.

Tilian was astonished. "You're ordering his death before a trial?"

"Far from it. Caelin is innocent of treason, and I want him restored to his royal rank," ordered Harold.

"Are you mad, Harold?" barked Morcar. "Did I not give you enough evidence for the crime he's committed against you?"

"Enough, Morcar. Count it a blessing that you still have your earldom even though you stationed spies in Winchester Castle, spies of Norman descent. And yes, of course, I found out he was Norman."

Harold then turned to the thane, Tilian, to continue. "The

trick will be capturing him unharmed or at least finding a way to communicate his restoration. He still thinks there's a price on his head, and his skills of being undetected are the best I've ever seen, so this will be difficult. I want you to consider various means of communication to inform him of his innocence so that we can avoid spilt blood."

"His?" asked the thane.

"Yours," responded Harold. "So, use Wessex men. If you approach him yourself, your body would not be found for centuries. Now, let's talk ranks, numbers, time and costs."

Though somewhat unnerved by the king's assertions, and Morcar seemingly powerless to protect him, which was unusual, Tilian stepped forward and spread a large parchment map across the table in the middle of the tent.

"Here, today, we have the bulk of what is ready across the kingdom," he declared. "Which is seven thousand thanes and huscarls of various rank and skill. Mounted and foot swordsmen, two-handed axemen, pikes and archers. I've stationed them in peerages across the coast from Bosham to here in Hastings, and we have smaller posts toward the east, so we can be alerted quickly once the Norman fleet is insight. The fyrd, we have five thousand. Their camps are stationed behind the huscarls and thanes."

"How long have the fyrd been here?" enquired Harold.

"Thirty days. They cost little to feed compared to the others." Tilian was prepared for his king's questions.

"And the other costs? How much are we outlaying for the huscarls, thanes and horses?"

"About ten pounds of silver coin per week."

"So, we have about one month remaining to retain the fyrd before I'm expected to release them and about four months before the king's coin store is bone dry," concluded Harold. "Now, gentlemen. Let's talk position. Position is everything."

CHAPTER 49

ORKNEY ISLANDS, SCOTIA

From the view of his longboat approaching the coast, Tostig could see the scurry of islander men, women and children moving in a panic from the beach back to the village to inform the clansmen. Behind him was the largest gathering of Norsemen longboats he had ever heard of, a fleet of five hundred or more approaching the beach of the Orkney island.

There's no turning back from here, he thought as he looked across to Hardrada's longboat, also drifting into the beach just thirty yards away.

Tostig jumped off his longboat with rope in hand, assisting several Norsemen secure it on the sand before heading to Hardrada's boat to do the same. It was the largest of the fleet, holding twenty men and supplies. Hardrada's English-speaking soldier jumped out and headed towards Tostig.

"You are not needed here, Tostig. These Orkney people are subjects of King Hardrada, not the King of the Scots as you expected. Most of them are of Norse heritage. Here we keep supplies, fighters, treasures and more boats. Your knowledge will come in handy once we reach northern England."

Tostig nodded as the wild Orkney shore winds flicked his dark hair around his concerned face.

CHAPTER 50

THE MOUTH OF THE RIVER DIVES, NORMANDY

Thirty miles north of Falaise, where the River Dives opens to the channel, Duke William arrived on horseback at the top of a hill overlooking the inspiring view. He was accompanied by Bishop Odo, Count Eustace, twelve Norman knights and several servants from Chateau de Falaise.

Though the afternoon sun reflected like diamonds off the calm sea, it wasn't the view across the channel that caught the Duke's eye, but the build of an immense fleet of five hundred longboats on the brink of completion, along with the gathering of six thousand warhorses, three for each knight. The hand-selected horses were all required to be the type known locally as the destrier warhorse. Along with most kingdoms on the continent, the destrier horse was the pride of Franks. Though they could be any number of breeds, they are selected for size at foal and then trained for strength, agility and, most importantly, effectiveness in the joust charge.

William took a moment and beamed with pride before he headed down to the ranks below.

"Duke William," said Count Eustace as they rode through, waving at nobles, knights and foot soldiers they passed by. "Though this is ... impressive, I can't help but think of practicalities and the voyage across the channel."

"How did I know this conversation was coming, Eustace?" laughed William. "I could hear your brain ticking over the number of boats, horses, men and supplies while we on the hill."

"Not just the numbers, William. The weather," argued Eustace. "The larger of these tightly packed longboats will be heavy, with ten to twelve horses, four to six knights and their supplies. They will need more than an autumn offshore breeze to get moving; it will need to be a significant southerly wind to move north across the channel. Norman autumns are not known for their strong southerly winds; it's usually northerlies."

Though he couldn't argue with Eustace's pragmatic perspective, William was far from appreciative of the sudden move from the excitement of progress to the dim realities of the weather.

"Ah, Rufus," he bellowed as he recognised his new loyal knight a few yards away, a welcome sight. Rufus left the conversation he was having and headed in the direction of William as he dismounted.

"Duke William, I'm honoured." Rufus bowed and kissed the papal ring on William's finger. "We have much to show you, which should all be ready within a few days. Come, come."

William followed Rufus but couldn't resist the temptation to give Eustace a look, to imply that Rufus was an example of a proper attitude.

A proud Rufus drew William's attention to an almost completed longboat as William and Eustace followed him up a ladder onto the timber dock.

"As you can see, Duke William, these larger design boats can be tightly packed without pushing the limits as the old designs did, keeping the horses distracted and calm. Though they are stable, my liege, they are still heavy in the water. We need to talk about the weather. We'll need a strong southerly before we consider pushing out to sea. I believe we could be here for some time before we see that wind." Explained Rufus

Eustace also couldn't resist the temptation and turned to William with a raised eyebrow.

"How long, Rufus?" enquired a frustrated William.

"From my experience on the shores of Brittany at this time of the year, it could be weeks."

CHAPTER 51

SAINT PETER'S MONASTERY, THORNEY ISLAND, LONDON

"Good morning, Abbot Edwin. I hope this isn't a bad time." Announced Aldred, Archbishop of York, as he let himself into the monastery's scriptorium, closing the door behind him. "I was told I could find you in here."

"Archbishop. An honour." Edwin closed a bound script on the table and approached, kneeling at Aldred's feet and kissing the ring on his finger.

"Rise, son. Come, let's sit." Aldred invited Edwin to join him on the short stools at the corner of the extensive reading table, which was used for spreading out large or multiple scripts.

"I'm glad you're here alone as I need to discuss a couple of things with you in private," began Aldred. "I saw you briefly at Harold's coronation, but I've meant to come and visit you since that week."

"I see," responded Edwin, under no illusion as to where this conversation was going.

"I assume you saw the fascinating hairy star in the clear night sky a few days after the coronation?" asked Aldred.

"Yes, I certainly did. I think everyone did."

"On that night," continued Aldred, "shortly before we noticed the star, Archbishop Stigand and I were discussing with Harold a certain relationship he has with the Normans, specifically with Duke William."

"I see."

"He mentioned a sacred oath he took. In which the reliquary of Saint Foy or Faith of Agen was involved," said Aldred as he lowered his voice.

"Ah, I see." Edwin threw his head back and looked to the roof's timber beams as certain pieces in the puzzle came together in his mind.

"From the look of things, Stigand was right to suggest you were the person to approach about this," Aldred asserted with a subtle smile as his eyes moved to the other corner of the reading table.

"From the look of things?"

"My eyesight is still quite good at this age, Edwin. From here, I can see Jerome's *Book of Martyrs* over there, the *Martyrologium Hieronymianum*. And next to Jerome's book, I can see the *Liber Miraculorum Sancta Fidis*. The *Book of Miracles of Saint Faith*."

"There's no hiding from you, Archbishop," smiled Edwin.

"Yes. The thing is, Edwin. Archbishop Stigand and I are two of only a handful of people in England who know about Harold's encounter with the Saint Foy reliquary. How is it that the abbot of London's largest monastery is up here in the scriptorium taking significant time to research that very saint?"

"Aldred, it's no secret that I experience more … spiritual encounters than the average abbot," Edwin said carefully. "I not only treasure them, Archbishop, I seek them, like nectar. King Edward was no different; may God rest his soul."

"King Edward?" asked Aldred, curious about his involvement in this discussion.

"Yes. Edward was, of course, inexperienced when he first turned to serious prayer ten or so years ago. But in the year leading up to his death, he was more spiritually discerning than I have ever wished to be. Edward's ability to connect with God, to see and hear God, was astounding. He really did pray without ceasing, as Saint Paul instructs us. He often said that his prayers would continue in his sleep and wake him for the Matins service. The desert monks spoke of this in their writings hundreds of years ago, but few of those hermits ever achieved it. Edward's experiences opened my eyes to see and hear new things also."

"Go on, Edwin," pushed an increasingly curious Aldred.

"He related a strange vision to me while on his deathbed. He said that a Norman monk came to his bed and said that God had given England over to evil spirits because of her sins. He asked, 'Will God not have mercy?' and the monk replied, 'Only when a tree cleft in two by lightning will come together of its own accord and grow green again. Only then will there be pardon'."

"And you also were having similar visions?"

"Well, yes. I had experienced a similar sense of God's anger. So, Edward's vision gave me plenty to fear and pray about."

"And what about since then, Edwin? What have you seen, and how did Saint Foy come to your attention?"

"On the day of Harold's coronation," Edwin continued, "I

experienced the most vivid scene of a dark wrath being poured out on this land, devouring all but one thing."

"What thing?" Aldred leaned in.

"Well, not a thing, Archbishop," continued Edwin. "An innocent young child, a girl. In my vision, she walked this land untouched and oblivious to the destruction going on around her. She approached me and said that she was Faith, and that she was coming."

"And so, obviously you've been prayerfully studying Saint Faith since that night? So, what have you discovered?"

"Correct. Saint Faith, Saint Foy. From what I've read, Foy's relics can be a blessing, a trick or even a curse, depending on who has it or who venerated her relics. Cases of both healings and people being driven to madness are reported within days of each other, Archbishop. I understand the reliquary was stolen from Conques Abbey by a disguised novice not long ago and brought to Falaise. I feel the Normans intend to use the power of the relics in their conquests, and England is in their sights. You mentioned a sacred oath, Archbishop. Perhaps that is where it all started."

"Perhaps. Anything else, Edwin?"

"I'm reluctant to say this, but I feel the relics of Saint Foy will not only lead the Normans into battle but will ultimately bring them victory ... for a time," concluded Edwin.

"Why, Edwin? Why do you feel that Foy will bring the Normans victory?"

"Because she has her own conquest, Aldred. Something holy."

Archbishop Aldred's face fell into his thin, ageing hands.

"Tell me more about the sins of this kingdom you mentioned, Edwin."

"I do not believe I am the right person to answer that question."

CHAPTER 52

HASTINGS, ENGLAND

"Of course, I don't want to release the fyrd; I need them here, ready with the others. But I don't have a choice, Morcar. I've already kept these men thirty days more than their forty-day obligation to the crown." Harold and Morcar were standing on a windswept grassy hill overlooking the movement of five thousand soldiers heading north, away from the army camp along the coastline.

"You're their king, Harold. Releasing the fyrd is a weak move, even for you. You'll lose half your infantry strength. You could demand more time," insisted Morcar.

"Just like I said to you before, you have no idea how to lead an army. It's harvest time, Morcar. These men need to go home and feed their families. You're right about one thing; I am their king. But a king who robs men of their ability to feed their children is never worth defending. They're not completely gone; I can pick up the fyrd after the harvest. But they'll be strong and more loyal."

"So, where's William?"

"I expected him to strike quicker than this." Harold stared

out across the calm channel sea. "It's been months. He seems to be biding his time; he could be waiting for more men or supplies. It's possible that waiting is his strategy to catch us off guard later. We'll see, but we'll have to stay on alert."

Enough moments passed to calm the tone between them, then Harold enquired, "Has your Northumbrian thane come back with any word on Caelin?"

"Yes, he has. He reported last night that he had successfully passed on a message to Caelin, informing him of your declaration and the restoration of his position."

"And?" urged Harold.

"The spy who managed to contact Caelin indicated that Caelin wasn't convinced and that he considered the information as a trap for his capture before he disappeared again."

"Damn you, Morcar. I could be benefiting from Caelin's knowledge right now if you had not have ruined everything with your cheap tactics and lying Norman spies. Caelin may know things that we don't about William and other threats? But I can't get to him," blasted Harold.

"This is useless talk." Morcar waved his hand at Harold before turning to head down to the camp. "I'm taking my men back to York; I have Northumbrian matters to attend to. Send word when your Norman liege arrives."

CHAPTER 53

VILLAGE OF RICCALL, TEN MILES SOUTH OF YORK

"Mama, Mama, look," yelled a young Northumbrian child as he pointed toward the River Humber.

"Dear God," sighed the child's mother as the sight of countless enormous longboats filled with soldiers sailed up the peaceful Humber. "Quick, we must head back to the village. Go."

The mother and child dropped their firewood bundles and ran through trees and thickets towards their village of Riccall. As they turned sharply around a high, thick bush, they came upon a frightening sight of four prominent and armed Norse soldiers heading their way and so quickly changed direction.

"This way, my love," beckoned the mother, as they continued to run down an alternate route which took them past old unused fort ramparts around the village before heading toward the north entrance. The child knew the area well and ran past his mother to reach the gate.

"Son. Wait."

As she ran to catch up, the boy could be seen arriving at the turn at the end of the rampart, but instead of continuing to the village, he stopped and took a step backwards. Once his mother arrived behind him, she understood why he didn't proceed. The scene before them was not what they left just a few hours prior; the entire village was overrun with at least one hundred Viking raiders—taking, burning, slaying, working their way through everything and everyone in their path. Villagers screaming, running here and there as dozens of bodies littered the village centre. Almost every house and barn were ablaze, sending billows of smoke into the clear autumn afternoon sky.

As they stood and watched, frozen with fear, the mother woke herself from the shock as she realised the need to think quickly. They had not yet been seen.

"This way," she ordered as she grabbed her son's hand and headed west away from the village and further down the Humber. Staying low and taking advantage of nearby bushes and shrubs for coverage, they ran, covering almost a quarter-mile.

"Down," whispered the mother as she suddenly pulled her son to the dirt and sand of the riverbank under a bush, thick with foliage.

After a moment, the mother signalled to her son to remain quiet before moving his attention to the river. Several men were already on the riverbank, taking ropes from the giant longboat amongst the fleet and securing it to the bank as they talked in a strange foreign language. As the mother and child lay silent, they watched several men disembark from the elaborate and enormous longboat, the first of whom was the largest man the child had ever seen, sending a shiver of fear to the back of his neck.

"Tostig. Tostig. Come and advise. Hardrada has ordered," yelled a Norse warrior, as the mother and child watched on under the bush, surprised to hear familiar English all of a sudden. A man emerged from the group of foreigners on the riverbank, but he wasn't dressed like them. He looked like an English noble.

"Tostig?" the mother whispered. "Surely, it's not the old earl, Tostig Godwinson. My God, it is."

"York is ten miles north," Tostig advised Hardrada's translator. "That's where you'll find what you're after. Prisoners and provisions. You don't need these little villages around here."

Upon hearing the translation from his man, Hardrada squinted, and his expression changed as though he had been insulted. He stepped forward and struck Tostig in the jaw with a powerful strike from his right fist, which sent Tostig to the ground. Tostig immediately jumped to his feet and attempted to strike Hardrada back but instead collided with two solid red raven shields that blocked his attack. Tostig found himself on the ground again, but there he remained. Looking up, he could see two of Hardrada's elite blocking his view.

"Du forteller meg ikke hva jeg kan ta!" yelled Hardrada in his rough, rasping voice as he walked past with his men following behind.

The Norse translator headed over to Tostig and offered him a hand to help him up, but Tostig brushed it away.

"I do not like my job, telling your English to the king," the translator said, with his limited English and a wry smile. "You say the wrong things."

"What did Hardrada say?" asked Tostig as he picked himself up and brushed off the sand and dirt from the riverbank.

With a smirk, the translator responded. "He said, 'You do not tell me what I can take.'"

As Tostig and the Norse translator continued to speak on the riverbank, the mother and child were still hiding under a nearby bush, listening. They turned their attention to other sounds from their village, some distance behind them—the crackling of the fire and the screams of women and children. The initial shock was fading, and the reality of what was happening was dawning on the child. Tears appeared. His mother noticed, but she shook off her instincts, reasoning that there would be time to mourn and comfort later, and the situation still required an astute plan if they were to survive.

"Son," the mother whispered, "I have an idea, but we need to stay sharp, do you understand? Your father is garrisoned south, in Selby. We can head the long way around the village and then down to Selby to alert them. These men are heading north to York."

CHAPTER 54

THORNEY ISLAND, LONDON

Harold paced swiftly through the corridors of the palace; his long tunic and robe flowed and lifted behind him as each servant he passed stopped to bow. His younger brother, Gyrd, the Earl of East Anglia, trailed behind, struggling to keep up.

"Harold, without the fyrd and the bulk of Morcar's men on the south coast, we're unprotected if William's fleet appears."

"Gyrd, William can land on our shores; we can't stop that. While he's distracted gathering food and provisions from the coastal villages, we can gather our forces and meet him inland before he reaches London. Trust me; we've done this before. We can discuss more in the morning. Go, rest." Harold slapped the concerned Gyrd on the shoulder before leaving him in the corridor and entering the king's private quarters.

He entered the large room, closed the door behind him and proceeded to strip off his royal robes and sword, casting them over a table near an open window. This window provided Harold with a view over the courtyard, abbey, and the river as he undressed. Lights in the east could also be seen on this clear night, from the populated side of town, which Harold took a moment to enjoy as he exhaled and leant on the table.

Suddenly, Harold's mouth was covered with a hand, and a blade was held to his throat by a hooded figure behind him.

"Shh, not a word Harold. Not a sound," spoke the unidentified man from behind. "Don't worry. I'm not staying long. You just need to listen, and then I'm gone. Now move away from the window, so we can't be seen."

With both hands slightly raised, Harold slowly shifted away from the open window, which allowed the assassin to move closer to it, with Harold unable to speak and still under threat. The voice and accent of the assailant were not recognisable, and though he could tell that this was a well-planned attack, he wasn't convinced it would be his end. He concluded that a move to protect himself would cause more problems.

"I have no reason to kill you, Harold, but if you make a sound or move to break free, you'll be dead. I have no reason to lie to you either. So, listen well. Your brother Tostig and the Norwegian king, Hardrada, have landed on the northeast coast near York. An enormous fleet, maybe five hundred ships. No doubt you've heard tales and legends about Hardrada? They call him the Land-Waster, and for good reason, I'm sure. They've probably wiped out Morcar's army by now, and if they have, I imagine they'll be heading south soon."

At this point, Harold twisted his body slightly to see his assailant.

"Uh uh, Harold. I'm sure your head is full of questions. Let me help. Who am I? You may find out, but not now. Why am I telling you this? Even though the thought of Morcar being cut in half by the axe of a Norseman is amusing, the prospect of those same Norsemen heading south is not so amusing. You need to mobilise north, pick up more men along the way and meet Tostig in battle. You can believe my report or waste three or four days until the same report reaches you from royal sources. It's up to you."

Harold's head was full of questions, but he was mindful of not making matters worse for himself.

"Now, I'm going to remove my blade and my hand, but I'm drawing my sword. You'll stay with your back to me, and you'll stay quiet until you can no longer hear my footsteps on the courtyard's cobblestones below. If you move or make a sound, my archer in the abbey's tower will have an arrow through your neck. Is that clear?"

Harold, with his mouth still covered and his open palms raised, gently nodded. The assassin slowly released his grip and removed the blade from Harold's neck. An unmistakable sound of an unsheathed sword was heard, followed by the gentle prod of its point felt in Harold's back.

"Remember the archer in the tower, Harold."

The sword's point was gone, and with the slightest sound of moving timber on the floor, Harold knew he was alone. A moment passed as Harold listened to the running footsteps gradually fading across the courtyard towards the river; as soon as they disappeared, he turned his head swiftly. The room was empty, as though no one was ever there. Harold rushed to the window and looked down to see an open courtyard and the abbey's tower also empty.

Harold was shaken but calm. Turning away from the window and heading back toward his bed, he noticed something on the table. He picked up the large lit candle and placed it on the table, where a small but elaborately decorated blade was stabbed into the timber with a pilgrim's medallion of Saint Edmund the Martyr wrapped around its handle.

"A Wessex blade, and the medallion from Edith." He sighed as he picked up the blade and the Wessex dragon impression in the leather became apparent in the candlelight. "Caelin."

Harold dropped the blade and medallion and immediately headed for the door to find his brother Gyrd, still near, talking flirtatiously to a handmaiden in the dimly lit corridor.

"Brother, we need to get moving. Now!" Harold returned to his quarters to grab his robe and sword.

"What is going on, Harold? I thought you were asleep." Gyrd turned to Harold as the handmaiden disappeared down the corridor.

"I'll explain later. We need to send word to the garrison in the south. You and I are heading north," ordered Harold.

As the loud and constant discussion between Harold and Gyrd Godwinson gradually faded down the corridor towards the stables, Edith Swanneck emerged from behind a large stone column within Harold's sleeping chamber. She wrapped a fur around her near-naked body – she had intended to seduce her husband – but the events of the night had not unfolded as Edith had planned. Instead, she witnessed her husband escape unscathed from a cunning assassin who, it seems, was also hiding in the same room.

Edith headed over to the table and picked up the blade that she had watched being held to Harold's throat. *A Wessex blade?* She thought before she placed it back down on the table and noticed the medallion of Saint Edmund the Martyr.

It had been weeks since she gifted her token of unwavering faithfulness to Harold, and by wearing it, it was supposed to signify his acceptance, his forgiveness. But there it sat, on the table.

Edith drifted her fingertips across her glowing white cheek, wiping the tear that trickled down. The pain of her husband's rejection was far more potent than she expected. She thought she was stronger than this. Edith dropped the medallion on the table, flicked her gold hair and spun around to exit the room. Her bare feet made no noise on the timber floor as the long fur flowed behind her.

CHAPTER 55

FULFORD GATE, YORK

"Kneel!" roared Hardrada at Earl Morcar, who duly obeyed and dropped. His knees squashed the deep blood-filled mud of the marshes beneath him. Hardrada knew the Norse word for kneel was much the same in some other languages. He had used it many times before.

"Du presset min hær for en tid, men vi beseiret deg. Nå vil vi ødelegge byen din," declared Hardrada with his enormous sword drawn, as his interpreter relayed in English, "You pushed back my army for a time, but we defeated you. Now we will destroy your city."

Hardrada stood over the kneeling and defeated Morcar.

Morcar, injured and covered with blood and mud, looked at the corpses around him, the remnants of his York barracks. Nearly one thousand young men now lay dead or were still being finished off, most of whom were terrified and had never seen battle before. Morcar also watched as Hardrada's men nearby laughed as they crossed over swamp pools by stepping on the dead to avoid the mud. The bloodstained muck beneath him was soaking into his tunic; he felt as though hell had arrived at York and death was drawing him down into the earth.

Surely, this is the end, Morcar thought.

To his surprise, the enormous Norwegian king who stood in front of him lowered his sword and stepped aside. Morcar looked up to see someone he never expected to see again.

"Tostig?" asked Morcar in shock.

"You know, it wasn't far from here," Tostig beamed at Morcar, "where you captured me and slaughtered my men. I remember it like it was yesterday, and now here you are kneeling before me." Tostig proceeded to walk around the humbled Morcar.

"See this all before you, Morcar? This hell?" he continued. "You've brought this on yourself, and this same punishment will now be unleashed on York. Now that you're unable to defend it. But don't worry, I will keep you alive so that you can witness its beauty."

"You bastard. You're killing your own kin for the glory of some foreigner?" sneered Morcar, which caused Tostig to strike him with a Norse shield, sending Morcar face down in the bloody mud.

"A kingdom that banishes me is no kingdom of mine," responded Tostig, as he leant down to whisper in Morcar's ear to continue. "I would have allied with anyone for this, and I will enjoy it."

Tostig stood up and stepped on Morcar's back before walking back to the Norse ranks.

"You don't need to raze York," spluttered Morcar as he helped himself back to his knees.

"Careful, Morcar," warned Tostig as he joined the gathered group of Norse captains. "The Norse king doesn't like being told anything."

The interpreter could be heard relaying Morcar and

Tostig's conversation to Hardrada as he watched on, somewhat disinterested.

"York has more men, slaves, supplies. Under my orders, the city can recognise Hardrada as king. The remaining men will join your march south," declared Morcar.

"How many men?" yelled the Norse translator from the back of the gathered group of Norsemen, discussing options.

"Two hundred in York, and almost five hundred in a small village eight miles east. Stamford Bridge."

After some discussion amongst the Norse captains, Hardrada raised his hand, clearly indicating he had come to a decision, which silenced the group. He declared to his men that the added boost of seven hundred men would be valuable as they march south, and that the opportunity would be seized. The captains were instructed to order their ranks to set up camp back at Riccall where they had landed, while Tostig, along with three captains, were to take Morcar to York to collect the promised soldiers and prisoners and return with them to Riccall.

"If you are wrong about any of this," yelled Hardrada's interpreter, "you and everyone in York will die."

CHAPTER 56

NORTHAMPTON, ENGLAND

"About one hundred and fifty miles to York, my king," declared thane Tilian of Northumbria.

"Yes, I know how far we are from York. What progress have you made to gather the fyrd from the shires?" enquired Harold as he dismounted from his horse and headed over to Tilian.

"They're moving in, rather quickly, actually. The messengers we sent are way ahead of us. They should be beyond Nottingham by now, and the fyrd will file in as we pass through."

"Good to hear, we should get moving then," announced Harold as he headed for his horse.

"One more thing, sir. We've just received word that Tostig and the Norse have taken York, which means—"

"They headed north after they sailed down the Humber, not south," interrupted Harold as he turned back, perplexed by the news.

"That's right. It's a good thing we left when we did. Caelin's unconventional delivery of information was fortunate."

"Yes. He is probably still tracking us," suggested Harold.

"Let's hope so. The message we received was from a garrison in Selby. They also indicated that the Norse have set up camp in Riccall. I know Tostig; I watched him over the years under his service. I would wager that he is taking his time enjoying his revenge over Morcar and the Northumbrian thanes that betrayed him. But Tostig is cunning. I believe he'll take the time to gather strength in numbers by taking Morcar's garrisons surrounding York before he heads south."

"I think you're right, Tilian," responded Harold. "You know, it was in this town I last saw Tostig several months ago. I assure you that his anger will be at its peak when we meet next, and anger is rarely effective in war, Tilian. So, we must be cunning."

"We will be, my liege."

"Good work. Let's move out. We'll head to Selby and then make plans if we can get there before Tostig does. I want to be there in four days, with our full strength," commanded Harold.

"Yes, Good King."

CHAPTER 57

VILLAGE OF SELBY, FIFTEEN MILES SOUTH OF YORK

"But father, I want to stay here with you," cried the boy as his father held him tightly.

"Son," said the father with love in his eyes, "you were so brave running away from the scary Vikings with your Mama, and I am so glad you're both here safe. But I need you to stay safe, and the best way to do that is heading to your Mama's family. I will head south and be with you soon, but for now, I need to stay here and keep this village safe with the other soldiers. Remember I promised I would teach you to ride a horse? I will keep that promise, you hear?"

The boy nodded through tears before turning to the arms of his mother, who in turn embraced her husband affectionately.

"Go now. Head south to your family," he said lovingly to his wife. "Stay off the main roads. You should have enough coin to get through the next couple of months."

The father turned and headed back towards the Selby barracks.

"Sir," yelled a fellow Northumbrian soldier from the outpost above. "We have information."

"I'll come up," the father responded before waving again to his wife and child as they walked off into the distance. He then headed up the tall timber outpost and entered a room where several Northumbrian thanes and soldiers had gathered.

"We have just received new information from the north. The Norsemen have set camp at Riccall and have taken York. Morcar is handing over the remaining men from York, and he also plans to hand over the garrison at Stamford Bridge, eight-mile east," said the Northumbrian thane.

"What is our plan?"

"There's more. The Norsemen have Tostig Godwinson with them. So, they will have Tostig's knowledge of the north, and Morcar won't be able to lead the Norsemen astray with false information. I'm sure they'll be heading here after Stamford Bridge."

"What about King Harold? Last I heard, his army was stationed along the south coast, waiting for a Norman invasion, which never came."

"That's right, but they somehow received word that Tostig is here with the Norseman, and so they're heading north, as we speak."

"All of them?"

"All of them. Picking up the fyrd as they go. They could be here in two or three days."

"Would it be too much of a risk if we rode out to meet Harold?"

"Leave Selby unprotected?"

"Yes, but if we can steer Harold's ranks towards Stamford Bridge quick enough, with Harold's army, we could pull off a surprise attack in Stamford. Then Selby would be safe. But we would need to leave now. All of us."

CHAPTER 58

THE MOUTH OF THE RIVER DIVES, NORMANDY

Bishop Odo's hands were shaking, sweat dripped from his cheeks, his entire being gripped with fear. Using a small blacksmith's tool, Odo moved tiny bone fragments from the reliquary box to Duke William's shin greave armour.

He wore a long bishop's robe, which billowed around his large frame as he bent over a table in the middle of his tent with the delicate reliquary box of Saint Foy on one side, and various pieces of Duke William's armour piled on the other. The reliquary had become the centre of Odo's life since it turned up that strange night by the hands of his spy monk, Brother Hugh. But Odo had never looked inside the box itself, and he had never wanted to. Since the night it arrived, followed by that strange vision, the thought of seeing inside the reliquary never crossed his mind. He feared the unknown consequences.

But Pope Alexander instructed that William could wear fragments of Saint Foy's relics on his armour to assist him in battle. Though Odo tried to discourage the duke from adopting the Pope's idea, as the relics had a reputation for inflicting harm on people Saint Foy saw as unfit, William shrugged off the suggestion. He ordered that Odo carry out the rite on every main piece of his armour as soon as possible. Especially now, considering that the southerly winds were picking up. Consequently, with a great deal of uneasiness, Odo ordered the reliquary be transported from Falaise to where William's ranks were gathering for the invasion, at the mouth of the River Dives.

Opening the box was a fearful enough experience, and Odo was resolved that he would not touch the actual pieces himself. Alternatively, he seized a small instrument from the blacksmith and used it to move the bone fragments. Most of William's armour pieces were complete, with the delicate bone fragments held on with intricate but strong iron clasps. The smaller pieces would be applied to arm and greave armour, but a larger bone fragment would be fixed to William's breastplate. Each fragment embedded in the armour required a liturgy of prayers and chanted psalms, which Odo meticulously followed, resisting the temptation to carry it out in haste or miss sections. So far, the pieces had been successfully extracted and fixed to four armour pieces.

The breastplate was the last remaining piece to be blessed with a relic. Odo placed the plate on the table and prepared the blacksmith tool to extract the selected finger bone from the box. He dug the tool deep into the reliquary box and emerged with a small, frail, discoloured bone. His hands began to shake more than usual as he started to quote the rite from memory.

"In nomine Patris, et Filii, et Spiritus Sancti ..."

At that moment, his sweat-filled palms made the tool slip from his grip, which caused the tool and the bone to spring free from Odo's hands into the air above the table. Time seemed to stand still as Odo's near-perfect eyesight allowed him to lock his gaze on the falling bone fragment, ignoring the tool. The urgent

need to prevent the bone from touching the unholy ground over-
came his fear of touching the holy object itself, forcing him to
reach out and catch the bone in his bare right hand. As the bone
rested in his palm, the relief of saving the object moved to fear
that his mortal soul was more unholy than the ground ever was.

Odo let out a groan as he held on, falling back from the table
onto the ground, clutching the bone close to his chest. With his
head suffering a significant impact, he lost consciousness, and
his mind shifted into a dreamlike state. Odo's vision launched
him soaring through the clouds far above Normandy and across
the channel. Fierce waves crashed beneath his flight as he flew
towards the English coastline's dramatic and unmistakable
sheer-white cliffs. Across a patchwork of bleak farmlands and
frostbitten villages until landing in the dark town of London.
Odo found himself in a courtyard of stone, surrounded by a sea
of hundreds of men, women, children, and all ranks of church
clergy. He could see novice monks, archbishops, and popes,
all looking up at the towers of London's immense new Saint
Peter's Abbey on Thorney Island. The doors of the abbey flung
open, and everyone fell to their knees. Light beamed through
the entry and flooded the courtyard as though the sun had
just appeared through the clouds. A vision of Christ himself
stood at the doors in a simple but glistening white robe and
gold sandals. Suddenly a young girl appeared and stood beside
him, taking his hand with a smile on her face that could only
be described as happiness from another world. Odo recognised
the girl from the visions he had experienced. It was Foy.

The beaming figures of Christ and Foy proceeded through
the doors into the multitude of people in the courtyard. Kneeling, Odo needed to hide his face on the ground as the light became blinding and painful to his eyes. Moments later, he could
hear the footsteps of the two walking past where Odo knelt,

Christ's simple sandals and the skipping of the happy child gently scraping on the cobblestones. The intensity of the light subsided, and Odo was able to unfold from his humble state and look around. He noticed that the people in the courtyard were no longer worshipers but vile evil creatures. They were no longer interested in the figures of Christ and Foy who were walking off into the distance; instead, all their attention was on Odo, speaking of his past and present sins, reminding him of his unworthiness.

"Lies. Greed. Adultery. Theft. Oppressor of the innocent. Murderer," they whispered, causing Odo to cover his ears and shriek in guilt and sorrow.

In desperation, he turned again towards the figures of Christ and Foy, who he could still see in the distance, surrounded by light and unaffected by the dark that covered Odo. He watched on as Foy released her hold of Christ's hand and continued to skip joyfully into the rolling hills of England, lighting up people, villages, and nature from their former dark and wintery state as she went.

Christ then turned his countenance towards Odo, who was still tormented by the dark creatures surrounding him. Fear gripped Odo's entire being, but he could not look away. Christ's expression was that of grace and acceptance, but his eyes felt as though they were piercing Odo's chest like a sword. He fell on his back to the courtyard's cobblestones with a painful scream, clutching at the pain in his chest.

Suddenly Odo found himself awake, lying on the ground in the bishop's tent, still clutching at the finger bone fragment.

CHAPTER 59

STAMFORD BRIDGE, YORK

Tostig and the Norse translator rode their horses behind Hardrada and his guard of fifty or more Norse warriors. They were riding horses provided by the York garrison. Morcar rode alongside Hardrada. His hands were bound, and he was still covered in mud and blood. His humble and defeated posture slumped over his leather saddle.

"From the few Norse language words I have learnt," enquired Tostig to the Norse translator, "I noticed that Hardrada only ordered five hundred men to follow us towards Stamford Bridge, leaving behind most of his men. Surely, more will come than those five hundred?"

"He also told them only to take weapons, to leave behind the heavy war armour," smiled the interpreter.

"I don't understand. That is a risky move. I know we're only going to Stamford to pick up the rest of Morcar's men and some prisoners, but what if the Stamford garrison is more than the five hundred Morcar promised, and they launch an attack?"

The Norse translator gave a hearty laugh. "Do you know which rank our king ordered for this march east?"

"No, and why would it matter?"

"You have probably never heard the name of this particular Norse soldier. Berserkers. Hardrada ordered those five hundred berserkers to follow us to Stamford Bridge," said the Norseman.

"Berserkers? Whatever they are, five hundred men are still just five hundred men, regardless of the rank or name you give them. And they're on foot. There's only fifty of us on mounts," responded Tostig as he continued to ride along.

"You English know nothing of the ways of the Norse," responded the translator. "A berserker is not one man; he is like five of your English hired men. He is like ... half-wolf, half-man. Trained from childhood and raised like hermits, they are rarely seen under the command of a king. They are usually seen fighting on their own, like a one-man army for a family against raiders. But they have come together and flocked to Hardrada because he is like one of them. Hardrada fights like a berserker, only much stronger."

Tostig shook his head as the Norse translator continued to laugh at his ignorance.

"You better tell Hardrada that Stamford is just over that hill. Morcar is probably trying to tell them now, without much success."

The translator rode ahead of Tostig and caught up with Hardrada and his men to find Morcar trying to communicate to the Norsemen, just as Tostig predicted. The translator cleared up the confusion and relayed Morcar's message about Stamford Bridge.

Hardrada acknowledged by speeding ahead of the group, causing the remainder to pick up their pace and follow their liege as he headed up the muddy hill to a crest that overlooked vast lush green pastures leading towards the impressive Stamford Bridge. An immense timber structure wider than any other bridge north of Nottingham. It spanned the broad and rapidly flowing River Derwent and was the gateway to the village on the other side.

Hardrada took some time to inspect the view toward the bridge, moving his horse back and forth. His aspect was limited; the path on the other side of the bridge leading to the village was still too far to see. He ordered his men to follow his lead to the bridge.

As the group slowed their ride to a canter and followed, Tostig's curiosity caused him to look back to see the five hundred berserkers approaching on foot in the distance, roughly two miles behind them.

One of Hardrada's guards began raising concerns in Norse, which sparked further discussion amongst the other riders as they approached. The bridge was still two hundred yards away. The Norse conversation ended with one rider breaking away, galloping at speed toward the bridge.

"What's going on?" enquired Tostig of the translator.

"One of the men, who can see further than the rest of us, noticed some movement on the riverbank across the bridge. No one believed him, so he went to see."

Moments later, the Norse warrior returned from the direction of the bridge, yelling with a clear tone of alarm.

"Du sa fem hundre," roared Hardrada at Morcar.

"King Hardrada has asked why you said only five hundred men were garrisoned here?" relayed the translator to Morcar.

"There are only five hundred here, I swear it," Morcar responded as they continued to canter towards the structure.

"Then what is that over there, across?" The translator pointed to the village across the river where the roar of thousands of English soldiers echoed.

"It looks like three to five thousand soldiers, Morcar. This is not what you said."

Hardrada himself rode over to Morcar's horse and raised his axe with a deafening roar.

"I swear I know nothing of this," Morcar cried. "It is likely Tostig's brother, Harold. God knows how he made it this far north so fast."

"He's right." Tostig stared across at the sea of men and steel reflecting the sunlight from the river. Hardrada lowered his axe as the translator relayed Morcar and Tostig's words.

"I can see Harold's standards raised at the rear," continued Tostig, "and I know how he forms his ranks. I'd recognise this anywhere, exactly what I feared. It's Harold. Tell Hardrada that we should fall back to Riccall and gather the full strength. We will not win here, but we have a chance back towards York."

As the translator finished relating Tostig's words in the Norse tongue, Hardrada started moving his horse around and looking at the terrain and the bridge before them. He then turned his horse back towards the west to see the five hundred berserkers approaching on foot, now less than half a mile away.

"Bind Morcar til det treet," Hardrada ordered one of his men. The solider duly dismounted before tearing Morcar off his horse and binding him to a nearby tree.

Hardrada then turned to the rest of his guard and announced his plan, which included one-word Tostig could identify. Berserker.

Tostig turned to look at the Norse translator with concern, expecting a translation.

"Are we retreating to Riccall?" Tostig asked.

"No."

"Tilian, it looks like we've shocked them. They're heading back," announced Harold Godwinson, yelling over the near-deafening noise of his enthusiastic four thousand-strong English army. Who were, at this stage, chanting a traditional English response to invaders. The old Saxon term for 'out'.

"OOT. OOT. OOT. OOT. OOT. OOT. OOT. OOT."

"You're right, my liege," yelled Tilian. "Although I believe we should hold fast rather than give chase. They'll be back, but we're yet to see how many they'll return with."

"Agreed," said Harold. "Even before we start, I'm proud of what we achieved here, Tilian. Following Caelin's information, the journey north as we gathered the fyrd was difficult for those on foot, forty miles a day. And the effort of the garrison at Selby to leave their post and meet us."

"It's been a significant feat, my liege. I'll make sure the men know how the king feels about their efforts," responded Tilian, who was also beaming with pride.

"I'll tell them myself," announced Harold as he kicked the side of his horse and proceeded to ride around the ranks. The men cheered as they saw their king ride. The easily recognisable king and his horse were adorned in flowing royal red material. Harold's head was covered with a crowned battle helmet. His breastplate and other armour pieces were mirror-like, reflecting the afternoon sun. He trotted his well-trained horse in front of the rank and held his sword high into the air, sparking an eruption of noise: the roar of men bent on the protection of their lands, the smashing of swords and axes against steal-centred shields.

"Men of England. Men of England," bellowed Harold with a raised sword as the roar settled. "Hear me. Today you are not the fyrd; you are not huscarls, thanes or noblemen. Nor are you Northumbrians, Mercians or East Anglians. Today, you are all protectors of our kingdom. The Norse invaders have smashed our eastern shores long enough. Today, we send them home in their longboats with one memory. That England is, and always will be, Saxon!"

The roar and clanking of metal immediately resumed, louder than before, and as the chants of "OOT" also recommenced, Harold locked eyes with the captain of the Selby garrison and gave the nod.

Harold stared off into the distance, where the Northumbrian landscape met the afternoon sky, and for the first time since his humbling and tragic voyage to Normandy, he felt confidence and pride burning in his breast. But as he turned to his position, he noticed something; a person staring at him in the distance. A lone figure, standing in a pasture. A hooded monk.

Not these crazy visions again. Not now. I'm past this torment, surely, Harold thought.

He turned back to his men, waving and keeping up their spirits, but as he turned back to the pasture, the monk was gone.

"Why are we not falling back to Riccall? This is suicide," shouted Tostig to the Norse translator as they galloped toward the approaching troop of berserkers.

"Your counsel is no longer needed today, Tostig," the translator informed him. "Hardrada thought your suggestion was … cowardly. We will fall behind the berserkers, and they will take the bridge. Follow my lead and do not break rank. I will bear the Raven Banner, so you should see where I am. Remember, King Hardrada will not hesitate to order your death if you disappoint him again, and I will not protect you."

Tostig and the fifty Norse riders arrived at the approaching group of five hundred berserkers and followed behind. Tostig found himself staring with eyes wide open as he rode around them. They were all enormously built men, wielding various designs of single and double-handed battleaxes. Some with simple, poor clothing while others wore wild animal fur draped over their muscular shoulders.

"Løpe. Skjold veggen broen," roared Hardrada at his men, ordering the berserkers to pick up the pace and shield-wall the bridge. The berserkers roared in response and immediately picked up speed, with the mounted Norsemen cantering in a line behind them.

"Here they come, Tilian," announced Harold. "Roughly five or six hundred, it seems. For now. Prepare archers."

"Archers!" Tilian shouted, prompting the archer standard to be raised.

"When they are ten yards from the approach to the bridge, unleash three torrents," commanded Harold.

"Very good, my liege."

"Holde. Berserkers fortsetter," yelled Hardrada, ordering his mounted personal guard to hold position one hundred yards from the bridge to allow the berserkers to proceed forward.

The berserkers slowed their run to a jog as they approached the bridge, which allowed them to move closer together into a square formation.

As Tostig watched on with intense curiosity, Hardrada

roared out another command to his warriors, loud enough to be heard by the English.

"Skjermskjold!"

The berserkers began using their shields to protect above the sides of the square formation. When the square form was complete, it was as though an enormous shield-covered box was approaching the bridge, with the leading side wide enough to block the width of the bridge entrance.

"Archers! Fire!"

Eight hundred skilled longbow archers launched their first volley into the afternoon sky. The sing of the bows and the ensuing whistle of the arrows could be heard by the Norse on the other side of the River Derwent.

As the barrage of arrows fell on the Norse shield box, only several arrows found their way through gaps in the shield wall, injuring several, slaughtering a couple.

"Archers! Fire!"

"Tilian. After the third volley, pull the archers back and send in the frontline ranks of the fyrd to break their line," commanded Harold as he watched the Norse line at the foot of the bridge, impressed by their tactics and disappointed by the archers' effectiveness.

"Yes, my liege. Archers! Fire!" responded Tilian.

As the third and final barrage of arrows landed, with only several Norsemen slain or too injured to stand, the berserker square formation remained unmoved. The silence that followed was enough to hear the gentle sounds of the River Derwent below the Norsemen's feet. The Norse shields and the timber bridge in front of them were covered with English arrows.

"Fyrd one!" commanded Tilian.

Three hundred sword-wielding fyrd soldiers charged towards the bridge as the berserker shield formation began to transform. Shields that once covered the heads of the Norsemen were dropped and moved to the front line. The box changed to a flatter formation to prevent English soldiers from breaking their line at the corners of the bridge.

As the initial frontline fyrd soldiers collided with the Norse shields, long spears protruded through the gaps, pushed by berserkers two lines back, quickly penetrating the fyrd's flimsy leather and material armour, slaughtering dozens in the initial blow. The fyrd who managed to avoid the spears were swiftly dealt with, their weak swords brushed away or shattered under the weight of superior berserker weaponry. Line after line of fyrd attacks were swiftly cut down and massacred by an unbreakable sequence of shields, thrusting spears and swinging berserker axes.

Almost half of the initial attack, three hundred soldiers, were slaughtered by the Norse line within moments.

"Pull back! Pull back!" ordered Tilian, as half of the fyrd rank who managed to survive the Norse line turned away. "Archers! Fire!"

At the sound of the arrow volley, the Norse immediately moved back into the box formation, again limiting the effectiveness of the archers.

"You see, Tostig? Five hundred berserkers are not the same as five hundred hired men," laughed the Norse translator.

Tostig's eyes had never seen such a finely tuned defence tactic executed so effectively in battle. He turned to Hardrada, and for the first time since Tostig began his journey, he noticed Hardrada branding a slight expression of enjoyment and pride as he watched his berserkers.

Harold's confidence was beginning to wane as the cries of the injured and dying fyrd soldiers on the bridge could be heard from his position.

"I've heard about these Norse tactics, Harold," said Tilian. "In Northumbria, we've suffered Viking raids on monasteries of late, but some monasteries were more prepared with archers and fire. So, over time the Norse developed this method of defence. Impressive; it requires a powerful attack to break. Especially considering the bridge, which is limiting."

"We could wait it out and see how long they want to hold the bridge. Once they're away, we should be able to flank them," suggested Harold.

"We need to move them ourselves. Push them back. Split them, divide them. Then a full attack," suggested Tilian.

"Send in a rank of huscarls, then back it up with another rank of the fyrd."

"Axes one!" yelled Tilian.

Three hundred single- and double-handed axe-wielding huscarl professional soldiers, with heavy armour, moved forward in formation before picking up pace and noise towards the bridge.

"Fyrd two! In position!"

Two hundred of the fyrd ranks moved forward, waiting for the final order to attack.

Unexpectedly, while huscarl soldiers were charging the bridge, the berserker front three lines confidently emerged from box formation to confront the attack with the clear intent for one-on-one skirmish.

The two forces collided with a brutal clash of metal and blood. It was clear that most English attackers were no match for the brute strength of the berserkers and their superior steel, which sliced through attacks and armour with ease. A handful of English soldiers were a challenge for the frontline berserkers, and despite their smaller axes, were disposing of several berserkers. Taking advantage of their minimal armour, they removed limbs with pinpoint accuracy before ending lives with a final blow.

The berserkers holding the bridge behind the attack line began slowly stamping their feet rhythmically on the timber bridge and mumbling a chant, which became louder and louder.

"Sjef skål. Sjef skål. Sjef skål. SJEF SKÅL! SJEF SKÅL! SJEF SKÅL!"

The frontline berserkers who we not injured or slain in the skirmish pulled back to disappear behind the shield wall, leaving the English confused and without a fight—again, staring at a strong wall of raven-bannered shields.

The Norse chants continued as three of the berserker men shifted their shields aside. Moments later, from the back of the berserker formation, a single warrior bent over as he made his way through the opening in the shield wall. Once he passed the shields, he stood, and it was clear to the English that this was the largest and strongest of the berserker rank. The very sight of this monster caused many of the English men on the bridge to take a step back. He stood more than seven feet tall and, without doubt, displayed more strength than anyone on the battlefield. Though there was little more than wild animal fur covering his bulging muscular body, his intimidating double-handed and double-edged axe was almost double the size and weight of any other axe seen.

The inspiring chant continued behind this chief berserker, beckoning him to slaughter all who stood in his way. He slowly stepped forward, raised the back of his right hand at the English before, and waved them toward himself, gesturing that they attack with all they have.

Immediately, five of the larger huscarls, strong axe-wielding English soldiers, advanced, flanking the berserker, whose initial swing opened the bellies of two, followed by the raising of his right foot, which sent another off the bridge entirely and into the river below.

———————

Harold watched on in awe of this enormous secret weapon of the Norse army as Tilian released the final fyrd rank, which was to be followed by another wave of huscarl axe wielders.

"Fyrd two! Axes two, follow!"

For a moment, Harold turned away from the battle and back towards the open field in the north, where he saw the lone monk earlier. The monk was not to be seen on the field, but as Harold spanned the area further, he spotted the hooded monk again, though he had moved to the riverbank upstream from the bridge.

Despite the battle that continued to rage, Harold curiously watched the monk as he stepped into what looked to be a small timber boat and pushed himself out into the river's flow, drifting toward the bridge. The monk then bent down, which made the boat seem empty or inconsequential.

Harold moved his horse a little to gain a clear view of the monk in the boat, moving at speed along with the current, almost reaching the bridge.

Harold trotted back to where Tilian was, following the boat's journey meticulously with his gaze, down the River Derwent.

"Are you all right, my liege?" enquired Tilian.

"That small boat on the river, do you see it?" asked Harold.

"The one that has just drifted under the bridge?"

"Yes, that was the one. So, I wasn't dreaming. I believe it has someone in it."

Tilian and Harold watched the seemingly empty boat emerge from the other side of the bridge and continue to float down the Derwent.

───────

The chief berserker, who continued his slaughter on the bridge, carried few injuries while dozens of brave but lifeless English soldiers lay around him. However, the bridge made it difficult to wage an effective attack.

Suddenly, the enormous chief berserker dropped his heavy axe and roared out in pain as blood sprayed from his lower leg and groin. The calf muscle of the Norse warrior was almost completely removed from the leg, held on by only a few threads of flesh. More blood was flowing from a separate and more damaging groin puncture, which could have only come from a sword. For a moment, the English soldiers were seen stepping back in shock, amazed as to how it had happened. But before the English could think of capitalising on the injury by mounting a final blow, a hooded figure emerged from the side of the bridge. He was dressed in the long dark habit of an ordinary monk and wielding a double-edged sword covered in blood, evidently from the blow he launched from beneath the bridge, through a gap in the timber.

The hooded monk moved to face the injured and unarmed berserker, who, while in immense pain, reached for his axe and swung. The monk almost casually stepped aside to evade the attack, and the axe thudded deep into the timber. The monk quickly shuffled behind the Norseman to deliver a decisive slice of his sword across the giant's back, which sent him crashing down on the timber.

The monk struck another blow to the berserker with his sword, which removed the head in full view of an increasingly shocked and furious berserker army, eager to attack but holding the line.

As he stood over the bloody body of his assailant, the monk turned towards the English, removed his hood to reveal his recognisable face, and shouted, "FOR THE KING!"

Tilian followed the scene by ordering all ranks to attack.

"ALL RANKS! FULL ATTACK!"

This released a wave of more than two thousand inspired English troops toward a fractured Norse rank holding the bridge.

Shocked and overwhelmed, Harold immediately recognised his dear friend Caelin, who was closer and more loyal than a brother ever was to him. Like many times since the night he heard the news of the alleged betrayal, he wanted to reach out and embrace him, thank him, restore the friendship. But now, all he could do was watch on and be grateful for Caelin's gesture and be in awe of his tactical mastery, which had allowed the English to break the line.

Harold and Tilian watched on as the sheer number of his troops mounted enough weight to break the berserker line and push the battle to the other side of the river. Amongst the chaos, Caelin was no longer visible.

<hr />

Hardrada began discussing options with his guard. Three dispatched to send word to the west back to the camp at Riccall to advance immediately. But as Tostig watched the rider disappear into the distance, he knew that the Riccall strength would arrive too late.

As the battle raged on just one hundred yards away, Hardrada moved his horse back and forth in front of his fifty strong personal guard, yelling Norse obscenities in response to their counsel, which on this occasion he found to be useless. He then turned to Tostig with a face of unmistakable rage and spoke.

The Norse translator moved in to join the conversation. "The king said that you have been useless so far, Tostig. Maybe now is the time for your counsel."

"I gave my counsel before," shouted Tostig in frustration as the translator began to relate. "We needed to fall back to Riccall two hours ago. But you considered it cowardly. Now that option is useless. I say we pick up the Raven Banner and charge. Now. Make it through the English line and pursue Harold himself."

As Hardrada heard the translation, he gave a simple nod and turned to his men.

<hr />

"Harold, look," called Tilian. "The riders we first saw, they're heading back into the fray."

"You're right. The huscarls will see it coming. They have a reliable method for charging mounts."

"Is that Tostig amongst the riders?"

"Yes, I believe you're right. Let's head down towards the bridge."

"I don't think that is a good idea, my liege. If they managed to break the line, they'll head straight for you," suggested Tilian.

"They won't, Tilian."

As they slowly trotted down toward the bridge, it was becoming clear to Tilian that the huscarls were more than capable of matching the Norse mounted charge, swinging their double-handed axes in a circular downward motion, slicing through horse and rider with a single blow.

Harold kept his eyes on Hardrada and Tostig, and it wasn't long before both their horses were cut down. Hardrada picked himself and his axe up off the ground and instantly launched into a berserker combat style, aiming to inflict maximum pain on enemies rather than a quick death.

After defeating several English soldiers, Hardrada received a surprise arrow in the throat which stopped him instantly, causing the English to inflict several final wounds on the Norwegian king before he dropped face down to the earth.

Tostig and several Norsemen were fighting against some Northumbrian soldiers, who recognised him and became more inspired to be his end. While desperately fighting off the bloodthirsty Northumbrians, Tostig turned and spotted his brother, Harold, on the other side of the bridge. Their eye contact only lasted a few seconds but seemed like a lifetime.

Tostig was filled with anger fuelled by the pain of his

brother's betrayal, while Harold felt a deep sense of grief and personal remorse for what was about to occur. His wayward brother would not be saved and was about to be lost forever.

Tostig noticed in the corner of his eye that the Raven Banner had fallen, along with the Norse translator who lay dead beside it. He immediately dropped his sword, picked up the flag and headed in Harold's direction, keeping eye contact and roaring out his last word.

"TRAITOR!"

A moment later, Tostig received a slash across his back and a sword thrust through his chest from behind.

Harold slowly closed his eyes and dropped his head.

CHAPTER 60

THE MOUTH OF THE RIVER SOMME, NORMANDY

A gusty south wind filled sails, lifting spirits and effectively pushing the Norman fleet of five hundred heavily laden longboats north away from the Frankish shore. Boats littered the coast in and around the Port of Saint Valery after a failed attempt to launch from the mouth of the River Dives several days prior when the southerly was not strong enough.

Finally, Duke William's heart lifted as he stood on the bow of his boat, *The Mora*, and led the fleet north. *The Mora* moved faster through the swelling seas as they pushed out, as it only carried the Duke's provisions and horses, so it was much lighter than the main fleet of boats.

CHAPTER 61

YORK MINSTER, NORTHUMBRIA

With a burst through the elaborate timber doors, Harold entered the enormous stone abbey of York Minster. The Yorkshire winds blew his robe around amongst scattered leaves as he entered. He was followed by his two brothers on either side, Gyrd and Leofwine. The three Godwinson brothers were visibly exhausted and mournful. None looked up or spoke as they approached Tostig's casket, which was laid before the altar. The three Godwinsons stood around their fallen brother and bowed their heads. After a moment, Gyrd and Leofwine moved to the timber pews, leaving Harold staring at the casket alone.

The York weather outside made the abbey dark, despite the hundreds of candles that lined the long nave. The darkness was apt for Harold; it reflected his feelings of grief and failure to protect his brother, protect him from himself.

Standing behind the altar was Aldred, Archbishop of York, dressed in full episcopal robes and mitre. Morcar and several

Northumbrian thanes were standing in the timber pews with Harold's brothers.

Tilian, who after the victorious battle at Stamford Bridge was promoted to Harold's Chief Royal Guard and Thane, remained at the back of the abbey.

Harold stood unmoved beside Tostig's casket, staring down at the timber as though he was waiting for something, waiting for clarity, or waiting for the shock to subside. The elderly and somewhat unstable Archbishop Aldred waited patiently behind the altar, unwilling to hurry Harold, let alone commence the funeral liturgy until the king was done.

Harold knelt on the cold stone floor and, with evident grief, gently moved his clenched fist from his forehead to the top of Tostig's casket.

"Why? Why did you do this, you fool? You bloody fool!" Harold yelled as his head remained bowed, and his cries echoed off the stone walls.

A moment later, he quickly turned to his two younger brothers with tears dripping from his eyes.

"You two! Swear it! Swear to me now that you will never repeat this, that you will never do this to me. Swear!" Harold ordered.

Both brothers were shocked at the outburst but placed their fists on their hearts and nodded in Harold's direction nonetheless.

In an attempt to calm himself of the rage burning in his chest, Harold dropped his head and slowly placed his open hands on the casket, letting out an audible sigh. He then turned to Aldred. "Commence the rite. Pray for his soul."

Aldred was stunned by the somewhat spiritual request and commenced the liturgy immediately as Harold rose from his knees and proceeded down the nave towards the door, leaving the others in the pews. Tilian, who knew Harold would not stay, opened the door for his liege.

"Tilian. Prepare the troops. We ride south at dawn."

"Yes, my king."

CHAPTER 62

VILLAGE OF RICCALL, TEN MILES SOUTH OF YORK

There wasn't much left of the Riccall camp after Harold's army swept through it following Stamford Bridge. The remnants of the Norse army spared by Harold were given access to the body of their king and safe passage so long as they left England immediately.

Efforts were underway to commence the long journey north, home. Provisions were being loaded onto boats, and everyone paused their work without a word as Hardrada's body too was brought onboard. The rough timber funerary box was a poor reflection of the honour the Norse king would receive at his burial in Tonsberg.

Hours later, many villagers watched from the riverbank as twenty-four ships sailed east towards the coast, leaving behind over two hundred empty vessels. The timber would be useful for years to come.

CHAPTER 63

PEVENSEY, SOUTH COAST, ENGLAND

As William's fleet approached the daunting white cliffs of the English south coast, they diverted east until they found harbour near the village of Pevensey. Though Count Eustace and many of the knights were suspicious of how easily they were able to approach and land on the coast, William was full of confidence.

As the beach was so vast, dozens of longboats at a time were able to unload their men, horses, battle supplies and provisions. William stood onshore where the lush green grass met the white sand. He was enjoying the burst of activity; his fleet had now overrun the entire length of the once-peaceful beach.

"My liege." Rufus of Brittany was returning from a scout of the area.

"Yes, Rufus, what have you found?"

"There seems to be an old stone Roman castle in the middle of a village just over that hill. But it is empty. We approached with caution, expecting it to be some sort of surprise attack by the English, but nothing. We sent scouts, and there are no reports of English troops within the vicinity, only civilians. We managed to get some of the villagers to talk. They said that Harold's army was here two weeks ago but have left."

"Perhaps the delay waiting for the southerly winds has worked in our favour, Rufus," responded William. "Set up timber forts on the grounds of the old Roman site. Then send men to the surrounding villages to stock up on food, horses and horse supplies. We need provisions fast; we need to take advantage of this lack of pressure from the English. Burn whatever we can't take. Go!"

Rufus bowed and turned toward the village.

"Rufus, one more thing. Send some men to locate the road that heads north to London. It should be an old road with either Saxon or Roman markings. The land behind this village is a swamp, so we may need to head northeast."

Rufus bowed again and rushed off toward the production line of Frankish soldiers carrying provisions to the village of Pevensey.

William turned his attention to one of the boats to see Bishop Odo struggling with a crate as he disembarked. Instead of simply stepping off the boat onto the sand, the crate caused him to lose balance and fall fully immersed in the shallow water.

William laughed as he watched one of Odo's aides rush to assist the soaked bishop, his wet episcopal robes barely covering his shame as he emerged from the water.

CHAPTER 64

THORNEY ISLAND, LONDON

Harold emerged through the large double timber doors that were opened for him, into the Great Hall on Thorney Island, where the members of the Witan Council were waiting. As he entered the hall and took his seat, council members bowed their heads in his direction while they remained standing. In attendance stood Harold's brothers Gyrd and Leofwine, along with Morcar, Archbishop Stigand, Tilian and three other royal Wessex thanes.

"Gentlemen. We showed our mettle at Stamford Bridge. We were victorious and managed to finish off their broken ranks further at Riccall ... wait, where is Aldred?" asked Harold.

"Archbishop Aldred was taken ill just after you saw him in York, my king," responded Stigand, Archbishop of Canterbury.

"I see."

"But he has requested that someone take his seat at the council, for this one occasion," continued Stigand.

"Witan council members do not send delegates, Stigand. Nor

have they ever done so in the history of this court," responded Harold.

"But, are they permitted to, my king? Aldred has not merely asked that someone come and stand amongst us because of his absence. He believes his delegate has counsel for the king. I understand you hold Aldred in high esteem. He has asked that you consider his request. May I send for Aldred's delegate?"

"Very well, Stigand."

Archbishop Stigand turned and motioned to a royal attendant who stood between two royal guards at the door.

A moment later, Abbot Edwin entered the hall. Upon reaching the circle of council members, he bowed in Harold's direction.

"Edward's abbot? From the monastery across the courtyard? Is this some sort of a joke, Stigand?" laughed Harold.

"I asked the same question, my king, but this is no joke. Archbishop Aldred has asked that we accept Abbot Edwin as we would Aldred himself. Just this once," responded Archbishop Stigand.

Harold rubbed his head and let out a sigh of confusion. "Granted. Shall we move on?"

"Brother, we have confirmed accounts from the southern shires. William has landed at the harbour Pevensey. Burning and plundering the local villages," announced Gyrd.

"Harold, didn't you release the fyrd as you headed south from York? Perhaps you should have retained them for the south defensive," Morcar suggested with a smile.

In fierce anger, Harold launched to his feet and headed to face Morcar. "Morcar, I should have left you where I found you in Stamford, covered in mud and tied to a tree. While you were cowering to Hardrada's every demand, I was busy leading my men and yours to one of the greatest victories this kingdom has ever seen. So, don't you dare come in here and question the king's decisions on the fyrd or anything else."

Harold's raised voice echoed off the stone walls to the timber arches above.

"Gyrd. Do we know if he is heading north, or is he biding his time again?" asked Harold as he returned to his seat.

"From what we've been told, brother, it seems he's looking for provisions and an easier road north. The land around the village of Pevensey is a marshy swamp. Not ideal for moving a large army and horses."

"Horses?" asked Harold.

"There were accounts of seeing plenty of destrier warhorses, maybe five thousand or more," replied Gyrd.

The news drew a shocked response from everyone in the room.

"Five thousand destriers?" asked Harold.

"The fleet was enormous, brother. Maybe five hundred purpose-built longboats," responded Leofwine. "Gyrd and I had scouts along the coast, and their reports line up. This is a serious challenge."

"Your brothers are right, Harold. But there is something else," Abbot Edwin announced.

"This is more of a military concern, Abbot. I'm not sure what advice you can offer here."

"Have you had strange dreams lately, Harold? Or perhaps inexplicable visions since you returned from your time in Normandy?" asked Abbot Edwin.

"What would that have to do with this, Edwin?"

"Because the saintly relics over which you took an oath with the Normans was no ordinary village church reliquary containing nothing but pig bones. It was Saint Foy of Agen."

"The council knows about this, Abbot," said Harold impatiently.

"But there's more to it, Harold. This relic has become one of the most notoriously powerful but potentially troublesome pieces of western church mysticism in recent history. Those who encounter Foy's relics are often tormented with dreams, visions. Some can be led to madness. You've been seeing visions, have you not? Harold?"

Harold was alarmed by Edwin's foresight. His eyes were wide while Edwin's face of calm and confidence stared him down.

"Archbishop Aldred sent me here to ask you this question," continued Edwin. "He thought I could shed some light on what it could mean. I know you and I have not seen eye to eye over recent years, but let me help you, Harold."

"This is madness," dismissed Harold, trying to deflect the notion.

"It'll only get worse for you, Harold. These visions will increase now that she is here."

"Who's here?" asked Harold.

"His Holiness permitted the Normans to carry the relics of Saint Foy here, to lead them into battle, and the Normans are on this land with the relics of Saint Foy, now. Duke William was right to trust this power. She will be your undoing," declared Edwin.

"How is it possible that seven-hundred-year-old bones from Agen will be my undoing, Edwin?" laughed Harold.

"They are not mere bones, Harold. The bones of holy martyrs are like a window into heaven. You may have sworn the oath under duress, but you did encounter the relics, and now your fate is in her hands, God's hands. Now, tell me about these visions," demanded Abbot Edwin, as his voice echoed off the walls, leaving those around in shock.

Harold slumped back in his chair and gave a wry smile. "I'm impressed, Edwin. I've never seen you so ... assertive. As for the visions. Yes, I've seen a recurring appearance of a lone hooded monk. Always off in the distance, following me as I travel. Appearing and disappearing. However, once in a dream, this monk grew to the height of twenty men and attacked me. He said his name was Caprasius or Caprais. Something like that. There, now you have it. What does it mean, oh wise Oracle?"

"Caprasius was the young Foy's priest, maybe her bishop. He was also martyred in Agen a few hours after Foy. It seems these two saints have you and England insight," declared Edwin.

"But for what? Why don't these saints strike me down and be done with it?" asked Harold with a tone of mockery.

"Duke William may be setting out to conquer England, but these two saints have a different conquest. It's you, Harold. But God is not after your life, though he is after your contrition. Your faith. Your ... humility."

"I tell you, this is madness," mumbled Harold as he turned his tired eyes to the windows.

"There is something else. If you head south and attack the Normans while they have Foy, you will be defeated and likely die. But if you head north, allowing the Normans to take London, you will have the opportunity to face William on fair terms," suggested Edwin.

"Fair terms?"

"Because the Normans will not take Foy's relics north of London. The Pope did not permit it. Foy's relics will be rendered powerless north of the city—"

"Good King, this is something we should consider," interrupted Tilian as Harold rubbed his bearded chin, considering the idea. "The fyrd numbers we had at Stamford were grand but still not the full representation. If we head north and gather the full strength, it could be twenty to thirty thousand. But if we head south now to meet William, I estimate we will have less than we had at Stamford. The men were victorious, but they're tired, battered and bruised."

"Thank you, Tilian. Abbot Edwin, what does your plan have to do with my contrition or penitence to God?"

"God is more interested in getting your attention than just giving you victory. If you accept this plan, it'll be your first step towards … faith. Faith in God's strength, not your own."

"I understand, and I thank you for your time, Abbot," responded Harold. "But you must understand that the state of my faith has nothing to do with how I rule this kingdom. Right now, there is a Norman army laying waste to my villages, my people. Running for the hills and allowing William free passage to London, scorching as he goes, is not my way. It is not the Saxon way. We will meet the Normans head-on. William may still be expecting further reinforcements from Normandy, so we must strike now. Edwin, you will witness the Normans and their box of bones fleeing back across the channel, just as the Norsemen did."

Abbot Edwin closed his eyes and bowed his head.

"Men. We gather the ranks and head south in two days," Harold resolved. "I want at least three thousand huscarls and a new rank of fyrdsmen. If the Normans are in Pevensey, we'll head for Hastings to block their access north. Brothers, order the assembly at the ridge overlooking Senlach at Hastings. Morcar, establish a second line of defence here in London."

Across the courtyard from the hall where the Witan council was meeting, Caelin had managed to gain entry to King Harold's private quarters. Dressed as a monk and carrying a large woven basket containing habit cloth, Caelin moved into the room and closed the door behind him. He removed the material from the basket and gathered several items from the room; a set of royal robes, tunic, and a crowned battle helmet. Caelin knew that there were several versions of each item to be found at the royal armoury. As soon as the items were reported missing, they would be replaced within a breath.

With the basket now filled, Caelin covered the objects with the habit cloth, ensuring everything was sufficiently concealed before covering his head with his hood, picking up the basket and heading for the door. He stopped and turned back to see the pilgrim's medallion of Saint Edmund the Martyr still sitting on the table, where he had left it two weeks prior. He returned to the table, grabbed the medallion, buried it deep into the basket and headed for the door.

CHAPTER 65

HASTINGS, SOUTH COAST, ENGLAND

A common black raven landed on the point of a raised Wessex standard, providing it with an elevated view for potential morning prey. The Wyvern, the Gold Dragon of Wessex, flew in the wind beneath the raven's perch as it sat amid a sea of English soldiers unmoved on the brow of the hill. A sudden gust of wind caused the flag to flap, frightening the raven into flight. It picked up altitude as it circled the hillcrest before diving down the hill toward an opposing sea of soldiers and horses facing the English.

The Normans were given plenty of notice that Harold would block their journey north, past the unpassable swampland and the old Saxon road leading them to London.

Harold was also well informed of the Norman movements. He needed to move quickly to ensure his army would reach and secure their position at the crest of the hill with his lines of defence. Considering the mounted strength of the Normans, Harold knew their effectiveness would be dramatically reduced riding and attacking uphill.

Harold and his two brothers Gyrd and Leofwine, along with a dozen Wessex and East Anglian thanes, were on horseback behind the three thousand huscarl ranks. The front line reflected the morning sun toward the Normans with their intimidating shields. Behind them stood the rest of the huscarl ranks brandishing various battleaxes, swords, bows and long pike spears. Behind Harold and the thanes were the peasant soldiers of the fyrd. After the Stamford Bridge campaign, the hurried gathering of the fyrd left the thanes with only five thousand responding quick enough to meet the king's demands.

Down the hill, two hundred yards away, William was arrayed in full Norman livery, blessed battle armour, and proudly wearing the papal ring. He could see his flank captains, Rufus of Brittany and Count Eustace of Boulogne, to his right and left. Eustace's rank consisted of knights from the Flanders region, Rufus on the left flank, knights from Brittany. William, Rufus and Eustace were surrounded by at least one thousand mounted knights and three thousand foot soldiers and archers. William himself was accompanied by his own hand-selected Norman personal knights, who were also arrayed with steel. Many knights proudly held Norman standards with spear tips. Three knights at William's side were given the authorised papal standards.

With a nod from William and an acknowledgment from Rufus and Eustace, the Normans commenced their battle plan. Beginning with the archers moving from the rear to the front line.

"Shields," announced Harold to his brothers.

"Yes, I see it too, brother," responded Gyrd in haste before screaming, "Shields! Archers!"

This launched the English battle plan into action. All front-line ranks moved behind their own or the shield in front of them, while archers would shift into position immediately after the Norman volley of arrows had fallen. Harold and the fyrd remained out of range while the huscarl shields and archers braced for the volley of more than five hundred arrows.

"Au feu!" *Fire!* Ordered Rufus, Eustace and a knight by William's side, which sent a blinding view of arrows into the morning sky.

The sound of the volley landing on the wall of leather-covered timber shields was immediately followed by the screams of the English wounded by the arrows that found their way through gaps.

"Archers in position!" yelled Gyrd.

Rufus and Eustace moved their horses in front of their ranks and held their swords high in the air, which drew a roar of Norman fury from the entire ten thousand-strong invading force. As the noise continued, William himself took hold of a papal standard from one of his knights, moved his horse through the ranks and emerged from the front line in full view of Harold and the English. He then removed his battle helmet to show his face, imitating legends of the great Frankish king Charlemagne three hundred years before.

Holding the helmet at his side, he raised the blessed papal standard high towards the English army, screaming, "Ennemi de Dieu." *Enemy of God.*

The sight of their leader and the papal banner sent the Norman ranks into an even louder rage. Knights and infantry could be heard chanting "Serment menteur" over and over.

"Infanterie!" *Infantry!* Ordered Rufus, Eustace and a Norman knight near William as he moved back into the ranks.

———

"Can you hear that, Harold? They're chanting 'Oath breaker'," said Leofwine.

"No one makes a liar out of me, brother," said Harold. "Especially not a bastard Norman. Prepare shields. They're sending in a wave of foot soldiers, which I expect will be followed by a mounted charge. We need to hold the line, no matter what it takes."

Leofwine cried out the order across the ranks.

The English wall of immovable huscarl shields moved into place.

———

A few hundred of the initial Norman wave of foot soldiers marched forward ahead of their positions before starting to run, uphill toward the English line. Armed with shields and spears, their intent was to break the line and penetrate the shield wall while deflecting English archers.

"Archers ... Fire!" commanded Gyrd, launching a short-range volley of arrows from behind the huscarl front line toward the charging Norman infantry, reducing their numbers on the field before they clashed with the shields. Spears thrust from both sides as the weight of men pushed along the length of the wall. The dead and injured on the English side were pulled back behind the line by fellow soldiers to prevent the weakening of the wall. Norman soldiers thrust their spear attacks before falling under counterattack by the English.

"Première charge de chevalier," *First wave of the knight's charge*, commanded William to his knights as he could see his foot soldiers slowly diminishing beneath the English shields and spears.

William's knights' ensuing cry was instantly followed by orders from the right and left flank chiefs, Rufus and Eustace. A near impeccable line of two hundred heavily armoured Norman knights trotted their massive destrier warhorses into position. Their long spears pointed to the heavens, battle helmets reflecting the morning sun toward the English.

"Harold?" asked Gyrd.

"Yes, I see it, brother. This will test the frontline men. We've had nothing like this."

"Hold the line! Let nothing breakthrough! Archers in position!" yelled Gyrd.

The huscarls holding the shield line responded to Gyrd's order by commencing the old Saxon chant, which could be felt through the earth beneath the fyrdsmen behind their line.

"OOT! OOT! OOT! OOT! OOT! OOT!"

Harold turned to the five thousand fyrdsmen behind him as they joined in the chant of the huscarls. Amongst the fyrdsmen, Harold caught the eye of the Selby captain, who left their village defenceless so they could inform Harold of Tostig's movement to Stamford Bridge. Harold smiled, nodded and raised his clenched fist, which inspired the captain along with his men that surrounded him to hold their weapons in the air and roar in defiance of the challenge ahead of them.

Harold turned back to the view down the hill as the initial wave of mounted knights galloped fast up the grassy hill toward the English line. The expression on his face changed.

Fear brewed in Harold's stomach as the intimidating warhorses drew near the line. A few huscarl soldiers withdrew and fell back in fear as the knights were twenty yards away, causing the braver to cover the gaps with two shields.

The Norman attack fell heavily on the shield wall with a clash of metal and horses. Some knights successfully leapt their horses over the shield wall, which allowed them to attack several unprotected English huscarls from the height of their enormous destrier mounts before they, along with their horses, were taken down by English spears double-handed axes. The swinging tactics of the English axemen would often catch the Norman knights off guard, cutting through horse and rider in one movement. Though the initial mounted attack inflicted many more English casualties than the previous wave of infantry, the shield wall was unmoved.

In the hour that followed, William unleashed wave after wave of his triple formation strategy. Archers, followed by infantry and mounted knight attacks, though the tactics of the mounted attack changed to avoid the English axes. Instead, they drew close enough to launch spears before retiring downhill to prepare for another charge. But William's strategies were ineffective in breaking the English line and inflicting notable losses.

Harold's surprisingly effective defensive strategy alleviated fear and lifted his men's confidence as the battle progressed.

William watched on in frustration. *Very good, Harold,* he thought. The ride uphill was minimising the effectiveness of the Norman mounted attack upon the English defence. He needed a different approach, or his losses would start to add up.

"Rufus," he called. "It's time to distract the English on the left flank."

Rufus nodded at William's command before moving a line of his knights into position.

Eustace also moved a line of knights into position on the right flank, awaiting the order to proceed.

"Attaque!" yelled the flank chiefs in perfect unison, and their two separate lines drew closer to each other and the English line.

The Norman's left and right flanks of mounted knights slammed into the English shield wall once again. Eustace's knights covered the majority of the line's breadth. Rufus' attack kept to the English huscarl shield wall on the far left, allowing them to attack the line's end and the fyrdsmen behind.

"Reculer! Reculer!" yelled one of Rufus' higher-ranked knights, ordering the knights to retreat and head back down the hill immediately. But not toward the Norman position. They ran for cover in thick trees and shrubbery about one hundred yards to the west of the Norman ranks.

One group of fyrdsmen successfully dismounted and killed two of the knights who attacked the far-left flank. Upon seeing the retreating knights who were not returning to the Norman position, the young and inexperienced fyrdsmen were unable to resist the temptation to further their little victories.

The fyrdsmen broke rank.

Leaving their positions, around two hundred men bolted down the hill after their retreating foes, swords and axes raised above their heads.

"Hold your positions! Support the line!" yelled Gyrd and Leofwine as they noticed that the confidence of those who had broken rank was catching in other fyrd groups.

Amongst the confusion of attacking knights and fyrdsmen breaking rank, Harold turned to find the Selby captain and his men were not in their position.

"Brothers! Men of Wessex! With me," boomed Harold as he headed away from the English position and down the hill behind his charging fyrdsmen.

"Brother. This is not a good idea," yelled Gyrd as he motioned to his hundred or so Wessex thanes to follow, nonetheless.

William immediately sprang into action, kicking his horse and galloping in the direction of the left flank. Without needing orders, William's one hundred strong personal knights followed and surrounded their liege.

"We can't let these men be slaughtered. Those Normans are not retreating," yelled Harold to his brothers.

Gyrd looked back towards the English line, which no longer held a clean wall of defence. Ranks on the left and centre were carrying out their tactics without the direction of the Godwinson brothers.

In amongst the trees, Harold arrived aghast at a scene of Norman knights no longer fleeing in retreat but massacring the oncoming fyrdsmen with ease from the height of their horses.

Along with his brothers and the Wessex thanes, Harold immediately rode with swords drawn between the Normans and the vulnerable English fyrdsmen. Dozens of thanes and knights began combat, with King Harold himself in the fray. Harold's skilful swordsmanship, initially from horseback and then on foot as his horse was injured, swept aside Norman after Norman as they attacked. Moments later, Harold found himself fighting alongside the Selby captain.

"You disobeyed orders, Captain. You should have kept the line," berated Harold as he deflected a Norman spear before thrusting his sword into the knight's neck.

"My men were lured away by the false retreat, my liege. I only followed to protect my men. I'm sorry," responded the Selby captain, surprised but relieved to see his king.

"You mentioned at Selby that you have family in Riccall," recalled Harold as the two briefly made eye contact. "I came down here to protect you, brother. So, you better get back up that hill ... Now, soldier!"

The Selby captain walked backwards, staring at his king and in shock at what he had just heard and witnessed. His men were slaughtered, and he was honourably rescued by none other than the king. The captain followed his orders and moved away from the fight and up the hill towards the English defence.

"Stay alive!" yelled Harold as he and his men continued to fight off the knights.

―――――◦――――

A cry of "Le roi Harold est là" *King Harold is here* could be heard in the distance from the left flank, causing the entire Norman middle position of one thousand knights and foot soldiers to charge.

―――――◦――――

Except for the Selby captain, all the fyrdsmen who broke rank were slaughtered, leaving Harold and his outnumbered men losing the battle against the Normans. The English soldiers along the primary line of defence at the top of the hill were oblivious to their king's dangerous situation. They were unable to see through the thick foliage that surrounded him. Neither Harold and his men could see that William and the entire centre rank of knights and foot soldiers were approaching.

Though Harold's men were fighting bravely, they were falling one by one around Harold as the Normans fought ferociously, confident in their numbers, outweighing Harold's personal guard three to one.

A scuffle took place between four Normans and Harold's brothers, Gyrd and Leofwine. Harold could only watch while defending himself, seeing Gyrd slashed across his belly and Leofwine impaled with a Norman spear through the chest shortly after.

"Noooo!" yelled Harold as he, along with the dozen remaining thanes at his side, avenged his brothers by cutting down their assailants with fierce blows to their necks, which sprayed blood across Harold's face.

Harold turned to his next opponent, but before he could attack, an arrow whistled past his shoulder into the forehead of the Norman that stood before him.

Harold turned in the direction of the arrow to find a lone rider approaching arrayed in royal English robes and wearing one of Harold's battle helmets.

"Caelin!"

Caelin ignored Harold's call and fired a second arrow at another Norman nearby before riding past and out into the middle of the battlefield. He could see William and the Normans pursuing Harold's position on the left flank.

Caelin drew his sword and held it high, ensuring he would be the centre of attention for the Normans and the English. Raising his voice as loud as he could, his cry carried across the field. "William le bâtard. William le bâtard! Combattez-moi, lâche." *William the bastard! William the bastard! Fight me, coward!*

The entire English line of defence roared in support of their bold and courageous king.

"There is Harold. Go!" ordered William, as he and his entire rank of Norman knights and foot soldiers turned from their pursuit towards the left flank and headed toward Caelin and the English line behind him.

Harold watched on from the cover of the short trees, speechless and too far away to get involved. Furious that their army had just been fooled, most of the remaining Norman knights that surrounded Harold immediately mounted their horses and headed back to the Norman army line to alert them of the decoy. However, Harold was still left with four Normans to fend off himself, out of sight of the English.

"Ennemi de Dieu!" *Enemy of God!* Yelled William as he relished in the unexpected opportunity to face Harold himself, riding ahead of the rank and charging at Caelin, followed by his knights.

Caelin wasted no time and charged back at William. As their horses reached each other, Caelin dropped his riding position and successfully sliced William's horse with one skilful hit, causing William to fall heavily from his slain animal.

Caelin rode around and returned to where William had fallen, intending to finish him off if he wasn't dead already from the fall. Keeping his crowned battle helmet on, which covered most of his face, Caelin looked down on the fallen William, winded but very much alive. Knowing he had little time before the charging Normans would reach his position, Caelin dismounted and drew his sword. As he approached, he noticed William dragging himself towards an item on the ground which had fallen from either his horse or armour. Caelin was quick to pick it up before William could reach it, curious why it held such importance for the duke.

"Behold your guilt, Harold," declared the injured William on the ground near Caelin's feet. "The holy saint over which you swore your allegiance to me is here to collect her payment."

As Caelin held the bone fragment in his hand, his heart was instantly filled with peace and comfort as he turned his eyes to the sky above him to behold something he never dreamed he would see again: his dear sister. The sky had been torn apart, revealing a dreamlike and peaceful paradise with Caelin's sister smiling as she walked through its lush fields.

"You're safe. You're well. My dear sister, I can see you. Indeed, you are not in torment as I feared. My heart has found its rest now," Caelin cried to the sky, still holding the fragment and oblivious to the battle around him, which seemed to be frozen in time for this event of unmatchable importance.

Caelin's sister smiled back at him but remained silent. Her eyes then turned in the direction where Caelin last saw Harold. Caelin followed her eyes and realised he was being directed there. His expression changed as scenes of history flooded his mind. He could see it all: Saint Foy's martyrdom; Foy's relics journeying from Agen to Conques, then to Falaise where Harold took an oath, then to English shores.

He did not doubt what the relic was revealing to him. He not only knew the truth about Harold's oath to William, but he also could perceive the unseen strength behind William's conquest through the relic he held in his hand. To Caelin at that moment, it was beyond dispute that Harold would not be victorious on this battlefield while the relics were present. He understood that the relic was directing the battle's outcome, and no military strength or tactic would change it.

Caelin and William stared at each other, the moments passing like hours. Caelin said nothing, allowed the bone fragment to fall from his hand, mounted his horse and charged up the hill towards the English defensive line.

The Norman knights quickly headed to William lying on the ground, fearing he had been slain. One of the knights even announced to the rank that witnessed the blow and that William was dead.

Hearing the ill-informed call, William rose from the ground and threw off his helmet to reveal that he was very much alive before ordering his men to fall back to their position and re-form into ranks. A nearby knight dismounted and handed his horse to the duke.

Still out of sight and away from the battle, four Norman knights surrounded Harold and drew closer. He managed to deflect one of their attacks and counterstrike, sending his sword into the knight's belly. As the remaining knights approached Harold for their final move, a sudden single arrow from the trees behind the Normans shot them and into Harold's eye.

Harold dropped his sword and fell to the ground, causing the knights to turn and see several Norman archers behind them. The foot soldier archers had failed to see Caelin's earlier display and were still under orders to support the left flank.

The Norman knights congratulated the archers and headed back to the Norman position on foot.

As Caelin reached an enthusiastic and cheering English army, he continued his masquerade act and waved. Seeing that the ranks now lacked leadership without Harold or his brothers, he used his best Harold-like voice and ordered the huscarls to re-form the shield wall and the fyrd to re-form behind with the archers.

Caelin was eager to return to Harold's position on the left

flank. He knew he would be vulnerable but reluctantly decided that preparing the men for the next wave of attacks was more critical.

⋅⋅⋅⋅⋅⋅⋅⋅⋅⋅⋅ ❖ ⋅⋅⋅⋅⋅⋅⋅⋅⋅⋅⋅

Hours later, Harold regained consciousness and immediately writhed in pain from the arrow which had pierced his right eye, fracturing the outer eye socket but narrowly missing the delicate area behind.

Hearing the battle continue in the distance, he pulled off his helmet, removed his armour and robe and headed in the direction of some shrub cover to ensure he wouldn't be seen. Kneeling, Harold screamed in pain as he slowly removed the arrow from his eye socket. Blood poured down his face. Discarding the arrow, he slowly rose to his feet to see what he could from his blurry uninjured left eye.

In pain and shock, the vision he witnessed was as though he had awoken in hell. Bodies of the English covered the battlefield. In the middle of it all, Caelin himself, still arrayed as the king. He fought bravely alongside several huscarls, eventually surrounded and cut down by dozens of mounted Norman knights.

Moments later, William and his army passed nearby Harold's concealed position, heading up the hill, pursuing the remaining English fyrdsmen who were retreating north.

Harold's head dropped in despair. His failure to save Caelin, his men, his entire kingdom was a burden he was unable to bear. But the knowledge that the Normans would soon swarm the area kept his mind sober. He picked himself up off the ground and headed west, keeping away from the line of sight of any Norman ranks.

After walking for a few hundred yards, Harold came across a discarded monk's habit on the ground. It sat beside a pack that he identified as Caelin's. Through feelings of inconsolable despair and pain, Harold covered himself in the habit and pulled the hood over his head before continuing his slow journey west.

CHAPTER 66

THORNEY ISLAND, LONDON

"Edith Swanneck. Is that what they call her?" William asked as he slid his fingertip across Edith's glowing white cheek, wiping a tear away.

"Yes, my liege," responded Earl Morcar as he lowered his gaze. "She is also known as 'the fair'."

"I understand that she refuses to speak to me herself. I probably wouldn't understand her English anyway. What is she requesting?"

"Concerning what some of your men claim, that the man you killed was not Harold but a decoy, Edith insists that only she can identify Harold. By markings on his body known only to her. So, she asks to identify Harold's body herself on the battlefield at Hastings." responded Morcar.

"I see. Very well, she may go, but my men must accompany her," sighed William as he paced around the tearful Edith. "However, I must warn her that the markings she seeks may not be there. Harold did not see a clean death."

CHAPTER 67

THORNEY ISLAND, LONDON

Bishop Odo shifted his large frame and approached a wagon that had just arrived in the courtyard of the Thorney Island palace containing his belongings from the Norman camp at the Pevensey fort. Along with the shipment of Odo's belongings was the reliquary box of Saint Foy, in which Odo was required to return the bone fragments from William's armour.

A Norman servant was about to pick up the relic box but was quickly diverted by Odo. "Not that one. Fetch something else," he ordered in Frankish.

Odo pulled to dislodge the box himself but could not shift it from its position on the cart. Exhausted from his journey and frustrated by the spiritual and physical torment he believed was inflicted by Saint Foy herself, Odo stepped back from the cart and kicked its wheel with his muddy bishop's slippers.

Abbot Edwin emerged from the abbey and noticed a young girl in the courtyard who looked lost. He approached the child and offered to help her find her parent, who he assumed was a nearby English or Norman noble. The child took Edwin by the hand as they walked across the courtyard towards Odo and his cart.

Odo turned to see Edwin and the young girl approaching and fell to his knees as he watched them pass, his mouth open. The déjà vu scene was strikingly similar to the vision he experienced in his tent several days before. The girl looked like the young Saint Foy and Edwin like the figure of Christ himself.

Edwin and the child, oblivious to Odo's astonishment, continued a little longer through the courtyard in the direction of the palace as Odo watched on. Edwin eventually released the child's hand, sending her skipping towards someone she recognised. Edwin smiled as he turned back toward the abbey and Odo.

As he approached, Edwin noticed Odo and recognised his rank but was confused about why he was on his knees in the middle of the courtyard.

"You must be Bishop Odo, from Bayeux, is that right?" Edwin asked, recognising the Frankish episcopal attire.

Odo nodded without speaking.

"Are you all right? Can I help you with your things?" offered Edwin before he reached into the cart and emerged with the timber box containing the relics of Saint Foy.

"This is light. It must be just a few loose manuscripts in here. Where would you like me to take this?"

"It is Foy. Saint Foy," Odo mumbled, his eyes still wide open with fear.

"Oh, I see," replied Edwin. "That would explain why you're

down there on your knees, Bishop. I understand that this doesn't belong here, nor does it belong in Falaise. Is that right?"

"Conques," mumbled Odo.

"Yes, that's right. Conques Abbey," smiled Edwin. "Maybe I'll take it from here. I'll make sure it's returned safely to Conques."

Edwin effortlessly carried the light box under one arm as he passed Odo, giving him an assuring tap on the shoulder as he returned to the abbey, leaving Odo kneeling and sobbing on the cobblestones.

CHAPTER 68

HASTINGS, SOUTH-EAST COAST, ENGLAND

"It was somewhere here," announced the Norman knight, waving his arm around a general area as Edith and five Normans stood amongst thousands of fallen soldiers amid the Hastings battlefield.

As she shielded her mouth and nose with a delicate piece of material, Edith looked around for royal or Wessex livery colours amongst the bloody dead.

A few moments later, she ran over and fell to her knees beside one of the slain, distinguishably wearing a royal robe. There was a crowned helmet beside the body, which Edith knew was Harold's. She removed the loose tunic material that covered the face, but the injuries were so severe that Edith could not identify any facial features. Through her increasing tears, she moved her hands down the neck and found the pilgrim's medallion of Saint Edmund the Martyr.

Edith's tears progressed to sobbing. *He forgave me. He believed me,* she thought, relieved but overcome with grief and sorrow.

"This is Harold," she announced to the Normans as she moved away and attended to her grief.

"We will take care of his burial. Duke William asked that I inform you that you will be sent to a convent in the north before he is crowned. You won't have time to gather your things from Wessex. You leave tomorrow from London," said one of the knights.

Edith ignored the Normans and continued to grieve, kneeling beside the corpse and clutching at the pilgrim's medallion.

YORK MINSTER, NORTHUMBRIA

"Archbishop Aldred, you asked to see me? Is everything all right?" enquired a local abbot from a Yorkshire monastery.

"Ah yes. Come in," insisted Aldred.

"I am not accustomed to having an audience with the Archbishop. Forgive me; I'm a little nervous," said the abbot.

"Oh, it's nothing, I assure you, Abbot. Now ... I understand you have room for a new monk in your monastery at Selby, just south of York, is that right?"

"No, that is not correct, Archbishop. We are at capacity. Completely full. My monastery is popular with new novices, some even paying for their vocation. It's either the lodgings, which are more comfortable than your average monastery, or perhaps my quiet disposition, I'm not sure," replied the abbot.

"Well, I need you to find room for one more. Locate your

most comfortable room and assign it to the new novice I'm sending you. He'll arrive next month. Is that clear?"

"Of course, Archbishop. But who is this new novice of yours?"

"The son of an old friend."

VILLAGE OF SELBY, FIFTEEN MILES SOUTH OF YORK

E dith Swanneck moved slowly through the market stalls that lined the village square of Selby, selecting fruit for her convent. Though a Norman knight had been given control of Riccall and Selby villages, the townsfolk continued with their lives as though little had changed.

She took a moment to breathe in the fresh, crisp northern air, which was cooling as winter approached. She smiled as she watched a boy being taught to ride a horse as his father, the captain from Selby, proudly led him through the market and out into a neighbouring field.

"Are you interested in the apples, sister?" enquired a hooded monk behind the stall.

Edith knocked over several apples from the stall as she clumsily turned to address the novice, sending them to the ground. "Oh, forgive me, Father. My mind was miles away. Let me pick these up," she exclaimed.

"All is well," replied the monk as he emerged from behind the stall, pulling back his hood. "All is well, I forgive you," he continued, as Edith looked up, shocked to see the monk had an injured face, with one eye covered with a bandage. She recoiled and looked away, hoping to avoid staring.

Before Edith could walk away, the monk grabbed her hand.

"I forgive you, Edith," he said.

"How do you know my name … Harold?"

CHAPTER 71

CONQUES ABBEY, AQUITAINE

Abbot Edwin led an entourage of delegates commissioned to return Saint Foy's reliquary and statue to Conques Abbey as ordered by Pope Alexander. The newly crowned King William, seeing that his own Bishop Odo was unfit for the task, ordered Edwin to lead the official delegate south, including a dozen Norman knights, monks and other royal officials.

After making their way across the channel and journeying through the lush plains of Normandy and the mountainous terrain of Brittany, they arrived in the deep green valley of Conques village in the prosperous region of Aquitaine.

Abbot Etienne and the monastic community of Conques Abbey were informed of their impending arrival two days prior. Consequently, they were ready to receive the English delegates but, more importantly, prepared to receive their beloved Saint Foy.

The monks and villagers of Conques lined the streets, kneeling as Edwin led four monks carrying the bust reliquary past them towards the abbey. The gold statue beamed as it reflected the Aquitaine afternoon sun.

Abbot Etienne stood at the abbey's large timber doors as Edwin approached and fell to his knees.

"Abbot Etienne. King William and Bishop Odo of Bayeux, with great sorrow in their hearts, beg for your forgiveness for the theft of the relics of Saint Foy and the murder of Brother Michel. And as instructed by His Holiness, do penance by returning the holy treasure to its rightful place here at Conques. Please accept this act of contrition and pray for their souls," petitioned Edwin.

Abbot Etienne made the cross over Edwin and reached down to lift his counterpart from his humble position.

"My forgiveness and prayers are granted, dear brother Edwin," acquiesced Etienne with a smile as the two exchanged a warm embrace.

As the English monks proceeded into Conques Abbey with the reliquary bust and the Norman knights guarded the closing abbey doors, the gathered villagers burst into cheering, filled with joy at the safe return of their beloved saint.

"Come," said Etienne to Edwin. "Your journey has been long. You must rest and take refreshments."

"Thank you."

Edwin walked with Etienne down the nave and watched the reliquary being shifted back into its place behind the high altar by the Conques clergy.

"Edwin, I heard that the relics of Foy caused substantial disturbances to many people and events along its various journeys."

"Yes, indeed. More than anyone dared to anticipate."

"How is Bishop Odo? I understand he ... struggled with Foy."

"Well ... let us say the bishop has rediscovered an eagerness for prayer and reflection, now that the relics are off his hands," smiled Edwin.

"And what of your new King of England?"

"William is responding in his own way, building new stone churches as thanksgiving for his victories. But he seems to believe that his victory was a gift from God because he was more worthy, which is a dangerous conviction."

"And yourself, Edwin? Did God teach you something through our blessed Saint Foy?" Etienne held a door for Edwin at the rear of the abbey, leading to the vestry.

"Yes. I discovered that there is never only darkness. There is always light. There is always mercy. And it always wins," said Edwin before he proceeded through the door.

"But where sin abounds, grace abounds all the more," responded Abbot Etienne, quoting from Saint Paul as he closed the door behind him.

The end.

Printed in Great Britain
by Amazon